maybe
the horse
will talk

Elliot Perlman is the author of five books, including the internationally acclaimed bestseller *The Street Sweeper* and an award-winning collection of stories, *The Reasons I Won't Be Coming*, a national bestseller in the US.

His first novel, *Three Dollars*, won the *Age* Book of the Year Award, the Betty Trask Award (UK) and the Fellowship of Australian Writers' Book of the Year Award. He co-wrote the screenplay for the film of *Three Dollars*, which received the Australian Film Critics' Circle Award for Best Adapted Screenplay as well as the AFI Award for Best Adapted Screenplay. His second novel, *Seven Types of Ambiguity*, was a *New York Times Book Review* 'Editor's Choice', a *New York Times Book Review* 'Notable Book of the Year' and was shortlisted for the Miles Franklin Literary Award. It was made into an award-winning TV series for ABC TV.

He has been described by *Lire* (France) as one of the '50 most important writers in the world'.

BY ELLIOT PERLMAN

Three Dollars
The Reasons I Won't Be Coming
Seven Types of Ambiguity
The Street Sweeper
Maybe the Horse Will Talk

(Plays)
A Friend in High Places

(For Children)
The Adventures of Catvinkle
Catvinkle and the Missing Tulips

elliot perlman

To dear Stephen,
Hoping this finds you
well and thriving in
these crazy times.
Warm wishes,

maybe
the horse
will talk

PENGUIN BOOKS

PENGUIN BOOKS

UK I USA I Canada I Ireland I Australia
India I New Zealand I South Africa I China

Penguin Books is part of the Penguin Random House group of companies,
whose addresses can be found at global.penguinrandomhouse.com.

First published by Vintage, 2019
This edition published by Penguin Books, 2020

Text copyright © Elliot Perlman, 2019

The moral right of the author has been asserted.

All rights reserved. No part of this publication may be reproduced, published, performed in
public or communicated to the public in any form or by any means without prior written
permission from Penguin Random House Australia Pty Ltd or its authorised licensees.

Cover design by Alex Ross © Penguin Random House Australia Pty Ltd
Cover images courtesy best pixels/Shutterstock (skyline), Darq/Shutterstock (figures),
CSA-Printstock/Getty Images (horse head)
Typeset in Adobe Garamond by Midland Typesetters, Australia
Printed and bound in Australia by Griffin Press, part of Ovato, an accredited
ISO AS/NZS 14001 Environmental Management Systems printer.

A catalogue record for this
book is available from the
National Library of Australia

ISBN 978 0 14378 148 6

penguin.com.au

For Za

The law hath not been dead, though it hath slept
William Shakespeare

part one

I

'I am absolutely terrified of losing a job I absolutely hate.'

This realisation came to Stephen Maserov when he woke suddenly at around 3.30 one Wednesday morning. He wondered whether any of the other second-year lawyers who also worked at the prestigious commercial law firm, Freely Savage Carter Blanche, felt this way. If they didn't, how was it that he, an English literature major, former high school teacher and now a law graduate, did? In any event, lying there in his rented one-bedroom apartment, he found this unspoken articulation of his lose–lose predicament perversely liberating.

Among the equity partners of the vast legal empire that was Freely Savage Carter Blanche, the most feared was Mike Crispin 'Crispy' Hamilton. Maserov had heard the name even before he'd joined the firm. Hamilton sat in a corner office so high above the ground that a prolonged and studied stare out of either of the floor-to-ceiling glass windows would never permit identification by the naked eye of even the *species* way, way down on the street let alone its individual members hurrying to work for what would never, not ever, come within a light year of the annual salary, much less the partnership dividends, much less the private extra-legal entitlements and the trust fund accruals of Hamilton, who sat in the corner office no more inclined to imagine the lives of the people on the street than he was inclined to imagine the inner life of a bat.

And so he never looked down when he looked out the window. He certainly couldn't remember ever looking down and if it wasn't on his time sheet, where each hour was divided into ten billable units of six minutes, then he hadn't done it, not even when Joy was standing next to it. Joy, a young woman he had instructed to allow herself to be known as 'Joy', was his personal assistant. She was to be known as 'Joy', he explained when she started working for him, because her predecessor had been known as 'Joy' and this would avoid confusion.

It was in Hamilton's corner office that Malcolm Torrent sat in a plush chair with his back to the window – Hamilton had the window view – watching Joy pour them both a glass of Perrier from Hamilton's office minibar. Malcolm Torrent was the CEO of Torrent Industries, a giant company in the construction industry locally and internationally with a market value that hovered around $37 billion. They were waiting for the second-year lawyer, Stephen Maserov, who had just been summoned to join their conference. Mr Torrent was paying for every second Hamilton's Joy sashayed to the minibar, poured the water and sashayed out of the office again. Hamilton observed that it also served to distract Malcolm Torrent from the stress of whatever it was that had brought him there. Hamilton felt Maserov was taking far too long to arrive but Joy's comings and goings eased the ninety seconds they had to endure before his arrival.

Few lawyers below the Fifth Years ever spoke to Malcolm Torrent in person and all of the First Years were instructed not to engage with him if ever they should come upon him anywhere in the building. There was an unwritten rule within the firm that costs and disbursements that the lawyers couldn't otherwise hide should be buried in one of the many hundreds of files the firm had opened under the name of Torrent Industries.

As a second-year lawyer, Stephen Maserov knew of this unwritten law and thought that – since no lawyers below Fifth Year had ever been known to attend a conference with Mr Torrent – he must have been caught putting disbursements on a Torrent Industries file that properly belonged somewhere else. Perhaps the unwritten rule was not a rule but a myth. But with his own eyes he had seen other lawyers, senior and junior, billing Torrent Industries for non-Torrent costs and there had been no repercussions, none that he'd been aware of. Maybe it was an unwritten rule that had been implemented by so many at the firm so often that Torrent Industries had got wise to it. Perhaps Mr Torrent had been alerted to it by one of Freely Savage's disgruntled former staff members – there were five disgruntled former staff members for every current staff member. They had even formed a support group, the 'FSS', the Freely Savage Survivors.

Stephen Maserov was worried that an example was going to be made of him. This would explain why he, a Second Year, had been summoned to Hamilton's office for a meeting with Hamilton and Mr Torrent. The firm was going to offer him up as sacrifice to Torrent. What other possible explanation could there be?

Joy knocked at the door, stood at it without entering and announced, 'Stephen Maserov is here,' whereupon Stephen Maserov entered Hamilton's corner office.

'Maserov, I don't believe you've met Malcolm Torrent.' Of course he hadn't met Malcolm Torrent. He'd spoken to Hamilton no more than six times and on most of these occasions when he had gone home at the end of the day and told his wife about it she had poured him a double Scotch to help him recover. This was in the days before they had separated, or, more precisely, before she had asked him to leave.

'Pleased to meet you, Mr Torrent,' he said as he and Malcolm Torrent shook hands.

'Maserov, I want to thank you for your work on the Hoffner file.'

Stephen Maserov's forced smile froze as did the layer of sweat that adhered to his back, a miniature vertical Dead Sea that no shirt or suit jacket could be trusted to hide. Stephen Maserov had not worked on the Hoffner file. Not only that, he had never heard of the Hoffner file. Should he accept thanks for work he hadn't done in the hope that it would help him or should he immediately volunteer that he hadn't worked on the Hoffner file and hope for praise for his honesty or at least a quick and neutral return to the position he was in when he had walked into the room? There was no time to consider it, no time to call his wife, even assuming she was free and agreeable to taking his call. Following the birth of their second child she had resumed teaching on a part-time basis and he knew she would probably be teaching at that very minute.

They had met when they had both been teachers. They had married and, soon after putting a deposit on a house, reached the conclusion that at least one of them needed a better-paying job. So Stephen Maserov got himself into law school as a mature-aged student and Eleanor supported them both on her teacher's salary. The arrival of their first son, however, and the years and money sacrificed so that Stephen could study law took a toll on their marriage. They thought things might improve when Stephen took a job at a prestigious city law firm but they were wrong. The long, gruelling and bewildering hours Maserov spent at work only deepened the chasm between them. In an attempt to save their marriage, he mounted a case for having another child which was an especially heroic offer given that he barely saw his wife anymore and hadn't seen his libido since the previous financial year. Sure enough another son was born. He was loud and healthy but the marriage was, by Eleanor's reckoning, terminally ill. Describing herself as a corporate widow in all but liberty, one who had contracted a sexually transmitted debt, Eleanor suggested a trial separation. 'If you keep a clean shirt in your office you won't even notice,' Eleanor advised.

But Stephen Maserov didn't have an office. He lived in a collapsible workstation in one of the interstices between other people's promising careers in the glass and steel tower that caged Freely Savage Carter Blanche. Most nights since they'd separated four months earlier, Stephen

4

Maserov, now aged thirty-two, would visit the marital home to help put their two young children to bed with the additional not-so-well-hidden hope of reconciling with Eleanor. Then he would return to work for a few hours to try to make the day's budget. Then he would return to his recently rented one-room apartment.

Now, as the early morning sun streamed through the windows of Hamilton's corner office, he was being thanked by the firm's most important client in front of its most feared partner for work on a file he had never before heard of. Telling the truth had for him always been entirely autonomic, but he had been at the firm long enough to learn that the truth was actually just one of a number of options open to someone. It was always good to have options but one needed time to consider them otherwise one could choke on them. Malcolm Torrent of Torrent Industries and Hamilton were waiting for a reply concerning his work on the Hoffner file, a file Maserov had never heard of.

There was no Joy in the room. Her presence could have bought Stephen Maserov some time. What harm could there be in admitting the truth? It wasn't as if he had done anything wrong on the file. He hadn't worked on it at all. But credit from Malcolm Torrent, especially credit given in front of Hamilton, could be the genuine launch of a career. It could deliver him from obscurity, nay anonymity, and then later, once his tenure was more secure, the truth could be wheeled out like an overlooked driving infraction.

'Maserov?' Stephen Maserov heard Hamilton say, interrupting Maserov's terror-fuelled internal debate with himself and forcing him to imagine how he must have looked standing there mute in response to Malcolm Torrent's praise. This imagining itself took a few seconds and that, too, suddenly dawned on Stephen Maserov. 'I wish I could accept your thanks, Mr Torrent, but I didn't work on that file.'

Hamilton and Malcolm Torrent looked at each other in surprise.

'Is this true?' Torrent asked.

'Then why are you here?' Hamilton asked.

'I had a message from Human Resources late yesterday to come here but perhaps there's been some mistake,' Maserov volunteered before clearing his throat.

Hamilton picked up a file from his desk and started scanning it.

'Perhaps there's another Maserov in the firm?' Stephen Maserov said, as though he needed to explain not merely his presence but his existence. 'Perhaps *he's* the one who worked on the Hoffner file?'

Stephen Maserov knew there was no one else with his surname working at the firm.

Without looking up Hamilton spoke quietly, 'Yes, it's the other Maserov. Not this Maserov.' Stephen Maserov was astonished by the speed with which Hamilton had made the misinformation his own. 'I don't know why this Maserov is here. I'm sorry, Malcolm,' Hamilton said.

'Shall I get a message to him, Mr Hamilton . . . to the *other* Maserov?' Maserov asked nervously.

'No, you just go back to your workstation.'

'Just a minute,' Malcolm Torrent said. 'I like the fact that you didn't even for a moment try to get credit for something you didn't do.'

'You *like* that?' Hamilton asked, perplexed.

'I do. I like the look of this particular Maserov. I smell integrity of some kind. What level are you? I haven't seen you before.'

'I'm a Second Year, sir.'

'Aren't you a bit old to be only a Second Year? There must be some kind of a story attached to you, am I right? Integrity can hold you back, you know.'

'I was a teacher before I studied law.'

'A *teacher* – that's actually something socially useful!' Malcolm Torrent exclaimed.

'What do you mean, "socially useful"?' Hamilton asked.

'He doesn't even know what it means,' Malcolm Torrent laughed, addressing Maserov.

Stephen Maserov was stunned to be having a conversation like this with Malcolm Torrent, of all people, and in Hamilton's office. None of his colleagues would believe it. His wife wouldn't believe it.

'What made you give up teaching to practise law?' Torrent continued, to Maserov's amazement.

'Well, before we were married, Eleanor, my wife, and I used to joke that there was an inverse relationship between the social utility of one's job and one's salary so we decided that one of us better —'

'Joy, will you get in here please?' Hamilton said with agitation over the intercom.

'Actually, it's no joke,' Malcolm Torrent interrupted. 'Look at what teachers, nurses, social workers, child care workers, aged care workers and paramedics earn. When you think of the help, the vital service they provide, every day, and then think of what they earn. How do they live? What the hell kind of society is this? And it's not just them —'

'Social workers!' Hamilton spat out. 'Joy, will you get in here, please, *right away*?'

'I have to go,' Malcolm Torrent said, looking at his watch, 'but whichever Maserov you are —'

'It's Stephen Maserov.'

'Stephen, I'd like you to assist with *my* legal work, not the company's legal matters but *my* personal ones. You'll arrange that for me, won't you, Hamilton?' Torrent said as Joy entered the room.

Hamilton focused all his agitation on his personal assistant. 'Joy, I want you to find the other Maserov who works here.'

'Mr Torrent,' Maserov began, 'I'm really very grateful for the interest you're showing in me. Frankly, I can't believe this is happening.'

'It's not,' said Joy.

'What?'

'This isn't really happening,' she reiterated to Stephen Maserov as she kneaded Hamilton's shoulders from behind his chair. 'You *do* have a meeting with Mr Hamilton and Mr Torrent this morning,' she continued, 'but *this* isn't it. This is an anxiety-related dream you're having in the very early morning before the real meeting.'

'You're kidding?'

'No, I'm not. Ask yourself, which part of this, given what you know about the world, seems real?'

'Oh my God! None of it does!'

'No, the fear you brought in with you to Mr Hamilton's office truly reflects your reality. But have you ever known me to talk so freely, so eloquently and so analytically?'

'No, *no* I haven't! Oh God! What happens now?'

'Well, you *had* felt in the dream that it was all going well but that was only because thinking of me had given you a testosterone rush. You're about to wake up desperately out of breath. It will feel like a heart attack but that would get you out of this morning's meeting so you won't be that lucky. See the daylight sneaking in through the gaps in the curtains and the cracks in your squinting, crusty eyelids, uncaring, bright white light lying in wait for you? Here comes your real life. See the hot red numbers on the digital clock, the seconds sizzling contemptuously on the time allocated to *you* like an angry skin condition? Those numbers are not there to help you. They're there to chronicle your torment. Staring at your reflection in the toilet bowl before you urinate in it, which you are about to do, will somehow trigger fond memories of the days when your son would wet himself in the bed you used to share with your wife. Then you'll picture her already up making his school lunch in the marital home you're still helping to pay off. But right now you haven't even lifted your head from the pillow. It won't be easy. Your lower back's going to hurt you on your left side and you won't know why. *There* it is, feel it catch on your left side? Quite young for that, really, aren't you? Counting you in now. Four, three . . . Know you're running late. Here you go. Sharp pain, back *and* chest. Is that the beginnings, the faint stirrings of a headache? Is it? Can you hear its gallop growing ever louder and louder? Okay, mouth dry, desert dry, tumbleweed dry, tongue a tumescent swatch from a fetid shag-pile carpet of pathogens. Have to scrape it off to join society. Bladder full as an ocean. Paid off the house yet? Running quite late. Own that chest pain. Two, one . . . All on your own now . . . Breathe!'

II

When he had finally got home from work the previous night, exhausted as he was, Maserov's inability to stop imagining the impending morning's meeting had kept him awake till the early hours of the next day. The exhaustion had already sabotaged the new day and possibly his career and it wasn't even 7 am. He'd slept through his alarm. Stephen Maserov, a mere Second Year, was about to be late to a meeting, one he had been informed about the previous day, with Mr Malcolm Torrent of Torrent Industries and Mike Hamilton, the partner among partners, the first among unequals, *il Duce* of Freely Savage Carter Blanche.

Everyone in and around the firm feared Hamilton. His clients feared him and so continued to hire him believing that their commercial competitors would fear him even more than they did. Their fear would often explode into admiration as they witnessed his brazenness, even to them, as he explained in a chilly nonchalant manner that, while he billed for his services in units of six minutes he might, at his own discretion, also bill them by taking a lien on the client's property. A client, often unsure what a 'lien' was, but sensing that, whatever it meant, it bode ill, might smile uneasily as though perhaps it was a joke.

'I'm sure you understand this,' Hamilton would say about taking a lien, returning the smile to show he was serious and that he didn't care whether the client had understood him.

'I'm also billing for the time I spend telling you this. We both know I have to.'

'You *have* to?' a client had asked.

'If only to remain competitive,' Hamilton had explained.

'Competitive? With whom?'

'My partners.'

His partners feared Hamilton because he had more power within the partnership than anyone else. This was so because he had more voting rights than any of the other partners and he had more voting rights because he billed more than anyone else. And this because he was listed on more files as the 'partner responsible' (the partner responsible for bringing the work to the firm and thereafter for keeping the client happy). The more a partner billed the more votes he got at partnership meetings. It was as simple as that.

But it was more than just fear. Hamilton's partners also hated him. One had asked a Catholic priest whether it was wrong to pray for a man's death if it could be painless and was certain to bring comfort to others. When told Catholicism could not condone prayer for a man's death, the partner thanked the priest for his time but said he would continue his spiritual quest with a more accommodating religion. Yet another partner regularly role-played his interactions with Hamilton with his therapist. None of these people worked for Hamilton. They were not his employees; they were his partners. The employee lawyers could not afford the pleasure of hating him but the depth of fear they felt for him was uniformly unfathomable.

Maserov could almost fathom it. Riding up to the fifty-first floor, he could sense internal organs whose presence he had never previously been conscious of. By the time he reached Hamilton's office he still hadn't managed to catch his breath entirely. As the Joy in his dream had predicted, he was late, by less than five minutes, for the meeting but it put him in the wrong before he had even opened his mouth.

He didn't know they had started the meeting forty minutes earlier. When he knocked on the door in advance of the quotidian Joy announcing him and apologised for being late, around 270 seconds late, both Malcolm Torrent and Hamilton looked at him as though they had no idea who he was or what he was doing there. Human Resources had forgotten to remind Hamilton that he was obliged by the rules of the firm to have a second-year lawyer sit in on a conference once every two months. This was the only reason Stephen Maserov was there.

'What did you say your name was?' Hamilton asked.

'Stephen Maserov.'

'And why are you here?'

'Human Resources told me you wanted me in this conference?'

'Why?'

'I don't know.'

'But . . . you work here, right?'

'Yes.'

'What's your name again?'

'Stephen Maserov.'

'Is he a relative?' Hamilton asked Malcolm Torrent.

'Not of mine,' answered Torrent.

'Why did Human Resources send you here? Are you a Second Year?'

'I'm not sure. Oh, yes. I'm a second-year lawyer and —'

'Oh, he's a Second Year! Okay, well, sit over there and don't touch anything. Joy, bring me the records of this Second Year. Maserov, I think it is.'

'Yes sir, Stephen Maserov,' Maserov tried to help.

'Let me know how long until he's a Third Year,' Hamilton directed Joy before returning to Maserov. 'Well, just sit over there.' Then Hamilton turned back to Torrent. 'We have to do this. It's an HR thing,' he said by way of explanation. Malcolm Torrent continued as though Maserov wasn't there.

'Isn't there something called a "vexatious litigant"? Can't you get them declared a "vexatious litigant"?' Malcolm Torrent asked.

'For a court to declare someone a vexatious litigant the person or company instituting proceedings must be found to be doing so "habitually, persistently and without any reasonable grounds" merely to harass, annoy or embarrass the person being sued. None of these women can be said to be harassing you. Their claim is that you, or rather your employees harassed, sexually harassed, *them*. Don't worry; we'll see to it that Torrent Industries vigorously defends the accusations.'

'Mike, this is a *spate* of sexual harassment cases. It speaks to the culture of the whole business.'

'Malcolm, it's the construction industry. Boys will be boys.'

'Is that going to be your defence?'

'No, we'll tailor a separate defence in each case. We'll take care of it, but litigation takes time. You know that. You know how often things settle on the steps of the court and it can take years to get there. In the meantime you do not need to be thinking about this.'

'It's no good saying "it's the construction industry" and that "boys will be boys",' Malcolm Torrent countered. 'We're not talking about allegations of sexual harassment on a building site. That wouldn't be so bad. The allegations are that my executives are sexually harassing secretaries and support staff right there in my building, under my nose.'

'I understand your being upset by these women using their wiles – their bodies really – to attack the integrity of the company to gouge out some cash for themselves like so many unmarried mothers do but it's not a spate. Four cases hardly constitutes a spate. Nobody knows about this, it won't affect the share price and, anyway, we're going to make it all go away.'

Malcolm Torrent was not so easily convinced. 'You said that when the first case emerged and then two more popped up. And nobody knows about this *yet*, but they could at any time and if it goes public it very well might affect the share price,' he contended.

'No, trust me Malcolm; it wouldn't affect the share price. People don't care about this sort of thing, investors don't, certainly not the institutional investors.'

'I think you're wrong. I think investors do care about this sort of thing. There exist now what they call "ethical investors". This kind of investor scares the life out of me.'

'Ah yes, ethical investors,' Hamilton chuckled. 'I always enjoy the emergence of these faddish niche markets. Malcolm, I've never met anyone who would forgo an extremely healthy dividend in a blue chip company with tremendous growth potential because a lassie made a fellow jump out of his skin. Quite right too. This sort of thing happens every day. The economy can't stop every time someone pops their cork. Listen to me, things are very good for you. You've got all those Middle East deals and, of course, there's India. It's not a spate, maybe a little cluster. There's nothing that should worry you in this. You're making a mountain out of a boner.'

'Is this *all* you can say to me, Hamilton?'

'Relax Malcolm, it's the best advice I can give you.'

The two men exchanged an uneasy handshake and walked towards the door of Hamilton's office. It was only then that they remembered Maserov was in the room. Stephen Maserov stood up and nervously gave a half wave to Malcolm Torrent.

'Bye,' he said meekly, regretting it as the sound of the one-syllable word was leaving his mouth. He hadn't been expecting to have to speak, and he hadn't until then. Completely enervated by his frenzied effort to get to the meeting on time after waking up late, the silence demanded of him by his total superfluity to the meeting suited him perfectly. He would never know whether Torrent was going to respond because at the moment he might have been expected to reply he was distracted by the sudden appearance of Joy, who walked him out.

'You still here?' Hamilton said to Stephen Maserov when they were alone.

'I'm sorry Mr Hamilton, was I meant to have left the meeting sooner?'

'You're a Second Year, right?'

'That's right.'

'And when do you become a Third Year?'

'In about five months.'

'Probably won't ever have to see you again then,' Hamilton said to himself as he sat down and began checking his email.

'I'm sorry, did you say something?' Maserov asked.

'You can go.'

'Did you say something?'

'No. You can go.'

'You *did* . . . about not having to see me again?'

'That wasn't meant to alarm you.'

'Why not?'

'You weren't meant to hear it.'

'But I *did* hear it.'

'Apparently,' Hamilton said quietly, scrolling distractedly through his inbox.

'Why will you probably not have to see me again?'

At this Hamilton looked up. 'Because you'll probably be gone in a matter of months.'

'Why? I'll be a Third Year by then.'

'I know.'

'But doesn't the firm cull at the end of first year?'

'Traditionally, yes, but now we also cull at the beginning of Third Year. It's an innovation; I *innovated* it. It came to me in the back of a cab. Then I tabled it at the partners' meeting the next morning and they really went for it.'

'But how do you know *I'll* be one of the ones culled?' Maserov asked.

'Well,' began Hamilton, 'I'm not aware of any of the partners pushing you forward, grooming you, preparing you for an exciting dynamic future. Is there anyone at partnership level doing that?'

'Well . . . Mr Radhakrishnan —'

'Radhakrishnan?'

'Yes.'

'From Emerging Markets?'

'Yes.'

'How much of your billings come from Radhakrishnan?'

'Do you mean what proportion?'

'Yes.'

'At the moment?'

'Integrated over the last twelve months, yes.'

'Integrated over the last twelve months . . . I'd have to say . . . about . . .'

'You know I can check. I can have Joy find out the proportion of your work that comes from Radhakrishnan before you can say —'

'None,' Maserov admitted by way of interruption.

'Integrated over the last twelve months *none* per cent of your work has come from Radhakrishnan in Emerging Markets?'

'Yes.'

'Then why did you mention Radhakrishnan?'

Maserov tried to clear his throat. 'I've felt for a while that he's probably going to try to get me in on a few things.'

'You think he's probably going to try to get you in on a few things?'

'Yes.'

'Why do you think this?'

'Well, he . . . Whenever we . . . When we pass each other . . . in the hall . . . he generally . . . He pretty much always . . . smiles . . . at me.'

'He smiles at you?'

'Yes. I think so.'

'You think Radhakrishnan of Emerging Markets is going to bring you in on a few things because when you pass each other in the hall he always smiles at you?'

'Yes, he generally . . . That's been my feeling . . . for a little while now.'

'What do you *know* about emerging markets?'

'Well,' started Maserov, trying to swallow despite a dry mouth, '. . . they're markets that haven't finished, they, they haven't *quite* finished . . . *emerging.*'

'Have you ever seen Radhakrishnan's face when he's *not* looking at you?'

'When he's *not* looking at me? I don't think that's possible, is it?'

'If it's not possible then you can't have done it.'

'No, that's true.'

'Do you know where Radhakrishnan's from?'

'Emerging Markets?'

'Let me tell you something, I've seen his face when he wasn't looking at you. Guess what? He was smiling.'

'He smiles at you too?'

'He smiles at everyone! He's from India! It's an emerging market. They smile there, especially the ones who get out. Are there any other partners at the firm helping you avoid anonymity? Anyone smiling at you who *isn't* Indian?'

'Not regularly . . . Not intentionally,' Maserov replied.

'Do any of the partners here even know your name?'

'*You* know my name, don't you?'

'I don't know your name.'

'Well then —'

'Then *none* of the partners know your name, do they?' Hamilton said.

'No,' answered Maserov.

'So who will be here to argue that you shouldn't be culled?'

'No one.'

'That's why you'll be gone in a few months. You can go now.'

Maserov stood on the spot for a moment in shock and Hamilton looked up from his computer screen, surprised to see the second-year lawyer still there.

'Nothing personal . . . prob'ly. It's . . . you know . . .' Hamilton said, ripping open a novelty-sized envelope, 'Darwinian. *Might* be personal . . . Don't know.'

'Is it personal?'

'No, can't be personal. No one knows you're here. We're done now,' Hamilton said with a flick of his hand.

Maserov left Hamilton's office holding his pen and legal pad with nothing written on it but the date and the names of the people present at the meeting. As he walked past Joy's workstation he thought he felt a wave of sympathy emanate from the warmth of her perfumed bosom and up her neck to the smooth painted skin on her face, becoming for a moment a smile that winged swiftly and gracefully up across her face like a beautiful and rare bird away from its natural habitat, which then flew off in panic the instant Hamilton called her name. He had summoned her to clear the glasses he and Torrent had used. Hamilton would bill Torrent for the time it took Joy to clear the glasses as well as for the time he spent watching her do this. It was the same time counted twice but it was, Hamilton reasoned, occupied by two actions.

III

Stephen Maserov stood waiting for the elevator that was to take him down the three floors to where he would be sitting at his workstation for many hours over the next few months, trying to make budget in units of six minutes from the scraps of work people only slightly above him in the hierarchy would sprinkle haphazardly around him like breadcrumbs tossed to pigeons in a public square. There was no one in the firm looking out for him and so all the time he sat there he would be waiting to be told that he was through, that the end had arrived. Many others above and below him in the firm and in the neighbouring competing firms in the adjacent steel and glass towers were in the same position but they didn't know it. Some might have suspected it but Maserov knew it with certainty, almost to the date.

He looked at his sadly almost blank legal notepad and read all of the words written on it, his minutes of the meeting: 'Hamilton (partner), Torrent (client), Maserov (me)'. He had written this on arriving at the meeting and then had simply sat there listening without writing anything else. He was finished at the firm. It was widely known though little discussed that other law firms were not hiring, in fact they were shedding staff as quietly as they could to avoid the appearance of anything other than success. Even so, all of Maserov's contemporaries spoke to each other as though things were fine for them and fine for the firm. And not just among themselves but privately *to* themselves as well.

There was an increasing trend for legal jobs to be sent offshore to where so many other people's jobs had gone many years earlier. Now it was happening to lawyers and accountants. Now their jobs were going on a one-way trip to emerging markets as part of the global freeing up of everything. Soon would come the day when only the elite would be employed, and they did no work at all. But before the dawning of this diaphanous day, offices hummed with strip lights and anxiety twenty-four seven. With all of this spinning in his mind, Stephen Maserov, second-year lawyer, former teacher, estranged husband of Eleanor, with a five-year-old son and a two-year-old son, was waiting in shock for the elevator to take him to a brief stay in purgatory.

It was then he was struck to see, walking alone towards him from the other end of the hallway as though appearing in yet another dream, Mr Malcolm Torrent of Torrent Industries.

The elevator arrived and Torrent and Maserov got inside. They were the only ones in it. Maserov realised that Malcolm Torrent didn't recognise him from the meeting that had ended no more than ten minutes earlier. The elevator doors were closing. As both men stood facing the door Maserov wondered if he should say something. This was an opportunity, what kind of opportunity he didn't know, except that it was fleeting. It would last no longer than the time it took Torrent to get to the ground floor, unless it ended even sooner than that should Torrent get out before the ground floor. This was Maserov's chance. It could, he thought, end any second should someone else enter the elevator. Someone probably would. So he should say something. Another man would grab this opportunity. Another man would know what to do with it. Did he have anything to lose? There wasn't time to calculate this. What should he say? Maybe nothing. He could lose his job. But he was going to lose it anyway. He could lose it sooner. They were alone. It was now or never, and now was here already. And it wasn't coming back.

'Mr Torrent.'

'Yes?' Malcolm Torrent said distractedly.

'It's me . . . Stephen Maserov . . . The Second Year?'

'Do I know you?' Torrent asked.

'I was the second-year lawyer in Mr Hamilton's office with you . . . Just now?'

'Oh yes.' There was a silence. Maserov could see that Malcolm Torrent was heading for the ground floor.

'Mr Torrent?'

'Yes.'

'I'll bet you're pretty time-poor.'

'You got that right.'

'And, if I might say, I'll bet you didn't leave Mr Hamilton's office fully satisfied.'

'I didn't leave even slightly satisfied.'

'Sir, I think I can summarise what went on in that office. You had an appointment with Mr Hamilton to tell him in person, I mean face-to-face, that your company faces a delicate legal problem that concerns you. You told him that you're appalled by these sexual harassment cases, that one has become four, that you're worried there might be more and that you have concerns as to what it might do the share price of an organisation you've single-handedly built to be a giant of the construction industry. And you left with him telling you, essentially, that there's nothing to worry about, that he'll take care of it, which is probably what he said when you told him about the first of the allegations.' By this time the two of them had reached the ground floor. The doors had opened and Maserov's heart was pounding. There was no coming back from this. But Malcolm Torrent was smiling.

'What's your name?'

'It's Maserov, Mr Torrent. Stephen Maserov.'

'Go on, Maserov.' By now the two of them were in the foyer of the building. People were walking past and around them.

'Sir, this is going to sound both pathetic and ridiculous because it *is* both of those things but I can't talk to you anymore. I mean, I'm not permitted to talk to you . . . Not permitted by the firm.'

'I *pay* the firm. I'm the head of its biggest client. I can talk to anyone I want.'

'But *I* can't.'

'Walk with me.'

'Outside?'

'Yes.'

'Sir, I could lose my job just for talking to you without a partner or a senior associate present. If they knew what I'd just said to you I could be —'

'Ah, that's my driver,' Malcolm Torrent interrupted. 'Get in with me. I want to hear the rest of what you were saying.'

Torrent's driver double parked in front of the building, came out to open the door for Malcolm Torrent and both Malcolm Torrent and Stephen Maserov got in.

'Go on,' Torrent exhorted.

'Uh . . . where is he taking us, sir?'

'Back to my office. Continue with your analysis. I'm interested in where you're going with this.'

Maserov found himself in the back of Malcolm Torrent's limousine as Torrent poured himself and Maserov each a Scotch with ice from the minibar. He couldn't believe where he was or with whom. Or what he was doing. But he couldn't stop now.

'I know it's early but I always need a drink after seeing Hamilton. You'll join me. Continue with your point,' Malcolm Torrent said.

'Well, sir, as I see it, Mr Hamilton didn't give you any satisfaction. The problem is going to continue and he's counting on you to be so busy that you'll let it drag on. Sure, if he continually pays only lip service to your concerns you could ultimately take all your business to another firm but Hamilton's got so much of it that he's counting on corporate inertia to keep things just as they are.'

'He keeps the clock ticking and charging me for every damn thing,' Malcolm Torrent lamented.

'Well, you see, that's because the status quo is in his interest. You keep engaging him to put out all these spot fires. Even these sexual harassment cases are, so far, spot fires, albeit they could burn out of control at a moment's notice. None of them, by themselves, warrant moving your business to another firm.'

'Yeah, it's true. We *do* have all our files with Hamilton and it would take one hell of a logistical effort to take all our work away from Freely Savage and give it to a new firm. The time we'd lose waiting for a new firm of lawyers to get up to speed with all our work would end up costing us an enormous amount of money. And that's even assuming no one at the new firm dropped the ball.'

'Hamilton knows this, and knows you know it so there's no incentive for him to fix things in any great hurry and every incentive to maintain the status quo.'

'You make a good point, young man. And he's so damn smug!'

'Mr Torrent, I want to put something to you. I'm only a second-year lawyer, with all the inexperience that entails, but if you give me twelve months to get on top of this, to do nothing but work on these sexual harassment cases, I will find a solution for you. Mr Hamilton talked about the possibility of settling with the plaintiffs on the steps of the court. Maybe, but that could take years, with all the attendant risk of a public relations disaster in the media before the case gets anywhere near court. Mr Hamilton, in my opinion, isn't sufficiently sensitive to the potential for damage through social media. And who's to say these cases settle on the steps of the court, anyway? What if evidence is given in an open court that prejudices your share price before any possibility of a verdict? Even an ultimate judicial finding favourable to

Torrent Industries might not be able to stop the damage if the horse has already bolted. Sir, if you give me the chance to work on nothing but this, by the end of twelve months you won't have these problems anymore.'

'Son, you're taking an awful risk. Why're you doing this, Mister . . .? What's your name again?'

'Maserov, Stephen Maserov. The firm is going to get rid of me in a few months when I become a Third Year.'

'Why?'

'Well, as far as I can tell it's because, despite both the market and recent movements in the dollar, the economy, the *real* economy is in hopelessly bad shape. The firm is shedding lawyers and I don't have a champion or a backer at the firm. In fact, few people there at a senior level even know who I am.'

'Why should I trust you?'

'Okay,' said Maserov before inhaling, holding the breath and gently letting it go. 'Why should you trust me? Well, um . . .'

It was a miracle to be in a conversation with Malcolm Torrent let alone to be with him in his car. But what was the point of it? Would it have any effect on Maserov's life? Would it be a positive effect? Here lay Stephen Maserov's chance, in the next sentence, possibly the most important sentence he'd uttered thus far in his life.

'Sir, first, no one else has seriously offered to help you with this. Your concern about this is not being matched by the firm. Second, you admire people who take calculated risks. And third, the cost to your business of a year of my billings will not be felt. It would be so statistically insignificant that it wouldn't show up on a document important enough for people even three tiers below you to see. But the benefit of my ridding you of these cases, the avoidance of damage to your company's reputation and to its share price, would be plain for you personally to see in twelve months from now. And what have you got to lose?'

Eleanor Maserov, Stephen's wife, stood in the kitchen with her mouth open forming a perfect 'o' as he told her what had happened that day.

Their five-year-old son sat at the kitchen table and called for their attention. His two-year-old brother was asleep in another room.

'Who will read my bed-night story tonight?' he asked.

'Just a second, Beanie,' Eleanor Maserov said. 'Daddy's telling Mummy how he committed career suicide at work today.'

The Maserovs' eldest son, Benjamin, had been referred to as 'Beanie' from the day the sonologist had told his parents they were going to have a boy. Maserov had said he would take the technician's word for it but the ultrasound image looked more like a bean to him than anything else, and the name had stuck.

Maserov explained to Eleanor that after the short car journey to the headquarters of Torrent Industries he was invited up to Torrent's office, where he convinced Malcolm Torrent to send an email to Hamilton concerning the morning's conference. The email instructed Hamilton to direct Maserov to work on the sexual harassment matters to the exclusion of all his other duties – without exception – for twelve months and that at the end of the twelve months Torrent would personally review the situation. Maserov knew that the email was more than vaguely threatening because, despite the distraction of a palpitating heart and the effects of a double Scotch before lunch, he'd drafted every word of it very carefully himself. Maserov had asked Malcolm Torrent if he wouldn't mind sending it in the evening after he, Maserov, had left for the day. Torrent acceded and had Maserov blind copied so he knew all of this was really happening. When he'd seen the email in his inbox he knew this was no dream. It was too late to turn back.

'Hamilton's going to be apoplectic!' Eleanor exclaimed as she bathed Beanie.

'Probably,' said Maserov, from the kitchen, helping himself to his third beer from the fridge before joining them in the bathroom.

'Probably? *Certainly!* Are you out of your mind?' she asked her husband.

'Eleanor, didn't you hear me? I had months left. Hamilton told me directly this morning.'

'And *now* you're going to be out of work immediately. Great thinking!'

'I don't think so,' Maserov countered philosophically.

'What in your right mind possessed you to do this?' his wife asked incredulously.

'What *should* I have done?'

'I don't know but . . . not *this*. How are you going to fix this? You can't do it. Do you know how to do what you've promised to do? And anyway, you shouldn't be stitching up some poor woman who's had to deal with God knows what kind of vile executive you'd be defending. It's not even moral.'

'You can't say that,' Maserov countered. 'You don't know the facts of the case.'

'You don't know the facts of the case *either*!'

'Not yet but I will soon.'

'And in the meantime you've already promised to get the guy off.'

'I don't need to get them off. They're not criminal cases . . . I don't think they are. That's a good point. I should check that.'

'There's more than one?'

'There are four . . . four cases that I know of.'

'Four! There's an epidemic of sexual harassment at this place.'

'Yes, four's a lot better than one when you think about it, more work. Makes me more needed, potentially, if I can do something about it,' said Maserov, sipping his beer.

'Stephen, listen to yourself. You've promised to do something potentially unethical and, even if it's not, something you don't know how to do.'

'I've promised to do it four times. You're deliberately seeing only the bad in this.'

Eleanor began, 'You want life to go on for these executives as though nothing ever happened. It takes guts for a woman to bring an action like this, especially against her boss. Sexual harassment needs to be taken seriously. It's not a chip to be bargained with for your career advancement.'

'Career advancement! I'm talking a roof over my family's heads! Okay, it's no longer over *my* head but —'

Eleanor repeated, undeterred, 'These women shouldn't be bought off, conned or coerced into dropping their claims for the sake of your career advancement. That's just wrong!'

'Well, would you would mind if these women were bought off, conned or coerced into dropping their claims for the sake of your mortgage?'

There was a slight delay, uncharacteristic of the rhythm of her previous argument. Then as if refreshed by a fresh wave of resentment, Eleanor continued the conversation. 'I never thought I'd marry a man who'd defend sexual harassment.'

'I never thought you'd leave him,' Maserov replied.

By this stage of the conversation Beanie was in his pyjamas and tucked snugly into bed with a menagerie of soft toys and three books for one of his parents to choose from as his 'bed-night' story.

'Who will read me a story?' Beanie asked.

'Daddy will, sweetheart,' Eleanor told him, 'Mummy needs to revisit her life choices.'

Maserov sat down on Beanie's bed. He picked up each of the books and examined them in turn. 'Sweetheart, we've read all of these,' he said to his eldest son. 'I'm not going to read you a story tonight. I'm going to *tell* you one. Don't you want to hear something new?'

'No.'

'Really?'

'No.'

'Beanie's on the right track, Stephen,' Eleanor called from the hall. 'We're going to have get used to re-using everything.'

'What if I made one up for you? What if I made up a story for you?' Stephen said, ignoring Eleanor, loosening his tie and now sipping on a glass of wine that he'd brought in from the kitchen with the bottle it came from. This had been a momentous and alcohol-rich day. Tonight he was not going back to work when his children had been put to bed. Tonight there was no reason to go back to work. A turning point had been reached in his legal career today. Either Malcolm Torrent's protection would buy him a year of safety to find a new job and save his marriage or no quantity of billable hours on any time sheet was going to save him from Hamilton now. So he drank with a drink-and-be-merry-for-tomorrow-we-may-die attitude because tomorrow Hamilton might have him killed.

'No, Daddy, don't make up a story. Read me one I like.'

'But what if I made it really good? Wouldn't you like to hear something new, if it was a really good one?'

'But I like the ones I know.'

'Where's your spirit of adventure? Beanie, listen to this. Just try me. See how we go. Once upon a time, in the thirteenth century in a far-off land now called Turkey, there lived a jester whose job it was to entertain the king. This jester was an excellent jester, known not just in this kingdom but in every kingdom as far as the crow flies, which is very far indeed. He would tell the king jokes, put on funny voices, transform himself into characters, tell the most fascinating stories and perform all sorts of magic tricks that would boggle the mind. He'd been doing this for many, many years. He'd gone to court jester school years earlier to learn how to be the best court jester he could be.'

Beanie's eyes were fluttering heavily as his mother came to the room and stood by the door listening to the story. 'His wife had put him through court jester school on a teacher's salary,' she interjected.

'One day the king summoned him and in the presence of all the guards, the knights, the entire nobility, the maids of honour, the concubines, the lobbyists, the flunkies from HR, the team-players, the change-makers, the thought-leaders, the social-media influencers and several dozen futurists, he told the jester that he had something important to tell him. A hush fell over the entire assembly as the king announced that, while he had been very amused by the jester for a long, long time, he no longer found the jester amusing. Accordingly, the king, in his majestic wisdom, decreed that he would have to let the jester go.

'Now, what you have to know, Beanie, is that because royal jesters were so close to the kings they amused and knew so many of their intimate secrets, their downsizing invariably led not merely to the loss of their jobs but to the loss of their heads.

'The jester panicked. Desperately seeking to save his life, he told the king that he had a trick that would astonish him, a trick that no other jester or magician had ever been able to do. The jester said he could do it but it would take a whole year to perfect. "What is this trick?" the king asked, intrigued.

'"Under the right circumstances, I can make your horse talk."

'Everyone including the king himself gasped. "You can make my horse talk?" the king asked.

'"Yes, sire, that's the trick. It's an astonishing sight. But I need your very best horse, not just any horse but your best, and I'll need him for a whole year if I'm going to get it right. It's not easy, you know. Horses are very shy animals. They're naturally resistant to talking."

'"My best horse . . . for a whole year?" asked the king.

'"Yes, sire, if you can let me have your very best horse, by the end of the year I will have trained him to talk."

'The king was very taken with the prospect of his best horse being trained to talk and he happily agreed to the jester's suggestion. The jester went home and told his wife all that had occurred. His wife, however, was terrified . . . and angry. His wife, as it happened, was called Eleanor, the same name as Mummy, and she was often angry with the jester and sometimes stupidly thought she'd be happier without him. She yelled at the jester. "You can't make a horse talk!" she cried. "Are you out of your mind? You don't know how to do that! *Nobody* knows how to do that!" said the jester's distraught wife. "When you fail the king will have you killed."

'"Listen," the jester said to his wife, "he would have had me killed soon anyway. I've just bought myself a whole year. In a year many things can happen. The king might die. The horse might die. I might die."'

By now, Beanie was fast asleep and breathing in a nice steady rhythm. Stephen Maserov looked over to his wife who had been listening intently to the whole story from the doorway of her son's room.

'Or, maybe the horse will talk,' Maserov suggested softly.

part two

I

Stephen Maserov had never got used to walking through the cavernous entry foyer of Freely Savage Carter Blanche, which swallowed him each morning and when he returned there at night in an attempt to make budget, after having visited his two young sons and estranged wife.

The sound of his shoes on the marble floor as he walked to the bank of elevators would trigger an anticipatory visceral reaction to the frustration and humiliation that defined his work days. And, by arithmetic induction, his hatred of his job. He would either be starved of any files to work on, or he would be allotted more files needing immediate attention than he could handle in a week, let alone a day. Or he would be given mutually contradictory instructions on a matter by two different partners. Or he would have an allegedly urgent file he'd worked on till late the night before suddenly taken over by someone else the next day without any explanation. Or he would be summoned to report on a matter to a meeting of partners but in the event not given an opportunity to say anything. Or he would be given a menial task like collecting a partner's dry-cleaning.

All this, including being continually on call, continually contactable, was to be accompanied by the need to feign exuberant fealty to a firm where downsizing was a regular event.

As he came into the building that morning he wondered what had changed since Hamilton received the email written by Maserov himself and sent by Malcolm Torrent. As far as he could tell, nothing seemed different. He rode the elevator up to his floor and was making his way to his workstation, which he was heartened to see still existed, when he saw a flicker of something – concern, understanding, warning, perhaps a recognition of bravery – *something* in the eyes of another Second Year, a well and softly spoken young lawyer named Emery. Emery was the only other Second Year who Maserov felt possessed an undercover agitator's sense of irony. As far as Maserov could tell, Emery hadn't yet adopted the Stockholm syndrome mindset of the other Second Year quislings.

He'd already passed Emery's workstation and was about to sit down at his own, just long enough to breathe in his new circumstances, when he realised that the slight widening of Emery's eyes meant that Emery must know something of what had happened. Maserov and Emery had never openly discussed with each other their utter disenchantment with the firm and their working conditions but Maserov knew from subtle tells in Emery's demeanour over the last two years that he was mentally recording the whole thing. While each of them was powerless to help the other, they recognised that the other was the closest he had to an ally. Other than the support of tiny facial gestures, in reality all Emery could really offer Maserov was a capacity to bear witness, at least as long as he, Emery, lasted, which, statistically, was going to be another few months. But that morning Emery's flicker told Maserov he hadn't dreamed the email from Malcolm Torrent to Hamilton. The slight adjustment of Emery's facial muscles as Maserov passed by confirmed to Maserov that indeed the world had changed.

Maserov sat down at his workspace and took in a breath. Malcolm Torrent's personal assistant had forwarded a return email from Hamilton acceding to Torrent's request, subject to Maserov's continued observance of the Freely Savage HR department's requirements. He looked all around him. There were muted voices, the quiet competitive clacking of keyboards (always fast, since slow typing suggested uncertainty or thinking) and of course the occasional loud conversation from a partner's office. Nothing was out of the ordinary and yet everything had changed. Maserov reached into the one drawer provided by his desk and took out his red tartan glasses case. His mother had given it to him before a high school exam he'd dreaded but which he'd done well in. She was dead now but she was often with him, as was that glasses case. He had taken it into every exam he'd ever had and, armed with it, he had done well enough each time to ultimately gain admission to legal practice, a vitamin D deficiency, and a recurring chilli-red skin condition. Then he'd smuggled the glasses case into the drawer of his collapsible office desk. Some of the more senior lawyers had seen it but rather than considering it juvenile they had just assumed it was where he was keeping his stimulants and anxiolytics. They made a mental note of it.

The twelve months Maserov had bought himself to solve Malcolm Torrent's company's sexual harassment problems, secure some kind of employment beyond the twelve months and save his marriage had begun. He was leaving his workstation when he noticed a small piece of white paper that had fallen from the seat of his chair to the floor. He picked it up. It read, 'Stephen, please call Human Resources.' It was signed with the initials HR. Either it was from someone working in HR with the same initials as the department or it was from someone who could sign a memo with the full imprimatur of the department they worked for.

Maserov looked at the note for a moment and, putting it in his pocket, decided he would call HR from the offices of Torrent Industries. He would feel safer there and, anyway, he wondered, how urgent could it be? After all, he had Malcolm Torrent in his corner. Emery coughed as Maserov reached his workstation which Maserov took as a signal to stop, crouch and pretend to do up his shoe.

'Hamilton's out to get you,' Emery whispered.

'All of us,' Maserov answered without deviating his gaze from his shoe.

'"All of us"? What do you mean?'

'There's going to be a cull of Second Years.'

'When?' asked Emery in an alarmed whisper.

'When everyone assumes they're a Third Year.'

'But I thought they only cull —'

'New policy,' Maserov interrupted.

'Have they fired you already?'

'No,' Maserov answered. 'I've been seconded to Torrent Industries.'

'That could be good,' Emery said, before adding, '*Is* that good?'

'I hope so,' whispered Maserov. Then he stood up, patted Emery gently on the back and walked towards the elevator and the unknown. It occurred to him that someone watching might think him brave. It was a novel thought and it dissolved like a yawn as the bell rang for the elevator doors to open.

II

As the cab pulled up outside Torrent Industries headquarters, Maserov realised that he had forgotten to get a Cabcharge voucher to pay for the ride. But he didn't care. He felt both employed and free. This must have been how people with jobs felt in the sixties when, his parents had told him, you could quit your job in the morning and have an equal or better one in the afternoon. He even tipped the cab driver the whole cost of the ride, so pleased was he by his changed circumstances. He had no idea how he was going to solve Malcolm Torrent's problems but he had a year with a salary to do it and nobody on his back. He could, if he chose, spend half his time looking for other jobs.

As the cab pulled away, Maserov, having first wished the cab driver *Eid Mubarak*, several months too early, affected the sort of corporate facial set he felt was the sine qua non of a lawyer who could solve Torrent Industries' sexual harassment problems. As he rode the elevator to Malcolm Torrent's office it occurred to him that Torrent might have had second thoughts about paying him for a year. Or he might have forgotten all about their arrangement, one that while life changing for Maserov touched Malcolm Torrent's world like the wings of a butterfly, no, a moth, a second-year moth.

Not likely, Maserov thought. He had a folded printout of the email to Hamilton. But what if Hamilton had persuaded him to renege? Then he, Maserov, would be in the same position he had been in before the conversation with Malcolm Torrent. No, he wouldn't be. He'd be fired. But there was no intimation back at his workstation that he'd been fired. The door opened and Maserov walked towards Malcolm Torrent's private office. There was the note from Human Resources asking him to call. Was that what it was about? Was he to be quietly fired?

'Good morning, I'm Stephen Maserov,' he said to Malcolm Torrent's private secretary, Mrs Joan Henshaw, a woman with a pleasant but not easy to read face. Nearing retirement, she gave nothing away. Would she remember him? It was only yesterday that he wrote an email from her desk. Email! If Human Resources at Freely Savage wanted to fire him with urgency they would probably also send him an email, not merely leave a handwritten − scrawled, really − note on his chair. There had been no email when last he'd checked. Maybe he should check his email from his phone now. Didn't want to. Talking to saviour's private secretary. Can't be rude. Better do it for peace of mind. Soon as possible. No. Don't want to.

'Oh yes, Mr Maserov,' Malcolm Torrent's private secretary said and internally Maserov celebrated wildly her remembering him. He thought of his sons. 'Mr Torrent has asked me to direct you to Human Resources.'

'What?!' screamed a raucous voice inside the cavity of his mind.

'*Your* Human Resources, right?' Maserov asked her involuntarily in the low voice one uses when there's no oxygen to be found on the planet you've been seconded to.

'Well, yes,' she replied with slight hesitation, unsure who else he thought she could have meant. 'They're on the fiftieth floor. Ask for Jessica Annand. I'll write it down.'

As he got out of the elevator he checked his email. There *was* a message from Freely Savage Human Resources. Was this it? Was he going to have to tell Malcolm Torrent that Hamilton had already broken his word? Don't open it. You have to. Suddenly Jessica Annand was standing before him.

'You're from Freely Savage?'

'Yes,' he said in a tone that couldn't hide his own surprise. It was unusual to consider himself in this light, as the representative of his own oppressor.

Of Indian heritage, she was beautiful, frighteningly, with dark, soft eyes and the sort of bouncy black hair one only sees in advertisements for hair conditioners, lustrous yet manageable. It was not simply that he could imagine how he looked to her, with his pale, creased face, in need of a shave though he had shaved not two hours before, and his small exhausted red eyes, portals into a world of anxiety not quite hidden by something like a cross between conjunctivitis and strabismus. No, worse than this vision of himself through her eyes was the sudden panic which assaulted his sentience. Would this beautiful woman in her elegant corporate bodycon dress realise that he was there to, in effect, defend certain men in the company she worked in against accusations of sexual harassment by women, her former colleagues?

No doubt some of these men had looked at her in a way that intimidated or at least nauseated her. And here was he, Maserov from Freely Savage, with a brief to frustrate the litigation these women had launched. He heard his wife Eleanor's voice, 'You want life to go on for these executives as though nothing ever happened. It takes guts for a woman to bring an action like this, especially against her boss. Sexual harassment needs to be taken seriously. It's not a chip to be bargained with for your career advancement.' Maserov didn't need Eleanor's take on what he was doing. He had enough qualms of his own.

'I'm Jessica Annand,' she said, extending her hand. He took it to shake. Do it quickly, he thought. Don't patronise her with a weak grip but nothing so firm it could be misconstrued as misogyny or neo-colonialism. Her tone was friendly and relaxed. This was going to be terrible, asking this beautiful woman for help and waiting for her to realise what he was there for.

She said there was a vacant office waiting for him with a phone and a computer. He wondered if it was a real office, a room with a door, or if 'office' was, like at Freely Savage, a euphemism for a collapsible workstation. She led him down the hallway and, as he sneaked glances at the executives in those offices with the door open and tried to avoid looking at Jessica's moving three-dimensional form lest he fix on it and get caught staring, she turned for a moment and gave him a gentle smile.

She gestured for him to enter an empty, pristine office with a door and a window view of the universe. 'Here's my card with my extension on it. Call me if you need anything.'

'Thank you,' Maserov said, looking at her card.

'I should get you a security pass if you're going to be here for a while. If you have a card it'll stop them getting your name wrong. Happens quite a lot around here.'

'Yes, of course,' he said, pulling out his wallet and taking out a business card to give her. Now there was perhaps the hint of an intimacy between them; him and her against the unthinking automatons who make security passes and get names wrong.

'How long do you expect to be here?'

'Oh, I'd say, give or take, in the vicinity of about . . . a year.'

'A year!'

'Unless they fire me . . . then it will be less than a year.'

'Why would they fire you?'

Maserov looked up at Jessica from his new desk as she stood in the doorway of his new office. 'You work in Human Resources, don't you?'

'Yes,' she said.

'Then you should have access to a list of reasons.'

'Reasons why you should be fired?' she asked.

'Not me in particular. I don't work here.'

'Other than for perhaps the next year,' Jessica added, intrigued.

Maserov looked at Jessica's business card in his hand then up at her before continuing earnestly, 'Ms Annand, may I call you Jessica?'

'Yes, Mr Maserov.' She smiled.

'You look puzzled. Okay, well I work for Freely Savage.'

'So your business card says,' she added.

'Which makes you my client,' Maserov finished.

'You mean it makes Torrent Industries your client, not me.'

'For the purposes of this conversation I'm treating you as the representative of Torrent Industries.'

'Okay, as long as it's only for the purposes of this conversation.' She smiled again.

'Well, you're in HR, so . . . At Freely Savage we have a certain . . . well . . . There is a common view of the human resources department.'

'What view is that?'

'You won't be offended?'

'Why should I be? You're not talking about our HR department, you're talking about yours. Aren't you?'

'Yes.'

'So I can't be offended, can I?'

'No, I guess not.'

'But don't let that stop you coming to the point.'

'I'm sorry, I'm not used to coming to the point first thing in the morning.'

'I can show you where to get coffee if you think it will help.'

'Oh God yes, please!' Maserov said, rubbing his eyes with the palm of one hand.

'Okay but first, what's this common view of the Freely Savage HR department and who holds it?'

'Everyone below partner level at Freely Savage considers the firm's HR department to be . . .'

'Yes?' Jessica asked.

'To be the equivalent of the Stasi.'

'The Stasi?'

'Yes, I'm afraid so.'

'The East German secret police?'

'Yes, that's the Stasi we have in mind. Similar methods, similar goals, similar staff.'

'Don't be afraid. You're here now,' said Jessica Annand, amused.

'Yes I am.'

'For a whole year, possibly?'

'Yes, for a whole year . . . unless they fire me.'

III

Maserov, alone in his new short- to medium-term office at Torrent Industries headquarters, took out the slip of paper that read, 'Stephen, please call Human Resources' and was signed 'HR'. It had, he thought, certain characteristics that would have been at home on a comparable note from the Stasi. There was the comma after his name, the use of only his first name (the feigned intimacy being ultimately more frightening than some impersonal document) and then the sign-off being the initials of the department itself, rather than someone working in the department. Should he call them? He didn't know who he was meant to call but he realised it wouldn't take long to find out and so he delayed calling. He didn't open the email from HR either. Maserov decided that he would feel better, less fraudulent, if he first made at least some headway and came up with a plan, a road map, for tackling the problems he'd talked Malcolm Torrent into assigning to him.

To begin with, he had to read the Freely Savage files on the allegations of sexual harassment at Torrent Industries. His difficulty lay in not having the files, or access to the files, or even access to the name of the

Freely Savage lawyer who was handling the cases. But somewhere in the offices of Torrent Industries, in a database on a hard drive, there had to be the name of the lawyer. The simplest thing was to ask someone at Torrent Industries. He knew only three people there, the CEO, Malcolm Torrent himself, Torrent's stony-faced private secretary, Joan Henshaw, and Jessica Annand from their HR department. He would start with Jessica.

With a continuation of the feeling that he had nothing to lose, he picked up the phone and invited her to show him her idea of the best coffee in the neighbourhood. Her response brought an immediate return of the feeling that he had lived with for much longer than the feeling that he had nothing to lose – namely, that he had everything to lose. Jessica sounded strange, cold and distant, almost as though she didn't remember who he was or didn't like what she remembered. She said she wasn't able to meet him for coffee, or more exactly, 'That's not going to work for me.'

Maserov felt as though he'd asked her for a date and she had declined. She was far from the first woman who had. The last woman he'd asked on a date had been the woman who had become his wife, Eleanor, and she had not declined then. But after years of marriage and two children, Maserov was confident she'd decline if he asked her out now. The sudden Proustian rush of rejection sheeted home to Maserov just how fragile his what-the-hell-I've-got-nothing-to-lose attitude really was.

Perhaps Eleanor had been right. Perhaps he should have stayed at Freely Savage, biding his time until they culled the Second Years who had just become Third Years and him among them. He was doubting the wisdom of having even approached Malcolm Torrent when the phone on his desk rang. The only person who knew that he occupied that room was Jessica.

'I'm so sorry,' she said. 'I was trapped in an executive's room and couldn't speak freely.'

'Didn't I call your office extension?' Maserov asked.

'Yes, you did, but I had to transfer my line to his office, so I was talking to you from there. I've only just sneaked out and I have to go back in there. I can't meet you for coffee. Sorry.'

'No, I gathered that. It's fine,' Maserov said.

'But I was thinking of lunch,' Jessica volunteered. 'Do you have lunch plans?' Maserov's emotions now lurched the other way. They hastily arranged to meet at the bottom of the building at 12.55 pm. Maserov put the phone down and just sat there for a moment. Although he didn't understand why, he thought he might cry.

It was a warm and sunny autumn day and the city streets were blooming with lightly dressed women, lycra-clad superheroes cunningly disguised as bicycle couriers on amphetamines, ripped-off foreign students hopelessly lost and staring at their smartphones, avant-garde art students from the south-eastern suburbs clutching their caffeine fixes, street musicians sustained by the hope of reaching somebody, and a multitude of homeless people hopped up on cocktails of anti-dandruff shampoo, nail-polish remover and methylated spirits. Stephen Maserov awkwardly shook Jessica Annand's hand when they met in the foyer of the building.

'We've met, remember?' she said, looking down at his hand taking hers. 'Do you shake the hand of people you have lunch with at Freely Savage?'

'I can't remember. I mostly eat alone.'

'You're not very gregarious, are you?'

'No one there is very gregarious, really. Sociability is not a trait they tend to value. It can't be measured in six-minute billable units. Nor is it consistent with the competition between employees the firm works so hard to cultivate.'

They sat down opposite each other in the nearby Nashi sandwich and coffee bar, each ordering a handcrafted sandwich with fillings the establishment promised were exotic. It was noisy and crowded but their table was in a slightly darkened section that recommended itself to

professionals with an inclination towards a midday fix of alcohol, anxiolytics and office intrigue. Nobody spoke for a little while. Maserov was
not afraid of silences. Jessica was less comfortable with them.

'I hope you don't mind my asking,' Jessica began once they had
ordered, 'but what's the nature of the work that's led you to our offices?'

'No, I don't mind your asking. And . . . I'm thinking I'm going to
need *someone's* help.'

'So it might as well be me?' Jessica asked.

'Yeah, that didn't . . . um . . . that didn't really come out right. Can
I . . . Let me just . . .'

'You want to tell me the whole story?' Jessica asked.

'A lot of it, yeah.'

And so Maserov told her what had happened the previous morning
with Hamilton and how he had learned that within a few months, when
the Second Years were becoming Third Years, there was going to be
another big cull and that he would be included and why. He told her
how he had buttonholed Malcolm Torrent, correctly guessed the sweet
spot of his discontent and, in return for twelve months' job protection,
promised to rid him of his problem.

'It seems to have worked but I think I'm going to need a Torrent
Industries email address.'

'Why?'

'I don't know what Hamilton's going to do but he's not going to take
this lying down. He could try to shut me out or terminate my email
account. He could do anything.'

'You really think he would sabotage your attempt to solve the problem
of his most important client?' Jessica asked.

'Definitely. It's just a matter of when and how. He might even fire me.'

'I thought you said he agreed by return email to Mr Torrent to give
you twelve months to work on nothing but Mr Torrent's problem.'

'He did. I have a copy of that email. But if push comes to shove, and
with Hamilton shove usually arrives first and in a limo, how am I going

to enforce this deal? I'm entirely dependent on the goodwill of Torrent and he's only just met me. There's no reason he should have any regard for me,' Maserov said.

Jessica thought for a moment. 'Should push come to shove, you need to remind Mr Torrent of how little Hamilton, in contrast to you, cared about the problem.'

'You're right,' said Maserov, impressed.

'I can get you a Torrent Industries email address. That's easy. I can do that after lunch. What else do you need?'

'Well, I realised that I don't know the names of any of the alleged Torrent Industries staff members involved in the . . . any of the people Mr Torrent wants me to look after.'

'You haven't told me precisely what you're looking into.'

'Oh, it's pretty dry, boring legal stuff . . . building codes, regulations,' Maserov lied. He was worried that if she knew that he was trying to protect alleged sexual harassers he'd kill any chance of her helping him. Worse, she'd probably consider him the enemy and a creep.

'Really? Building regulations, and Hamilton won't look into it? That doesn't make any sense. Why won't he look into it?'

'I don't know yet. I may never know. Look, I realise this whole thing probably looks pretty cloak and dagger, especially to someone who's happy with their professional situation.'

'Happy with my professional situation; are you kidding?'

'You seem —'

'Look, a lot of your description of the mood or the atmosphere of Freely Savage applies to Torrent Industries too.'

'Really? It seems so . . . I don't know . . . benign.'

'That's because you've been at Torrent Industries for two hours.'

'You're not so happy there?'

They barely knew each other but that didn't seem to inhibit her.

'Oh Jesus, where do I start? I had all these plans when I first came here. I've got a Masters in psychology. I never intended to work here or not for long. My career ambitions are wilting before me like lettuce leaves.'

'Hmm . . . lettuce leaves,' echoed Maserov.

'I had plans for a career in organisational psychology but I got sidetracked by the need to eat and pay rent. There weren't any other jobs, not ones commensurate with my education and the debt it left me with. Torrent Industries kind of seduced me with its capacity to satisfy my need to sleep under a roof and eat on a semi-regular basis. I'll be honest, at first I was fooled by the opulent offices and the way the money automatically appeared in my bank account every two weeks. But the disappointment began in earnest when I found I was spending significant parts of my day ensuring there was sufficient alfalfa on each side of the sandwich platters I was instructed to order and sometimes to deliver for in-house seminars. This was not what I had aspired to. I had always imagined a robust, exciting career, perhaps blossoming into life as an academic. Can I tell you what my ambition used to be?'

'Please do.'

'No, I probably shouldn't. I've only just met you.'

'Well, I don't want you to feel uncomfortable,' Maserov said, hoping she'd tell him everything as soon as possible, the more personal the better.

'I saw myself giving TED Talks.'

'TED Talks?'

'Yes, my plan was to gain insight into the corporate coalface at Torrent Industries and roll that into one or more TED Talks and eventually into a book.'

'Forgive me, but that's your ultimate ambition, to give a TED Talk?'

'I already have an MA in psychology.'

'Yeah, that's what I mean. I would have thought that was much more impressive than giving a TED Talk.'

'More people have an MA than give TED Talks,' Jessica explained.

'Yes, and more people have an MA than open a McDonald's franchise.'

'Do you think so?'

'On a global basis, I'd say that's probably right.'

'Accepting that this is true, which I don't unequivocally, what's your point?'

'My point,' Maserov explained slowly as he tried to remember his point, 'my point is that it's a mistake to think that something being rarer than something else makes it more intrinsically valuable.'

Jessica was enjoying having her ambition gently challenged by Maserov's logic. He was the first person in the work environment to whom she'd confided this. She looked down at her plate briefly and moved some salad around slowly in a clockwise direction before looking up and continuing.

'You do realise I mean the *real* TED Talks, I don't mean any of your locally organised, community-forum-type talks. I'm talking Vancouver, I'm talking Clintons; Hillary *and* Bill . . . and Chelsea.'

'Oh, you *are* serious!'

'Are you perhaps laughing at me?'

'Um . . . Yes, I think so, but gently.'

'The TED Talk would be a stepping stone. Did I mention that?'

'Yes.'

'To a book,' Jessica continued.

'You said.'

They sat looking at each other.

'Why are you looking at me like that?' she asked him.

'I'm not aware of the way I'm looking at you, only that I am looking at you. And I'm thinking you've already achieved something greater, more impressive, than your stated ambition.'

'Look,' said Jessica, 'I'm Indian. Do you know what that means?'

'Um, not in this context, no.'

'It means my parents are Indian.'

'Yeah, so?'

'They can't see a Master of Arts degree. I mean they can't show it to friends and family. They can show a piece of paper but that's not going to cut it with extended family in Richmond Hill, Harrow and Bangalore.'

'But a TED Talk they can see,' Maserov said, feeling the weight of the penny dropping.

'Yes, they can watch it over and over again, each time my parents pretend that they haven't already sent the link to this or that aunt, uncle or cousin who in turn might send it on even further.'

'Forgive me, I now see the importance of the TED Talk, a considered and even noble ambition. You want to please your parents,' said Maserov sympathetically.

'Yes,' said Jessica, unable to hide her sense of defeat. 'But after two years at Torrent Industries, these ambitions seem no nearer to realisation than when I started. The way it looks right now, I'd have enough trouble getting them to *send* me to a TED Talk.'

'They're anti-TED Talk?' Maserov asked. 'I had no idea.'

'It's worse than that,' Jessica continued. Now she was almost whispering. 'Do you know who Frank Cardigan is?'

'No,' answered Maserov, also in a whisper. 'Who's Frank Cardigan?'

'He's a Torrent Industries executive, a rising star. Everybody there loves him, or at least those above him do. He's recently been moved to the Urban Infrastructure department to restore its viability after they experienced some crushing losses. In just eighteen months he managed to return Urban Infrastructure to profitability.'

'That sounds impressive,' said Maserov, not terribly impressed. In truth, she didn't seem to be either.

'Yeah, everyone is just so impressed with him, he thinks he's earned the right to pepper his conversations with, "I'm a great believer in . . ." He's a great believer in *this*. He's a great believer in *that*. He made the company some money and now he's developing *ad hoc* belief systems.'

'It sounds very annoying, I realise, but why is he your problem?'

'Yeah, he shouldn't be my problem. He became my problem a while back when he was required to write a regular column for a bimonthly professional publication, a newsletter for the construction industry, *Construction News*. It's sponsored by Torrent Industries and all employees, all those at corporate HQ, are expected to read it.'

'I've never known whether bimonthly denotes something that happens twice a month or every two months. Sorry, that's probably not relevant,' apologised Maserov.

'Actually it is relevant. I'll explain. When Frank Cardigan's star began to rise it was none other than Mr Torrent himself who chose Frank to write this column. As you might have guessed, Frank's unctuous gratitude to Mr Torrent for choosing him was followed by a call to HR to ask for assistance.'

'He wanted someone to write it for him and they chose you.'

'Exactly.'

'Why did they choose you?' Maserov asked.

'Because . . . Okay.' Jessica took a breath. 'I'd written some discussion papers for the department and Aileen van der Westhuizen, the director of HR, knew I could write. So when she started getting pestered by Frank Cardigan in his search for a ghostwriter she volunteered me. She said I really had a way with words.

'And that was the beginning of my Frank Cardigan problem. I had to start writing his shitty columns for him. Mr Torrent read some of them, liked them, and so now I was really stuck. Frank Cardigan, elated, became obsessive about his "audience reach". He wanted to know who in the firm was really reading his articles, the ones I was writing.

'I did manage to get him to agree to "write" the columns every two months. Citing my background in psychology, I put to him that adopting the every-two-months definition would leave people hanging out, plain desperate to read them.'

'He accepted that?'

'He's astonishingly stupid. And arrogant. So anyway, now he considers me his "lucky charm". He's even called me that.'

'To your face?'

'To any part of me he can get near.'

'Is he sleazy?'

'He works at it but so far I've managed to keep a certain distance between us. But it's not easy. He wants to run every decision he makes past me, which is crazy because I don't know anything about infra-structure; urban, suburban, rural or extra-terrestrial.'

'How do you write his columns for him?'

'We have these meetings where we scan the business pages of one or other newspaper – local, interstate, international – it doesn't matter. There he selects a topic, which he gives me. I write it down and go back to my office and there I consult Wikipedia. Then I change the verbs. Then I add adverbs. Then I go to the thesaurus and I change as many nouns as I can.'

'Are the columns a success?'

'Well, he's turned the division around so people think he knows what he's talking about.'

'Does he?'

'How can he? I'm writing it and my background's in organisational psychology. So he thinks I'm his lucky charm and I can't seem to break away from him, not completely.'

'You can't appeal to your higher-ups?'

'I haven't got a case. He keeps recommending pay rises and bonuses for me.'

'So that's good, right?'

'Yeah, but I can't be dependent on his good graces for my employment. What happens when they find out he's an idiot, which they eventually will? Not only that, this isn't how I imagined my career, alternating between organising bagels and alfalfa for thirty people and ghost-writing for an asinine construction executive. And he's not merely asinine. Frank Cardigan is a vain, self-obsessed, sexist, manipulative careerist who values people only for as long as he needs them. He's a great user of people.'

'They're everywhere, let me assure you. I don't have any ready advice. I wish I could help you.'

'You might be able to. If whatever it is you're working on here is so important to Torrent then maybe you could ask for my assistance in which case your stuff would take precedence over his crap.'

Maserov tried to hide his discomfort. It was not that he didn't want to help her. He really liked her. But if she became involved in his work in any way she'd soon learn that he was working for alleged sexual harassers and she'd share the contempt for him Eleanor felt when he'd told her about his arrangement with Malcolm Torrent.

'Yes, of course, if it's at all possible I can definitely try to get you involved,' Maserov heard himself say. Maybe he wouldn't be able to. Maybe he would be, but in a way that hid from her what he was really doing. Maybe the horse would talk.

IV

Armed with a Torrent Industries email address Jessica had supplied, Maserov was able to obtain the names and the files of the alleged sexual harassers employed by Torrent Industries and the name of the Freely Savage lawyer assigned to clear up the mess or at least to pretend to. He was a man called Featherby, an eighth-year lawyer who lived in one of three pinstriped suits. Maserov had had very little to do with Featherby but he'd been struck by his extreme thinness, his near two-dimensionality, and by the tenacity with which he clung to the pinstripes and they, in turn, to him. Featherby seemed unconcerned that no one else in the developed world was currently wearing pinstripes in a corporate setting without irony and he would, no doubt, remain unaware when he would one day appear at the vanguard of their triumphant return to boardrooms everywhere. He had straight, stringy, thin hair that wasn't yet grey but had been rehearsing for its autumn all his life. Maserov could tell it was a life that had begun in an expensive private school with its own carefully nurtured grand tradition of manicured gardens, rote-learned Latin, extreme orienteering, vast tracts of perfectly cut, moist, lush grass to cradle participants in various blood sports and random extracurricular outbreaks of non-consensual sodomy – a school that had taken great pains to attenuate its students' vowels and stiffen their consonants. It had inflicted these and other torments on him and had billed his parents handsomely for the trouble and for his board.

Now Featherby was an eighth-year lawyer at Freely Savage, living on a diet of Diet Coke, anything with doxylamine succinate, selective serotonin reuptake inhibitors and the amphetamines that he either bought or bartered for on the black market at Freely Savage. He managed to smile in bursts of a few seconds at a time whenever people in his department gathered around the high-speed photocopier for sponge cake and two-dollar-ninety-nine spumante on the occasion of a department member's birthday. It had been an initiative of HR several decades earlier that many departments had quietly abandoned. On careful examination of dusty cupboards in even these departments an archaeologist could still sometimes find the plastic cutlery and polystyrene cups that had been so essential to the ritual. Featherby was one of the fee-earners still forced to engage in it. He would stand there zombie-like, all pinstripes and brittle greyish lifeless hair, his face alternately, like a blinking neon sign, affecting a tortured smile then catatonia, a tortured smile, catatonia . . . He had a wife who in the middle of the day he had trouble picturing.

This was the lawyer in charge of the Torrent Industries sexual harassment files. This was the man Stephen Maserov called on the afternoon of his first day working out of the offices of Torrent Industries.

'Featherby,' responded the eighth-year lawyer when he picked up his phone.

'Hello, is that Bruce Featherby?' Maserov asked from his new office.

'Yes, it is,' said Featherby.

'I'm calling from Torrent Industries,' Maserov said. 'I've been asked by Malcolm Torrent to have a look at all the files concerned with allegations of sexual harassment levelled against executives of Torrent Industries.'

There was a pause. Maserov knew what it signified. Featherby was processing what he had just heard. Featherby was unlikely to feel that what he had just heard would be good for him. It probably wouldn't be neutral either. Had Featherby billed too much? Had he taken too long? Had he overlooked something? A man with a perennially dry mouth suffers more than most when his mouth becomes Sahara dry.

'I'm sorry, what's this about?' Featherby asked over the phone, trying to keep his heart, which was beating like that of a rabbit, inaudible to his unknown interlocutor.

Maserov repeated, 'Yes, I'm calling from Torrent Industries and I've been asked by Malcolm Torrent to have a look at all the files concerned with the allegations of sexual harassment that have been levelled against executives of Torrent Industries.'

'I'm sorry, who is this?' asked Featherby.

'My name is Stephen Maserov.'

'You're from Torrent Industries?'

'Yes, I'm calling from Torrent Industries. Mr Torrent has asked me personally to peruse the files and —'

'Maserov, did you say?'

'Yes.'

'Would you mind terribly spelling that?'

'Not at all. I spell it as well as anyone. M-A-S-E-R-O-V.'

'Thank you. Can I ask the general purpose of your perusal, Mr Maserov?'

Featherby's politeness told Maserov that he thought Maserov was working for the client and not a junior lawyer in his own firm about to be flicked to the job market like a piece of lint to the floor.

'Yes, of course. Mr Torrent has asked me to conduct what you might call an audit of the files for Torrent Industries.'

Through the silence at the other end of the phone line Maserov heard Featherby hurriedly alighting on and then off and then back onto the possibility that all the hours he had ever worked, all the indignities, everything he had endured to become an eighth-year lawyer at Freely Savage, it had all been for nothing. But you don't get to be an eighth-year lawyer at Freely Savage without picking up a few tricks.

'Mr Maserov, would you be able to shoot me your request in an email and include the best number for me to reach you and I'll be delighted to help you.'

You had to admire the shimmy, and Maserov did. Featherby, despite his terror, had managed to stall for time, time to think and gain confirmation of Maserov's identity, and still affect a willingness to help without actually promising anything. And it was all delivered with an immaculate politeness that would have made the housemasters of his alma mater give him a standing ovation.

They got off the phone and Maserov began the email Featherby had requested. Though he would be sending it from his new Torrent Industries address, Maserov knew Featherby would discover he worked for Freely Savage. What he didn't know was whether that would help or hinder his getting the files.

Maserov now had no legitimate distractions to take his mind off the email from the Freely Savage Human Resources department. It was sitting in his inbox like an unexploded bomb. He took several deep breaths and allowed his mind to go for a walk through the field of possible outcomes. There beneath the long dry grass lay the barely hidden tombstone of his tenure at Freely Savage. This was the worst that could happen. Human Resources might be executing Hamilton's order to have him terminated. If this were so there would be nothing for it but to test the strength of Malcolm Torrent's commitment to him as the anti-Hamilton, as Jessica had named him. Could it be something else, something worse? Had somebody died?

Both his parents were already dead so they couldn't be bursting at the seams to tell him that. Suddenly he thought of Eleanor and the boys. Could they be trying to tell him something about them, some horrible news? The dread of this and the need to be relieved of it led him to open the email without further delay. It read, 'Dear Stephen, Could you please make a time to see Bradley Messenger at your earliest convenience?' It was signed by someone he'd never heard of, said to be the executive assistant of Bradley Messenger, director of Human Resources. So it had nothing to do with his wife or children and it didn't, in and of itself, end his employment. The suspense wasn't killing him but he suspected something associated with the email would try very soon. He would have to make a time to go back to Freely Savage to see Bradley Messenger, the Gauleiter of Freely Savage HR.

Within an hour of Maserov's email Featherby responded with 'Dear Sir, Thank you for your enquiry. Unfortunately it's not possible to accede to your request without jeopardising the prosecution of these matters. Yours, Bruce Featherby, Freely Savage Carter Blanche.' Maserov knew at once that Featherby knew who he was. He decided it was time to go for broke with Featherby.

'Bruce Featherby,' said Featherby with an upward inflection in 'Featherby' when he answered his direct line.

'Bruce, Stephen Maserov. Thanks so much for getting back to me,' Maserov said, referring to the email but making it sound as though it was Featherby returning his call.

Featherby tried to take pre-emptive measures. 'Maserov, we can't send you the files.'

'But I'm their lawyer,' said Maserov.

'Whose lawyer?' asked Featherby, slightly confused.

'The alleged sexual harassers',' answered Maserov.

'No, *I'm* their lawyer,' shot back Featherby.

'We are *both* their lawyers,' said Maserov in an attempt to sound conciliatory. 'We are both Freely Savage lawyers.'

There was a pause while Featherby held his breath, a skill he had honed in his youth while on a series of terrifying school camps in remote locations. He and Maserov both knew that Featherby would have been told directly or otherwise that Maserov was Hamilton's enemy. There was no conflict in this for Featherby. It was not a subtle matter. Maserov was a second-year nothing who no one knew existed twenty-four hours earlier. Hamilton was omnipotent.

But this second-year nothing with his own Torrent Industries phone number and email address was so inexplicably brazen in his attempt to get hold of the sexual harassment files that Featherby wondered if the whole thing was a trap engineered by Hamilton. Perhaps, Featherby thought, he had failed to make sufficient progress on these or some entirely different files and possibly now he was being audited by Hamilton for suitability for the status of 'former person'.

'Former person' referred to a category of lawyer in the firm who had fallen off the partnership track but who for some reason hadn't yet been fired. There weren't many of them but the other lawyers, in fact everyone who worked at Freely Savage, knew a former person when they saw one.

A former person might have a Body Mass Index that would embarrass the firm should they ever get out of the building or be seen by a client. Alternatively, a former person might wear clothes with the outline of a hard-to-shift food stain of which they're unaware because their eyesight has deteriorated in the course of the years trying to make budget. A male former person might have facial hair not reflective of any current fashion among young men but reflective of a man who weeps alone at night into the depths of his pillow. The distance between the tip of his tie and his belt might be between three and five centimetres greater than mandated by an unspoken new fashion diktat.

A female former person might wear too much perfume or else she might wear a perfume marketed at her grandmother, or show too much cleavage in a manner that her tormentors usually welcome but don't in her case because of her age or a vague sense of desperation that clings to her, which they exploit to ridicule her just far enough out of earshot for them to be able to pretend, in a shining micro-corporate example of plausible denial, that they didn't think she could hear them. She might be kept on because she understands a particularly difficult provision of the Tax Act no one else can understand but if that provision should ever be amended she'd be out faster than you can pour stale water out of a vase.

Featherby wondered if this whole attempt by an apparently rogue Second Year called Maserov didn't prefigure his banishment, his re-categorisation to the status of 'former person'. So he held his breath, as evolution had taught him to do in moments of possible danger.

'Maserov, I know who you are,' Featherby said quietly and seemingly without emotion over the phone.

'Good, good, then you know I'm under instructions to peruse all the sexual harassment files.'

'You won't be getting them,' Featherby said, but as he was putting his phone down to prematurely end the call he heard Maserov's voice and the words were enough to get him to put the phone back to his ear.

'Featherby, you know you're instructed to make the files available to me. Let's not play games.' Maserov could hardly believe that it was him saying this. It seemed to come not from him but directly from somewhere around the orbitofrontal cortex region of his brain.

'What do you mean *instructed*? Who do you think you're instructing?' Featherby snapped back like a rubber band. 'You're a Second Year.'

'Featherby, you can think of me as a second-year colleague or, if it's more helpful, you can think of me as the client.'

'How can you be both? You can't be both?' Featherby asked, genuinely perplexed.

'You can see . . . on your phone . . . the number I'm calling from. I'm calling from the client. I'm at Torrent Industries. I'm on the inside,' Maserov continued.

Maserov could almost hear Featherby thinking. No question he had made the much more experienced lawyer sweat but Featherby held his nerve.

'I shouldn't even be talking to you,' Featherby fended, and with that he hung up.

Maserov decided to do the only thing he could think to do. He wrote an email on behalf of Malcolm Torrent addressed to Featherby and copying in Hamilton, requesting the files be sent to Maserov at Torrent Industries. It was bold but necessary. Whether it worked or not, Maserov would know where he stood and if he really did have Malcolm Torrent's backing. He took the letter to Malcolm Torrent's private secretary, Joan Henshaw, told her what he had done and asked her to put it into Mr Torrent's inbox for him to forward. Within an hour he saw that Malcolm Torrent had indeed sent it. What he couldn't see was Featherby's face when he received an email from Malcolm Torrent.

The arrival of the files on the desk of his Torrent Industries office triggered a release in the tension in the muscles in his back and chest Maserov had thought everybody always felt. His eyes moistened and he felt he was in danger of falling asleep. The evaporation of fear can have that effect. Whether or not he could ultimately do anything to assuage Malcolm Torrent's concern about the allegations of sexual harassment, it looked as though his plan to buy himself twelve months was working. He could barely believe something he had thought of and acted on in a moment of acute stress was actually working. If only Eleanor could be made to appreciate the daring and the brilliance of it.

Walking up the incline of Collins Street towards the Paris end in this relaxed state for a one on one with Bradley Messenger, the director of Human Resources at Freely Savage, Maserov considered what he'd been able to glean from the files thus far on the basis of a very cursory reading. There were four sexual harassment claims by former Torrent Industries employees. Was it a spate, a pattern, the tip of an iceberg of a still-to-be-revealed culture ranging from off-colour, uncomfortable, embarrassing and degrading sexist banter to career-damaging misogyny to, in the worst cases, sexual assault and rape? Yes, of course it was, if Torrent Industries was anything like the law firm handling the complaints.

All but one of the alleged victims were representing themselves, he noticed. Only one of them had engaged a lawyer. This particularly piqued Maserov's interest. Why would three out of the four alleged victims sue a construction behemoth without engaging a lawyer? Yet judging from a brief glimpse of their files, each one of the three had a statement of claim that read perfectly. It was as though a lawyer, a good lawyer, had drafted them. Not surprisingly, none of the three self-represented plaintiffs worked at Torrent Industries anymore and neither did the one plaintiff who had a lawyer on record.

'Stephen! Stephen Maserov!' Bradley Messenger exclaimed theatrically when Maserov entered his office. 'We in HR are very glad to see you here.'

'Thanks. I'm just visiting,' Maserov said, accepting the invitation in the HR director's gesture to sit down.

'Absolutely! Just visiting. *You're* the Second Year who caught the eye of Mr Malcolm Torrent, no less. We'd already had our eye on you. Marked you down as one to watch, a Freely Savage no-nonsense, go-getting, type A personality.'

Maserov sat there for a moment slightly stunned by the welcome. 'You know, the whole division of people into type A and type B personalities is a bogus one. As a Human Resources professional, that would probably interest you,' he responded with unusual abandon. After all, he'd stood up to Hamilton and was still breathing. Who was Bradley Messenger compared to Hamilton?

'I think you'll find the categories of type A and B are accepted everywhere.'

'Like American Express,' added Maserov, 'which isn't actually accepted everywhere. My dry-cleaner won't touch it.'

'No, if you do a *little* more reading you'll see these personality types were devised by doctors so I'm *very* comfortable using them,' said Bradley Messenger.

'Yeah, they were cardiologists,' Maserov said. 'They weren't psychologists or psychiatrists. And they were funded by the tobacco lobby.'

'Well,' began Bradley Messenger, starting to get ever so slightly exasperated through his smile. 'We at Freely Savage represent many pillars of the tobacco establishment. In fact, they have us on a retainer, don't they?' he asked rhetorically. 'If it weren't for the tobacco lobby and its vigorous defence of the attacks on them we'd probably never have developed the much-imitated Document Retention Program, one of a number of litigation tactics that have made us market leaders.'

'That's the one where we hide, lose, throw out or destroy a client's incriminating documentary evidence and then charge them for it. That's how the Supreme Court saw it,' Maserov continued.

'"Winnowing for relevance", wasn't that what it was called in his honour's judgment?' asked Bradley Messenger.

'No, that's what *we* called it on appeal. And we lost,' explained Maserov.

'Well, you can't win everything, although don't quote me on that. Stephen, you know your stuff because *you're* the lawyer and that's why we've called you in to see us. How would you like to be the Second Year representative in our fee-earner fact audit?'

'I don't really know what that means.'

'You know what *most* of it means,' Bradley Messenger volunteered.

'I know what most of the words mean on their own. All of them, actually.'

'You see, there you are!' said Bradley Messenger triumphantly. 'And this is only the first time we've ever discussed it and already you're pretty much on top of its meaning. Anyway, Stephen, we're asking how you'd like to be the representative of the Second Years.'

'In what?'

'In our comprehensive audit of the needs, wants and proclivities of the fee-earners.'

'What exactly do you want me to do?'

'Well, for our first fact-finding audit we want to know what the second-year fee-earners think of hot-desking.'

'What's hot-desking?'

'It's a system of office organisation that does away with permanent workstations for employees, thereby freeing them up to sit next to different colleagues.'

'So people have to continually move desk?'

'Yes, and often without warning,' expounded Bradley Messenger enthusiastically.

'Why would anyone want to do that?'

'Change, they get to experience change. We want to be change-makers here at Freely Savage, don't we? And that's just for starters.'

'Change-makers?' echoed Maserov unbelievingly, ignoring as best he could the never-ending corporate need to convert nouns and verbs into each other or force them into unhappy marriages in order to create the illusion they are technical terms in a learned discipline.

'To exploit the invigorating effect of change.'

Maserov reminded himself that he had twelve months' protection with pay so the insanity of hot-desking, of continually moving people from workstation to workstation, wouldn't affect him personally. But he was nevertheless affronted by the madness of it.

'So you want me to find out what the Second Years think about hot-desking?'

'Yes.'

'Will their opinions carry a lot of weight?'

'Probably not. We haven't decided yet what to do with them.'

'I can tell you already, without asking,' Maserov said. 'People, fee-earners, will hate it.'

'Do *you* hate it?' Bradley Messenger asked.

'I've never done it but it sounds like a stupid idea, especially for lawyers. By the way, when you ask me how I'd *feel* about being the Second Year representative . . .?' inquired Maserov haltingly.

'We're *asking* you to do it.'

'And when you're *asking* me to do it . . .?'

'We're *telling* you to do it. It's been a pleasure talking to you, Stephen.'

With that Bradley Messenger stood up and the meeting was over.

V

'It sounds insane. Who on earth could possibly be in favour of hot-desking?' Eleanor asked her estranged husband as she knelt over the bath to wash the soap off two-year-old Jacob Maserov, the younger of their two children.

'People who will never themselves have to leave the comfort of their own desks, people who have to prove they deserve their salaries, have to come up with new ideas to foist upon the already terrified,' said Maserov as he knelt beside her, bathing their older son, Beanie.

'How can hot-desking possibly improve efficiency?'

'It can't. But you're missing the crux of what I've told you.'

'What's the crux?' Eleanor asked.

'That they asked me to be the Second Year representative,' Maserov explained while wrapping Beanie in his favourite blue towel with the head of a bear at one end.

'So what does *that* mean?'

'No idea.'

'Is it because you stuck your neck out with Malcolm Torrent?'

'It's got to be, no one knew I existed before that.'

'Is it good?'

'Well,' said Maserov, thinking. 'It's too soon to tell but it's definitely annoying, 'cause it means I have to go into the Freely Savage office to ask people stupid questions that will make them angry at the person conducting the survey, me, when I could be working back at Torrent Industries.'

'Trying to give aid and comfort to their band of sexual predators,' Eleanor interrupted.

'Yes, and working to pay off the mortgage on the house you live in with our sons. I really don't think you should look at my work as saving sexual predators.'

'I wouldn't think you'd want anybody looking at your work that way. But what other way is there to look at it?'

Maserov started gently towel-drying his older son's hair with the bear head part of the towel. 'Eleanor, we don't know exactly what these guys did and, anyway, even people accused of murder deserve to be defended.'

'You *wish* it was murder. Murder you can defend. Everyone understands murder,' she said, pat-drying her youngest son, Jacob, using the closed toilet as a seat.

'Are you saying sexual harassment is worse than murder?' Maserov asked.

'I'm saying murder is more understandable.'

'Well, actually the sex urge is more frequent in people than the urge to kill.'

'Not when *we* lived together.'

'Anyway, these are so far just allegations,' Maserov said, dragging the plastic stool over to the basin where he would encourage Beanie to brush his teeth.

'You mean they're unfounded?'

'Well, I don't know yet.'

'Why don't you know yet?'

'I've only just moved offices. I'm trying to survive. It's complicated.'

'So you have your work cut out for you, is that what you're saying?'

'Yes,' said Maserov. 'I do. I have my work cut out for me. Not too much toothpaste, Beanie. You don't need that much.'

'I do,' said the five-year-old Beanie.

'No, not *that* much.'

'I need only *this* much,' said Beanie, 'but I want the rest.'

'That's a fine distinction,' said Maserov.

'Thank you, Daddy,' said Beanie, applying the bristles of his toothbrush to his small pink tongue.

Eleanor bounced Jacob wrapped in a towel on her knee. 'So you'll still have to go back to work at night there too . . . probably,' she said.

'Well, no, actually. I don't have to rush off tonight. I can read the kids a story, maybe two.'

'You probably shouldn't,' said Eleanor, fumbling in a small wicker basket for Jacob's nappy rash cream.

'No, it's alright.'

'But don't you need as much time as you can get to solve Malcolm Torrent's problems?'

'Well, one of the advantages of my new situation is that it's task oriented. There's no one watching me, noting when I come and go, so as long as I feel I'm making progress I can be satisfied with the day's work. It's almost like I'm working for myself.'

'But you wouldn't want to be complacent.'

'I'm not complacent. It's just that I'm now in a position not to have to race back to work every night, away from my sons . . . and away from you.' Maserov reached his hand out to stroke his wife's arm but she slowly pulled away.

'Eleanor, I'm more my own boss than ever. For the first time in years I don't have to rush off anywhere, don't have to study. You'd said you wanted more time together and —'

'Yeah, I did, but now we're separated.'

'I know and I don't like it. I don't like being separated.'

'It's a transition,' said Eleanor. 'It's still new. All transitions are hard. It's only been four months. You need to give it time.'

'I need to give it time?'

'Yes. We were together many years, you know.'

'I know. I was there.'

'Not for all of it,' Eleanor said.

'Even when I wasn't there I was still . . . there.'

'You need to give the separation another chance,' Eleanor explained.

'That's what people urge with respect to a marriage, not a separation.'

'Well, I'm saying it with respect to the separation.'

'Don't you find it difficult?'

'Perhaps I'm coping better than you.'

'Perhaps you are. But can I read the kids a story tonight?'

'No, not tonight. Tonight's not good.'

'Tonight's not good?'

'No.'

'Why isn't tonight a good night for me to read a story to my children?'

'I've . . . um . . . I've got . . . Someone's coming round.'

'Who?'

'A friend.'

'Are they *my* friend too?' asked Maserov.

'I don't think you would think so.'

'Would *they* think so?'

'I don't think they would think so.'

'So we have that in common, me and your friend?'

'Yes,' said Eleanor.

'This friend, the one who's coming over who would agree with me that we're not friends, are they animal, vegetable or mineral?'

'You don't need to worry.'

'It sure sounds like I do.'

'It's Marta. Marta's coming over.'

'Marta?'

'Yes.'

'You could've just said "vegetable". I would have got there eventually.'

'I know you don't like Marta. That's why I thought it might be better if *I* read the kids a story and then you won't run into her.'

'*She* doesn't like *me*.'

'It's not you.'

'It feels like *me* when I say hello and she doesn't answer.'

'It's men. She doesn't like men.'

'She married one, sort of.'

'No, they *were* legally married.'

'No, I meant he was sort of a man.'

'He *was* a man before she married him,' Eleanor said.

'Yeah but three years after she left him he still hasn't thawed out.'

'Well, that's a man for you,' Eleanor replied.

Maserov kissed his children goodnight and went outside to wait in his car to see if Eleanor's visitor was indeed her friend Marta, the divorced geography teacher who hated him because he reminded her of men. When he saw that it was, he was relieved and exhaled quietly though his nostrils.

part three

I

There were four women, former employees of Torrent Industries, suing the company for sexual harassment. But only one of them had engaged a lawyer. The other three were apparently unrepresented. At least this was on the face of it what their pleadings suggested. This piqued Maserov's interest. Why would three out of the four of them sue the construction behemoth without engaging a lawyer? How would they know where to start? Even from Maserov's earliest glimpse of their files, and it was a mere glimpse, nothing in them appeared to him *un*-legal. Each one of the three unrepresented women had a statement of claim that read as though they had been drafted by a skilled and even motivated lawyer.

It seemed likely that the three had actually engaged a lawyer to draft their pleadings but why, wondered Maserov, would their lawyer hide his or her identity behind the clients? Since their time at Torrent Industries coincided, it was likely that all four women knew each other, and yet only one, a Carla Monterosso, had a lawyer acting for her who was willing to admit it. Maybe the one lawyer was acting for all four of them? But then why be open about it in Carla Monterosso's claim but not in the others?

Maserov was confident Bruce Featherby would have some information or at least a theory about this, which was why he picked up his phone from what felt to him like the sanctuary of his office at Torrent Industries headquarters.

'Bruce Featherby?' whispered Featherby anxiously, almost breathlessly, down the phone when seeing the prefix of the incoming call from Torrent Industries. But it wouldn't have taken a call from Torrent Industries to stimulate an autonomic fight or flight response in him. No, ever since his first encounter with Maserov over the phone he had begun to speculate that he, Featherby, was being considered for the category of 'former person'. In fact he might already have been consigned to it. If not, perhaps his every move now was being scrutinised to determine whether or not he should be allowed to stay on the partnership track or else, like a wart, be frozen off the body politic of the competition for partnership at Freely Savage.

Why did this inexplicable Maserov thing have to happen to him? If only someone else had been handling the Torrent Industries sexual harassment allegations. And perhaps former personhood wasn't the end of this, not even the worst of it. Maybe he had already signed his last departmental birthday card for someone he saw every day and didn't know.

'Bruce, it's Stephen Maserov. How're things? This a bad time? I got the files, thanks. Tell me, why are three out of the four plaintiffs representing themselves or seeming to? What do you make of that?'

'I can't talk to you, Maserov,' whispered Featherby, as though even telling him that might be bad for him.

'This a bad time? I can call you back. I just thought you might know something about their lawyer. The unrepresented plaintiffs' files have the fingerprints of a lawyer all over them.' Maserov wasn't meaning to fan the flames of Featherby's anxiety but that's what he was doing.

'I can *never* talk to you,' answered Featherby with a low quiet steadiness to his voice.

'Featherby, we've been through this. Okay, I got the files but I hope there are no hard feelings between us.'

'*No one* will talk to you,' said Featherby quietly as he placed the phone down into its cradle. Maserov was going to have to figure this out on his own.

II

It was time to read the affidavits to see each plaintiff's case. For no reason other than it was first in the pile, he read the affidavit of Lilly Zhang. For Lilly, a cheerful but shy 24-year-old, it began with an invitation to lunch from the man for whom she was working, Brian Weeks, in Compliance. Out of a sense of unease she declined the invitation with great embarrassment but it led only to more invitations, until she finally accepted. When that first lunch passed without incident she agreed to let the man take her out again at the end of three very long days. This time the executive wanted to buy her a drink and so took her to a bar. Maserov read that, while Lilly Zhang drank only mineral water, Brian Weeks had at least four drinks, two of which were spirits, and this was when he began making suggestive comments about Lilly's body. He told her, 'I like Chinese.' Lilly was uncomfortable but he was her boss and so she just sat there as he commented on her rear. Then he put his hand on the back of her blouse so that it was resting on her bra strap. She gently moved his hand away and told him that she was due to meet her boyfriend and had to leave.

That night was the night Weeks started sending her lewd text messages in which he claimed to be able to feel that she was attracted to him. At work over the ensuing days he would go in and out of work mode. He would be in work mode when he wanted something from her quickly but would slip out of it when he himself had finished a task and was taking a break, even if his finished task had now given her new work.

She deposed that he seemed to delight in trying to distract her with suggestive text messages even after he had given her work to do that he had described as important and urgent.

Maserov read that on one occasion Weeks had texted that he wanted her to do to him what she did to her boyfriend. She ignored this but it didn't stop him. Within two days he had texted her that he wanted her to fellate him right there under his desk. She ignored this text too but was having trouble sleeping at night for fear of what might come next.

She began dreading coming to work. Early one afternoon, he returned from lunch smelling of alcohol and began to massage her back as she sat at her desk, very quickly moving his fingers to the front of her blouse and touching her breasts. At this she began to cry, got up from her desk, and ran down the corridor to the elevator. Lilly deposed that the executive called out in a voice for everyone to hear that if she 'didn't want it' she should have said something sooner. Lilly, frightened, humiliated and aware that everyone could see her, waited for the elevator to take her down to the ground floor where she ran out, breathless, to Flinders Lane. She went into the Grain Store cafe where a few people were still finishing their lunch. Without waiting to be seated she sat down at a corner table and buried her head in her arms and cried. Maserov took a break to splash water on his face. He had to read these affidavits but he was starting to realise just how much he didn't want to.

Next he read the affidavit of Carla Monterosso. It began with the date Carla had started working at Torrent Industries and then the date she was transferred to Mike Mercer in Urban Infrastructure. She had heard rumours about Mercer but then one heard rumours about so many of them. If you listened to them all you couldn't work for anyone. Maserov was already impressed with the affidavit. While nothing specific had been alleged yet, the scene had been set, a milieu, an environment had been established that felt entirely real to him.

So Carla began working for Mike Mercer. He would comment approvingly or sometimes with mock disapproval on her choice of clothes, setting the tone of one-sided informality that had her permanently off-balance. She remembered the first time he came to her workstation to read over her shoulder. She could smell him. She waited for him to touch her but he didn't, not that day or the next time he read over her shoulder or the time after that. Then, a few days later, he was reading over her shoulder again and this time she felt his hand, the flat of his palm. At first it rested on her shoulder. Then as he was reading her typed words out loud to himself she felt his index and middle fingers fiddling with her bra strap. No one walking past would have detected anything untoward.

Maserov winced and screamed to himself, 'Stand up! Get up now.' Carla had screamed but no sound came out. The screams had bounced around inside her head like a pinball.

A team of people, a subset of the Urban Infrastructure department, was working back late on a tender proposal for a bridge in Iraq. It involved long days and late nights. There was an urgency due to a looming deadline and among the team a sense of excitement, even among some of the support staff. They were lucky to have been asked to work late nights and long days, privileged to be chosen to be on the team. If the tender was successful the team – the whole team, not just the team leader or his executives, everyone – would be minor heroes within the department and, it was said, within senior management. One wanted to think that everyone was in this together, pulling in the same direction, part of a group, part of the Torrent Industries Urban Infrastructure bridge tender team. The support staff were told several times a year, and always at the office Christmas party, to feel a sense of pride every time they saw a crane with a Torrent Industries logo on it reaching way up to the heavens somewhere in the city, in a magazine, or on television. 'We couldn't do it without each and every one of you,' they were told.

You wanted to believe it. Maserov had seen people at Freely Savage wanting to believe similar corporate professions of gratitude. You wanted to buy in. You felt better if you did and so many did, as much as they could for as long as they could, and you tried not to pay too much attention to other things you heard unofficially and on the grapevine. There was overtime pay and your name would be recorded as a team member.

Yet none of the support staff in the team wanted to be the last one there despite the overtime, no one wanted to be alone. 'You want witnesses,' Maserov whispered to himself.

Because Mike Mercer was the senior member of the team, the team leader, he would be the person signing off on the whole endeavour, he would determine when the tender was ready to go. There were some typos in the document but essentially it was done. Some beers were shared in another office along the corridor. You could hear occasional laughter. Job well done, everyone. Carla would tidy up the typos.

She was alone at her workstation and could hear the festive sounds coming from down the hall. She had three pages to go when Mercer came back to his office, looking over her shoulder at her progress as she went. 'Nearly there,' she said in a tone that tried to give the impression she felt she was part of the team. She *was* part of the team. It was just that she didn't feel like it. He asked her to print it out and bring it to him when she was finished.

By the time it was all printed the noise from down the hall was dissipating and when she sat down opposite him as instructed while he read through it she could hear nothing at all. But perhaps, she thought, there was still someone there. Mike Mercer had closed his office door. It was hard to know for sure who was still there.

It was 2.20 am. Mercer was pacing his office pretending to read the document. Each time he got close to her Carla could smell the beer on his breath. She could feel him behind her.

'You've done well, my girl,' he said. He let the document drop to the ground and began kneading her shoulders.

'Get up!' Maserov shouted after the event and to himself.

Carla did get up. With his hands on her shoulders, Mike Mercer turned her around. She was facing him.

'You want this as much as I do,' he whispered.

'No! No, Mike, this is a mistake. Stop!'

'You'll like it.'

He pushed her down flat on her back on the carpet and put his mouth over hers. He was hard. She could feel it as she tried to get out from underneath him. He deliberately misinterpreted her movement as simulated sex and he began to dry hump her even more vigorously.

'I know you're liking this,' he said quietly between breaths.

She wanted to scream but nothing came out of her but air. This was a nightmare, *the* nightmare. Reaching his hand between her thighs, he attempted to feel whether he had excited her but her stockings and underpants gave nothing away and she pulled his hand from her crotch before he could go inside the garments to get to flesh, membrane.

'Mike, are you fucking crazy?' she managed to say between gasps. Ignoring her, and breathing hard like a jogger in a marathon, someone on a mission, he tore the buttons off her blouse and ripped off her bra with one hand. He shifted his position upwards so that he was sitting on her chest and, with her breasts exposed, he leaned forward with his fly undone. Her words were useless now. Her consent was irrelevant.

'I know you've wanted this for months.'

Leaning forward, he attempted to place his fully erect penis in Carla's mouth. When writhing, squirming, her eyes screwed tightly shut, she refused, still with his leaden weight on her, he rubbed himself back and forth on top of her until he ejaculated between her breasts. In this state, with his ejaculate on her chest and Mike Mercer now relaxing the pressure of his weight, she slid out from underneath him and ran terrified out of his office, down the now empty and silent corridor, to the women's bathroom. She looked at herself in the mirror, alone there under the strip light at almost three in the morning, dishevelled, make-up smudged, clothes torn, and splashed water on herself in an attempt to get clean enough to go out into the street, to catch a cab, to escape. What would the cab driver think? What kind of man would he be? Did he, himself, know what kind of man he would be when he looked at her? He would be waiting for her at a cab rank in King Street outside the Spearmint Rhino Gentlemen's Club.

Maserov could see it all. There was nothing in the affidavit that did not ring true to him, not even Mike Mercer asserting that he knew Carla had wanted this. But how could Carla have wanted it? This had nothing at all to do with sex. The paragraphs in Carla's affidavit told a story, not of sex, but of humiliation and power, the arbitrary exercise of power with the expectation of almost complete impunity.

Maserov read that Carla had, subsequent to the attack, resigned from Torrent Industries by the month's end and was, at the time of swearing the affidavit, receiving ongoing psychiatric care at her own expense.

Maserov thought he might be sick. He knew men like this, had seen them. When he had grabbed his chance to do something for Malcolm Torrent and buy himself some time to look for other employment, the plaintiffs were nameless, faceless victims. Now, on reading Lilly's and Carla's affidavits, they were real people to him. He wondered what he was doing defending Torrent Industries against these sexual harassment claims. This wasn't why he had gone to law school.

The affidavits of Ms Carla Monterosso, the plaintiff with the lawyer, had been prepared by a certain A.A. Betga. Maserov stared at the name, Betga, because, unusual as it was, it was strangely familiar to him, although he couldn't say why. He said it to himself a few times sitting at his desk. He said it to himself walking to the men's room and then a few more times at the urinal. Then he remembered.

A.A. Betga was August Anselm Betga. He had been a few years ahead of Maserov in law school and was famous, almost legendary, for two things. First, it was said that he earned the money to put himself through law school by working several seasons as the entertainment director on a cruise ship. Second, he was unequivocally brilliant, apparently almost freakishly so. He came either first or second in every single subject he took and topped his year every year of his degree. He was a winner of the Supreme Court Prize, the most prestigious academic award available to law students, frequently won by young lawyers beginning their journey to great legal distinction and often culminating in a judicial appointment to one of the higher courts.

It was the only A.A. Betga he had ever heard of and the only one it could be. Maserov didn't know him, although Betga had been pointed out to him in his first week of law school. He might even recognise him. Maserov's problem, he learned after a day and a half, was that none of the phone numbers and none of the addresses given by Betga in the relevant affidavits were current. When he contacted the Law Institute, the address of Betga's practice in their records corresponded with that of Carla Monterosso's house. The email address they had for him, which was the same as that on the affidavits, wasn't operative.

The only way of getting hold of Betga, he realised, would be to visit him at Carla Monterosso's place, which was ironic since he was seeking Betga only to have him speak on her behalf. There was, however, a problem with that. Maserov knew there was a no contact rule, which forbade him from communicating directly with the client on the other side of a civil matter. There were, of course, exceptions to the no contact rule, just as there were to every rule (except the ones that permitted no exceptions, at least until other smarter people had found them) and so, to cover himself, Maserov hastily wrote a letter to Betga that he presumed Betga would never receive and sent it to all the addresses Betga had listed in the relevant court documents, informing him of his wish to speak, ideally, with Betga, and if not with him then directly with the client, Ms Carla Monterosso.

III

He waited ten days, suspecting this was long enough to cover him should he need an exception to the no contact rule. When, as expected, he hadn't received a scrap of evidence that Betga was still handling the case or even alive, he headed out to the East St Kilda terrace house of Carla Monterosso one evening on a wing and a prayer, in a 27-year-old Saab, the sight of which induced in most people surges of *Weltschmerz*, and in Eleanor Maserov something approaching contempt.

Unlike her lawyer, Carla wasn't difficult to find. She still lived in the property listed as her address in her affidavits.

Maserov rang the doorbell and waited in what would have been the dark had it not been for the valiant strivings of an intermittently on streetlight nestled inside a cushion of branches and exhausted powerlines. He could hear what sounded like a television game show that was, on closer listening, the news, as well as a small child crying and a woman's voice alternating between addressing the child in coos and addressing an adult in more exasperated tones.

'No, *I'll* get it . . . Why not? I can get the front door as well as you. Okay, you get your hand on your holster and cover me.' That was the last thing Maserov heard before the door was opened just enough to reveal a tall woman somewhere in her late twenties to early thirties with large dark almond-shaped eyes framed by thick jet black hair and wearing silver-grey compression leggings. The woman was holding a little girl who looked likely to grow into the woman holding her and whose age Maserov guessed at somewhere between one and two.

'Yep?' Ms Monterosso said through the gap in the door.

'Hi, my name's Stephen Maserov. I'm a lawyer and I'm looking for Carla Monterosso?'

'*Who* are you?'

'My name's Stephen Maserov,' he said, holding one of his business cards up to the screen door between them, 'and I was wondering if you could help me. I'm trying to contact Mr Betga, A.A. Betga, whom I understand to be your lawyer.'

'He's not here.'

'Who is it?' called a man's voice from inside.

'I don't know . . . a lawyer,' Carla called back to the man.

'No, I didn't think he was here,' continued Maserov, 'but I wondered if you could help me find him. You're Ms Carla Monterosso?'

'*Where'd* you say you're from?' she asked him.

'What does he want?' the man's voice called to her from inside and down the hall.

'I don't know. Will you let me talk to him?' Carla called back, holding the little girl tightly within her arms and bouncing rhythmically for her benefit via shallow squats.

'Where'd you say you're from?' she asked him again.

'My name's Stephen Maserov. I'm a lawyer with Freely Savage Carter Blanche and I'm trying to find —'

'I got nothing to say to you,' she said, closing the door.

Maserov stood there frozen for a moment, looking at the closed front door, and heard Carla say, presumably to the man's muffled questions, 'How should I know? Said he's looking for Betga.'

Maserov realised that, although technically she hadn't actually admitted it, this was almost certainly Carla Monterosso, and she had opened the door only to close it on hearing he was with Freely Savage, so she knew who A.A. Betga was. So Maserov tried twice more at different times of the day to visit her, having left phone messages that went unanswered. On both occasions his visits were unsuccessful.

How hard could it be to track down this woman's lawyer, he wondered to himself. How could he even dream of solving Malcolm Torrent's sexual harassment problems if he couldn't do that? And why wouldn't Carla Monterosso agree to speak to him, not even long enough to tell him where Betga was or even just how to contact him? As he sat in his car he could see himself using up the precious time Malcolm Torrent had gifted him and drawing a salary for it, but without making the slightest progress towards solving Torrent's problem or securing alternative employment. He was squandering the gift. The car smelled of him and even he knew it. It wasn't an intrinsically unpleasant fragrance but it used to smell a little of Eleanor. Had he squandered his life with her? A tiny cinder of self-regard waved at him and then surrendered to the gale of anxiety he kept beneath all his business shirts.

He was parked outside Carla Monterosso's house two days later, waiting for her to come home, when he realised that few people would consider what he was doing anything other than stalking. Here was a lawyer, a man, acting for a client she was suing for sexual harassment and he himself could be regarded to be stalking her, at least by the ethics committee of the Law Institute. When he saw her car pull up he took a breath and opened the door of his car.

'What do you want?' she said, taking her little girl out of the car. 'I'll call the cops. My partner's a cop,' she said as though just remembering.

'I'm sorry, I'm just trying to find Betga.'

'Fuck off, whoever you are,' she said, propelling Maserov back into his car. If only she'd seen the reassuring sight of the children's car seats in the back seat. How non-threatening is a man with two kiddie car seats behind him wherever he goes? But he didn't have kiddie car seats, they were in Eleanor's car. What about a young mother and two kiddie car seats? Carla Monterosso might respond less defensively if she was approached by a woman.

IV

'Let me get this straight. You're trying to co-opt me into coming with you to the home of a victim of sexual harassment in order to convince her to give you the whereabouts of her lawyer. Is that right? And you think she'll talk to me because I'm a woman?' Eleanor Maserov was standing in the kitchen of their marital home with a glass of twelve-month-old Shiraz in her hand and an expression that was the perfect cross-fertilisation of astonishment and contempt.

'Well, I hate to say it but this isn't just a problem for me. It's kind of your problem too,' answered Maserov.

'Now you're going to tell me again how if you don't keep your stupid job we can't keep the house.'

'Eleanor, where did all this anger come from?' Maserov asked and then immediately regretted it and swallowed the air as though this might be what one does when trying to un-ring a bell, one that had become untethered in one's head. The clock ticked in the otherwise silent kitchen they once shared and he looked more closely at his shoes than he had since she had asked him to move out. But it was just as he'd thought, they were no more interesting than they were when he lived with her and their children. And still the silence whizzed around his ears as he waited for her to say something, something that promised to be not good.

Maserov moved in towards her and tried to put his arms around her.

'In what universe does that seem like the appropriate response to this situation?' Eleanor asked him.

Maserov drew breath but he had a ready answer. 'Well, we're both tired. We know each other very well, we're under pressure and, most importantly, we love each other,' he said with a vulnerability that couldn't have left him more open if he'd tied his hands behind his back and approached her with his chin pleading, 'Please hit me.' But before she had a chance to lean in for the kill, he threw her off balance with, 'We have two children, two little boys whom we each love more than anyone and anything else in the world. And no one will ever love them ahead of everything else other than you . . . and me.'

In the twenty minutes it took for the inside of the wine bottle to reach bone-dry Eleanor came around to asking what it was he thought she could do to help him get the details of Carla Monterosso's lawyer, A.A. Betga, that he couldn't do himself.

In the backseat of Eleanor's car sat the two Maserov children in their respective car seats, little Beanie and the even littler Jacob. There had been no one to look after them so they'd had to accompany their parents. While Maserov went to see his children every night to bath them, read them stories, and put them to bed, the longer Eleanor's mandated separation, her 'much-needed time apart', lasted, the more he worried that the separation might become permanent simply through inertia, even if it was never deemed permanent as a matter of any articulated policy. It would be a kind of *status quo post bellum*, a *bellum* whose *casus* was a mystery to him. One morning he had woken up and there it was, a *bellum*, resting on his wife's face.

This led him to worry that his children would grow up with little memory of his being around much at all. Nothing else worried him more than this, not even the unemployment, underemployment or economic humiliation he was tightrope-walking to avoid. These were, after all, increasingly the norm everywhere he looked, although seemingly better hidden by people who weren't him. And anyway, at least theoretically, they were reversible. But your children not remembering your being around, not loving you, that's irreversible.

Maserov drove. Eleanor was sitting next to him. It had been a few months since she'd been in the Saab they used to share. Now, since asking him to live by himself, she had a much newer car, which she shared with a finance company that agreed to let her drive it, fill it with fuel, clean it and insure it, on the condition that she would pay an exorbitant undiminishing rental while the car depreciated to worthless.

When they pulled up not far from Carla Monterosso's worn weatherboard terrace house Maserov could see a look of unease settle gracefully on his estranged wife's face.

'You want me to go in?' Eleanor asked uncertainly.

'Not if you can get her talking at the front door.'

'You think just 'cause I'm a woman she's going to give me the where-abouts of her lawyer when for some reason she wouldn't give them to you?'

'She won't even let me *talk* to her.'

'She doesn't trust you because you're a male lawyer representing the company that's protecting the man that sexually harassed her.'

'That's right,' said Maserov. 'She's entitled not to trust me. I'm not blaming her.'

'That's big of you,' offered Eleanor.

'If I can talk to her lawyer I won't need to bother her directly ever again.'

'What are you going to say to her lawyer?'

'We don't have to get into that now.'

'Will it be fair?'

'That's what she's got a lawyer for.'

'So it won't be fair?'

'If it's within my power it will be fair.'

'Do you have any power?'

'No, I don't think so.'

'This is crazy!' Eleanor said. 'What do you want me to say to her?'

'Okay,' said Maserov. 'You go up to the front door and ring the doorbell. She opens the door and sees you with Jacob in your arms —'

'What! You want me to take Jacob to the front door?'

'Sure, she's not going to slam the door on a mother holding a little boy.'

'But what if it's not safe?'

'Of course it's safe. There's no reason to think it's not safe. She hasn't any history of anything but alleging sexual harassment. She's unlikely to accuse Jacob. Look, she's an innocent victim, *allegedly*, remember? And anyway, her partner or boyfriend is a cop. She told me.'

'A cop!'

'Yeah, a chivalrous cop, apparently.'

'What makes you say he's chivalrous?'

'Once when I came to the door she asked him to *cover* her.'

'With a gun?'

'I assumed it was a gun but it could have been a piece of halibut.'

'She asked him to cover her! You're willing to risk not only my life but Jacob's life in the quest for —'

'Eleanor, nobody's risking anybody's life. You can't really think I'd send you into any kind of danger. You go to the door. When she sees you're holding Jacob she won't slam the door on you. Explain who you are and by all means you can slag me off to get her trust. Talk to her that way you do to Marta.'

'What way?'

'You know, *that* way, about men. Then tell her you can't believe I've sent you here like this and then get her to tell you how to contact her lawyer, A.A. Betga. It will take less time than it's taken to talk about it.'

Maserov watched as Eleanor got out of the car with Jacob in her arms. Turning back towards him she whispered, 'This is the last time I do something like this for you.'

'Why couldn't *I* go with Mummy?' asked Beanie.

'That would have been overkill,' said Maserov.

'Overkill,' said Beanie, momentarily assuaged by his father's tone rather than by the words.

'Do you want to tell me about your day at school today?' he asked Beanie, keeping his eyes firmly on Eleanor's progress.

'Not today, Daddy.'

'Okay, what day *would* you like to discuss? What about last Tuesday?'

'I don't remember that day.'

'Sure you do, came after last Monday.'

Beanie was considering the question as he watched his father watching Eleanor in conversation with Carla on the doorstep in the distance. Carla was talking to her. She hadn't slammed or even slightly closed the door on her. So far, so good. Maserov was heartened. With good fortune like this there was no question he had a bright future ahead of him, he told himself.

Carla was holding her daughter to her chest with one hand and seemed to be reaching out to stroke Jacob's wispy hair with the other. The kid was a success. Eleanor too seemed to be doing well. He wondered what they were talking about. Maybe Eleanor would come to feel invested in the case, in his career? 'How about that!' Maserov couldn't help saying out loud. Carla had invited Eleanor to come inside the house. Eleanor and Jacob were going in.

'Daddy!' said young Beanie from the back of the car.

It had been a good idea to get her involved. She'd already spent more time talking to Carla Monterosso than he could have hoped for.

'Daddy!'

The only other woman he could possibly have asked was Jessica Annand but that would have entailed disclosing the true nature of what he was doing at Torrent Industries. He winced at the thought. Sooner or later she was going to find out and she was going to hate him for it. That was coming, sure enough.

'Daddy!'

'What is it Beanie?'

'I need the toilet.'

'Are you sure?'

'Yes.'

'How about a drink? Have you got your water?'

'I need the toilet, not a drink.'

'Oh shit!' Maserov swore.

'Yes, that's right,' said his son.

'Really? Really *now*?'

'Yes.'

'Standing up or sitting down?' he asked the little boy.

'Dad, it's the sitting down kind. I need to go now.'

A thin veil of perspiration lay on Maserov's forehead. He told his son to hold on and then walked him to the front door of Carla Monterosso's house, where the little boy was instructed to knock loudly at the door and ask for his mother when it opened. Maserov moved just out of the line of sight of whoever would open the door and he heard a man open the door and speak to Beanie.

'Hello young fella. How can I help you?' The surprised man was a slightly rotund but tall uniformed policeman.

'I need the toilet. My mother's in here.'

'Oh, you'd better come in then. Second door on the left.'

Beanie ran in before anybody had a chance to change their minds.

'Which way is left, again?' the little boy called as he ran inside in desperation.

'The side with your watch on,' Maserov called out to his young son who was unknowingly sacrificing his dignity for his father's career.

'I suppose you'd better come in too, Mr Maserov,' the policeman said. He closed the door and led Maserov down the hallway to where Carla Monterosso, holding her daughter, and Eleanor Maserov, holding their son Jacob, were sitting at a wooden dining table of Scandinavian design, staring at him each with a glass of wine in front of them.

'Okay, I understand you've got to keep your job to keep your house. And that was a brave thing you did with your boss,' Carla said to him.

The policeman leaned in and offered his hand to Maserov, 'Acting Sergeant Quinn.' He looked at least twenty years older than Carla and the nature of the relationship wasn't immediately clear.

'Oh for God's sake, Ron, just let him call you Ron.'

The policeman, now duly berated, nodded his agreement. 'Ron, then.'

'I can't tell you where Betga is. I hate the son of a bitch but I'm not the kind of person . . .' Carla said, resuming her conversation with Eleanor.

She paused, not quite sure what kind of person she was. 'Look, I think the sleazy, dishonest bastard was at least once trying to help me so I don't want to get him into any trouble.'

'He's not in any trouble, not as far as I'm aware, not from me,' explained Maserov. 'I only want to talk to him in his capacity as a lawyer, as *your* lawyer.'

'So just talk to me,' Carla offered pragmatically.

'I can't. If he's still representing you, I'm obliged to talk to you through him, ethically obliged. Is he still your lawyer, at least for this matter?'

'I don't have any other matters.'

'Okay, sure, but is he your lawyer in your case against Torrent Industries?'

'Yes,' Carla said. 'Yes, I suppose he still is.'

'Well, how can I negotiate with him if I can't contact him?' Maserov asked.

'I don't mean to be rude,' Carla replied, 'but that's *your* problem. I'm planning on taking this to court.'

'It *is* my problem but it's also *your* problem. I can't help you if I can't get hold of him.'

'I'm no lawyer, Mr Maserov, but isn't it your job to help the people I'm suing?'

'It doesn't have to be like that; it doesn't have to be a zero-sum game,' answered Maserov.

Carla Monterosso poured herself and Eleanor Maserov each a second glass of wine and asked, 'It does, doesn't it?'

From down the hall came the sound of young Beanie Maserov flushing the toilet.

'It doesn't, actually,' said Eleanor. 'You know, you could do a lot worse than having my husband as the lawyer acting for Torrent Industries.'

Carla took her gaze from her glass and gave it to Eleanor. 'You're a teacher, right, not a lawyer?' she asked.

'That's right,' said Eleanor.

'I can't tell you where he is but sooner or later you'll find him, or at least someone who might know where to find him . . . at one of two hotels: the Dick Whittington or the Grosvenor,' Carla said, as though hoping some or other deity would forgive her for divulging this, even if Betga wouldn't.

'Pubs . . . in St Kilda?'

'Yep, sorry, it's the best I can do. Don't tell him it was me. Case the place for regulars and choose one. It won't be him but they'll know how to find him.'

V

'Are you interested . . . in craft beers?' the man growled haltingly. The speaker had a scar that ran cheek by jowl towards a neck decorated with tattoos of over-endowed women fawning over apocryphal beasts from no mythology Maserov could recognise.

Maserov was taken aback. Sitting towards the rear of the main bar in the Grosvenor Hotel, the day after his conversation with Carla, this was not how he remembered Betga. What had life done to him, Maserov wondered. Hair colour could be changed easily, yes, but how does one compress a body so much? The man was squat but taut with muscles that insisted on grudging respect if not outright admiration. And Maserov remembered Betga to have been tall and lithe.

'Am I interested in craft beers?' Maserov asked incredulously.

'Was that right?' the man asked more fluently in the direction of a third party Maserov couldn't see. The third party revealed himself only when Maserov turned around.

'Well, you got the *words* right but the tone was appropriate only if you meant to intimidate him.'

The third party was A.A. Betga, still tall and lithe, in a crisp white shirt open slightly at the collar and lightly checked pressed trousers pleated in the style of the late forties. This was Betga's style. No one else dressed like this and yet here he was, carrying it off without ostentation.

'You're . . . Betga?' Maserov asked a little hesitantly.

'Yes, A.A. Betga,' said Betga, shaking Maserov's hand. 'And this is Kasimir. Did you *mean* to intimidate him?' Betga asked Kasimir.

'No,' Kasimir replied.

'Then you fucked up. Kasimir comes from a big family with a long, proud tradition, several of them, families *and* traditions. They were a very big name on the Melbourne waterfront at one time,' explained Betga. 'But things went wrong for the family ever since the Costigan Royal Commission into the Painters and Dockers Union in the eighties.'

'I've engaged Betga as my life coach,' explained Kasimir with something approaching pride.

'How's that working for you?' asked Maserov.

'Look, he can be a little condescending but I think we're making progress,' said Kasimir.

'I'll accept that,' said Betga.

'He *is* one of the best.' Kasimir smiled at Maserov. 'I shopped around. He's a lawyer too.'

'Oh, he knows I'm a lawyer,' said Betga. 'That's why Mr Maserov is here. Do you want to get the two of us a beer? And that's another one of those questions where the answer is assumed.'

'Ah-ha!' said Kasimir. 'I knew that.' Then, turning to Maserov, 'I used to misconstrue like a motherfucker.'

'Yes, I remember,' Betga agreed as Kasimir headed towards the bar.

Then Betga swivelled around on his seat to face Maserov front-on and without missing a beat he began, 'You work for Freely Savage. The partner responsible for these files is Mike "Crispy" Hamilton. You answer to him?'

'Everyone answers to him.'

'*I* don't,' said Betga. 'Used to.'

'You worked for Freely Savage?'

'You hadn't discovered that yet? Man, I'm surprised they're still paying your way through the nine circles.'

'The nine circles? Oh, right, Dante's nine circles of hell.' It had taken Maserov's mind a moment to transcend Kasimir and the miscellany of craft beers.

'It's a change to be talking to a former high school English teacher instead of Kasimir over there.'

'How do you know so much about me?' Maserov asked.

'Your wife told Carla everything. Don't you remember? I thought you were there.'

'Yeah, I was there,' Maserov said with a sigh.

'Well, I'm intrigued by what she told her about you and Hamilton,' said Betga. 'You're looking for me because you work at Freely Savage and you're acting for Torrent Industries, their most important client, as I recall, yet you've apparently done a number on Hamilton. Have I got it right?'

Just then Kasimir returned holding two pots of beer.

'Good work!' said Betga. 'What did you choose?'

'I can't say the name. It's from Czechoslovakia or some shit.'

'That's not a country anymore, but don't worry. You go home and I'll see you next week. Did you tell Keith to put the beers on my tab?'

'Yeah, he said you don't have one.'

'Well, that's wrong. He's wrong. That's a . . . That's an administrative error. I can fix that. Ignore it. Okay, take it off what you owe me for this month. Don't lose your temper between here and home and, if you do, don't express yourself with your fists *or* your feet. If you have to defend yourself try sarcasm. It's scalding but leaves no injury that can be picked up by an X-ray, CT scan or any other imaging device. And it's not illegal. Not yet, anyway. Now, if you'll excuse me, Kasimir, I've got some business to discuss with Mr Maserov here.'

Betga returned to where he'd left off before he'd accepted the free pot of Czech beer.

'What did you do to Hamilton?' he asked Maserov.

'You're the lawyer of record for Carla. Why aren't you admitting that you're representing the other three plaintiffs?'

'Who says I am?'

'I'm not quite as stupid as I look,' said Maserov.

'Someone needs to get you a mirror.'

'Hey, *I'm* not the Supreme Court Prize winner who's now Kasimir's life coach.'

'The two aren't mutually exclusive.'

'That's debatable.'

'I've got to ask you, Maserov, are you fucking with Hamilton?'

'I'm just trying to survive. Why are you so interested in Hamilton?'

'Why were you so interested in finding me?'

'I wanted to talk to the lawyer representing the women suing Torrent Industries.'

'They're not going to settle.'

'They'd be insane not to and you know it . . . For the right offer.'

'Do you have the authority to make an offer?' Betga asked. Maserov suddenly realised he didn't know the answer to that question. 'You don't have that authority, do you?'

'I'm not the client,' answered Maserov after his momentary hesitation.

'Exactly who are you, Maserov?'

'I'm a Second Year at Freely Savage who's trying to get to the bottom of these Torrent Industry sexual harassment cases.'

'You want to make them go away.'

'Preferably, otherwise we'll win them in court but it will be ugly . . . for everyone.'

'A Second Year; they wouldn't . . . Hamilton wouldn't normally let a Second Year anywhere near this. What the hell happened to Featherby?'

'What happened to you? Seriously, Betga, I mean no disrespect but when I was at law school, just as you were finishing, people were paying good money for your notes; *Betga on Contracts*, *Betga on Trusts*, *Betga on Tax*. This isn't a negotiating tactic. You're right, I'd need instructions from Torrent Industries before I could make any kind of offer and, anyway, technically you don't have the authority to be negotiating on behalf of any of them other than Carla and she's got a problem with you that's at least the size of any my wife has with me. But I want to know . . . as someone who admired you from afar. What the hell happened to you?'

Betga took a sip of his Czech beer, licked the foamy residue off his top lip and stared downward in the direction of his brown brogues in a manner Maserov could already tell was uncharacteristic of him.

'Hamilton,' said Betga.

'What?'

'Hamilton,' Betga repeated.

'What about Hamilton?'

'You asked what happened to me. The answer is . . . Hamilton.'

'What did he do?'

Betga sat for a moment without speaking, looked around the room and sipped his beer again.

'I tell you what,' Betga began, 'are you able to come back here tomorrow night?'

'Yes, I think so.'

'If you can get authority to negotiate on behalf of Torrent Industries, you come back here tomorrow night at eight. Then we can talk. You tell me what you did to Hamilton and I'll tell you what he did to me.'

VI

Maserov was back in his Torrent Industries office. There were both an email and a text message waiting for him from the Freely Savage Human Resources department. The message, innocuous in itself, was to the effect that Bradley Messenger, the head there, was waiting for Maserov's data from his survey of Second Years' attitudes towards 'hot-desking'. Maserov had forgotten about that obligation and the reminder was unsettling since the task would be both a complete waste of time and intensely unpleasant. Having successfully shut it out of his mind he had instead been preoccupied with his attempt to solve Malcolm Torrent's sexual harassment problems.

Maserov of course knew he'd need Malcolm Torrent's authority to make a deal with Betga on behalf of the four women suing the company. But each contact with Malcolm Torrent, however necessary, was also daunting, first, because he found any interaction with a man of such power, renown and unimaginable wealth to be intimidating no matter how well their previous meetings had gone and, second, because despite their agreement, Maserov could never quite believe or trust that Malcolm Torrent was going to take his advice, back him against Hamilton should the need arise, or even remember that they had an agreement. In fact, Maserov wasn't confident that Malcolm Torrent would even remember who he was.

He knew that any conversation about settling the cases, about money in general, and especially one seeking authorisation for Maserov to spend the company's money, ought to be held in person. So, after a cup of intensely strong black coffee that almost separated his palate from the rest of his mouth, Maserov picked up the phone to call Malcolm Torrent's private secretary, Joan Henshaw, to arrange a face-to-face meeting. The offer Maserov envisaged to settle the whole matter would be on a confidential basis and would concede no liability.

A loud banging on the door caused him to abort the call. It was Jessica and she looked distressed.

'You have to help me,' she whisper-shouted in exasperation.

'Why, what's wrong?'

'I'm in trouble . . . or I will be. Next week Frank Cardigan wants me to stay back after hours with him.'

'Why?'

'He wants me to work with him on his leadership skills.'

'Is that a legitimate request or is he just looking for a reason to be alone with you at night?'

'Oh God, where do I start with this? Even were he to ever be likely to lead anyone anywhere, I still wouldn't want to be alone with him at night.'

'I totally understand.'

'And the worst part of it is . . . it's kind of my fault, too.'

'How?'

'Well, when he has me alone in his office I'm so desperate to keep the conversation away from anything creepy that he veers it towards, personal stuff like his marriage or my private life or even my clothes, that I started waffling on about idiosyncrasy credit as a measure of one's leadership.'

'About what?'

'Idiosyncrasy credit.'

'What's idiosyncrasy credit?' Maserov asked.

'It's a concept in psychology. It doesn't really matter what it is.'

'No, what is it? What's idiosyncrasy credit?'

'It's used to explain why some people can get away with deviating from group norms where other people would be ostracised or at least criticised for the same behaviour. If someone is consciously or otherwise considered a leader by a group, not only will that other person's behavioural deviations be tolerated by the group, a true leader will find the behaviour emulated.'

'Interesting,' said Maserov. 'So if someone is a good leader their idiosyncrasies will be tolerated or even emulated?'

'That's right, according to some psychologists.'

Jessica's attractiveness cut through all the urgency, fear and rational thought that had been fuelling him just moments before. It wasn't so much that he wanted to touch her. He was too exhausted, socialised and married for that.

'It's actually very interesting,' Maserov repeated. 'It explains a lot of what's been happening around the world recently.'

'Well, Frank Cardigan finds this absolutely fascinating and he wants me to devise some deviations from standard behaviour for him to adopt within the company or at least within his department that will enable me to help him assess who considers him a leader and who doesn't. Oh, and I still have to come up with his stupid column for the stupid fucking industry newsletter. His vanity rivals his stupidity and I'm scared that alone at night they'll join forces and he'll make a pass at me or worse, especially if he drinks.'

'And you can't just tell him you're not available?'

'I can't be unavailable every night! You've got to help me.'

'*Me?* What can *I* do?'

'You've got to get me in on whatever it is you're doing for Torrent. You've got to make me an essential part of it. And you've got to get him to tell Frank Cardigan that my work on your thing takes precedence over his stupid shit. I'll help you come up with an angle that I can be involved in if you just let me know what it is you're doing for Torrent. I'll help you to help me but you've just got to give me more information. Why *are* you here, what are you doing exactly?'

VII

Stephen Maserov sat down at a table in the main bar in the Grosvenor Hotel and ran his hand over his face. It felt dry and hot and he wondered why. He was too young for menopause and also the wrong sex but he didn't want to rule it out. He of course knew that the aetiology of his symptoms was psychological and not biochemical. He had become someone who lived moment to moment in the gap between the certainties previous generations had taken for granted. Perhaps he could get used to this? With the fingertips of one hand gently caressing the skin on his face, he looked around the bar for Betga and knew that he would never get used to it.

He had told Jessica earlier that day that he wanted to get her involved in his work but it was confidential and he needed to get Malcolm Torrent's permission to get her involved. She left his office grateful that he was going to mention her to Torrent. Maserov saw the offer as the quick thinking of a drowning man. She said to call her as soon as he knew whether he was able to bring her in to assist him. She wanted to call off Frank Cardigan as soon as possible.

Maserov had wanted a face-to-face meeting with Malcolm Torrent anyway, to work out the parameters of any deal he might strike with Betga, but he had been unable to get one that day. Now he was in the awkward position of being about to negotiate with Betga when he had no authority to reach any kind of settlement whatsoever. He was worried he would look stupid to Betga and eventually duplicitous and immoral to Jessica when she found out what he was really doing there for Malcolm Torrent.

Should he have remained an English teacher? When he left teaching he was already living in a world where subeditors at major metropolitan newspapers had been fired and replaced by algorithms and most of his students sensed his ever-diminishing status even in their world, a world they were soon to bust out of.

He thought of the house he was trying to save. Situated near several small parks, it was a late Victorian red brick that had been rendered and painted white. It was protected on two sides by a veranda and in the front by an unassuming thirsty lawn and an iron picket fence painted a shiny black that stood guard for a phalanx of broom shrubs of green so light they were almost yellow. Along one side there was a pebbled driveway leading to an unpretentious Menzies-era brick garage that would hold no more than one car without complaint. The walls inside and the ceilings, replete with the original intricate plaster roses, were off-white, but it was the floors of polished Murray River red gum that had really sold it to them. There were three bedrooms, one of which was used as a study now that the two boys were sharing a room. The main bedroom was large enough to accommodate the Maserovs' shared aspiration of an en suite bathroom even if, had he stayed a teacher, it was always going to remain just that.

Now, as he often did lying awake in the early hours of the morning in his hastily rented cramped one-bedroom apartment in Elwood, surrounded by suitcases, boxes, and hillocks of laundry, all Maserov could picture were his two small sons playing Magna-Tiles together in their pyjamas, fresh from a bath and ready for bed. Their absence was gut wrenching.

Betga was late. Maserov had already bought and downed a craft beer that Kasimir couldn't pronounce and two double whisky chasers when Betga sat down at Maserov's chosen table with two more pots of allegedly Central European beer.

'I've got nothing,' said Maserov.

'What, not even a "Hello, what kind of a day did you have?"'

'Hello, Betga. What kind of a day did you have?' Maserov asked dutifully and to delay his embarrassment.

'I had quite a busy day, thanks for asking. Kasimir, it seems, has quite a few colleagues at the nearby Dick Whittington who are interested in my life coaching services. I was there making what I believe people in the creative sector, the *content providers*, call a "pitch" and so was consequently somewhat delayed. I do apologise for being a little late.' Betga took a moment to drink in the now unambiguously inebriated Maserov. 'But it looks like you've kept yourself busy.'

'Colleagues? What colleagues does Kasimir have, in what industry, what sphere of endeavour?'

'They adapt to the exigencies of their lives, often exigencies over which they have little control. They value flexibility. They do a little of this and a little of that.'

'And they make a living from being so adaptable?'

'Oh yes, enough to engage a consultant for the purposes of self-improvement, which many consider a tertiary need, at least in the sense of Maslow's hierarchy.'

'I should've studied adaptability instead of law,' said Maserov.

'You sound somewhat pissed off. I thought we were about to negotiate mutually satisfactory outcomes.'

Maserov looked at him blankly. 'I hate my job,' Maserov confessed to Betga. They sat across from one another at a small table at the back of the dimly lit bar where Betga seemed to be making Maserov a regular.

'I thought you were camping out at Torrent Industries?'

'Yeah, that's a temporary and insecure tea-break from my life at Freely Savage. It took me years to get that job, the one I'm working to save, and I hate it. I'm there working fourteen-plus-hour days without a net. Half the time I don't know what I'm doing. My wife doesn't know me anymore. The only people I ever see are people who work in the same building. I go there every morning and I . . . I forage,' Maserov continued, warming to his topic. 'I forage for scraps at the very bottom of a tall gleaming steel and glass enclosed secular hierocracy,' he said, staring out blankly into the middle distance. 'And I can't sleep at night because I'm terrified of losing my job.'

'The one you really hate,' added Betga, knowingly, quietly, like a therapist, as he put his beer down.

'The one I really hate,' Stephen Maserov confirmed sadly. 'To crawl haltingly towards a mirage of middle-class success that you *know* will always remain just out of reach, this can't be the natural way of things.'

'No, of course not,' said Betga, sipping his beer. 'The natural way of things is smallpox.'

'What am I doing it for?' Maserov asked rhetorically.

'Look, Maserov,' Betga exclaimed, 'you need to understand that there are now just two kinds of people in this city, the people who are relegated to selling crafts by the side of the road – called consultants – and the people who still have the option of not buying those crafts.'

'You're saying I sacrificed my marriage to work fourteen-plus-hour days in order to be free not to buy crafts by the side of the road?'

'Yes, that's what I'm saying.'

'So what about *you*? You were once in my position. How do *you* survive? How do *you* keep going?'

Betga looked around the bar conspiratorially before answering quietly. 'By acts . . . of sabotage.'

'Sabotage?'

'Helps with the breathing,' Betga whispered. 'Better than tai chi.'

The two men drank each other in, neither of them speaking, just letting the alcoholic vapour seep from their respiratory systems and linger in the air and although they were not equally inebriated they were both looking for themselves in what they saw of the other.

'What do you mean, "sabotage"? Who or what are you sabotaging?'

'I could say "the system",' said Betga, 'but you'd seek further and better particulars and then cross-examine me until I spat out names.'

'Yes, give me a name,' Maserov demanded weakly.

'It's Hamilton,' answered Betga. 'You know it's Hamilton.'

'Jeez, if Hamilton could fuck *you* up, what hope is there for the rest of us?'

'You know, normally I'm good at identifying rhetorical questions, better than Kasimir, but in your present state I'm not sure that *was* rhetorical. But I thank you for the implicit compliment. Anyway, haven't you outsmarted Hamilton in some way that's connected to Torrent Industries' defence of its culture of sexual harassment?'

Maserov ignored the question and asked his own. 'How are you seeking revenge on Hamilton?'

'My plan, at least in a macro sense, has always been a little like yours.'

'Like mine?' asked Maserov.

'Yeah, I recognised, as you clearly did, that the way to get at Hamilton is to get the CEO of his biggest client, your friend Malcolm Torrent, to fall out of love with him.'

'Okay, so how are you doing that?' Maserov persisted.

'Well, I'm the lawyer for the four women suing Torrent Industries for sexual harassment, the very sexual harassment accusations you're trying to protect the company from, the same accusations you're also using to try to hurt Hamilton.'

'You're making money out of this?' Maserov exclaimed accusingly.

'Well, I'm their lawyer, so of course I'm making money out of this.'

'No, no, I'm not talking about fees, Betga. You're trying to scam Torrent Industries. You and the women, this whole thing's a scam.'

'Hold on Maserov, I'm still a practising lawyer, an officer of the court. This ain't no scam.'

'You've virtually admitted it is,' countered Maserov.

'Have you read the affidavits?' Betga was showing a hint of irritation for the first time.

'I was trying to find *you*.'

'So you haven't read the affidavits?'

'Well, not all of them,' conceded Maserov with some embarrassment. 'But I guess the ones I've read do sound genuine. Actually, they're very moving. Okay, I accept this ain't no scam.'

'Well now you've found me, go and read all of them. What the hell kind of lawyer are you, anyway?'

'I'm a desperate one.'

'That's the best kind. But are you desperate for yourself or for your client?'

'I'm desperate to do a good job for my client.'

'Yeah, well so am I,' Betga shot back. 'Only I'm working for the victims. You're working to protect the sleazy pricks who grab what they can't get by consent.'

Duly chastened, Maserov sat there silently and then murmured, 'You sound like my wife.'

'Yeah? Well, I hear she's a good woman. No doubt got a good reason to kick your arse out of your own home. You want another drink?'

Maserov nodded, Betga raised one finger and a waitress came.

'Two more of the same?' she asked. Betga nodded. 'On Kasimir's tab?'

'No, this round's on my friend Mr Maserov.' Maserov nodded and the waitress headed off to the bar.

'But why didn't your clients go to the police?' Maserov continued. 'I mean, aren't these criminal offences?' Betga smiled at the question but his silence led Maserov to repeat it. 'Why didn't they go to the police?'

'Are you serious?'

'Yes, I am.'

'Now you're being naive.'

'Okay, walk me through it.'

'You know damn well what would happen. In a criminal case there's a higher standard of proof. In a criminal case it's the victim's word against the accused. The women, my plaintiffs, would have to testify in open court, in front of the media, and they would have their entire sexual histories, possibly including some fevered fabricated allegations based on scant evidence or just innuendo, levelled against them. The victims would be faced with the de facto onus on them to prove that they are not "easy" and that they should be believed. And all of it ventilated, to the titillation of the perpetrator and every man in the court, and all of it floating out there on the internet in perpetuity. Not only would they never get their privacy back, they'd find it hard to get a job of equivalent standing. This is why women everywhere keep taking this shit and not reporting it to the police.'

'Yes, of course. You're right.'

'Thank you.'

Maserov was impressed by Betga's passion and his sense of justice. There was, however, one thing bothering him about what Betga had just said.

'But there's one thing that still doesn't make sense.'

'What's that?'

'The burden of proof still falls on the women and the parading of the sexual histories, real or fabricated, the embarrassment, the eternal publication on the internet – all of that's still going to happen in a civil case.'

'Yeah,' smiled Betga, 'but you can *settle* a civil case. You can't settle a criminal case.'

'So you don't want a conviction. You want to settle these cases, you want money?' Maserov asked.

'Of course I do. Man cannot live by life coaching alone. *They* want money too.'

'But you, personally, would make more money if the four cases went to trial.'

'You might think so.'

'So how do you make more money if they settle?' The question hung in the air until, as drunk as he was and getting drunker on the beer Betga told the waitress he, Maserov, would pay for, he answered his own question with a slow realisation. 'You're getting a cut. You're taking a cut of whatever they settle for. That's your plan, isn't it? Try to settle and along the way scare the hell out of Malcolm Torrent and his share price and thereby put some heat on Hamilton. Make it appear that Hamilton is unable to stop the trickle of cases from aggrieved women, a trickle which might become a torrent, no pun intended, sink the share price and torpedo Hamilton.'

'Buy this man a drink!' exclaimed Betga. 'Where's Kasimir when you need him? He buys a good drink. Although you're not *quite* right, not entirely.'

'How am I wrong?'

'I'm not taking a cut from all of them, only three of them.'

'Which one gets to keep all of her damages?'

'Carla.'

'Why Carla? She seems to be none too fond of you. I would have guessed one of the others.'

'A good lawyer doesn't guess.'

'I never said I was a good lawyer. I'm just the one you've got here on the other side of this table.'

'Look, don't undersell yourself, Maserov,' said Betga. 'You're only a Second Year, you were scheduled for execution and yet somehow, against Hamilton's wishes, you've bought yourself time and a certain security from within the very jaws of the lion. That's not too shabby.

Anyone who can do all that from a position of absolutely no power gets my respect.'

'Thank you, Betga,' said Maserov. 'Which reminds me, what the hell did Hamilton do to screw *you*? You were the guy most likely to go places.'

'I'll tell you everything but first let's settle these cases. I've got four very deserving women as clients. Now, starting with Carla —'

'Okay then, back to Carla. Why aren't you also getting a cut from Carla, assuming she could be prevailed upon to settle?' Betga sat there looking at Maserov like he was trying to decide whether or not to answer his question.

'Would you like another beer?' Betga asked solicitously.

'You're trying to get me drunk so I'll negotiate at a disadvantage,' objected Maserov.

'But you are still sober now?'

'I think so.'

'Okay, let me ask you this and please use all your currently accessible neurons. Don't hold back.'

'I won't.'

'Ready?'

'Ready.'

'Maserov, do you have any authority to settle any of these cases right here, right now in this bar?'

'None,' answered Maserov.

'So how would it benefit me to compromise your negotiating capacity even further than you yourself have compromised it so far this evening?'

Maserov pondered the question. 'I'm not sufficiently sober to answer that to my own current satisfaction. Perhaps you're trying to distract me from my last question. You're charging your clients fees and getting a cut of any settlement but only from three of them. Why aren't you also getting a cut from Carla, assuming she settles?'

'I don't think I can tell you.'

'Why not? You just told me I had your respect.'

'Do you have your wife's respect?'

'Not anymore. What's that got to do with it?'

'Nothing, I was checking your cognitive agility. You passed.'

'You're stalling,' pressed Maserov.

'Now you passed with honours,' confirmed Betga. 'You want to play on for the car?'

VIII

'Come on,' Maserov persisted, 'what's different about Carla? Why are you treating her differently?'

After a deep breath and a passing glance at the ceiling Betga told him. 'Three reasons, I guess. But with respect, why should this apparent distinction in my financial relationships with various clients be any of your business?'

'I don't know, let's say curiosity. Three reasons; what are they?' asked Maserov, ploughing on undeterred.

'Okay, first of all, I'm in love with her.'

'You're in *love* with her?' Maserov repeated unbelievingly.

'I know, it's a disappointingly conventional answer.'

'You're in love with her?'

'I love her romantically, platonically, diatonically, catatonically, domestically, if I had a more substantial line of credit I'd love her internationally, and perhaps most distractingly of all, I love her carnally. Don't get me started, Maserov. I'm not proud of it. I feel compromised by these emotions, all this caring, all this longing. It's an unusual sensation for me and, to be candid, quite out of character. Love gets in the way of things and ultimately makes you unhappier than you were when you weren't in love.

'I know what you're thinking, however slowly. You're thinking, "If this Betga, such a charming, erudite and handsome man, is in love with Carla, why does she insist on not having anything to do with him?"'

'It's a good question,' offered Maserov.

'It's yours,' said Betga without missing a beat. 'I met Carla while working on a Torrent Industries file when I was still at Freely Savage. I asked her out to lunch, then for a drink, we talked on the phone a lot, initially legitimately, and one thing led to another. And then another thing led to the one thing. And before either of us knew it, we were in exactly the kind of committed exclusive romantic relationship so unrelentingly celebrated by popular culture.'

'Until?'

'Until she discovered it wasn't exclusive. I mean, it was *emotionally*.'

'Not sexually?'

'No, a distinction she wasn't prepared to recognise let alone accept.'

'How could you fuck it up if you love her so much?'

'Listen, Maserov, many people enjoy being judgmental. But it could have happened even to you. After Hamilton got rid of me I went to a legal recruitment agency.'

'And?'

'I slept with the legal recruitment agent. It's a tight job market.'

'And now Carla doesn't want to have anything to do with you,' Maserov added.

'Although she's remained my client.'

'So you're in love with her; that's one reason you're treating her differently to the others.'

'Isn't that enough?'

'I would have said so but you mentioned three reasons. What are the other two?'

'Okay, the second reason? Read her affidavit, her case is different to the others. I can't talk about it now. It makes me too upset, too angry. Read her affidavit.'

'I have read hers. I'm embarrassed that I haven't yet read all the affidavits.'

'Yeah,' said Betga, stretching. 'You probably should be.'

'What's the third reason?'

'You went to her house, you saw her and the maladroit policeman, right?'

'The older guy who lives with her, yeah.'

'Oh, he doesn't live with her. He'd *like* to live with her.'

'Yeah, I saw them and their little girl.'

'It's not his little girl. Her name's Marietta.'

'Yeah, I saw them and Carla's little girl. Marietta?'

'Well, reason number three: Marietta is my daughter. She's my little girl too.'

'You *do* have a problem.'

'Even more than you know. Marietta is my daughter but Carla disputes this. She won't let me see her.'

'Who does Carla claim is the father?'

'She's not saying, or at least, not to me.'

'But you want to be in Marietta's life?'

'Of course I want to be in her life. I want to reconcile with Carla and be my daughter's father. Don't you want to be in your children's lives?'

'More than I am currently, yes.'

Betga looked over at Maserov, his new friend. 'You are reasonable, aren't you . . . for a desperate man. You want my clients to settle?'

'I think they should.'

'Okay, Maserov, here's what I'm going to do for you. I'll try to convince them it's in their best interests to settle. But first you've got to get Eleanor to make a play date for your kids with Carla and Marietta. You go with her and you get an ice-cream stick or a lollipop or something and you give it to Marietta to suck on. Then, when Carla's not looking, you take the item with my daughter's saliva on it and hide it in a ziploc bag. You give it to me and I prove my paternity.'

'I can't do that.'

'Of course you can.'

'Eleanor will never agree to come.'

'Why not?'

'Well, first, they've only just met and under awkward, artificially contrived circumstances. She didn't come willingly, let me assure you. And even if she comes,' Maserov continued, 'she won't want to get involved in your family disputes and she *definitely* won't want to trick Carla like that.'

'Are you really saying she won't want to help reunite a little girl with her father?'

'You're really the father?'

'I most certainly am. Have a look at her. She *looks* like me. And she's got that certain Betga style. You can't fake that. Besides, I'm almost certain Carla hasn't been with anybody since she found out I'd been unfaithful.'

'How did she find out?'

'Long story but the legal recruitment agent told her . . . over the phone. You get me some DNA for a paternity test and I'll do what I can to have my clients settle posthaste . . . quickly even. So will you try to pitch it to her?'

'I'll try,' said Maserov, not quite believing what he was agreeing to. 'Wait a second!' he continued hopefully after considering this for a moment. 'I don't need to do this. You can get a court order to compel Carla to allow a paternity test.'

'No,' coughed Betga, shaking his head, 'No, no, no. I can't do that. A court order would only infuriate her even more. We need your wife.'

'To trick the woman you love, mother of your daughter.'

'Exactly.'

'I'll see what I can do,' said Maserov glumly.

'That's the Maserov I've come to know these last two drunken evenings! Oh, there's one other thing. Even if we're able to get this done, I'll also require a face-to-face with Malcolm Torrent.'

'What?' said Maserov, astounded.

'I want to meet with Malcolm Torrent.'

'Why, what do you want to say to him?'

'I don't know, I haven't figured that out yet. But I'm definitely going to need to talk to him.'

part four

I

He thought a few glasses of wine once the children had gone to bed could perhaps improve his chances of getting Eleanor to help him. In a state bordering on delusional hope, one from which he would inexorably lurch after a short time to a kind of numb fatalism, Maserov walked himself through a list of the tasks confronting him.

Tonight's strategy, one born of desperation, was to pour Eleanor a glass of wine and then begin the kitchen-cleaning ritual by going down on his knees and vigorously scouring the floor under the kitchen table with damp paper towels.

'You want me to *what*?' Eleanor's disbelief was palpable.

Maserov had asked her to help him get a swab of Carla Monterosso's infant daughter's saliva for the purpose of proving that A.A. Betga was the little girl's father.

'I know it sounds appalling —'

'It's child molestation. It's a violation of the person,' interrupted Eleanor.

'Yeah, sure, I agree it looks like that but it's actually a highly moral thing to be doing,' Maserov countered from the floor underneath the kitchen table. 'We'd be reuniting a little girl with her father.'

'You want me to *trick* Carla into enabling you to get a paternity test done to determine whether the lawyer representing the victim can have all the rights of a father to her infant daughter. Establishing his paternity has become some kind of bargaining chip. It's wrong and I'm not going to do it. How do you expect her to trust you?'

'I don't expect her to trust me. I expect her to trust her own lawyer.'

'Yeah, but he started sleeping with her and then screwed around behind her back.'

'He wasn't merely sleeping with her, they were in a committed relationship.'

'That makes it worse, don't you see that? She was committed to him and he was committed to his own immediate gratification.'

'He slipped up, I'll grant you, and he's desperately sorry. He wants to be a father to her daughter, his daughter.'

'He *says* she's his daughter,' countered Eleanor.

'Yes, but isn't that better than getting Carla pregnant and then *denying* paternity? That *would* make him a deadbeat dad. But this, wanting to be in both their lives, it's kind of noble.'

'Noble! You're *good*.'

'Thank you.'

'And did you say he wants to be in both their lives?' Eleanor asked, sipping the pinot grigio he'd poured her.

'Yes.'

'So he wants to reconcile with Carla as well as be a father to Marietta?'

'Yes,' said Maserov, sensing that he was making some headway. 'And he only slipped up once,' he went on, which he recognised was counter-productive when the amount of blood flowing to Eleanor's face increased perceptibly.

'How many times *is* it acceptable to cheat on your partner?'

'None,' Maserov shot back. '*No* times.'

'Right,' snapped Eleanor.

'I'm just saying, as wrong as once is, surely once is much better than many times.'

'I'll grant you that.'

'Listen.' Maserov was not giving up. 'Let me take you through a few propositions and you tell me if you agree with them or not.'

'Okay.'

'Every child deserves the opportunity to have a relationship with his or her father.'

At this Eleanor looked up at him and he could see that this was really perhaps the only point worth making, that this was what made getting a paternity test right.

'Agreed,' Eleanor responded reluctantly.

'So don't see it as doing a favour for Betga but rather as giving a little girl another chance to have her father in her life.' Maserov could see that Eleanor momentarily looked at him with the tenderness she used to bestow on him before he'd embarked on a legal career.

'But why do we have to deceive her, to go around there with the pretext of a play date for the children and slip an ice-cream stick in her daughter's mouth when she's not looking? It feels so dishonest. Why can't we just tell her the truth?'

'It's just that if she knows in advance that you want to talk about Betga's putative paternity of Marietta she may not agree to the play date.'

'You realise you're pimping out your children now? You do realise that?'

'Do *you* realise,' Maserov countered, 'that you're scanning, ransacking your mind for reasons to not help me?'

'Why do you need your wife and children to prop up your career?'

'Eleanor, can we separate this . . . this suggested course of action, which is admittedly for my career but also for the house, the mortgage, for our family, from —'

'*Now* he talks about the good of the family,' she said to an invisible audience. 'I'm bringing up two kids on my own while you swan around the city in a suit with all those other corporate lawyers.'

'I don't swan, I flap, I flounder. I'm just trying to stay employed. It's not just for me, it's for all of us. And as for helping out more with the kids, you kicked me out!'

'I did, didn't I?' she said, almost with pride. 'You never thought I'd actually go through with it. You thought I was too scared to live without you, didn't have the guts.'

'Not because you didn't have the guts but because when your transient discontent with this or that subsided you'd realise that we love each other, that we're good together —'

'We were never together . . . well, not for years.'

'— that it's good for the kids. I'm a good father.'

'You *are* a good father,' she conceded.

'Maybe Betga would be a good father.'

That made her stop and think. 'Okay, I'll call Carla and see if I can set up a play date.'

'Great, it's the right thing to do.'

'But I'm not going to take any ice-cream sticks or plastic bags. I'm going to tell her the truth.'

'You've got to do whatever you're comfortable doing,' he said, knowing this was the best he could do.

'I think she liked me. I'll call you as soon as we've got a time and date.'

'She definitely responded to you . . . I could see that.'

'I simply chose to be honest. And I'm going to be honest with her again.'

'Yep. Sure. Go with your instincts,' Maserov agreed. 'But don't tell her why you're there until you're inside and she's closed the door.'

II

'Fuck off, Maserov.'

That was the way Maserov had expected a very high proportion of the subjects to respond and that *would* have been the first response to the questions that HR had mandated he put to his colleagues had he approached anyone but the closest thing he had to a friend at Freely Savage.

Emery gazed up at Maserov with a look that was equal parts relief – because a non-threatening person who somewhat understood him was about to engage with and possibly even converse with him inside the building – and disbelief, tinged with the preter-rational fear that Maserov, who he thought had been killed by Hamilton, was now shuffling back onto this mortal coil forty-eight flights up, against the very laws of nature.

'It's okay,' whispered Maserov, crouching beside Emery's black plastic waste-paper basket. 'I'm *meant* to be here talking to you. In fact, I've been *told* to.'

'Been *told* to?' Emery whispered fearfully. 'Are you firing me?'

'*What*? No, of course not! How can I be firing you? I'm a Second Year, like you,' Maserov reminded him. But Emery's vulnerability was ready for that.

'Maybe they sent *you*, an advance guard sort of thing . . . *I* don't know how it happens. You *can't* know. A Fourth Year got walked out last week. *Nobody* knows . . . except *them*,' Emery replied. Just imagining the trauma of getting fired was more than he could cope with.

'Emery, that doesn't make any sense at all.'

'No but . . . you said they're culling Second Years.'

'They *are* but they're not going to get *me* to do it. How does *that* make sense?'

'I don't know. How can you *be* here? That doesn't make any sense either. How can you still be here? Hamilton's out to get you. You know that,' Emery replied. 'Aren't you on secondment to Torrent Industries anymore?'

'Yes, I still am. I'm only back here to do something futile for HR, for Bradley Messenger.'

'What?' Emery asked, still unsure how scared to be.

'HR is making me go around to a selection of Second Years to survey them about hot-desking.'

'What does hot-desking mean? Making people move their work-stations around all the time?'

'Yes.'

'Isn't that kind of futile and counter-productive, time-consuming and generally conducive to disequilibrium among fee-earners?'

'Yes, of course it is.'

Emery thought for a heartbeat. 'Should I say I *like* it?'

'Not sure it matters what you say.'

'But if they do decide to introduce it and word gets round that I said I like it, people are going to hate me. They'll blame *me*. So maybe it does matter,' reasoned Emery.

'No one's going to believe your opinion mattered and, anyway, I don't even know if they're planning to bring it in.'

'Then why are they asking you to ask us about it?'

'I don't know but it can't be because they care what any of us think.'

'Who else are you going to ask?'

'I wasn't sure.'

'Ask Fleur Werd-Gelding. Then make my answer the same as hers.'

'Why Fleur Werd-Gelding?'

'She's a beautiful, well-spoken, pedigreed, sweet-smelling, vicious junkyard dog, immune to self-doubt and bred for success. To emulate her in any way I can seems to me the safest thing to do in most situations.'

Maserov did as Emery had asked and that's when it came, exactly as he'd expected.

'Fuck off, Maserov.'

Fleur Werd-Gelding was, among other things, very reliable. Like the rattlesnake, she was born ready to attack.

Fleur Werd-Gelding had never engaged in small talk. She had absorbed the overwork mania of the WeWork generation and its celebration of her indentured exploitation by the partnership. She was strikingly attractive with blue eyes and thick lustrous hair the colour of cruelty. And she was no slouch intellectually. She had a razor-sharp mind that smothered self-doubt before it gestated and this, along with a relentless need to succeed, led to a first-class honours degree. She had grown up around floodlit infinity pools, wineries, cattle stations the size of Luxembourg, and beach houses bequeathed to her parents and their cousins by previous generations of Werds and Geldings. She had gone to an all-girl private school like her mother and her mother's mother before her and, like them, she was expected to breed with a slightly older boy from the brother school and to share her genes with his in return for a share of his properties, shares and trust fund annuities. Maserov held no interest for her.

So when Fleur Werd-Gelding rolled her eyes at Maserov's enquiry he replied, looking down at his notepad, 'I'm going to take that as a "not in favour of hot-desking".'

Maserov returned to Emery's workstation, knelt down beside him and described Fleur Werd-Gelding's response. Emery looked at him with unexpected admiration. It was as though, without saying anything, he was trying to take in the full measure of the man he had started out with some two years earlier. Then he exhaled wistfully and with a slight smile in bewildered admiration of the somehow better man, he shook his head at the strength of what he perceived as Maserov's achievement.

'She has contempt for you, Maserov,' Emery whispered.

'Yes, I know.'

'*Me* . . . She doesn't even know *I* exist. But *you* . . . First this thing with Hamilton and Torrent Industries, which is incredible enough, and now . . . I mean, if I could just earn her contempt . . .' Emery trailed off dolefully.

'Don't give up hope, Emery. As long as there's life, there's hope.'

'You think?'

'Why not? Don't sell yourself short,' Maserov offered compassionately.

III

Maserov was in his new temporary safe haven, his office at Torrent Industries headquarters, when his mobile phone began to vibrate. It was Eleanor.

'Eleanor, is everything okay?'

'I did it.'

'What?'

'I called Carla and made a play date.'

'That's great. When is it?'

'Tonight.'

'Tonight? That's great!'

'Yeah, I figured: I like her, Jacob is around her daughter's age and I'm not doing anything wrong so . . . so what the hell. Right?'

'Right, you're definitely not doing anything wrong.'

'No, especially since I decided I wasn't going to mention anything about Betga and paternity.'

'You're not? Eleanor, that's the whole point of the play date.'

'I know. That's why you're going to do it.'

'How can *I* do it?'

'I've made the arrangements. I'll be at her house with both kids between about five and seven, then I'm taking them home to bath them. You come up with some pretext why you need to meet me there and then you do it.'

'Eleanor, how does that help? That doesn't help me.'

'Stephen, I can get you in the door. That's all I'm willing to do. You want to talk her into allowing a paternity test for your new friend Betga, *you* think of an excuse to meet me there and to ask her yourself. Why should I make myself uncomfortable?'

'We'll lose our house if I can't make a deal with Betga and this is what he wants.'

'Like I said, if you can think of a pretext, I can get you into the house.

After that it's down to your advocacy skills. We'll be there between five and seven.'

'Jesus, Eleanor! Why would I need to see you rather than just phoning?'

'Oh, *I* don't know. There could be something you have to give me urgently.'

'What could I have to give you urgently?'

'I don't know. Sleep Bear.'

'What?'

'Sleep Bear. Come over to deliver Beanie's Sleep Bear. I'll tell her that Beanie can't sleep without Sleep Bear.'

'It's true, he can't. But why can't I give it to you when you go home?'

'Stephen, she doesn't care. She won't ask.'

'What am I going to use for Sleep Bear?'

'Come by our place on the way to Carla's. I'll leave Sleep Bear in a plastic bag in the letter box.'

'Okay, I'll bring Sleep Bear.'

'Don't forget, 'cause Beanie can't sleep without him. Bye!'

Eleanor was right, he acknowledged. The mortgage and the house were their problem but all the ramifications of the deal he'd made with Betga, the precise details of which he now regretted, they properly lived at his door, the door to the rented one-bedroom. He needed to formulate a case to put to Carla. What could he say that would convince her?

His train of thought was abruptly terminated when the phone rang again. This time it was the landline.

'Stephen Maserov, it's Bradley Messenger from HR. How are you? I'll get straight to the point. We loved your work on the whole hot-desking issue.'

'Yeah, sorry, Bradley, it seems everyone hated the idea.'

'Yes, statistically that's true.'

'Is it untrue in some other way?'

'Well, that's just the thing, we're not sure. What *is* truth? Isn't that what all lawyers ask?'

'No, never. You're thinking of philosophers.'

'Well, get back to me when philosophers bill in units of six minutes, right Maserov? Anyway, I just wanted to let you know we were very, extremely, happy with your hot-desking work, so much so that we intend to call for your help again shortly.'

'To do what?'

'Haven't quite finalised the details yet. I just know you're the man for the job. We all do.'

'Bradley, why are you coming to me with these things? Why me?'

'You happen to have caught Hamilton's eye. He's told us to call on you whenever we need help. He says you're very capable. Talk soon.'

'He said that?' Maserov asked, but Bradley Messenger had already hung up. None of this made any sense to him.

Then it dawned on him. His secondment to Malcolm Torrent had conditions attached to it. Hamilton had agreed to let Maserov work for twelve months solely on Torrent Industries' sexual harassment problem on the condition that Maserov abided by the dictates of the HR department of Freely Savage. This was Hamilton using Freely Savage HR to sabotage his efforts to solve Malcolm Torrent's problems by giving Maserov useless tasks simply to take up his time. But they were tasks that he couldn't refuse. Malcolm Torrent wouldn't come to his defence over such trivial matters internal to Freely Savage. Maserov was confident he wasn't being paranoid.

He was in mid-speculation when a percussive sound infused with anger or desperation brought him back to the room he was in. There was no time to wonder who at Torrent Industries he could have annoyed. The sound of knuckles rapping at the door was followed by the door being firmly pushed open and then closed. Jessica sat down in the chair opposite Maserov's desk. She looked around the room furtively.

'There's no one else here. You can look under the desk. Are you alright?'

'It's got to be tonight,' Jessica whispered.

'Are we robbing a bank?'

'He's making me . . . Frank Cardigan's making me stay back *tonight*. So you have to get me involved in your thing *tonight*.'

'He can't order you, can he?'

'Yes, he almost can.'

'Almost?'

'I've exploited the gap between "almost" and "yes" as long as I can and now you have to get me in on your thing by tonight. What *is* your thing?'

'I haven't been able to clear it with Mr Torrent.'

'What?'

'You can check with his PA. He wasn't here yesterday. He's not here today.'

'He's got a phone, you know.'

'I thought I'd have a better chance talking to him in person.'

'I guess you would. It's just that by the time you get to talk to him in person I will have been frisked and filleted by Frank Cardigan.'

'Jessica, I'm so sorry to have let you down. I'll be able to help you tomorrow. Isn't there somebody else who can help you tonight?'

Jessica's response was to gaze up to the ceiling and close her eyes. When she opened them again it was clear they were glistening. Some combination of rage, fear, frustration and embarrassment had commandeered her face and transmuted her usual office hours corporate demeanour into that of a frightened young woman. It was only after a tear or two had fallen on her right cheek that she was able to speak.

'No. No one else can help me. I'm so sorry to be burdening you with this.'

'Jessica, you mustn't be.' His impulse was to leave his chair, go around to her side and physically comfort her by hugging her but under the circumstances that could easily have been misconstrued. There had been a time in his life when that might not have stopped him.

'We'll work something out. I've asked for an appointment with Malcolm Torrent to talk about seconding you to help me. But we won't let Frank Cardigan —'

'I have to be alone in the building at night with him . . . tonight, five-thirty actually.'

'How scared of him are you really?'

'You know, that's the kind of question only a man, even a well-meaning one, could ask. For a man, I know, the corporate world delivers all sorts of fear; fear of being frozen out, passed over, overworked, under-utilised, humiliated, being fired and ultimately unemployed. I really do understand that. I don't merely understand that intellectually, I understand it emotionally. I feel it myself. Women have all that too.

'But then there's a whole other level, a whole additional level of terror and disequilibrium that most men never really understand. A woman in the workplace has her clothes discussed by her male colleagues, her appearance, her body shape, *changes* in her body shape, her reaction to sexual innuendo, to off-colour jokes about sex, unwanted, unasked-for flirting and her reaction to that, fear of casual bodily contact all the way along the continuum, offers to trade sexual favours for career advancement and the consequences of rejecting them, blackmail and every conceivable permutation of sexual harassment and assault all the way down the line to rape. There's no overtime, no salary, no perks of the job that make any of that worthwhile.

'In addition, being Indian, I have to tiptoe through a minefield of racism that adds an extra dimension to the precariousness of my position within these hallowed walls. Sorry, you didn't ask for any of that.'

'You don't need to apologise for anything. I'm beginning to understand how hard this is for you. It's me that has to apologise. So you're meant to meet him at five-thirty. Where?'

'In his office. The place is still buzzing till somewhere between six and six-thirty. But by six-thirty it's quiet. It's too empty for a woman to feel safe alone with a man in his office, particularly if he's Frank Cardigan.'

'Has he ever touched you, been inappropriate?'

'No, but I've never been alone with him after hours. But he's commented on my appearance. And sometimes he . . . he talks to me while eyeing my breasts.'

Maserov suddenly feared that he'd done that too. He had no memory of having done it but this is what a lot of men do and he remembered having been a man. Admittedly, it was some time ago.

'Are you wondering whether my concerns are justified?' she asked him.

'No.'

'Then why did you ask that question?'

'Well . . . if he's already harassed you in some way, attempted something, you probably have the right within your terms of employment to decline to work with him after hours.'

'I'm sorry, Stephen, if I sound angry. I shouldn't be sounding this way, to you of all people.'

'There's nothing you've said that sounds at all unreasonable.'

'No, it's not the content but my manner. It sounds like I'm holding you accountable for the behaviour of all men around here, of pretty much all men. To be honest, meeting you has been like a breath of fresh air. You're honest, decent. You're not at all in love with yourself or arrogant like so many of the men here.'

'That's not a temptation I'm resisting, I'm afraid. I have nothing to be arrogant about.'

'Actually that's not true, you know,' Jessica said quietly.

Maserov didn't argue. She was going to hate him very soon. He knew he wasn't going to be able to delay telling her precisely what he was doing for Malcolm Torrent much longer. But it wasn't going to be then.

'Listen, I'm going to help you.'

'But there's nothing you can do, not tonight anyway,' she added, fatalistically.

'No, I'm going to help you tonight. You tell me where his office is and I'll wait in the office next to it. He won't know I'm there.'

'You'll hang around just in case I scream?'

'Yep, that's what we'll do tonight and then tomorrow I'll somehow get you in on my thing.'

'So what exactly is your thing for Mr Torrent, if I may ask?'

'There's one slight hitch though . . . with tonight.'

'Oh?'

'You have to find a reason why you can't be here till after, say, seven-fifteen, at the earliest.'

'Do you have to go somewhere?'

'Yes, I have to . . . see my kids.'

'You have kids?'

'Yes.'

'Are you married?'

'How much time have you got?'

'Isn't there a one-word answer?'

'Separated . . . if you want it in one word.'

'I'm sorry, it's none of my business.'

'You seem surprised.'

'I don't know why but . . . I just thought you were single.'

'Do I give off that air?'

'No, not at all. We tend to make assumptions about people. I'm sorry, I didn't mean to be rude.'

'It's understandable. I'm living on my own in a rented one-room apartment. I must smell of domestic dysfunction . . . to say the least.'

'Not at all. Actually, you smell . . . I like that aftershave. What is it?'

'I don't remember the name. My mother-in-law bought it for me. Or she got it for me with loyalty points from her pharmacy. Last gift I'll get from her, quite probably.'

'You possibly made assumptions about me.'

'No, I . . . How do you mean?'

'About my relationship status.'

'Well, no, I hadn't really given it much thought,' he lied.

'Oh,' she said, somewhat taken aback by his apparent lack of interest.

'I mean, I suppose, I kind of unconsciously assumed you were attached to some well-heeled son-of-a-gun.'

'Well-heeled son-of-a-gun? That doesn't sound like you.'

'No, it isn't me. It's just that I feel . . . awkward.'

'Why do you feel awkward?'

'This conversation's a minefield. I don't know . . . what I ought to say.'

'Nothing but the truth, I suppose. I'm single.'

'Oh, really? I hadn't expected that.'

'You said you hadn't given it any thought.'

'I lied . . . Of course I had. You're so . . . attractive young women aren't usually unattached. Isn't it a truth universally acknowledged that a single man in possession of a good fortune must be in want of a wife?'

'That's very good,' Jessica said, smiling. 'Not many male lawyers can quote Jane Austen.'

'I was an English teacher.'

'Really? There's so much I don't know about you. I suppose that isn't surprising. I was attached until . . . recently.'

'Should I not ask you what happened?'

'I discovered who he was.'

'Who was he?'

'An alpha male, a prick, vain, obsessed with his appearance, one of those guys who doesn't eat good food when he goes out to dinner because everything's bad for him yet he still does recreational drugs. One of those "my body is a temple" types.'

'Oh God!' said Maserov. 'My body is an abandoned warehouse out near the airport. It briefly had a pop-up shop in the far corner selling knock-off designer wear but now the electricity has been cut off.'

Jessica smiled. 'Your self-deprecation is amusing but it's unwarranted.'

'I'm serious. Show me where Frank Cardigan's office is and, I promise you, I will be in the office next door by seven-fifteen.'

'No, let's meet at your office, safer that way. You're a really nice man, do you know that?'

Maserov wished he could have recorded her saying that in order to play it back over and over once she came to hate him.

IV

Maserov was relieved to see Eleanor's car parked outside Carla's house. He rang the doorbell and when, after a moment, Carla answered, he held up the soft toy he had picked up from his erstwhile home. The gesture was meant to indicate that he came in peace. Maserov thought it had to be unprecedented in the legal history of every single negotiation that had ever been conducted in a common law country since the Magna Carta that the defendant's lawyer had to help the plaintiff's lawyer prove that the plaintiff's lawyer was the father of the plaintiff's child.

'Hi Carla, um . . . Eleanor probably told you I had to bring this toy for Beanie.'

'Yeah, she did.' Carla saw him not as the father of her new friend's children but as the lawyer engaged to deny her justice.

'Would you mind if I came in and gave it to him? This is my only chance to see the kids today.'

'No, come in.' He followed her down the hallway towards the living room where Eleanor was sitting on the couch with the children at her feet playing with Duplo. Beanie looked up and, on seeing him, ran towards him, passing Carla with arms outstretched, calling, 'Daddy!'

To complete the charade of innocence, Maserov leaned in to give Eleanor a kiss on the cheek. It was awkward not because of its assumed intimacy. That was the usual reason it was awkward. Today it was awkward because neither of them was a good actor and they both knew what they were there for. Still, the performance was good enough to secure a glass of white wine from Carla.

To break the silence threatening to discomfort them all, Maserov turned to Beanie and ceremoniously announced, 'I brought you Sleep Bear.'

'Oh, yes,' said Eleanor. 'We can't have a good night's sleep without Sleep Bear.'

Maserov noticed with concern that Beanie showed no interest in the arrival of Sleep Bear.

'What a good father you have!' said Carla in the direction of Beanie.

Impelled by her allusion to benign paternity, Maserov took the bit between the teeth and turned the subject to his real reason for being there.

'Oh, I don't know if you know but I've made contact with your lawyer. I wanted to thank you.'

'Yeah, I know,' Carla replied cautiously.

'He's a . . . Kind of larger than life, isn't he?'

'Yeah, a real laugh,' she said with discernible acrimony.

'He didn't tell me this but he was a few years ahead of me in law school and it was said that he put himself through by working as the entertainment director on a cruise ship.'

'That's what he says. Wouldn't surprise me,' said Carla unimpressed.

'Whereas Stephen put himself through law school by me working as a teacher,' Eleanor offered reflexively before realising she wasn't helping.

'Yes, by you and by debt,' said Maserov attempting to smile.

'I did it because he's such a good father,' said Eleanor uncomfortably.

'Talking about fathers,' Maserov cut to the chase, 'your lawyer says he's Marietta's father. Is that true?'

'Did Betga put you up to this?' Carla asked.

'Up to what?' Maserov played dumb.

'To finding out whether he is.'

'I'm not sure what you mean,' said Maserov.

'Yes,' said Eleanor. 'He wanted us to take a swab of Marietta's saliva.' Maserov winced.

'She knows, Stephen. She's not an idiot.' She turned to Carla. 'We were never going to do it. I did genuinely want to see you again. We're really separated. I'm not his agent.'

'Yes, we really are separated,' offered Maserov hopefully.

'But whatever problems I might have with Stephen, I never have to worry about him as a father. He's an incredibly devoted father. I knew he would remain one even when we separated.'

'Thank you,' said Maserov again, enjoying the unexpected praise and the respite from pursuing Betga's demand.

'Yes,' Eleanor continued, 'it made the decision to separate so much easier.'

'What?' asked Maserov incredulously.

'Knowing that whatever happened, you would always be a great father to our kids. He comes over every night to see them, feed them, bath them, tell them stories and put them to bed. Then he goes back to work to try to make budget.'

'Betga wouldn't be leaving to try to make budget. He'd be trying to make something or someone but not budget,' Carla snorted.

'It's obviously none of my business, and you know him and I don't. But if there's any possibility this Betga guy is Marietta's father . . . and that he'd be a good father, she deserves the chance to know him.' Eleanor was trying to help.

'He does seem pretty keen to be her father,' Maserov added. 'A lot of men try to shirk that responsibility. He's doing everything he can to take it on. Your daughter deserves to have a father, doesn't she?' Maserov asked, noticing that the little girl he was talking about wasn't actually in the room with them. He swallowed a lot of wine quickly and was shifting the glass nervously from one hand to another as Acting Sergeant Ron Quinn came out from the little girl's bedroom holding her against one shoulder and a disposable nappy bag in his other hand. Maserov tasted shame. The policeman must have heard and Maserov wanted the earth to swallow him. He glanced with alarm at Eleanor.

'They're right, Carla,' Acting Sergeant Quinn said quietly.

Carla stood up and walked over to take her daughter from the shoulder of the older man in uniform. The policeman opened the kitchen door that led to a small back garden and Maserov watched him put the nappy bag in the outside rubbish bin.

'He doesn't need her to have a paternity test. He's the father,' Carla said.

The policeman's step faltered just slightly when she said this but he kept on walking despite, as his colleagues might have described it, being wounded in the line of duty.

When Acting Sergeant Quinn came back from washing his hands, he poured himself a drink. Maserov wished some other person had poured it for him but it wasn't his place to come into someone else's house and start offering drinks. Embarrassed, he felt incredibly responsible for any discomfort his presence might have caused the policeman.

The children played quietly at the feet of their mothers. Maserov wondered why his sons had to choose this moment to be quiet.

'You seem to know what you're doing. You have kids of your own, I guess?' he asked Acting Sergeant Quinn.

'No,' said the older man, adding to Maserov's guilt.

Maserov stood up. He had what he came for so why did he feel so awful?

'You coming back to help me put the kids to bed?' Eleanor asked him.

'I can't tonight. I've got to head back to the city. I've got a meeting at Torrent Industries,' Maserov announced without confidence, knowing how it must have sounded.

'A *meeting*?' Eleanor Maserov couldn't help herself asking.

'Yeah . . . it's just come up.'

'Well, you'd better go then,' she said.

She had asked him to move out, showed little sign of wanting him around other than to help with the children, and yet news of this meeting angered her in a way neither of them would have expected. Hadn't she just helped him out professionally by getting him into Carla's house and then securing Carla's admission that Betga was the father of her daughter? She'd even praised him as a father. Within minutes of all of this he'd humiliated her by bailing on her to attend some fictitious meeting at work.

As Carla said when she opened another bottle of white wine a few minutes after seeing Maserov to the door, 'Who has a meeting at work at seven o'clock?' Now they really were bonded; two women with small children fathered by unfaithful bastards.

V

Maserov drove back to the city in an optimistic state of mind. He'd got what Betga wanted, Carla's acknowledgement that he was Marietta's father. On top of that, Eleanor, obviously suspecting he didn't have a work appointment but was seeing a woman, couldn't hide her hurt and anger. That had to be encouraging.

He hadn't lied to Eleanor. He *was* driving back to the city for work and he really did have to meet someone at a scheduled time, which is what is commonly referred to as a 'meeting'. But it was also true that he was driving back to the city to see a woman, someone whose company he enjoyed, who thought well of him and whom he found very attractive. She was also single. All in all, he felt better than he had at any time in recent memory.

In the car he decided to call Betga, who was beginning to seem more like an ally than a negotiating adversary. 'I have news for you, an update,' Maserov said over speakerphone while driving back to the city. 'It's not something one lawyer normally gets the chance to say to another.'

'I hope you don't charge by the word,' he heard Betga say. 'I'm due at the Grosvenor in ten minutes. Kasimir has a dear friend celebrating his statistically unlikely parole. The man is a prime candidate for life coaching. What's your news? You got authority from Malcolm Torrent to negotiate?'

'No, that's not my news. You're not going to need Marietta's saliva. Congratulations, you're a father to a beautiful healthy little girl.'

'What? How do you know?'

'Carla admitted it.'

'You're kidding?'

'No, I'm not.'

'Did you record it . . . on your phone?'

'No, but I've got witnesses.'

'Who?'

'Eleanor, my wife.'

'Anyone else?'

'The acting sergeant.'

'The sad cop?'

'Yep.'

'She said it in front of *him*?'

'Yep. She even said I can tell you.'

'Hell . . . she admits I'm Marietta's father!'

For a moment Betga really was speechless.

'Betga, are you there?'

'Yeah, I'm here.' Maserov heard a sniff down the line. Either a strain of cold virus had suddenly attacked a part of Betga's upper respiratory tract or he was choked up by the news.

'Are you alright?'

'Yeah. Where are you?'

'I'm in the car.'

'You want to meet me for a drink at the Grosvenor? I'm officially Marietta's father! My pitch to Kasimir's friend won't take long.'

'No, I have to head back into the office.'

'No, you don't. I know what you're working on. It's *me* . . . and my clients.'

'Well, yeah but something else has kind of . . . come up.'

'Hmmm,' said Betga, with a grin that was visible over the phone.

VI

Office towers, like Egyptian temples and Sumerian ziggurats in other times, are where the present waits to be discovered and interpreted by future archaeologists and historians. But for many that work in them, their current significance is unambiguous. They represent tiny corners of Agincourt, the Somme or Stalingrad. Even after sunset.

Jessica met Maserov at his office and told him that the room next to Frank Cardigan's room on the floor below was now empty. All he had to do was creep in there undetected and listen. In the best-case scenario Cardigan would never know Maserov had been there and Jessica would leave his office unharmed and unthreatened.

'How will I know if I'm meant to come in? We need a signal or something, don't we?'

'Okay,' she suggested, 'if I need you to come in I'll tell him I'm thinking of buying a new car and ask him if he thinks I should buy a VW Golf.'

'Does he drive a VW?'

'I've no idea what he drives. But if you hear me say VW or Golf in a loud voice, louder than the conversation had been previously, you should come in the room.'

'What should I say?'

'I don't know. It will depend on the circumstances. If he's taking his pants off you could say, "What the fuck do you think you're doing taking your pants off in the workplace?" If he's doing anything less egregious, just introduce yourself and tell him you've been looking all over for me 'cause you need me urgently for the thing you're doing for Mr Torrent.'

Maserov waited for two minutes after Jessica left before going to the room next to Frank Cardigan's. For a moment he had trouble with the door handle but it was just a matter of aligning the deadbolt with the hole in the strike plate on the other side by slightly lifting the door a few millimetres via the handle. It took only seconds for him to figure this out and enter but it was long enough for him to break into a sweat. Sitting there with the lights out and the door slightly open he could quite clearly hear Jessica's voice and that of a man he took to be Frank Cardigan.

'Frank, sorry I couldn't be with you sooner,' Maserov heard Jessica say.

'No matter, please sit down. Okay, let's get down to it; leadership, specifically *my* leadership.'

He heard the soft sound of a chair scraping against carpet and assumed this was Jessica sitting down across from Frank Cardigan with a desk in between them.

'How can I use my idiosyncrasies to become a better leader? That's it, isn't it, idiosyncrasy credit?'

'No, that's not what idiosyncrasy credit is.'

'What is it?'

'It refers to why some people can get away with behaving in a certain way when others would be criticised for behaving that way. If someone is considered a leader, not only will that person's behaviour be tolerated, it will be emulated.'

'Oh yeah, that's right. So to determine whether I'm a true leader I need to get them to emulate my behaviour.'

'No, you can't *get* them to emulate your behaviour.'

'No, I probably can, Jessica. I know *you* no doubt think of me as a friendly, kind of hunky, easygoing, successful type of guy, rising rapidly up the Torrent chain of command but, I have to tell you, the guys in my department are scared of me. I can probably get them to do almost anything. I think I'm a true leader.'

Cardigan's narcissism was remarkable, Jessica thought. Real presidential material. 'But Frank,' she replied, 'that's not how idiosyncrasy credit works. You're misunderstanding . . . I mean . . . that's a misunderstanding of the concept. It can't be used with compulsion. You have to deviate from group norms and *then* see whether, *without* compulsion, without threats, inducements or promises, people in your department follow your lead.'

'How do we do that?'

'So . . . you need to do something that's a little unusual and see whether anyone follows you, whether anyone emulates your behaviour.'

'What sort of unusual thing should I do? I mean, everybody knows I'm a pretty regular kind of a guy, other than, you know, my leadership and charisma.'

'Let me ask you, Frank, what time do most people in your department leave for the day?'

'Oh, I'd say . . . most guys around here knock off between six and six-thirty.'

'What if you knocked off earlier? That would be unusual, wouldn't it?'

'Yeah but —'

'What if they saw you leaving at, say, four o'clock?' Her voice rose with enthusiasm.

'They'd probably just think I was going to a meeting.'

'Maybe once or twice they'd think that. But what if you started leaving the office at four o'clock *every* day, day after day.'

'Leave at four . . . every day? But what about my work?'

'We won't do it for long. It wouldn't test your productivity, just your leadership credit.'

'So you'd want to see if any of the other guys were copying my idio-syncratic style of leaving work early?'

'Yes.'

'Okay, well, how long do I have to keep leaving early?'

'Well, we can't know that at such an early stage of the test. We have to be flexible in our design.'

'This is a real psychology thing, is it?'

'Oh, yeah, I can show you papers on it. There's been a lot written about idiosyncrasy credit. But I thought I'd save you all the hassle of doing the reading yourself by doing it for you and presenting you with the concept and a plan to test yours.'

'My what?'

'Your idiosyncrasy credit.'

'Right, of course. But there's one thing that still puzzles me. If I'm leaving early . . . every day . . . how will I know how many of the guys are copying me? How will I know *who's* copying me? How will I even know if they've noticed . . . that I'm not there, that I'm leaving early?'

'*I'll* tell you. I'll be your eyes and ears.'

'Could you do that for me?'

'Of course, Frank.'

'Well, when should I start?'

'As soon as possible.'

'So . . . tomorrow?'

'You could start now.'

'But it's late. Everyone's gone. If I just get up and walk straight out the building, there's no one here to see.'

'Frank, you're a hard worker. Everyone knows this. You're not going to find it easy to just pick up and walk out of your office and out of the building at four o'clock every day. It will feel strange. So I want to condition you to being able to just pick up and walk out of the building.'

'Just like that?'

'Just like that. So that tomorrow, when the time is right, you can just get up and leave and show the guys below you in the department just how idiosyncratic you are. Show them you can do it, that you're not afraid to do it.'

'Oh, I'm not afraid.'

'Go on then, walk out. Go to the elevator, press the button.'

'This is great, Jessica. I'm feeling really fired up about this whole "leaving at four" thing.'

'Great.'

'You want to have a drink with me?'

'That wouldn't be scientific.'

'Why not?'

'Because I won't be having a drink with you when you walk out at four tomorrow. Or the next day. I will never have a drink with you . . . out of commitment to the project.'

'So if I don't go ahead with this project?'

'You've just got cold feet. But a *real* leader . . . See if you can do it, Frank. Get up now. Go. Walk away.'

Maserov heard Jessica leave first. A minute or two later, he saw Frank Cardigan walk with purpose past the partly open door. Then he heard the elevator bell ring, and some seconds after that, its doors opening and closing. Frank Cardigan had left.

VII

'Brilliant, absolutely brilliant!'

Maserov was praising Jessica for having escaped the further attentions signalled by Frank Cardigan using only her wits.

'What else was I meant to use?'

They were sitting next to each other on a mahogany leather settee in a sparely lit bar in the Esplanade Hotel in St Kilda, affectionately called the Espy by its devotees, where Jessica knew some of the bar staff and felt sure that no one from Torrent Industries would run into them. She had ordered them each a cocktail known as the Celibate Screwdriver, which was served in a glass that had been coated with absinthe.

'I told you, Frank Cardigan's vanity competes with his stupidity to be the first thing you think of when you hear his name. It was the marriage of these two of Frank's attributes that I put my money on. Here, take a sip of this. You earned it,' Jessica said, handing him his drink. 'I must say though,' she said, taking a sip herself, 'the degree to which you seem impressed by my wiles suggests that you really have no idea what it's like for a woman to work at a place like Torrent Industries, to work nearly anywhere, actually.'

'You have to do this kind of thing often?'

'To plan my interaction with fellow staff members, to have an exit strategy up my sleeve? Yes, I have to do this pretty much every day. This has been building with Frank Cardigan for a while. It's probably worse at Torrent Industries than most places because of the high ratio of men to women. It's even worse if you're a waitress. You're working for tips. You have to constantly calculate what every little innuendo, leer, sleazy remark, outrageous request, touch or grope is worth.

'And you're making this calculation with your hands full, arms juggling a stack of dishes or a tray of glasses. Then someone tries to touch you and it throws you off balance physically as well as psychologically. I used to waitress when I was a student so I know. I've got it good now. I'm only trying to juggle the politics of the situation. That's what a woman buys when she graduates with a Masters. You get to fight back with your hands free. You don't have to balance a stack of dishes when the hands come. Worth every penny. But there is no question my longevity in the job and progress up the pay scale depends to no small extent on my being attractive to men. My boss might be a woman – sort of – but she's got her ear out herself for the panting heartbeat of all the men she needs to keep happy.

'Anyway . . . Listen, I don't want to hit you over the head with anything, not even the way things really are. You're one of the good ones. Stephen, I'm really grateful you were there tonight.'

'It turned out you didn't need me.'

'Well, neither of us could have known that in advance.'

'But you had a strategy ready to go and you carried it off with such great . . .' Exhausted as usual, Maserov tried to find the right word.

'Aplomb?'

'Yes, aplomb. You don't hear that word very often these days; aplomb.'

'That came from knowing that I was safe, I had you in the next room ready to pounce. Were you ready to pounce?'

'I was ready . . . as ready as I can be these days . . . to pounce. I'm kind of . . . I've been sort of ground down a little . . . recently . . . by a few things, and I've done very little . . . very little pouncing. Is that absinthe?'

'Yes, but you're not meant to lick the glass. You pounced on the opportunity to save your job, didn't you? You've got to tell me what you're doing for Mr Torrent.'

'Do you think they've got any more of that absinthe?'

'Yeah, but you're driving. Why don't you just suck on the rim for a bit longer?'

'Jessica, you're not going to like me anymore . . . any moment now.'

'Why, what are you going to do?'

Maserov leaned back, raised his arms above his head and stretched, looking for more relief than stretching ordinarily provides.

'I told you my wife and I are separated.'

'Yeah? What happened . . . if I can ask?'

'I was a teacher, an English teacher. She's a teacher as well. That's how we met, we were teaching at the same school. All went well at first. But after we'd put a deposit on a house we found ourselves on the verge of drowning, bobbing up and down beneath waves of financial insecurity, periodically swallowing water. Then the intervals between mouthfuls of water got shorter and we decided at least one of us needed to earn more.'

'As a drug dealer?' Jessica offered.

'No, drug dealers are nowhere near as stressed as we were. If I were a drug dealer I might still be living with my children.'

'You're just a lawyer.'

'Yeah, just a lawyer. We decided that I should study law and we'd live off my wife's income until I could start earning the kind of money the parents of children at private schools are rumoured to earn. But, to cut a long story short, between the hours I spent studying and then the hours I spent at Freely Savage trying to accumulate sufficient six-minute billable units to make budget, my wife said we had begun to drift apart. But by then we had two small kids and with work and the demands of the children, we never found the time to talk, not as a couple. She said all our conversations were merely transactional; who pays which bill, who picks up which child, that kind of thing. She was right.'

'And that's when you met someone else?'

'No!'

'That's when your wife met someone else?'

'No, at least she says she hasn't.'

'So why would she ask you to move out?'

'I don't really know, to be honest. I think she's just angry at the way her life has turned out, and in a fit of pique that she hasn't quite got over, she's sort of thrashing around trying to make some big change that will lead to . . . some big change. I go there pretty much every night to see my sons but after we've put them to bed she expects me to leave. Then I go back to work. But I miss my sons incredibly. When I'm finished at work for the night I go back to the apartment, get into bed and look at photos of my sons on my phone.'

'So why am I not going to like you anymore, any moment now?'

Maserov put his hands to his face and began the story of the meeting with Hamilton and Malcolm Torrent, of how he bumped into Malcolm Torrent alone at the elevator and of the reprieve he'd negotiated with him by promising to rid his firm of a serious legal problem. She already knew this.

'His problem,' Maserov finally admitted, 'the problem I offered to help with that Hamilton seemed intent on ignoring, was the spate of sexual harassment claims, allegations made by four women, clerical staff. I told him that if he gave me a year I could free him of the problem.'

'What sexual harassment claims?'

'You don't know about them? I thought Torrent's HR department would be all over this.'

'No, certainly *I've* never heard anything about any of this. I doubt anyone in HR has.'

'I can't believe the Torrent Industries HR department didn't know about this. That doesn't make any sense to me.'

'No, it makes perfect sense. The women would have known, instinctively perhaps, of the HR department's policy, unofficial policy.'

'What's the unofficial policy?'

'Don't ask, don't tell. The women would have been hesitant, even reluctant to come to HR with the allegations because they'd know their allegations would be buried, ignored, and they might possibly even suffer on account of having made them. It wouldn't do the women any good or the perpetrators any harm. So they don't come to us with their sexual harassment claims, almost never, and this assists the company in maintaining that it doesn't know about any problems with its culture, not in this area. Ever since the sexual harassment legislation was first enacted, that's the way it's always been handled. Don't ask, don't tell.'

'Well, I guess that isn't really that surprising if you think about it, which I must admit I never had. Anyway, that's what I've been avoiding telling you, that I'm the guy acting for the defence, that is, for Torrent Industries and the alleged harassers, in the sexual harassment claims cases being brought by these former female employees.'

Jessica swallowed what remained of her drink. 'So that's what you're doing at Torrent Industries, saving these . . . these *animals* . . .?'

'Well, I'm not actually saving *them*. These are civil cases. They're not facing any criminal sanction and it's the company that will have to pay out, not them, so —'

'So what?' Jessica was getting angry.

'Well, nothing, it's just that I'm not actually protecting them.'

'No, you're defending the company that employs them from liability for what is unequivocally assault. And you're doing this to save your own skin.'

'Well, um, I *guess* . . . you could put it that way.'

'Is there any other way to put it?'

'I'd been hoping like hell to find one because I was dreading the time when you —'

'When I what?'

'When you thought as little of me as I'm imagining you do now.'

Jessica was clearly upset. There was a battle going on inside her between sadness and anger.

'Fuck you, Stephen!' Anger won, as it so often does. 'You're as bad as them.'

'As bad as the perpetrators? No, I'm not!'

'Okay, you're not as bad as them but . . . You have no idea. It's a jungle out there and every day is . . . is jungle warfare. You're either with us or you're against us.'

'Jessica, you've got to believe me, I'm *with* you. I'm not one of those guys. I'm not like them. I just found myself —'

'Collaborating. You're a collaborator.' She grabbed her bag and stood up. 'I guess as long as there's money in covering up spasms of toxic masculinity, there'll always be weak men lining up to do it.'

'Jessica!'

She started walking towards the door and turned just to say loudly enough for anyone interested to hear, 'And I really fucking liked you!'

Maserov thought of trying to stop her from leaving but she walked too quickly towards the door and he was, in any event, hampered by the sudden realisation that people were looking at him. He wondered if they were trying to figure out exactly what he had done. He wondered if he should tell them, maybe canvass opinion. Would other women see him the same way? Would anyone, any other woman, think it was acceptable to save his house, to save his marriage, in the way that he was trying to do? And if his marriage was so important to him, what was he doing in a bar with a woman he was attracted to? Perhaps he really *was* a collaborator.

He walked to the men's room trying not to look at the faces of any of the people lest he trip over their condemnation. When he had relieved himself he washed his hands and then splashed water on a face the mirror confirmed was exhausted. Well, what did he expect, he asked the face. He had predicted she would no longer want to have anything to do with him when she found out what he was really doing at Torrent Industries. Wasn't it good to be right about *something*?

And anyway, was it really acceptable to say that if it wasn't him, someone else would be acting in these cases for the company? It was a defence that hadn't worked at Nuremberg. As he was making his way back to his table in the bar before realising there was no point to going back other than perhaps to finish his drink, which he hoped someone might have been kind enough to spike, it occurred to him that he wasn't really a collaborator.

He sat down to rehearse how he would make the point to Jessica the next day at work when he was startled to look up and see her looking at him from the doorway of the bar. Perhaps she was going to hit him.

Jessica walked over to him and said, 'I think I might have been too hard on you.'

'Jessica, I'm not a collaborator. It's true I talked my way into this position but I only ever wanted to try to get each of them, Carla, Pauline, Lilly, and Monika, the best deal I was able to get for them. All the more so after I read their affidavits.'

'Aren't you professionally obligated to try to shaft them?'

'I think I'm morally obligated not to. What I'm hoping to do, if I can, is marry my professional and my moral obligations here, at least to the very best of my ability.'

'Not everyone would do that.'

'I'm so glad you said that.'

'Yeah, I got into the street, cooled down a little and figured, based on what I know of you, that you might well be the best thing that's happened to these women since they quit. And if so, I owed you an apology.'

'Thank you.'

'Then I realised that if my first impressions of you were right —'

'Well, you really liked me . . .'

'If I was right about you,' she continued, ignoring his interruption, 'this could well be fantastic.'

'What?'

'This could be fantastic!'

'How?'

'Listen, this is how,' Jessica said, raising two fingers to signify a request for two more of the same to the bartender who'd been watching the whole thing. 'You're at Torrent Industries to fight against sexual harassment. This could be the start of something really important, a fundamental cultural shift.'

'No, you're not getting it. I'm meant to make these claims go away.'

'Okay, tell me if I'm getting this right,' Jessica said. 'There are three possibilities, the victims —'

'*Alleged* victims.'

'The alleged victims can drop the case, they can take their case to court or they can settle with Torrent Industries. Is that right?'

'That's right.'

'Well, the women clearly aren't going to drop them or you wouldn't be needed by Malcolm Torrent.'

'That's true.'

'So either you're going to defend them in court where the culture of rampant sexism will be ventilated for the public and the media . . .'

'The rampantly sexist public and salacious media, yes.'

'Or you'll settle the cases and the women will be compensated. Either way, you'll have the opportunity to make recommendations to Torrent that could turn the place around.'

'Jessica, I'm a second-year commercial lawyer. We mostly preserve the status quo. I'm not a royal commissioner. I'm not a civil rights lawyer or a poverty lawyer. There's no grand jury. I'm hanging on just to be *any* kind of lawyer. He's got me in to put out spot fires before they become raging infernos. Someone in my position doesn't get to make recommendations.'

'Maybe not, but *I* do. This is how you get *me* in on it. We can work together on this. This is a chance to do something that matters. You tell Torrent that the firm urgently needs a completely new policy to deal with sexual harassment in the company or these cases are going to keep coming.'

The bartender arrived with two more of the cocktails. Jessica picked up both of them, one in each hand, and clinked them together. She was ebullient.

'To cultural change!'

It was very late and Maserov went searching for the absinthe with his tongue.

part five

I

Sometime in the mid to late nineties Malcolm Torrent had ordered a huge watercolour artwork for the wall of his office opposite the floor-to-ceiling glass window. By his own admission, he didn't know much about contemporary art, but he did understand competition very well and was tired of being repeatedly outbid for large watercolours painted by the contemporary Danish artist Olafur Eliasson, most recently by UBS, the Swiss multinational investment bank. Malcolm Torrent had made his money creating things that were not previously there and so he gave his art dealer a simple instruction. 'I want something that takes up 90 per cent of that wall that looks like a cross between an Olafur Eliasson piece and something my granddaughter could have done if she was taller and had a bigger arm span. Make sure the artist is ethnically interesting with a name that makes people feel good about themselves once they've mastered it. When it's done, get it featured in all the appropriate journals and magazines and have the artist reticent to give interviews. I'm happy to pay extra for the reticence.'

Maserov was looking side-on at the result. He was seated in Malcolm Torrent's palatial office in a chair that was far too comfortable to accommodate his apprehension that the head of Torrent Industries would not remember who he was. He was distracted only by a disconjugated gaze that took him out the window and into a sunny sky, waiting for the older man on the other side of the desk to look up from the documents he was reading.

About three minutes earlier Maserov had felt confident he had Torrent's attention – some of it, not all of it – but for the previous two minutes he'd had none of it. Maserov was now in great danger of falling asleep. He'd experienced the same kind of intoxicating narcoleptic yearning in the face of anxiety previously when waiting to begin some particularly important task. He hoped that this was the sort of sleep that was waiting for you when you died, only without the need to perform or the burden of being assessed. Finally, Malcolm Torrent shifted the last piece of paper in his hand from one side of his desk to another and looked up at Maserov.

'Maserov, where are things now with these . . . *alleged* incidents?'

'Well, Mr Torrent, progress is slow when one is careful, I'm sure you'll agree, but we're definitely making some.'

'Some what?'

'Progress.'

Maserov had written and rehearsed that line in his bathroom in the shower and then while shaving. He had been struggling to satisfy the various and often conflicting demands of Betga, Eleanor, Carla, Bradley Messenger in Human Resources and his two small children and, in truth, there was little progress on the sexual harassment cases to report. Tracking down the other side's lawyer and commencing negotiations would not sound very impressive. And it would be hard to explain to Malcolm Torrent how he'd come to deliver a daughter to the smooth-talking yet pining lawyer on the other side, thus winning the other man's gratitude for life. Even if he had been able to convey the story in its entirety to Torrent, replete with the weight of Betga's paternal longing, Maserov knew that Torrent would ask what Betga's gratitude was worth to Torrent Industries in this instance. He didn't know the answer to this so he led by promising that the progress he'd made thus far was limited. Then it was time to bait and switch.

'I've got someone outside I'd like you to meet,' he told the construction tycoon.

'Who is he?' Malcolm Torrent asked, never considering that it might be a woman. It wasn't. Not yet.

'Well, he's a . . . good man. I think he's going to be a considerable help.'

'In the sexual harassment cases?'

'Yes.'

'You want to engage him?'

'Yes, I think it's a good idea.'

'Who is he? What does he do and why do I have to meet him?'

These were all excellent questions and Maserov's answers didn't really match them for quality. Sensing this, the recently arrived Betga bounded into the room, saying to Malcolm Torrent's exasperated private secretary behind him, Joan Henshaw, 'Don't worry, he's expecting me. I'm with Maserov.'

'Mr Torrent,' said Betga, reaching over to shake the CEO's hand. 'A.A. Betga. Your man Maserov has filled me in on the cases. I understand you're keen to make them go away, to settle, not to litigate, and I think that's definitely the way to go.'

'You are?' said Malcolm Torrent, looking at the hand of his that Betga shook as though to confirm nothing about it had changed.

'Betga, A.A. Betga.'

'And what do you do, Mr Betga?'

'I'm a private investigator, among other things,' said Betga handing over a card that read 'A.A. Betga, Private Investigator'.

'Among other things?'

'Yes, I'm also a lawyer, which puts me ahead of the competition.'

'The competition? Who or what's the competition?'

'Other private investigators you might be considering hiring.'

'I wasn't aware I was considering hiring a private investigator.'

'Well, Maserov considers it essential to the resolution of these sexual harassment allegations and that's why I'm here. Without putting too fine a point on it, Mr Torrent, you're going to find me indispensable and sooner or later you're going to want to meet me so, since I might be on a stake-out at the very moment you decide you need to meet me, I thought I'd show you the cut of my jib right from the outset and then I can report to you directly or, if your schedule doesn't permit it, I can report directly to Maserov.'

Malcolm Torrent took a moment to fix the squint he employed to convey scepticism as he scanned the private investigator–lawyer, who was dressed from head to toe in the style of a forties romantic lead. It was said he had put himself through law school as a cruise ship's entertainment director. Maserov wanted to kill him.

'Indispensable, Maserov?'

'Extremely useful, Mr Torrent, yes.'

'Why do we need a private investigator? Isn't this simply a legal matter?'

'For your share price and the general public and investor perception of your organisation, you obviously want to settle these cases, right?' Betga asked, sitting himself down in a chair beside Maserov, who was trying to hide his fury behind a fixed expression that was meant to suggest the meeting was going according to plan when in fact he had no idea what Betga was doing.

'Well, yes. We don't want these cases going to court.'

'And you want to settle on a confidential basis, expeditiously, but without throwing money away needlessly, am I right?'

'Well, yes, Mister . . .'

'Betga, A.A. Betga,' said Betga, smiling and pointing to the card, a gesture that challenged Maserov's restraint more than anything he would later try to remember. 'So what do you think is going to cause these women to settle?' Betga continued.

'A healthy offer, I'd say.'

'Yes, the bigger the offer, the faster the women will settle. That's true,' said Betga. 'That's unless you have something *on* them, something incriminating or at least embarrassing. The more you can make these women dread the litigation process the less you have to offer them to make the whole thing go away.'

'So that's why I need a private investigator. Okay, I see that. But why should I choose you. Mister . . .?'

'Betga, A.A. Betga. As you can see from my card, I'm not only a member of the Association of Investigators and Security Professionals, I'm also a lawyer. I'm a lawyer with a history of working on these cases from the plaintiff's side. I can get inside the minds, not only of the alleged victims, but even their lawyer.'

Maserov winced involuntarily.

'Anyone can have something printed on a card, Mr Betga,' Malcolm Torrent advised.

'That's right, Mr Torrent, but if I came in to your office *without* a card you'd no doubt ask for one or be troubled by my failure to have one, so I give you my card, for what it's worth, which as you very rightly point out, is not very much. What *is* worth a lot is a relationship, a relationship that generates trust and mutual respect. You can't buy that. We have only just met but I *do* have a longstanding professional relationship with your Mr Maserov. You're trusting him and he, obviously, trusts me, otherwise he wouldn't have called me in here to take up your time like this.'

The fingers of Maserov's right hand gently caressed his forehead in an unconscious effort to ward off an aneurism.

'You trust him, Maserov?'

'Wait, before he even answers that,' said Betga, 'I'm going to throw in the proverbial steak knives. Don't yet take me on for this. Wait. Give me ten days. In ten days I will make *this* go away. This is . . .' Betga reached into his inside jacket pocket. 'This is a copy of the statement of claim of one of the plaintiffs. She's a Ms Jane Ode. In ten days I or Mr Maserov will show you a Notice of Discontinuance with her name on it. I will make it go away and I won't charge for this.'

'How are you going to do that without making an offer?'

'Mr Torrent, a man in your position – and there aren't many of them – can't be too careful.' Betga looked around the room conspiratorially and Maserov looked deep within the crevices of his right hand.

'What I propose, Mr Torrent, is that I don't tell you anything about that, that I don't *ever* tell you anything about that and that you never again *ask* me anything about that. If I succeed as I intend, you should agree to have me work on these cases for the life of the cases, after which we can revisit my role in your organisation, should you decide that I should have one. If I successfully deliver Ms Ode's Notice of Discontinuance within ten days I will receive no compensation for it but thereafter I will be in the employ not of Torrent Industries, nor of its CEO in any private capacity, but of Mr Stephen Maserov. My remuneration will be equal, to the dollar, to the bonus you might wish to give him simply for finding me. It's nobody's business how or why one gives one's associate a bonus. I've always felt that governments and the tax office should show some decorum in this area, as befits a civilised society.

'If ever we need to speak directly before these sexual harassment cases have been resolved, you can simply arrange it via Maserov. There need be no record of you contacting me, employing me or associating with me unless or until you decide otherwise. I'm simply a private investigator and a qualified and experienced lawyer that Mr Maserov knows and is talking to on or about the time your problems are going away.'

There was silence until the voice of Malcolm Torrent's private secretary came through the speaker on his phone. 'Mr Torrent, I've got Beijing for you.'

Malcolm Torrent briefly closed his eyes and nodded at Betga before saying, 'I need to take this.'

Betga and Maserov stood up and as Betga was walking out the door Maserov added, 'Mr Torrent, there's still one thing I need to talk to you about.'

'Can you wait ten minutes? My secretary will get you a coffee. This won't take long.'

'Thank you, Mr Torrent.'

Outside Malcolm Torrent's office Maserov, once he could see that the inscrutable Joan Henshaw was occupied by both the telephone and her computer screen and very unlikely to be able to hear him, opened fire on Betga.

'What the fuck was that, bursting in and offering your services as a private investigator?' Maserov whispered in white hot fury.

'Don't worry, I'd say it went very well.'

'Went well? Are you out of your mind? How can you be a private investigator *and* the lawyer on the other side at the same time?'

'I admit it's a novel way.'

'A novel way to what?'

'To earn his trust?'

'By misrepresenting yourself?'

'Hey, I didn't utter a single untrue proposition. I *am* a member of the Association of Investigators and Security Professionals and I'm also a lawyer.'

'You're the lawyer acting *against* him. How can you be helping him?'

'You're seeing this as all adversarial. I'm being very creative here. It's a postmodern kind of alternative dispute resolution.'

'Betga, how the hell can you be a private investigator *and* the lawyer on the other side at the same time?'

'Maserov, listen to me,' Betga almost whispered. 'Sooner or later you or your replacement or someone from Torrent Industries is going to hire a private investigator to look for dirt in the private lives of these women so that entirely healthy, normal, human behaviour can be used to threaten or publicly shame them. Carla being a single mother, for example, will be used to send zeros flying off the page of any settlement document with her name on it. So it's better if there's a tame PI on the case who won't find anything, won't even look.'

'Betga, it's misleading and deceptive. We're adversaries. You represent the plaintiffs. I represent his company. You're *suing* his company.' Maserov said this with his hand literally covering his mouth as Malcolm Torrent's private secretary, Joan Henshaw, walked past to get herself a coffee. Then she started to double back and Maserov broke into a tiny imperceptible sweat suspecting she had heard something that would ultimately but soon lead to his unemployment and the end of all hope of reconciling with his wife.

'Can I get you gentlemen a coffee, water, anything?'

'That's kind but no thank you. *I'm* fine and *he's* going,' Maserov answered, leaving her to walk away to get a beverage for herself. Once she'd moved on, Betga's defence continued.

'Look, we're going to wrap this up very quickly to everybody's satisfaction, right?' Betga offered. '*He's* going to be happy, my *clients* will be happy; well, as happy as victims of sexual harassment can be, and *we're* going to end up happy. But before the whole thing is resolved I wanted to meet him, get him to trust me and show him I can be indispensable to him. I'm already looking to the post-settlement future and, frankly, if you don't mind my saying, Maserov, you should be too.'

'You didn't say anything about doing this.'

'You would have been unnecessarily uptight, I *know* you, seeing problems that aren't really there.'

'Problems that aren't really there! That's another thing. Who the hell is Jane Ode? That's not the name of any of the women alleging sexual harassment. There *is* no Jane Ode and what are you doing bringing her statement of claim into that meeting?'

'So you *have* been paying attention. That's good. No, she's a new one. I made her up. Ode is an anagram of Doe, Jane Doe, get it?'

'You made her up? Why did you invent another plaintiff? There are already four real ones, all of whom are really, genuinely your clients, even though only one of them admits it.'

'Relax, Maserov. You're very upset. Look, I don't know about you but I can't always control my real clients so I made this one up to bargain with. I've promised to bring Mr Torrent a Notice of Discontinuance within ten days and just in case it takes longer to convince my real clients to settle, I needed to have a fake one up my sleeve, one who I can guarantee will settle.'

'Because she's not real.'

'Exactly.'

'But weren't you afraid he'd catch you out? What if he'd read your new fictional statement of claim and your fictional client's fictional affidavits? He'd see your name as the lawyer on the other side.'

'Maserov, he's a big-picture man. He doesn't read the fine print. That's what he pays people like you for.'

'Are you out of your mind? You just took a huge fucking risk.'

'A calculated risk, yes. Just like you did back at Freely Savage.'

'But you took a huge fucking risk with *my* standing with him. You've got me vouching for you.'

'You *do* vouch for me, don't you?'

'I wouldn't have if I'd known you were going to pull a stunt like that.' Malcolm Torrent's private secretary was returning to her office walking briskly with a single cup of black coffee in one hand.

'My dear Maserov. You need to trust me,' implored Betga very quietly. 'I would never do anything to harm you. You've given me a child!'

The rhythm of Joan Henshaw's walking altered dramatically enough for some of the coffee to leap up and lick the exterior wall of the cup. She looked up at them and Maserov smiled at her reassuringly. There was a brief silence and she resumed her walk back to her desk in her office. Maserov was wincing, imagining what she was going to tell

Malcolm Torrent. When he allowed his vision to return to normal he saw Jessica getting out of the elevator and begin walking towards them.

II

Maserov realised he was going to have to introduce her to Betga. As Jessica, smiling the smile of someone starting their big day, got closer, it occurred to Maserov that her meeting Betga was a bad idea for a number of reasons, some of which he could feel but not yet articulate.

'Jessica Annand, this is A.A. Betga.'

'Very pleased to meet you, Ms Annand, Jessica, is it?' said Betga, holding her hand instead of shaking it and looking at her as though she were lunch.

'Don't even think about it,' said Maserov.

'Think about what?' asked Betga ingenuously.

'Are you working on the sexual harassment, Mr Betga?' said Jessica, withdrawing her hand.

'For all he's worth,' said Maserov.

'Yes, I am.'

'In what capacity?' Jessica asked.

'Betga considers himself a ladies' man. He's incorrigible. Just ignore him,' Maserov tried quickly to commandeer the conversation, to head it off at the pass.

'Well, I have a few capacities,' said Betga, ignoring Maserov. 'Lawyer, life coach. Today I'm here in my capacity as a private investigator.'

'Yeah, which was totally news to me,' said Maserov, still fuming quietly.

'You need to relax, Maserov. Everything's going well. You're a very tense man. Do you find him tense, Jessica?'

'Betga, I need you to get out of here,' Maserov whispered.

'Out of respect I'm going to adhere to your request but we will talk later, possibly with Ms Annand present if we're lucky, and you'll see everything is going to be fine. Good day to you, Ms Annand,' said Betga, reaching for her hand before Maserov pushed Betga's hand away from Jessica.

'He's overwrought,' said Betga, turning to go. 'More *wrought* than he should be. "Should" not in a moral sense but in the sense of a warrant for wellbeing and for the situation,' he added, heading towards the elevator.

'Who's Betga?' Jessica asked.

'I'll explain later. Torrent's going to call me back in when he gets off this call —'

'Why does he dress like it's 1946?' Jessica said, looking down the hallway to where Betga was just entering the elevator. There was no denying he made an impression, especially on women. No one but Betga could carry off Betga quite so well.

'Betga? I told you, ignore him. Torrent's going to call me back in when he finishes with this call and then I'm going to broach the topic, the topic of changing the culture.'

'You haven't talked to him about it yet?'

'I've been heading towards it . . . in the general direction.'

'Does he know I'm here . . . to see him?'

'No, not yet.'

'Have you mentioned me?'

'Not in so many words.'

'Stephen!'

'I'm going to do it now. I had to make sure Betga didn't blow us all up. I'll go back in and . . . I'll talk to him, tell him I need you . . . to work with me on this . . . when he gets off the . . .' Maserov's mouth was dry but under his arms and along the ridges of his spine were thin beads of water mixed with ammonia, sugar, salt and urea.

Malcolm Torrent spoke without looking away from the screen he was squinting at as Maserov sat down. 'Sorry, Maserov, that call took a bit longer than I expected.'

'Oh, no problem at all.'

'No,' interrupted the older man, 'I mean I no longer have time for you to sit down. What else did you want to talk to me about, other than your private investigator?'

Maserov stood up. 'Well, sir, I think these cases and the matter generally, and the culture surrounding it . . . I think we'd benefit from a woman's perspective.'

'What does that mean?'

'There's someone, someone that you already employ, that I'd like to have working on this; a woman.'

'We don't have any women working here, do we?'

'Um, in Human Resources you do.'

'Oh yes, there are women there. What do you want the woman to do?'

'A couple of things; it might happen that there could be some kind of face-to-face negotiation, not just between lawyers but with the plaintiffs there. We wouldn't seek that but it might be a condition precedent to settling, letting the women air their grievances in a secure environment. And having a woman there as part of our team could make the difference. A softer presence, seeming perhaps almost like an ally, expressing understanding, something along those lines.'

'So, if the women or their lawyers want a meeting, yes, of course, you can take one of the girls from HR. Not likely to happen though, is it?'

'It might and we need to be ready, so I'd like to have the female HR representative fully briefed and up to speed on each of the cases. Additionally, and now I'm thinking longer term, even if we can get rid of these particular cases —'

'Even if?'

'*When*, when we've dealt with these cases, *after* we've dealt with them, we need to address the culture of the corporation to prevent these things from happening again.'

'Well, boys will be boys, but you can draft a memo telling them to keep their hands in their pockets, not that they will, and I'll be happy to sign it. That it?'

'Not quite,' Maserov continued. 'In the event that anything remotely like this surfaces and reaches the market, the media, the shareholders, even the public, we want to be on the front foot with this.'

'Meaning?'

'We want to have a well-worded, carefully drafted anti-sexual harassment and anti-discrimination policy ready to put to everyone and anyone we need to show it to.'

'Do we have to enforce it?'

'It would definitely help if we can show that we took steps to enforce it.'

'Okay, make it look like we enforce it. What do you want exactly?'

'The same woman from HR whom I brief on these current cases can help me draft the policy and even, if necessary, be the public spokesperson for the company on these issues.'

'That's smart thinking, Maserov. Well done. Okay, get the head of HR, Aileen van der Westhuizen, to help you with all of this.'

'No, she isn't the one I have in mind.'

'Who've you got in mind?'

'Jessica Annand.'

'Which one is she?'

'She's got a background in psychology, very well-spoken —'

'Is she the um . . . the brown one, tall, big attitude in her . . . chest?'

'I wouldn't say she's tall.'

'Brown?'

'She's Indian.'

'Oh yeah, I know the one. She's a looker, alright.'

'She'd make a very good human face for the company should it ever come to it.'

'You're right.' Malcolm Torrent was thinking. 'But I don't want to put Aileen's nose out of joint. After all, she's the Indian girl's boss.'

'Yes, but my thinking was that Aileen needs all her time to run the department and this is going to need the relevant HR person to put aside everything else.'

'Really?'

'I think so.'

'Maserov, this whole MeToo thing; it's big, isn't it? I mean, it's not going to go away.'

'No, the change it's ushering in could well be profound. Torrent Industries needs to be on top of it, especially because it's a construction company. The potential for public relations disasters in a male-oriented industry is enormous, a minefield, really. You need to be ahead of the curve. Torrent Industries should become the poster child for correct practice in this area.'

'You really think it's *that* important?'

'I do, Mr Torrent. The world is changing.'

Malcolm Torrent sat back in his chair and glanced out of his floor-to-ceiling window as though checking whether he could see the world changing. His view was partially obscured by cranes with his company's logo on it.

'Well, Maserov, you're a younger man, younger than me and younger than Hamilton. I'm paying you to tell me what's up ahead.'

'You are, sir.'

'But tell me, Maserov, do you think there'll be a backlash against all of this MeToo stuff?'

'There probably will be,' said Maserov.

'Couldn't we be ahead of the curve on that?'

'On the backlash?'

'Yes,' said Malcolm Torrent, confirming Maserov's understanding.

'No, I don't think that's a good idea. Leaving aside the legal implications, because of course judges and juries walk into court with unstated preconceptions about different corporate entities before any evidence has been led, and leaving aside any moral implications, there are of course share price implications from these sorts of things.'

'Yes, of course, you're right, Maserov. And you think the Indian girl should be the human face of our response to this, should we need one?'

'Should we need one, yes.'

'Hmm, just between you and me and the lamppost, Maserov, Aileen, her boss in HR, she can be a pain in the arse when she gets her nose out of joint. You know what I mean; that classic female passive aggression? Can be a real bitch at times. She can't get to me directly, of course, but she pisses off my secretary.'

'I do, Mr Torrent, entirely. But then there's the anti-discrimination aspect of all of this. You could tell Aileen van der Westhuizen that for public relations reasons it would be better for the firm to have her lieutenant in the role, not to mention the benefit arising from the business the company does directly with India.'

'To hell with it, Maserov, you're right! Let's go with the Indian girl. If Aileen gets her rag we'll tell her she's simply not an Indian.'

'Oh and I'd like to draft a memo from you, if I may, that makes it clear to anyone in any department that *this* work is Jessica Annand's priority until you say otherwise.'

'Jessica, that's the Indian girl?' Malcolm Torrent said, picking up his phone to begin talking to Joan Henshaw about something else entirely.

'Yes.'

'Do it, I'll sign it.'

III

Having, together with Eleanor, fed, bathed, read stories to and kissed goodnight both Beanie and Jacob, Maserov was on his hands and knees in the kitchen for a second go at what seemed like a newly created rice paddy on the floor, when Eleanor told him not to bother about it. She would finish the cleaning.

'Oh, that's okay, I'm already down here,' he said, but Eleanor seemed even keener than she usually was that he leave.

'My mother's coming,' Eleanor said in a tone that suggested it was an explanation for wanting him to leave sooner than usual.

'Are you preferring your mother's floor cleaning techniques to mine?'

'No, it's not that.'

'Well?'

'I thought you'd prefer . . . not to see her.'

'Why?'

'I thought it might make you uncomfortable. You haven't seen her in a while.'

'I haven't seen her in a while because you kicked me out.'

'Let's not start that again.'

'You always say that, as though my drawing your attention to what you've done to me and indirectly to the boys is somehow the wrong that's been committed. You know what? I don't mind seeing your mother. It's *you* who doesn't want me to see your mother. You don't want me to see her because she always liked me and she wouldn't agree with what you've done. If she comes and has even a short chat with me, sees me cleaning the house with you, she's going to give you a hard time in the days to come. She's going to redouble her efforts to get you to reconsider this separation and, you figure, if I'm not here and she doesn't see me, it will make your life just that little bit easier.'

'If you want to see my mother, fine. Why don't you call her and ask her out on a date?'

'A *date*, where did *that* come from?'

'Stephen, my mother's coming to babysit. I'm going out and I need to get ready.'

'Oh,' said Maserov. All the possibilities contained in her last statement seemed to dance before him, above the former rice paddies and over the kitchen table where they had once eaten as a family every day.

'Are you going out with Marta, the woman who's taken the teaching of Geography to a new low?'

'What is it with you and Marta?'

'She's always hated me. Is that why you're going out with her?' Maserov was looking for confirmation that Eleanor's evening companion was indeed Marta with an urgency that bulldozed subtlety beyond the confines of a conversation whose agreed-upon subject was up for grabs.

'It might be Marta. What does it matter? It shouldn't matter who it is.'

Maserov wished for a service along the lines of Google Translate only instead of translating from foreign languages it would take something his wife had said and instantly tell him what it really meant. Forget the human genome project, where was the algorithm for determining what his wife meant?

'You want me to go before the kitchen is all done?'

'If you don't mind, yes.'

'I think I mind.'

'One day you won't.'

'Can I leave *then*?'

'Stephen, I need a shower.'

This was a bad development. It was unlikely Eleanor needed a shower to see Marta the geographer, although Marta probably had her standards. It was possible that the shower wasn't for Marta per se but was just the ablution Eleanor needed to wash her children off her before going out, just to be comfortable. It was also possible she wanted to be clean for someone who wasn't Marta, wasn't even a woman. She might want to be clean to go out with a man.

Maserov sat in his car discreetly parked across the street from the home he was trying to pay off, listening to a BBC podcast called *In Our Time* in which Melvyn Bragg took it in turns with various aspects of himself to berate mild-mannered, learned academics who had the audacity to say something he wasn't expecting. As comforting as it was, nothing could distract him from the anxiety in his stomach as he waited to see who it was that was coming to the house. It was dark but the street light illuminated his mother-in-law's arrival. He wanted to tell her that

Jessica Annand had praised the aftershave she had got for him with her pharmacy bonus points. Maybe his mother-in-law could pass news of Jessica's existence on to Eleanor and that would make his wife think twice about finding some other man. Some other man. It was unthinkable. Yet, there he was. Maserov watched in the half-light as some other man came to his house and left again soon after with his wife.

IV

'So your wife's dating the PE teacher,' said Betga. 'It's not the end of the world.'

'I don't know that it's the PE teacher. It could be the drama teacher.'

They were sitting in the front bar of the Grosvenor Hotel. Maserov had not known what to do with the information that his wife seemed to have a date with another man so he had called Betga.

'I think it's worse if it's the drama teacher. You'd better hope it's the PE teacher.'

'Why?'

'Because if it's the PE teacher it's almost understandable. You have the body of a lawyer or even an accountant. The PE teacher is, I imagine, someone with a body that's qualitatively different. The drama teacher, on the other hand, no matter his body shape, would pride himself on being well-spoken and somewhat cultured, if not steeped, in the written word. These ought to be your strong suits. If she's sleeping with the PE teacher it's just variety. If she's sleeping with the drama teacher, you're being replaced.'

'I don't know that she's sleeping with anyone,' said Maserov to Betga and to himself.

'Maybe not,' said Betga. 'Not yet, but you'll know.'

'How will I know?'

'There's always a tell, even when they don't want you to know. And she'll want you to know.'

'What kind of tell?'

'I don't know exactly. She might be less interested in sex.'

'We're separated. How can I know?'

'So you're not sleeping together, ever, not at all?'

'Betga, we're separated, of course we're not having sex with each other.'

'Oh, okay, I thought that was marriage. Separation, I imagined, might spice things up. You could maybe cheat on each other *with* each other. Too late to suggest that now, I suppose. Well, then she might spend more than usual on clothes, start exercising more or she might tell you she's fucking the PE teacher.'

'You're a lot of help. I don't know why I expected you to have any insight into this.'

'Or . . .' said Betga as though he'd just recalled something brilliant. 'She might show you unusual kindness. You'd better pray she doesn't show you unusual kindness. I'll see what I can find out from Carla. They're seeing each other a bit, talking on the phone.'

'How do you know?'

'She told me. I've been going over there ever since you got her to confirm that I'm Marietta's father.'

'How's that going?'

'Fatherhood is great but the circumstances are, as you'd imagine, a little uncomfortable. Carla is still pissed off with me for being unfaithful and the sad policeman is better at changing Marietta than I am. He's not lording it over me exactly but it hurts to be out-changed by a cop, especially a sad elderly one. He's devilishly clever, using that sad maladroit elderly thing to his advantage. It's a killer. I'm currently being outdone by pathos.'

'With Marietta?'

'No, with Carla. Marietta presents her own challenges. She doesn't know me and it's hard to bond with her in an hour or two in the living room with Carla watching me like a hawk and occasionally the sad cop too.'

'Incidentally, I've got something for you.' Betga pulled a piece of paper out of the pocket of his jacket, unfolded it and handed it to Maserov. It was a photocopy of a Notice of Discontinuance in the name of Jane Ode, signifying that the fictional character he had created had ended her litigation for sexual harassment against Torrent Industries.

'What am I meant to do with this?' asked Maserov, looking at it.

'You take it to Malcolm Torrent, show it to him from a distance and with your finger over my name and start my retainer. Tell him it's best for him not to ask any questions and that you don't know how I did this.'

'What if he now wants you to get rid of *all* the pending cases against Torrent Industries without paying anything to the plaintiffs?'

'Tell him I told you that I checked the other claims and that it's my considered opinion this is the only plaintiff whose case can be settled without an offer.'

'What if he reads the Notice of Discontinuance and sees your name as the lawyer acting for her?'

'He won't. He's a big-picture man, remember, and you'll be holding your thumb over my name. You want it just close enough for him to read the heading, "Notice of Discontinuance". Then be sure to take the document *with* you.'

V

It was night and Jessica was alone in her apartment, half-undressed and lying on her bed, her head propped up on a small pile of pillows that she would otherwise have deemed superfluous. She took a sip from her wine glass and then placed it down on the book her book club was forcing her to read. The novel was about a woman who eventually found love on a small boat that cruised the canals of Paris in search of bookshops only to dock, somehow, in Tuscany. It managed to have 'bookshop', 'Paris', 'Tuscany' and 'love' in the title. The book was written by a trusted and experienced author, someone who had written this kind of book many times before and could be relied upon to do it again. But this wasn't what she was going to read, not tonight.

Maserov had copied and given her all of the affidavits in support of each of the four women alleging sexual harassment at Torrent Industries. Finally, she was going to see what was done, or was alleged to have been done, and who it was that the women alleged had done it. She was hoping to see Frank Cardigan's name on the pages.

Each of the four women were support staff. With her laptop beside her on the bed, Jessica was able to log into the Torrent Industries HR database remotely and see a photo of each of the women within minutes. None of them worked there anymore. Jessica wondered if they had found work anywhere else. Was it any different anywhere else?

Jessica looked at a photo of the first plaintiff in the pile, a Ms Pauline Hart, twenty-six years old with mousey-brown hair and a diploma in secretarial studies and office management from McPhersons Secretarial College. She had seen Pauline, she recognised her from the photo, but couldn't remember ever having spoken to her. Jessica wanted to get a better sense of Pauline before reading her affidavit but there wasn't much about her in her file. She lived or had lived in Croydon, took the Lilydale line to Flinders Street. She had gone to Croydon Primary School and then to Lilydale High School, where she left at seventeen before undertaking a twelve-month diploma course that Jessica estimated would have cost somewhere around $18 000. She learned to type up to ninety-five words per minute before there was even slight diminution in her accuracy. She had worked at Torrent Industries since McPhersons Secretarial College had managed to get her placed there. When asked if she had any dependents, Pauline had listed her cat. She lived at home with her mother and certain minimal, never-articulated hopes that dared to surface only at night and on public holidays in the bedroom she had slept in all her life and she was not even infinitesimally responsible for what happened to her at the hands of an older, wealthier, more powerful man at the headquarters of Torrent Industries.

She had been working diligently and seemingly anonymously in Accounts when she was told that the secretary to an executive in Urban Infrastructure was on leave and that she had been chosen to fill in while the other woman was away. Frank Cardigan worked in Urban Infrastructure. Jessica felt sure she was about to read his name in the affidavit, any paragraph now. But she didn't. The executive Pauline was sent to work for was junior to Frank Cardigan, a man named Michael Mercer. Jessica knew Mike Mercer and, even before reading on, knew she would have no trouble believing whatever allegations she was about to read. Several years of attending the same office Christmas parties and having him leer at her, brush past her in the corridor, touch her arm lightly but unnecessarily, all of it had primed her to believe whatever was coming.

As it transpired, Pauline had not been working unnoticed. Having seen her in the elevator, Mike Mercer found where she was working. Then when the need arose for a temporary replacement for his secretary he asked specifically for her. How would she know this, Jessica wondered? The next paragraph in the affidavit made it clear. Mercer had told Pauline that she had been specially chosen by him.

On her first day working for him she arrived earlier than she'd been told to, just to ensure she wasn't late. She was nervous and wondered if this was a promotion of sorts or a test to determine whether she ought to get a promotion.

It was on that first day working for him, indeed, on the very first morning, that he asked her if she had a boyfriend. She had been taken aback by the question and, not having expected it, she told the truth. She didn't have a boyfriend. This led to the beginning of a line of questioning about her experience with men, beginning with questions about the existence and length of any previous relationships.

The questions, she said in the affidavit, made her uncomfortable but eventually she summoned the courage to ask why he was asking them. He told her that she had a sweetness, an innocence, that he found endearing but that if she was going to succeed in the corporate world she would benefit from a mentor, a protector, someone who would guide her through its alleyways. He said he would teach her how to get on, how to move up the ladder faster. She said she had smiled when he had said this but only because she was nervous. She didn't really know what he meant and didn't really know the appropriate way to respond. He made her feel uncomfortable but, she said, she didn't really know how to describe why. She had wondered if she was being uncharitable to him and if she should consider herself lucky.

Then Mercer started asking her about her previous sexual experience. She pretended she thought he was joking and didn't answer. This went on almost every day. And the questions became more and more explicit. Jessica poured herself another drink and shifted on the bed before reading the precise nature of the questions Pauline Hart had sworn under oath she had been asked by her boss, Mike Mercer, of Urban Infrastructure. Was she a virgin? Did she like performing oral sex? Did she like receiving oral sex? Had she ever had anal sex?

She said in her affidavit that when she refused to answer, pretending, she said, that she thought he was joking and wasn't really interested in her answers, Mercer became less clinical in the language he used and this compounded her discomfort. Did she take it up the arse? Did she swallow? Had she ever had a man spell her entire name in cum on her tits? These words were there in black and white in the affidavit.

Alone on her bed in her apartment, Jessica asked out loud, 'Why didn't you come to me? Why didn't you tell anyone?' Then, as though answering her, in the very next paragraph of the affidavit Pauline Hart stated that at that stage she didn't tell anyone because, she explained, the very language embarrassed her. It was not, she said, how she talked.

One night when she was working back on some urgent matter, a presentation he had to give, Mercer called her from her workstation outside his office and told her to come into his office and offered her his seat behind his desk. She was made uncomfortable by this because there was, as far as she knew, no one else on the floor at that time of night but she didn't think she could refuse. She saw that he had been drinking wine and he poured her a glass, praising her diligence. Then he started praising her dress sense. Then he started commenting on her body. 'Nice tits, great arse, but you're letting it all go to waste. If you're telling me the truth, you're in your prime and not using any of your assets. Is it that you don't know what to do?' Mercer had said. By this stage he had closed the door. She stood up saying that she needed to get home and in standing up abruptly from his desk, spilled her wine on some of his papers.

He came over to where she had been sitting, grabbing some tissues and telling her not to worry about the papers or the mess. He said there had been bigger messes in his office and then she saw that his erect penis was exposed through the open fly in his pants. He grabbed her hand and placed it on his penis. The affidavit said that she managed to get out of the room before he could stop her and when she turned around in the corridor to see if he was chasing her she saw he was standing in the corridor masturbating. Not wanting to wait for the elevator, she ran to the fire-escape door and down five flights before waiting for the elevator to take her to the ground floor.

She called her mother from the street in great distress but was not able to explain what had happened. The next day she called in sick and the day after that she came into work but did not go back to Mike Mercer's office. Instead she went back down to Accounts, where she told her supervisor, without mentioning Mike Mercer's name, that she wouldn't be returning to Urban Infrastructure. The supervisor, a woman, didn't ask any questions, nodded and made space for her back at her previous workstation. The other women in Accounts looked at her but none of them asked any questions either.

Pauline Hart became withdrawn after that. The speed and the quality of her work suffered. Within three weeks of this she had ceased to be an employee of Torrent Industries. But she was there long enough to see another woman pack up a few personal possessions – some photos of her family, a fluffy stuffed cat – into her handbag and make her way up to Urban Infrastructure as the other women looked on in silence.

VI

'Thank God you're here, Maserov!' Betga whispered when he opened Carla's front door.

'Where's Carla?'

'She's gone out.'

'Gone out? I thought the whole point of me coming here was to talk to her, for both of us to talk to her . . . about settling. She does know I'm coming, doesn't she?'

'She knows, she knows. She's gone for a walk with the sad policeman. He came here unexpectedly and found me. We almost had a bit of a scene.'

'Was he violent?'

'No, are you kidding? No, he was more . . . He was very sad, quite aggressively sad.'

'What a bastard!'

'Exactly! No man can expect to appear attractive to a woman if he's responsible for that degree of sadness in a much more pathetic man. He's got it all figured out. It's Darwinian. He's exploiting the one natural advantage he's got over me.'

'Abject sadness?'

'Yep.'

'Is that why you were so relieved when I got here?'

'No, it was because I need you to show me some dad tricks.'

'"Dad tricks"? Where's Marietta? Isn't she with Carla?'

'No, she's in there,' said Betga, pointing to the living room.

'By herself?' said Maserov, running down the hall to the living room. The little girl was sitting on the coffee table about to tumble off, head first and backwards. Maserov swooped in and picked her up off the table and held her in his arms.

'Okay, first dad trick. You can't leave her alone unless she's in her cot or in a playpen of some kind. She's too little. The cardinal rule of fatherhood is to never, *ever*, stop being terrified your child is going to hurt herself. Okay? And there's only one thing worse than her hurting herself and that's her hurting herself when *you* were the one supposed to be taking care of her, protecting her against harm, including harm that you haven't even thought of, harm that is *so* unlikely to come to her that its anticipation will expose an imaginative genius in you that you never knew you had. Got it?'

'Got it!'

'You need to wake regularly in the middle of the night, night after night, imagining terrible things happening to her, which are all your fault, that haven't happened yet but that probably will happen unless you think of them first. It's *only* if you think of them that you can have *any* chance of stopping them from happening. That's the first rule of father-hood. Jesus, Betga, you're nowhere near anxious enough for parenthood.'

They heard the sound of Carla's key in the front door. She walked in alone without the policeman and saw Betga in the living room standing beside Maserov with Marietta in his arms. She smiled wanly at the sight of Maserov holding her daughter, the little girl's arms around his neck.

'You see?' she said to Betga. 'That's the way to hold her. How come he can do it?'

''Cause he's never been sent away from his child.'

There was an uncomfortable silence as the three of them realised that was not true.

'The acting sergeant, he's gone, has he?' Betga asked, changing the subject to one he would very soon realise was not going to help him.

'I know you laugh at him but he's a very decent man.'

'Would you like a cup of tea?' Carla asked Maserov. 'I'm not going to settle with Torrent Industries but you're welcome to a cup of tea.'

'I'm not here to talk to you about settlement.'

'You're not?' Betga asked.

'No, I actually came here to tell you some news, some good news.'

'Oh really?' Carla said with her back to Betga and Maserov as she filled the kettle and Betga mouthed the words, 'What are you talking about?'

Carla spoke before Maserov had a chance to answer. 'I must say, it can't happen very often that the lawyer for the company you're suing holds your baby daughter better than her own father.'

'Who happens to be your lawyer,' Betga added. 'I'm not beyond learning. He's had more experience being a father but I plan to be around a lot more now so that Marietta feels more comfortable with me. It won't be long before she's comfortable enough with me to let me take her out alone.'

'Where are you going to take her, the Grosvenor?' asked Carla.

'Not yet, although I think she'd like the decor. It's got quite a surprisingly soothing ambience during the day. No, before that I thought I could take her to the park. But I understand that it will take a little time for her to be comfortable alone with me so, for the time being, I'll just hang out here with you as well . . . if that's alright with you.'

'You'd like to spend more time here, would you . . . to get Marietta more comfortable with you?'

'Yes, I would. And if that has the unintended benefit of allowing me to spend more time in your company that's no bad thing.'

'Okay,' said Carla, in a tone that implied a sudden good idea. 'If you want to spend more time around here there might be a way we can make that happen.'

'Yeah?' asked Betga.

'I'll need you to agree to do something for me.'

'Sure, you name it. Anything.'

'Well, you haven't yet heard what I want.' Then, surprising Betga, Carla turned to Maserov, who was still gently swaying and holding the now almost sleeping Marietta. 'Ron, the policeman Betga makes fun of, he's a very sweet man. I met him through or perhaps I should say *because* of Betga. When I found out about Betga's extra-legal contact with the legal recruiter I told him I never wanted to see him again but Betga, being the kind of child-like pain in the arse he is, wouldn't accept that I meant it. He kept coming back. In the end I went to the local police station and that's where I met Ron. And, in the state I was in, I probably over-shared. I definitely cried a lot. I told him all about Betga and how I didn't want to see him again or want him anywhere near me or the baby when she was born. He gave me his card and told me to call him if ever I was afraid or needed him for any reason at all.'

'They give cards now to acting sergeants,' Betga interrupted. 'It's irresponsibly profligate.'

'Okay, cut that shit, alright?' she said with a sudden flash of anger that was never very far from the surface. 'That's what I'm talking about. He's not the most dynamic man in the world but he was there, reliably there . . . if I needed him. And you, for all your intelligence and smart talking, you were a weak prick who let your constant need for a self-esteem top-up, for an ego boost, lead you down the path of instant gratification when we had a chance to build something here. And you did it even knowing what I'd been through, what had been done to me. So don't you dare laugh at him!'

'Carla, alright, I take your point but there's no need to canonise him. It's pretty clear what he was hanging around for.'

'Maybe that was true in the beginning, maybe he carried some hope. But I made it pretty clear pretty early that that was never going to happen. And do you know what? He hung around anyway, which is more than you would do. So if you want to hang around now, you're going to do something for me. I want you to be his life coach.'

'*What?*'

'You heard me. He often needs advice with respect to his career, handling people. He needs confidence, one thing you've got too much of. So here's the deal. You're going to be his life coach and you're going to do it for free.'

'You've got to be kidding!'

'I'm not kidding. You do this properly and you help him, you can start coming around here and learn how to be a father.'

'Carla, I can try, but I can't guarantee it will help him. He's got to *want* to be helped. I mean . . . I don't even know if he'd *want* me to be his life coach. He might find that, frankly, humiliating.'

'That's why you're going to approach him, make the offer out of gratitude for all he's done for your daughter and for the mother of your daughter.'

'And if he doesn't want it?'

'You're going to talk him into it.'

'And if I can't?'

'Betga, if you can't talk him into it that just means you didn't really try. Now, Mr Maserov, what's your good news? I could use some.'

Maserov explained how Betga had conned Malcolm Torrent into trialling him as a private investigator without revealing that he, Betga, was simultaneously the lawyer acting for the aggrieved women, a conflict of interest as large as the building in which the con took place.

'To demonstrate to Malcolm Torrent how good a private investigator he was, Betga concocted another woman, a fictitious plaintiff also suing Torrent Industries for sexual harassment, who he would persuade not to pursue the case. I was to present a Notice of Discontinuance to show that within a couple of weeks he had indeed got rid of the case. Betga hoped this would convince Torrent to take him on as a private investigator, off the books, that is, with no record of him or Torrent Industries employing him.'

'And?' asked Betga expectantly.

'The good news is,' said Maserov, 'it worked. You are now hired as a private investigator on the strength of your work for the period it takes to make the real cases disappear.'

'So he has a financial incentive to make them go on and on and last as long as possible. How is this good news for me?' Carla asked.

'Carla, relax. I'm going to help you out financially,' answered Betga before continuing. 'So what salary did you negotiate for me?'

'It's 75 per cent of mine.'

'That doesn't seem fair,' said Betga.

'I was fine with it,' answered Maserov.

'I still don't see where any of this is good for me,' Carla interrupted.

'You've got to take the long view here, Carla, although admittedly Maserov's negotiating skills on our behalf are disappointing.'

'No, no, she doesn't have to take the long view here. I'm here with the short view,' Maserov interrupted.

'What does that mean?' asked Carla.

'Okay, Malcolm Torrent doesn't want any record of him or the company paying Betga because he doesn't have any idea how Betga, as his private investigator, is getting rid of at least that one case. So, at Betga's suggestion, Mr Torrent pays me a "bonus" that constitutes his payment to Betga. So I'm responsible for this money. Knowing how keen Betga is to atone for his misdeeds and to be offered a second chance, I know that he's going to want this money to go directly to you.'

Maserov pulled out an envelope full of hundred dollar bills.

'This is for me? Oh my God, thank you!'

'Don't thank *me*.'

'I won't,' muttered Betga.

'It's Betga here you should be thanking.'

VII

'Torrent Industries would hire a private investigator to spy on us, on *me*? What the hell for? It's not like one of those personal injury cases where someone says they can't bend over anymore after a workplace accident and then they're caught red-handed on camera bending down to pick up a fifty-dollar bill. What, do they want to catch me out suing *other* corporations for sexual harassment?' Carla asked Maserov.

'No, they'll want to look into your past,' offered Maserov by way of explanation.

'My past what?'

Betga, who knew Carla better than Maserov did, drew breath to explain. He drew breath because he knew the force of the fury the explanation would draw. 'They're going to want to dig into your past romantic life, really they're going to want to dig into your sex life. They're going to want to bring up the fact, for example, that you're an unmarried mother.'

'What the hell has that got to do with anything?'

'Nothing, but since people are so often irrationally at least suspicious, if not downright condemnatory, of unmarried mothers, it's likely to be prejudicial.'

'That doesn't make any sense to me. What has my marital status and the fact that I'm a mother got to do with anything that was done to me in the workplace?'

'As a matter of fact, law and logic, it has nothing at all to do with it,' said Maserov.

'But as a matter of painting a picture for a jury,' Betga continued, 'Torrent Industries will try to make it have everything to do with it. Carla, you know what they'll try to do to you. They're going to try to paint a picture of a loose woman, a woman who sleeps around casually, with a history of sleeping around casually. They're going to cast aspersions on the way you dress.'

'The way I dress? You mean they're going to try to give the jury the impression that I was asking for it?'

'Yeah, begging for it, a bitch on heat,' Betga explained. 'They're going to try to make it look like it was . . .'

'It was *what*?'

'Consensual.'

'You are fucking kidding me?'

'No, we're not,' said Maserov.

'That's what Torrent Industries is going to say. They're going to say you didn't fight back, that you took your time reporting it. They're going to say that you stayed on good terms with your boss.'

'He was my boss!'

'They'll try to find holes in your story. They'll say that you don't *act* like a victim.'

'How does a victim *act*?'

'You're still working.'

'I'm temping two days a week wherever I can get it.'

'Shows resilience. That's got to hurt you.'

'You have *got* to be kidding me?'

'No, Carla, sadly he's not.'

Carla was cutting bananas into ever smaller pieces for Marietta. 'But wait a minute, aren't *you* Torrent Industries? *You're* the lawyer acting for Torrent Industries,' she said, with an upturned hand in the direction of Maserov, a hand that was still holding the knife. 'And *you're* the lawyer acting for *me*,' she said to Betga. 'And you're *also* the private investigator you said they've got to go digging about in my past.'

'Yeah, *that* can't last,' said Maserov quietly. 'He can't keep doing both.'

'Well, that's between you two,' she said. 'But surely it can last long enough for *you* not to dig,' she said to Betga, 'and for *you* to tell Torrent that he dug deep and came up with Mother Teresa.'

'They're finding stuff on Mother Teresa now,' said Betga, helping himself to a small piece of banana.

'It's not sexual though. Is it?' Maserov asked.

'It's not sexual *yet*,' cautioned Betga. 'They won't stop till they find something. That's what happens when you take a vow of poverty, chastity and obedience. Everyone knows poverty's the easy bit. With chastity and obedience you just become a target. It's a disincentive to being Mother Teresa nowadays.'

'Will you forget Mother Teresa? Are you even listening to me? Fuck, I hate lawyers!'

'I'm listening to you,' said Maserov sympathetically.

'What about you? *You're* my lawyer!' Carla shouted at Betga.

'I am listening to you, even when I'm not here.'

'Don't patronise me, you unfaithful arsehole!'

Betga's mobile phone rang. 'Don't worry, I'm not going to take that.'

'You're not taking it 'cause it's probably a woman,' said Carla.

'I don't care *who* it is. I'm not taking it because I'm in conference with my client.' By now he had the phone in his hand. He glanced at the number and winced. 'I'm *definitely* not taking that,' he said under his breath.

'I think we should return to the matter at hand,' said Maserov, a little uncomfortably.

'Who was it?' demanded Carla.

'Couldn't tell you,' said Betga innocently.

'It's a common tactic of the defence in sexual harassment cases,' Maserov ploughed on, 'to trawl for any evidence at all, however slight, that might suggest the plaintiff was promiscuous. Then, armed with that evidence, they try to suggest that the behaviour that forms the subject of the harassment claim was consensual.'

'Well, that's just absolutely disgusting,' said Carla.

'I agree completely,' said Maserov.

'Then don't do it,' Carla shot back.

Betga and Maserov looked at each other.

'He won't be doing it, Carla. Someone else will.'

'What do you mean?'

'Okay,' said Maserov, beginning his explanation. 'Eleanor told you how I came to be the lawyer Malcolm Torrent's got handling this.'

'Yeah, you found out your boss was going to fire you and in a chance meeting in the men's room with Mr Torrent you leveraged a hunch that he was pissed off that your boss wasn't taking Betga's claims, *our* claims, seriously enough.'

'It was in the corridor, not the men's room, but otherwise that's pretty much it.'

'So?'

'So Maserov's gamble didn't save his job, it only bought him time, some of which he's used up already.'

'Well, I'm sorry to hear that, for your sake, but how does that change anything for me and the other victims?'

'Carla,' said Maserov, 'a moment ago, you said it was disgusting to use the plaintiff's prior sexual history to suggest that the alleged harassment, that behaviour that forms the subject of the harassment claim, was consensual. And I agreed. But the decision to use it or not won't be mine because I almost certainly won't be running the case by the time it gets to court, if it gets that far. Because of the slow pace of these things —'

'What things?'

'Litigation, the legal system,' Betga chimed in support.

'Because of the slow pace of litigation,' continued Maserov, 'it almost certainly won't be me calling the shots. Whatever's going to happen to me will have already happened by the time your case gets to court.'

'Carla, what he's trying to say is that the lawyer who takes on the defence of Torrent Industries *after* him won't be anywhere near as reasonable as he is and that *that* lawyer, probably a man, is likely to come after you with all guns blazing. He's going to try his damnedest to paint you as a slut so that when Mercer testifies that there was "unfortunately some regrettable sexual activity" between you and Mercer in the office, it was just two hard-working employees letting off steam.'

'That's not what happened at all. I thought lawyers weren't allowed to lie to the court?' Carla was close to tears.

'The lawyer doesn't *have* to lie to the court. It will be Mike Mercer who lies to the lawyer. The lawyer is merely acting on his client's instructions. Then it will be Mercer's word against yours and they will have done all they can to blacken your reputation.'

'So what are you saying, exactly?'

'I'm saying we should try to settle with Torrent Industries while Maserov is still the face of the other side.'

Betga's phone rang again and nobody in the room was happy about it. He went into Marietta's room to answer it.

'Carla, he's right. I know this seems incredibly unfair to you. And it is. I know you're angry and you're hurt. You know, they teach us at law school that a damages payout, money, is meant to compensate the plaintiff to the extent of putting them back in the position they were in before the damage occurred. I know that in this instance you *can't* be put back in the position you were in before it happened. I'm not supposed to say things like this to you, not as the lawyer representing Torrent Industries but . . . well, the whole situation here is pretty unusual.'

'You're a decent guy, Stephen. You know that? I really do like Eleanor and I think she's smart but I don't think she's in the real world in so far as men are concerned. Maybe she married you too early, didn't experience enough of men, the way they can be. Guys like you don't come around every day, not round here, anyway.' She pointed to Marietta's room from where Betga's voice could be heard.

'I told you, I can't talk,' said Betga into the phone.

'She's crazy to think that guy can hold a candle to you, frankly.'

'What guy?' shot Maserov. He was meant to be mollifying Carla. Suddenly, a thin film of sweat announced itself on his forehead and under his arms. Carla was tuning into Betga's conversation.

'I can't talk to you. Not now,' they heard Betga say.

'Who's he talking to?' Carla asked herself out loud. 'Betga, you shit, stop hiding in your daughter's bedroom, taking calls from women when you're meant to be advising me.'

'Got to go. Now,' said Betga hurriedly into the phone. He was still putting the phone in his pocket when he became visible again to Carla and Maserov.

'That was a woman, wasn't it? You pretend you want to be back in our lives but take time out from giving me legal advice to take a call from a woman. That's the sort of stunt Ron would never pull, nor Stephen, here, for that matter.'

'I *do* want to be back in your lives and that wasn't a woman.'

'Would you try that shit on Eleanor?' Carla asked Maserov.

'If it was a woman? No, I wouldn't.'

'Carla, it wasn't a woman.'

'He says it wasn't a woman,' Maserov offered weakly in Betga's defence.

'I swear, that wasn't a woman!' offered Betga.

'Yeah, prove it. Prove it or you can leave right now and I'll get some other lawyer to represent me against Torrent Industries.' Maserov didn't know what was going to happen next. He was still reeling from the announcement of a man in Eleanor's life that couldn't hold a candle to him.

'Well, how do you want me to prove it?'

'Put your phone on speaker and redial the number that called you.'

'I can't. It's unprofessional. And it would betray a confidence.'

'You're totally full of shit.'

'Carla, it's a man. I was talking to a man.'

'Then call him back.'

'Look, how about this. You see the number here?' Betga walked over to her and showed her the number of the previous two callers. 'You see that number?'

'Yeah, I see it.'

'Okay, I shouldn't be doing this but I'm going to play you a voice message left for me on my phone from this guy's number. You see it's the same number?'

'Yes, it's the same number,' Carla said suspiciously.

'Okay, listen.' Betga played the voicemail message from the number and turned his phone speaker on so that the message was broadcast to the room. Then came the voice.

'Look, I don't know your name but I've been given your number. Well, given *this* number. I think . . . I need to talk to you.' It was a man's voice. Maserov could see Carla was comforted by this but he wasn't. He knew that voice but couldn't quite place it.

'He sounds like he needs help,' Carla said. 'Are you going to help him?'

'I don't know if I can.'

'I know that voice,' said Maserov. 'That's Featherby.'

'Who's Featherby?' Carla asked.

'He's the lawyer from Freely Savage that was handling the sexual harassment cases before me.'

'Why are you talking to *him*?' Carla asked.

'Okay, look, I'm not meant to tell you this. It has nothing to do with you. It has nothing to do with *either* of you.' Betga hesitated, looking at his fingers, which Maserov interpreted as meaning that either he was trying to come up with something both he and Carla could live with or that he was weighing up whether the situation called for a betrayal of confidence. Then, evidently having made up his mind, Betga continued. 'As Maserov knows, there's a group, a support group, called the FSS, the Freely Savage Survivors. It helps former lawyers, former employees of Freely Savage, to get over the trauma of having worked there. I'm currently the chair of that support group.'

'You're chair of the FSS?' Maserov asked incredulously.

'Yes, why does that surprise you? I'm a very caring and sensitive man. The tragedy is that in the absence of other people knowing this, I'm forced on occasion to say it myself.'

'Why's Featherby calling you? Doesn't he work there anymore?'

'No, he *does* work there but he wants to join the FSS. He wants to meet with the group.'

'I was never sure it really existed. Isn't it supposed to be for *former* employees?' asked Maserov.

'It exists. It's exhausting trying to heal all these people, believe me. I do it pro bono. I keep telling him that he can't join until he's a former employee but he says he thinks he's on the way out.'

'God, that's a lawyer at Freely Savage?' asked Carla. 'He sounded desperate. I didn't think someone way up there at Freely Savage would ever sound like that. He sounded like he was about to cry.'

'This shouldn't surprise you,' said Betga, 'of course he sounds like he's going to cry. He probably *is* going to cry. He's a lawyer in the corporate sector. Sooner or later all lawyers cry. Seven per cent of the general population have a drinking problem. Twenty-one per cent of lawyers do. Seven per cent of the general population suffer from depression. Twenty-eight per cent of lawyers do. These figures come from the American Bar Association. It's probably higher at Freely Savage. But I can't help him. I've told him that the FSS exists only for people who have left the firm. The lawyer has to be in recovery. I told him that if they get rid of him, *then* we can talk. So you see, I wasn't talking to a woman.'

'No, you were denying help to a desperate man.'

'Yes,' said Betga.

Both Carla and Maserov felt much better.

VIII

Jessica was simultaneously compelled to continue reading and repelled by what she was reading. The compulsion came from a sense of guilt. She was employed in the one department in the company with a heavy concentration of women, even a female boss, the one department with the explicit mandate to look after the wellbeing of staff. She had gone into the office day after day, week after week, half suspecting that this kind of thing was going on but never knowing the specifics and never making it her business to ask. As she had explained to Maserov, the whole culture there was one of don't ask, don't tell.

She felt too small, too powerless, to *ask* the people who also felt too small and too powerless to *tell*. She was a young woman, Indian too, in a white males' world, almost as likely as any of the female support staff to be a victim. Almost. It was the almost that got stuck in her throat. She had got herself an education which she had used to gain a marginally less vulnerable position. When she interviewed and was offered the job she hadn't known that what she would be doing was serving the interests of the people who allowed her to be slightly safer than the less-educated women at the front line. That, and ensuring there was sufficient alfalfa on the sandwich trays that were served at lunch during in-house seminars.

As she lay on her bed in her apartment reading the affidavits, she felt that the company's regular salary payments into her bank account were in fact dependent on her *not* voicing her concern with its treatment of women and she started to wonder in what sense she was complicit with its underlying culture. It was a culture she put on a brave face to negotiate every day, right after she applied her make-up in the safe space of her own bathroom. But after reading this, how was she ever going to look at herself in the mirror again? She had been terrified of being in the position in which these women had found themselves but had managed with guile and deft manoeuvring, sometimes deft physical manoeuvring, to avoid the worst that could happen. These women had not been so lucky.

Jessica knew that there were men who, after they loosened their ties at the end of the day, turned their attention to the women who, having groomed themselves first thing that morning after choosing their clothes carefully the night before, had fought their way to the Torrent Industries tower through impatient morning crowds clutching coats and bags, fingers tight around the dignity they brought from home for pay that would have left the pack cold. It was an attention these women, these stress balls for the men they worked for, could each feel in the air. In a touch, a look, a remark above the chatter of keyboards they would hear the subliminal sounds only feral dogs make. And soon, here and there, the teeth would emerge from behind a rapidly vanishing dissembled smile. The bite was coming, any moment now.

And if ever the taste turned sour, they would say she *asked* to be bitten, that she *wanted* it, she wanted the imbalance of power, the humiliation, the uncertainty as to her future prospects and earning capacity, the instant evaporation of self-esteem, the torn clothing, the smeared make-up, the sleepless nights, the counselling, the whole thing. You could just tell what she wanted, your honour. It was consensual. Jessica knew all of this, had seen it herself.

Having read what had happened to Pauline Hart, Jessica read what happened to Lilly Zhang, twenty-two, and then Monika Galea, twenty-five. There was another reason Jessica felt compelled to read on. She wanted to see what could happen to her.

Jessica remembered talking to Monika Galea at end-of-financial-year drinks. Though she'd seen her many times in passing, until that night they'd never really said much more than 'hi' and 'good morning' to each other. But even then there was something bright, something engaging and sympathetic in Monika's eyes that made Jessica feel that they might get on, that she might be someone nice to have lunch with if the prospect of eating with someone from HR didn't put Monika in a difficult position socially with the other secretaries in her department.

That early evening at drinks Jessica had made a point of approaching her and they had talked about food, cafes in the area, restaurants, and the best places to buy fresh produce for cooking at home. Monika had dark shoulder-length, wavy, almost curly hair and a ready smile. Jessica remembered she was warm and easy to talk to. But when one of the executives from Mining, her department, called Monika over to a group of other Mining people, Jessica had taken the opportunity to slip out of the boardroom and go home.

Now, on reading the affidavit, she remembered Monika privately raising her eyebrows to her when called over as if to say, 'Sorry, I have to go.' That had been the last contact she had ever had with Monika. And while it made perfect sense, Jessica was shocked to deduce from Monika's affidavit that this was the very night she was assaulted by Jim Duffy, one of the executives from Mining.

From Monika's affidavit Jessica learned Duffy had made suggestive comments before that night, many times, about her body, about her chest, and had even brushed up against her several times, pretending each time it had been an accident. So should she have seen this coming? That's what Jessica could imagine being put to her in court should Monika ever find herself giving evidence of Jim Duffy's assault on her that night. It would be put in a hostile tone as though it was Monika who had done something wrong and now she was trying to ruin the career and even the marriage of a good, hard-working man.

Jessica read on. Fuelled, emboldened, by alcohol, he had followed her out of the boardroom as she was leaving to go home. Walking two flights down via the fireproof stairwell, back to her desk in order to pick up her things before going home, where she lived with her parents, younger brother and sister, she hadn't even realised he was behind her in the stairwell. It certainly hadn't ever occurred to her that it would be unsafe for her to take the stairs in her own place of work. But it was unsafe.

Jessica read that Jim Duffy had come up behind her in the stairwell and pushed her against the concrete wall of the otherwise empty stairwell. The back of her head banged against the wall. She was in shock. He tried to kiss her, to invade her mouth with his, but failed and then started tearing at her blouse. She screamed but there was no one there to hear her. It seemed like ten minutes as she struggled to break his grip with her heart beating like a bell inside a fire alarm but was probably no more than two minutes before she managed to break away and run out of the stairwell at the next floor. Her shirt was torn and she had a scratch along one side of her chest from Duffy's fingernails.

Monika Galea no longer worked at Torrent Industries. Jim Duffy was still there, a highly regarded member of the Mining team.

By the time Jessica had finished reading the last of the affidavits, she had tears in her eyes. Was anything ever going to change?

She texted Maserov to say she had just finished reading the last of the affidavits, Carla's, knowing he had read them all. It had sickened her, she told him. She asked how negotiations with Carla and Betga had gone. It was eleven o'clock. She waited for a response and when nothing came back she suddenly worried that she had made a mistake by texting him so late.

Maserov was awake, alone in his bed, when the text came in. How should he tell Jessica what had happened at Carla's house? To his and Betga's surprise, Carla had said she wasn't interested in talking about settlement.

'This isn't about money!' Carla had said. 'This was a fucking crime. Ron said it's criminal assault, maybe even attempted rape. I want Mercer punished. I want him to go to jail. Then we can talk about money.' Maserov and Betga had looked at each other.

'It's complicated. Do you mind if I tell you tomorrow?' Maserov texted Jessica from his darkened bedroom.

'No, not at all. Sorry if I woke you.'

'No, you didn't at all.'

The leafy streets of Elwood and St Kilda were hushed as Maserov and Jessica lay in their beds, alone in their respective apartments, reading and re-reading their last messages to each other.

'Sleep well.'

'You too, sleep well.'

'Good night.'

'Good night.'

'See you tomorrow.'

'See you in the morning.'

part six

I

'Carla wants revenge. Of course she does. I understand that completely,' said Jessica, sipping a craft beer at a table under the soft light of the semi-private cocktail bar in the Grosvenor Hotel. On one side of her was Maserov. On the other was Betga.

'Yeah, I understand that too,' said Betga. 'But we're not in the revenge game. We're not assassins. Sadly. We're only lawyers.'

'You're *her* lawyer,' she said, looking at Betga. 'And *you're* her tormentor's lawyer,' she said, pointing at Maserov. 'And yet you're sitting opposite each other having not the first of a number of drinks together.'

'Yes, and for not the first time,' Betga clarified.

'Strictly speaking, I'm not her tormentor's lawyer. I'm the lawyer for her tormentor's *employer*.'

'But, if you don't mind my asking —'

'Jessica, you should feel free to ask me anything,' Betga volunteered in a manner that had served him well previously. 'Maserov too, probably. Ask him anything, about his marriage, for example. He's very forthcoming, even about his shortcomings,' he added.

'But aren't you bound by lawyer–client privilege, confidentiality, or something . . . to Carla?'

'Oh yeah, I'm bound by that,' said Betga, taking a sip.

'And you're not just Carla's lawyer, you're also her . . . estranged husband?'

'No, I'm not her husband,' he spat out flatly and immediately.

'But he'd *like* to be,' Maserov interjected. 'Their relationship hit a snag when she discovered he was a philanderer.'

'I'm not a philanderer.'

'He was unfaithful with a legal recruitment consultant.'

'It's a tight job market. A lot of people don't know that. And it was just once. The recruiter misinterpreted the terms of our arrangement. Wilfully too, in my opinion. I told her I had a daughter, or that I was almost certain I did.'

'How was that relevant to the recruiter?' Maserov asked.

'It suggested I need the job more than a person without dependants does and it also served to make me less desirable as a partner. It was meant to.'

'Yes, any reasonable woman would have deduced that you were an unreliable philanderer.'

'I *was*, the operative word being *was*.'

'He's reformed now,' Maserov explained to Jessica with the conviction of a lettuce leaf, not one from the core, an exterior one.

'I'm *recovering*. I'm in recovery.'

'Still,' said Jessica, 'You're on opposing sides, the two of you. Is it common for lawyers on opposing sides to be drinking together?'

'Alcohol is the first and oldest tool in the armoury of alternative dispute resolution, dear Jessica,' Betga proffered. 'It's the great conciliator.'

'Really? I thought it provokes,' she said.

'What did Shakespeare say, "it provokes and it unprovokes"? Right Maserov?'

'So it also provokes?' added Jessica rhetorically.

'Yep, has been known to.'

'Shakespeare was talking about lechery, not conciliation,' Maserov corrected.

'He was right about that too,' said Betga.

'Something you'd know about,' added Maserov.

'I *do* know my Shakespeare,' Betga replied.

'Didn't he also say "kill all the lawyers"?' Jessica asked.

'Yes, he borrowed the line from Maserov's wife.'

'Listen, there's got to be some advantage to you two being the lawyers negotiating all of this,' Jessica persisted.

'Well, not if Carla won't settle,' said Maserov. 'It's like you said, she wants revenge.'

'And you can't somehow structure that into the settlement agreement?'

'Revenge?' asked Maserov.

'What, like an exchange of money and fifty lashes?' Betga suggested.

'Torrent Industries can't be seen to be punishing Mike Mercer lest it be seen as an admission,' Maserov explained. 'Part of the value in a settlement is that it goes away without the company having to deal with allegations that it has a toxic sexist culture.'

'Of the kind it has,' Jessica interposed.

'Apparently, yes. You're better placed to comment on that than me.'

'Well, take it as a comment.'

'Duly taken.'

'What if Mercer is punished, sanctioned in some way but it's *not* publicised?'

'How do you mean?' Betga asked.

'I don't know; what if in addition to a payout, he was fined, or better yet, fired, but in confidence?'

'I don't know that I can get that. Malcolm Torrent won't fire one of his employees as a condition of a private settlement just to satisfy a plaintiff.'

'What about a few plaintiffs?'

'It would need to be more than three or four. It would need to be a class action, and even then . . .'

'So Mercer hasn't harassed or molested quite enough women?'

'Not for that. And anyway, he's too productive an employee. He's done too well for the company.'

'So between the two of you, there's nothing you can do to satisfy her need for some kind of revenge on this arsehole.'

'No, I don't think so.'

'Where's the justice in this?'

'What we're trying to achieve is a legal settlement. It's a negotiation between parties. Only *after* it's concluded do we even think of using words like "justice" and even then only to make the ripped-off party feel better.'

'But I don't *want* her to be ripped off. I don't want *any* of these women to be ripped off!' protested Jessica.

'Neither do *we*,' said Maserov.

'Then you've come to the right place,' said Betga. 'The first thing we have to do is get Carla to agree to settle.'

'Why, because it's in both your interests for her to settle?'

'It is,' said Maserov. 'But it's also in her interest to settle.'

'Yeah, while Maserov is still the lawyer on the other side of this thing.'

Jessica turned to Maserov and suddenly imagined a time when Maserov wasn't at Torrent Industries anymore. It was a thought she'd not yet entertained and its effect on her surprised her. She felt bereft. A strange feeling took hold of her, a cocktail of emotions akin to those felt when a much-loved friend, the only one who understands you, leaves to go to a new school in another state or when your parents announce that they're separating or when a pet dies. It was a visceral sensation that came to her pre-rationally. 'What are you going to do when —'

'When I'm forced to walk the plank?'

'Yes.'

'I'm supposed to be figuring that out while I work on these cases.'

'That's what I keep telling him,' Betga chimed in.

'My initial plan, to the extent that I had one after I buttonholed Malcolm Torrent, was simply to buy time before my execution. But now I want to do more than that. Although I've spent much of my life watching civil society going to hell in a handbasket I'm ashamed to say I've never given much thought to what women had to put up with till I saw what had been done to these women. So before I'm axed I want to get some justice for them.'

'But Stephen,' Jessica said, momentarily placing her hand lightly on his wrist before realising it and taking it away again with slight embarrassment, 'there can't be any justice, not of the kind she's looking for, if guys like Mike Mercer get away with it scot-free.'

'Jessica, I must be one of the least powerful people you know. I can't get any kind of sanction against Mike Mercer. I'm still not used to Malcolm Torrent remembering who I am.'

'You undersell yourself, Stephen,' she said quietly without looking at him directly.

'No, I think he's got it about right,' said Betga. 'Which is, you know, healthy, extremely healthy.'

'I can't make these incidents go away and I can't mete out or have the company mete out any retribution. The best I can possibly do is try to get these women a decent settlement before I'm gone.'

'But Carla's totally opposed to a settlement.'

The three of them sat around the table in silence. In the distance a crowd of people could be heard singing happy birthday to someone called 'Kayden'.

'Do you think it would help if *I* spoke to Carla? I'll tell her I'm from Torrent's HR department, if she doesn't already know, and I *know* that's not exactly going to endear me to her but I'm a woman who's experienced the culture of the place. Maybe I can, I don't know, I can . . . apologise.'

'Apologise? Why would *you* apologise?' Betga asked, and then added, 'Oh yeah, you're in HR.'

11

There was someone else whom Betga thought Carla should hear from before Jessica, someone who might help convince her to accept a settlement offer from Torrent Industries. A meeting with Jessica was too uncertain a prospect to be the next step. Carla might react negatively, seeing Jessica not as someone genuinely sympathetic from whom to take counsel but rather as a representative of Torrent Industries' HR department, a softer face of the heartless behemoth. Maserov and Betga mulled it over and agreed that Betga should try meeting with that someone else first.

It was a meeting that was inherently uncomfortable for Betga and *its* outcome, too, was far from certain. First, there was no certainty the man would even show up. Over the phone he'd sounded very dubious about the prospect of sitting down with Betga. When the appointed time arrived and the man had not appeared Betga glanced at his watch and said to himself under his breath, 'No appearance, your honour.' He experienced but did not allow himself to acknowledge the small relief in which one briefly luxuriates when a difficult or at least unpleasant task is removed from a person's schedule through no fault of one's own. But when Betga heard the crowded bar hush around him he knew his rendezvous had entered the bar even before he could see him. Acting Sergeant Ron Quinn stood hesitantly before Betga's table. Betga stood up and shook the policeman's hand but was unable to hide his disappointment.

'What?' the Acting Sergeant said defensively.

'You're in uniform.'

'So?'

'Didn't you hear the silence ripple through the bar as you walked in?'

'I told you I'd come straight from work.'

'Yes, you did but . . . I don't know,' Betga said, gently shaking his head in bewilderment. 'I didn't think you'd come in uniform. These are good people,' Betga said, gesticulating around him, 'relaxing at the end of their day. They don't want to be drinking around the police. Any decent citizen would be unnerved by it.'

'Are these people, in fact, citizens?'

'Citizens, permanent residents, asylum seekers, student visa holders de facto *and* de jure, entry-level frequent flyers and even some American Express card holders craving acceptance; unlike so many these days, *this* institution doesn't discriminate in issuing invitations to the public to partake in convivial libations in this non-judgmental yet still immensely tasteful setting that subtly pays homage to many of the aesthetic traits of the eighties, traits that helped to make that decade what it is today.'

'What is it today?'

'Gone; completely gone. The eighties, the decade that taste forgot. But that's not my point. Look, Acting Sergeant . . . and I mean no undue disrespect, *none* of these people would take comfort from the visible presence of the constabulary at the end of their day.'

'Is that why you've invited me here, to insult me?'

If only it had been, Betga thought wistfully. After apologising, he ordered Acting Sergeant Quinn a craft beer said to have come proudly from the Košice region of Slovakia and less proudly from certain laneways in Abbotsford. For the first time he looked into the eyes of Acting Sergeant Ron Quinn. There they were, just a few feet away from him, two shallow reservoirs of disappointment.

'I know that in certain respects you and I might be seen as adversaries but —'

'How so?' the policeman enquired.

'Well, first there's the law, and then —'

'We're both officers of the court, aren't we?'

'Yes, but I interpret and interrogate the law in a frankly highly creative manner while you stolidly uphold a draconian version of it in that way that makes people around you want you to drink somewhere else. You bow down to the chain of command whereas I answer to a higher power.'

'Do you mean God? You don't strike me as a religious man, Mr Betga.'

'No, I don't mean God.'

'Then what higher power?'

'Well, Acting Sergeant,' Betga began philosophically, 'it's more a repository of certain values than a deity marketed by any commonly venerated, state-sanctioned vehicle for tax relief, and I admit to remaining agnostic as to its name. But it sure as hell isn't the chief commissioner of police.'

'Well, yes, he's had his problems.'

'Yes, I'm glad we can agree on this. That's a good start. But then, of course, there's our different standing with and approach to . . .' He paused. 'Carla.'

'Yes,' said the policeman, 'I treat her honourably, while you . . .'

'Well, now, you see,' said Betga, shaking his index finger as though it were a recalcitrant thermometer or salt shaker, 'there's that tendency of your vocation again; judging someone harshly according to just one prior conviction, one to which I pleaded guilty.'

'Mr Betga, the way I heard it, she caught you. Wasn't there a woman who called Carla and —'

'Okay,' Betga said, drawing breath while a flat palm of his was raised in the air about level with Acting Sergeant Quinn's eyes. 'Now don't take this to mean I wouldn't *ever* be interested in your version of this aspect of my life, but this isn't really the reason I suggested we meet. The reason I invited you to meet me was to talk about Carla's future.'

'I would . . . I suppose . . . like to have some part in her future,' said the acting sergeant.

'You *suppose*?'

'Well, yes, I'll admit that.'

'No, no, it's not the admission that causes me to emphasise the word "suppose" as though an accurate transcript would italicise it. It's your very tentativeness.'

'I'm afraid I don't really get what you're talking about, Mr Betga.'

It was at this moment that the Slovakian craft beers from just north of Richmond arrived. The bartender put them down on the table diplomatically and Betga forthrightly shifted them both towards Ron Quinn, almost whispering to the bartender, catching him before he headed back to the bar, 'I'll have one too.'

'Look, Acting Sergeant,' said Betga and then, 'Do you mind if I call you "Acting"?'

'You can call me Ron when I'm off-duty.'

'How will I be able to tell?'

'When I'm off duty I'll probably be settling your daughter.'

'Now that's good, Ron,' said Betga, pounding the table with his fist. 'That's the first damn thing you've ever said to me that's got any kind of spunk, any kind of pushback.'

'Mr Betga, I don't go looking for confrontation.'

'It's not a matter of looking for confrontation, Ron. It's a matter of not looking for a way out when it finds you. It seems to me that you walk through your life as though wearing a sign that reads "I'm done. It's over for me", which makes you carrion flesh for others to devour.'

Ron Quinn thought for a moment. 'I've never thought of myself in those terms. But whether I do or not, what concern is it of yours?'

'I can understand you asking that question, especially since its answer may surprise you.'

'Go on.'

'Ron, I've come to realise that I owe you a debt of gratitude. You clearly know I'm Marietta's father.'

'Yes.'

'What you might not know is that I'm in love with Carla, have been ever since my days at Freely Savage, when we met at Torrent Industries HQ, right from the first time we flirted over the document shredder.'

'I'm not sure she'll believe you . . . because of your . . . affair with the legal recruiter when you —'

'I know what I did . . . was wrong. But even then, I loved her,' Betga interjected more angrily than he'd intended.

'While sleeping with another woman?'

'Ron, we're talking man-to-man here, aren't we?'

'Er . . . Yes.'

'It was a tight employment market. A man has to do whatever he can in difficult circumstances to provide for his family. Yeah? In terms of the economy it's like a time of war. Some of the things we do for our family . . . well, they're not pretty.'

'So the legal recruitment woman, she wasn't pretty?'

'No, she was smokin' hot, but morally, ethically, I know I was on shaky ground.'

'Shaky ground! You were cheating on Carla. I'd say that's pretty cut and dried.'

'Yes but, no offence Ron, there's that constabulary thinking again. One could argue that had I got the job and been able to support her and Marietta without Carla knowing the lengths to which I'd gone to get the job, well, then I'd done the greater moral good. In fact, one *did* argue that as I recall.'

'It didn't work though, did it?'

'No, I wasn't able to raise her mind off the sordid details she kept imagining. I couldn't stop her re-living a scene she'd never seen. Carla is a very jealous woman and when a jealous woman owns a vivid imagination it's possible for a man to have recurring nightmares without ever being allowed to fall asleep.'

'What does all this have to do with owing me a debt of gratitude?'

'During the time I speak of right up until very recently you took care of her, watched out for her, and gave her very impressive hands-on help with Marietta. You even helped her with money. I will forever be grateful for that, Ron.'

'Thank you Mister . . . What should I call you?'

'Betga's good.'

'*Mister* Betga?'

'No, I'd like to think we're friends now. Just Betga's fine.'

'What kind of name is Betga?'

'It's German but the spelling was changed to help English speakers. Very thoughtful family.'

'How long has your family been here?'

'My paternal grandfather was a physicist back in Germany. Tried to get into America after the war but they didn't believe he was a Nazi so they wouldn't let him in. Others got in, much stupider men, not him. It's always been "who you know", hasn't it? Had to come here instead.'

'Why didn't they believe he was a Nazi?'

'He didn't really carry himself like a Nazi. Tried to say he was just a bit flat 'cause they lost the war but US Immigration wasn't buying it. Not only that, he couldn't adequately explain why he'd been in hiding for twelve years. Wasn't expecting the question. Put him on the spot. He was still jet-lagged too. I imagine he was. Can't be sure because I was still very young when he died. But let me ask *you* something.'

'Yes?'

'How did you learn to change toddlers and babies, to settle them and that sort of thing? Do you have kids?'

'No, sadly.'

'You're not married?'

'No.'

'But you've been married?'

'No, never married.'

'So how did you learn to be so good with small children?'

'Well, I learned from being an uncle to my sister's kids. Always hoped to be a father but it never . . .'

Betga was in danger of choking up. This policeman was ruthless. He spun platinum-plated pathos the way Spider-Man spun webs. But Betga was saved from lachrymose capitulation by the sight of Kasimir who, although some distance away, was unable to hide his astonishment and disgust that Betga had not only brought in a cop but was sharing a table with him and, even worse, drinking with him. Betga could see Kasimir shaking his head. He knew he would have some explaining to do when this was over.

'Well, you've learned very well from your sister's kids,' Betga mused, returning to the topic of the policeman's facility with pre-verbal children. 'So listen, Ron, despite meeting Carla under different circumstances, I think you'd agree that we both have respect and affection for her.'

'Most definitely.'

'And we both want what's good for her and Marietta.'

'Yes, of course.'

'And we both know that she's struggling with respect to money at the moment and could use a break, financially speaking.'

'Yes, I don't know the precise circumstances but . . . yes.'

'Well, I don't know how much, if anything, she's told you about the work I've been doing for her in my capacity as her lawyer negotiating a settlement on her behalf against Torrent Industries.'

'No, whenever she *has* talked about you it's been mainly . . . other things.'

'Okay, but be that as it may, I'm on the verge of delivering her a settlement that I suspect will be in the hundreds of thousands of dollars.'

'Gee, that's fantastic, Mr Betga.'

'Please, Ron, you can drop the "Mister". Betga is fine.'

'That's fantastic . . . Betga.'

'Yes, it is, it *would* be, but one of my last remaining obstacles is her.'

'What do you mean?'

'She's reluctant to accept a settlement offer.'

'Why on earth wouldn't she accept it?'

'Because she wants the guy punished and the settlement would almost certainly contain no sanctions against the perpetrator. It would be a confidential settlement and it would be paid not by the animal that sexually assaulted her but by the company that employs him.'

'Well, that's okay. The perpetrator would face his justice in the trial, the criminal trial. I told her, what he did was a criminal offence, probably several of them.'

'Ron, have you ever been to a sexual assault or a rape trial? Ever sat in on one?'

'Actually, no, I can't say that I have.'

'Do you know what the defence would do to her? To save time, that's a rhetorical question so don't feel under any pressure. Since she knows her assailant, they would try to do two things; they would try to make her out to be sexually promiscuous *and*, even more cruelly, they would try to make any of the physical activity that formed the basis of the assault appear sexual and consensual. The first issue is clearly irrelevant but highly prejudicial. We would, of course, try to keep all evidence of her past sexual history and evidence of the way she dresses, how she has recovered from the assault and is working now, et cetera, out of evidence, but we wouldn't be completely successful, certainly not enough to keep all of this evidence out and —'

'Well, *I* could testify,' interjected the sad policeman with the eagerness of an earnest puppy, an eagerness Betga had never before known the man to possess. '*I* could testify that I made my romantic intentions clearly known quite early in our friendship and she didn't feel that way.'

Betga didn't know where to look after hearing this. He let Ron Quinn's words glide gracefully downwards like an ageing seabird all the way down to the depths of one of his two already drained Slovakian craft beer glasses. What was he to do with that admission given he was trying not to offend its maker, a man no jury in the land would convict of being sexually enticing at any time to anything, living or dead, in any universe, known or hitherto undiscovered.

'Trust me, Ron, your testimony, even sworn on the deed to the land on which the bible was first printed in Mainz, Germany, back in 1455, even *that* wouldn't quite cut it.'

'That's impressive, Betga, how you just know things that aren't . . . aren't even really what we seem to be talking about, unless I've somehow missed something. This bible printing business . . . Do you know about this from your family history, you know, back in Germany?'

'No, Ron. We Betgas fled Mainz sometime around 1282, leaving all property deeds to the archbishop's treasurers. Pity that. Still, Gutenberg wasn't much of a tenant. Never had any money. And, boy, was he messy! Fingers, everything. Very messy. But be that as it may, and notwithstanding the value of the sterling evidence of her stoic resistance to your entreaties that you would tender to counter the previous sexual indiscretions the other side would try to impute to Carla, the real damage would come when the perpetrator gives his evidence.'

'Why?'

'Because he's going to say they were involved in a consensual relationship that, to his regret, passionately spilled over into the workplace. Inappropriate, yes, but not assault.'

'But that's simply not true!'

'You don't get to court much, Ron, do you?'

'No,' the acting sergeant said somewhat sheepishly.

'The bastard is going to lie and the standard of proof required in a criminal case, "beyond reasonable doubt", is higher than that required in a civil case, so he's going to get off. He would be found not guilty.'

'So Carla's more likely to win a civil case than a criminal case,' said the policeman.

'Exactly,' said Betga, 'which is why I can see the company settling, just to ensure the case never comes to court. The company would pay handsomely to keep the allegations out of the news. So then, you see, Carla wouldn't have to testify.'

'Right, so you want her to sue the company in a civil case but not to have the police charge the perpetrator in order that she be spared the rigours of a criminal trial?'

'Ron, you've now grasped the whole thing. I'm trying to get her some compensation and at the same time keep her from going through the agony of a criminal trial where the other side will spend up big in order to lie about the events of the night, forcing her to publicly re-live her torment as both the victim and a witness, and where they would also drag her name through the mud with respect to the most private part of her life; all of it in public, recorded by the press to be saved on the internet in perpetuity where everyone in the world can read it and where one day Marietta could also read what was done to her mother.'

'Yes, I suppose that does sound like the way to go, Mr Betga. Er, sorry, Betga. Why isn't she listening to you?'

'Because, Ron, you filled her head with dreams of retribution via a criminal trial.'

'Well, it's understandable she'd want the man punished.'

'It *is*, Ron, but there are certain things I can't do. Although, between us, I'd rather you didn't say that around *here*. She's not factoring in the ordeal of going through a criminal trial.'

'Yes, I see.' Everything was slowly sinking in for the man in blue. 'And you want me to talk to her?'

'Yes.'

'But I can't tell her his actions weren't criminal because they were.'

'No, but you can tell her what she'd have to go through in a criminal trial and that, even after that, the guy is likely to be found not guilty.'

'What about the perpetrator getting punished? He deserves to be punished. How will he be punished?'

'I'm afraid we'll have to find the answer to that somewhere within Gutenberg's handiwork.'

'I'm not with you.'

'Ron, do you know who Gutenberg was?'

'Well, from the conversation . . . I just sort of assumed he was a relative of yours.'

'Ron, if you'll help me in this way, to take care of Carla, I'd like to do something for you.'

'Oh, Betga, really, there's no need to —'

'No, I'd like to. You might not know this, Ron, but I'm a highly sought-after life coach.'

'A life coach?'

'Yes. And I'd like to offer you —'

'But I'm not in training for anything.'

'You don't know what a life coach is, do you?'

'A life coach?'

'Yes, Ron, this is another one of those occasions you've probably experienced before where repeating the term you didn't understand a few seconds earlier yields no further discernible enlightenment. That's the kind of thing I can help you with.'

'Oh Betga, I don't know, really.'

'Ron, let me ask you, how long have you been an acting sergeant?'

'Just hit eleven years last month. We had sponge cake down at the station. Not everyone could make it.'

'Are there any consequences to being an *acting* sergeant as opposed to a real one?'

'Just superficial things, really.'

'Like the way people treat you?'

'Hardly notice it. Water off a . . . bird, a water bird.'

'Any financial consequences?'

'To an extent.'

'To what extent?'

'It changes.'

'Does it ever change in your favour?'

'I'm not . . . aware . . . of that . . . having happened.'

'Will it affect your retirement?'

'The department's never . . . in so many words . . . broached that directly with me.'

'Ron.'

'Yes?' The policeman looked up slowly from the table, like a child crouching behind an older man's face, and into the eyes of a younger, more handsome man who had fathered a daughter with a beautiful woman the policeman had helped and never even kissed.

'We'll make time, Ron. I can help you. You've been a great support to Carla and to Marietta. Let me do this for you. Free of charge.'

Betga thought the policeman was going to cry and that, if he did, he himself didn't know what he would do. He couldn't be seen in the Grosvenor Hotel offering aid and comfort to a serving uniformed member of the Victoria Police. As it was he was going to have a lot of explaining to do. Thankfully for him Acting Sergeant Quinn managed to keep speaking.

'Betga, you know, I think that despite yourself, you managed to learn something from your uncle.'

'My *uncle*?'

'Gutenberg. You'll have to tell me about him.'

'Okay, I'll throw that in too.'

III

'What's *she* doing here?' Carla asked.

'Perhaps this wasn't a great idea.' The reality of accompanying Maserov to Carla's house was suddenly dawning on Jessica. Betga was there minding Marietta while Carla finished her shift in the office of a cosmetics wholesaler. She was temping and considered herself lucky to get the work. The agency through which she sought work had been deluged by people, almost all women, clerical workers of varying degrees of experience and training, needing work. There was a massive imbalance between the demand and supply for clerical and administrative workers, even those who were highly skilled and experienced. The imbalance was weighted against the women with labour to sell.

So Carla was forced to take shifts far across the other side of town. Today she'd had to go out near the airport and even this had been possible only because she was able to leave Marietta with Betga. So when Carla at long last walked into the house, having first emptied her letterbox of the stack of envelopes with corporate logos perfectly formatted by the computers of the various companies to which she owed money, she wasn't at her most conciliatory.

Maserov, Betga and Jessica wanted Carla to reconsider her decision not to settle her sexual harassment suit with Torrent Industries out of court. But Jessica had gone with the additional intention of apologising as a woman, a female member of the Torrent Industries HR department, for not having done anything to protect Carla from a predator like Mike Mercer. She had not formulated a clear picture of what it was she, acting on her own, could have done but this hadn't dampened her need to apologise. The matter of how much of this need to apologise was for Carla's benefit and how much for her own was something that lurked away from the footlights of her consciousness behind a curtain of other needs, the need to assuage guilt being only one of them.

'You have a beautiful daughter,' she said to Carla, who was taking off her coat.

'Thank you,' said Betga.

'She's your daughter . . . too?' Jessica asked Betga.

'Haven't *you* ever made a mistake?' came the bullet-like reply from Carla.

'Actually, I have, a lot of them, one of which brings me here now. I hope you don't mind my being here. I don't have to stay long.'

'Well, it's just funny that I never saw you when I was working at Torrent Industries. Could it be 'cause you want me to settle? I mean, suddenly you show up in my house uninvited.'

'I invited her,' Betga owned up.

'So now you're inviting people into my house?'

Jessica looked momentarily perplexed until Betga explained, 'I'm Marietta's father but I'm not currently living here.' Jessica looked at Maserov, who knew her to be thinking, 'You *also* don't live with your children. What is it with you guys?' Maserov was anxious to distinguish himself from Betga as fast as he could but nothing was coming to him other than the screaming need for immediacy. It was Carla who helped him out.

'Stephen doesn't live with his kids but he's not a philandering shithead. So anyway, Ms Human Resources, why are you here?'

'Well, first, I want to apologise.'

'Why, who did *you* sexually assault?'

'Carla, there's no need to be rude to her,' Betga said, trying to sound simultaneously familiar, husbandly and also gallant. Within seconds the results of this attempt were audible and unambiguous.

'Shut up Betga, you unfaithful prick.'

'No, I didn't sexually assault anyone, but I stood by in a climate where I knew sooner or later that this kind of thing was likely to happen if, indeed, it hadn't already happened. And I did nothing.'

'Let me guess, somebody at Torrent HQ thought it was a good idea to get a woman to come around and sweet-talk me into settling. You're a woman protecting Mike Mercer. You're sucking up to the company. You'll do anything to save your own sweet arse. And you're dumb enough to really think that's going to save you when they come looking for your exotic pussy some wet and rainy night. So I don't have words to describe how low you are.'

'No, Carla, I swear, I'm not protecting him. That's not why I'm here. Nobody sent me. In fact, no one from the company knows I'm here. It was only by chance that I happened to be working with Stephen and found out what happened to you, what Mike Mercer did. As Stephen knows, I'm trying to leverage his good standing with Mr Torrent to try to bring in some changes, policies, to make it less likely this kind of thing happens to any other women.'

'I don't know what policies you got in mind other than chemical castration, with or without the chemicals, but a lot of good your policies are going to do me.'

'I know, that's why I'm here. I'm not here representing the company or even the human resources department, who *would* want to protect Mike Mercer. You're right. I live in fear of people like that. I hate them. Even if you had come to me in HR and reported Mike Mercer, to be honest, I don't know what I would have done if the people above me took his side. But that doesn't mean I shouldn't have let you know that there were sympathetic people, women, who would at least try to talk to those with the power to help.'

'Okay, you feel guilty, thanks. I can't bank that but I'll take it to my psychiatrist. We could probably get a good thirty minutes out of that. Maybe she can give me the number of someone who could help you with that guilt.'

'Carla, I'd be angry too.'

'Now what exactly would make you angry? Would you be angry if someone tried to rape you in your workplace? Would you be angry if HR ignored it? Would you be angry if someone came into your house uninvited and started shilling the joys of a settlement that allows Mike Mercer to prosper in his career as though nothing had happened while I'm up at night worrying about how to pay my rent and feed my daughter?'

'Carla,' Maserov said calmly, quietly and without any condescension. 'None of us in this room have the power to punish him, to deliver the retribution he deserves. Look, I don't know how long I'll be in this position, a position where, in effect, I'm trying to help you while acting as Malcolm Torrent's point person on this. But your turning down the money that I could get you just because it doesn't hurt Mike Mercer is crazy. And it really hurts you. I don't know what Betga's told you but I'm hopeful I could get Torrent Industries to pay you as much as five hundred, maybe even six hundred thousand. And you wouldn't have to go through it publicly in court. There'd be nothing about it on the internet.'

'Think what you could do with the money,' said Betga. 'Think what you could do for Marietta.'

'Is this why you want to be back in our lives, Betga? You want to mooch off us?'

'Carla, I'd hoped you knew me better than that.'

'No, I know you as well as that.'

'Okay, let me prove it to you. I'm making money, which I'm allowing Maserov to give to you because of my unshakeable love for you. I'm getting paid by Malcolm Torrent, every week you *don't* settle. When you and the others settle he stops paying me. Isn't that right, Maserov?'

'It's true, Carla.'

'Whereas the settlement money, if you settle, goes directly to you. I don't get a cent. I want to be adding to the net wealth of this family, not detracting from it.'

'Family?' Carla asked, but without the anger that had characterised everything she had said since she had come home.

'Well, yeah,' said Betga quietly. 'Whatever a family is, we're probably one. Don't you think?'

Maserov felt that last characterisation was somewhat unhelpful so he attempted to distract her from it by returning to the main issue. 'If I can get an offer of the kind I think I can get authority to make, you should take it,' he said, looking at her and knowing that the look on her face meant that she wanted to trust him.

She had left the front door open and the sound of footsteps along the passage gave way to a voice that was heard before its owner could be seen. 'He's right, Carla. You should take the offer.' It was Acting Sergeant Ron Quinn. He walked slowly into the room and Carla turned to him as he whispered 'Hello, baby girl' to Marietta, who reached out to him from within Betga's arms.

'But do you know . . . they're saying if I accept the offer, Mercer won't go to trial? There'll be no criminal trial. You told me he'd committed offences. You said the criminal law was on my side.'

'It is drafted to help you but something's wrong when . . .'

'When what?'

'I did some research today at the station. In the data for the most recent year I could find there were 3500 rapes reported in the state. Only 3 per cent resulted in a conviction. You know I only want what's best for you. Take the money.'

Everyone in the room looked at Carla looking at her daughter in the policeman's arms. A tear was sliding down her cheek. Nobody said anything. 'Okay,' she whispered. They almost didn't hear her say it.

Betga walked over to her and she let him hug her, eliciting more tears, some simply born of exhaustion. He held her for a long time and when the embrace was over Maserov spoke.

'Carla, I will do everything in my power to get you the best deal I can. Please know I will.'

She looked up from Betga's shoulder. 'I know you will, Stephen.'

'Carla,' Jessica began. 'Did you say before that HR ignored what happened to you? Did somebody report it to HR?'

'Yeah, I did.'

'Really? I didn't hear anything about it.'

'Yeah, I went straight to the top. Reported it to your boss, Aileen van what's-her-name.'

'Aileen van der Westhuizen, you reported it to her?'

'Yeah, I even made a note of it. I wrote down everything that happened within a week, certainly two weeks, of it happening. Gave it to her in person. I don't know why. I knew she wouldn't do anything. Said she would talk to him. For Christ's sake! Fucking waste of space! No offence.'

'Oh, I'm not religious.'

'No, but you're in HR.'

'Who's staying for dinner?' Betga asked suddenly, joyously, and without authority.

'Well, *you're* not, for starters,' said Carla. 'No one is. I've got a friend coming over. So I'm afraid you all have to leave.'

'A friend? What do you mean by that?' Betga continued.

'I think we should go, Betga,' said Maserov diplomatically.

'Did you hear that, Ron?' Betga asked the policeman. 'She wants you to go. Says she's got a friend coming over. *You're* her friend. What do you make of this, being displaced by someone ostensibly of equal rank?'

Maserov, Jessica and Acting Sergeant Ron Quinn quietly said their goodbyes and walked out into the darkening street. The policeman went to his car on his own while Jessica and Maserov went to the one car, Maserov's.

Betga was not far behind them, much to his displeasure. He saw the friend coming and was relieved to see it was a woman. In this he had it over Maserov, whose wife had had a male friend come to the house not long after he, Maserov, had left. What Betga couldn't have known was that Carla's visitor was, in fact, Maserov's wife, Eleanor. She had arranged for her mother to babysit and was visiting Carla without her children for the first time.

Eleanor could see that Carla had recently been crying. Once she'd been assured that Carla was now fine, she turned her attention to that which was suddenly uppermost on her mind. There had been people leaving Carla's house. She'd seen them leaving while she was parking her car. She couldn't tell exactly how many but she was surprised to see that her husband was one of them.

'Was that Stephen just leaving?'

'Yeah, some kind of a delegation.'

'And that . . . woman?'

'Yeah.'

'She was . . . Who was she? They left together . . . in his car. Did you know that?'

IV

'And what about the other three victims, Lilly, Monika and Pauline, Betga's other three plaintiffs?' Jessica asked. 'Their experiences weren't as bad as Carla's but they were still pretty bad.'

'Betga said that if Carla settles, the other three will too.'

'Are they all in touch with each other?' Maserov indicated that he didn't know with a slight movement of his hands and a gentle shrug of his shoulders. Somehow his not knowing this and his not pretending to know lifted Maserov even more, just slightly, in Jessica's estimation.

They'd had dinner together and then had gone to Jessica's local haunt, the Ghost of Alfred Felton, the cocktail bar at the Espy, to toast Carla's agreeing to settle. The bartenders there were famously egoless, an attribute in a bartender, waiter or any other man that suited Jessica perfectly. They were allies, not predators. But for all that, when Jessica left the bar that evening, the place she and Maserov had gone to toast Carla's agreeing to settle, one bartender couldn't help but notice the regard his favourite late-night corporate regular had shown Maserov, not through any conversation, which amidst the crushed and shaken ice he could not hear, but through her body language and proximity to Maserov.

He might well have been one of the famously egoless bartenders but Jessica's fondness for Maserov shook him and left him ever-so-slightly depressed. And that she was always so friendly and didn't act as though she was aware of the power of her beauty only made it worse for this man who, for a moment, hated Maserov as much as Hamilton now did.

The side street outside the cocktail bar was quiet but for the faraway sounds of Gogol's distant relatives girding and ungirding their threadbare overcoats, sometimes in company and sometimes alone, in the uneven, potholed seaside laneways that waited for social archaeologists who had not yet been born. It was cold but at least it was no longer raining.

'So tomorrow you'll go to Malcolm Torrent to get the authority to offer, what, five hundred or even six hundred thousand for Carla?' Jessica asked Maserov.

'Yep, tomorrow's the big day.'

'Have you checked that he'll be in?'

'Yep, no getting out of it.'

'Are you nervous?'

'I'll tell you honestly, I'm nervous every time I speak to him.'

'But he listens to you. It's always gone well with him.'

'Yeah, that's true. When I started this I was winging it just for myself, just trying to buy time to figure out what to do when they got rid of me, what to do with my life. But now I'm . . . involved.'

'Involved?'

'Emotionally involved.'

'You're emotionally involved?' Jessica said, edging imperceptibly closer to him.

'Yes, I haven't used the time to secure any options, to find work, when Freely Savage gets rid of me. I've just been working with Betga and you and getting emotionally involved.'

'I think it's great that you can say this, that a man can feel comfortable admitting that he's become . . . emotionally involved.'

'Well, only a heartless shit could know what happened to these women and not become emotionally involved in the outcome.'

'Oh . . . you mean emotionally involved in the cases.'

'Yeah, what did you think I . . .?'

Jessica turned her head to one side so that her face was pointed away from him. She was surprised to feel the fingers of one of his hands combing the hair on the side that was turned away. Maserov was surprised to be combing. But emboldened by gin and absinthe and the sudden increase in the force of the wind, he turned her face back to his, leaned in and slightly down to kiss her.

It wasn't a tentative kiss or one whose intent could be the subject of plausible deniability at any later time. He found the smallest space between her lips and used all the power of his longing to let her know how much he wanted her and when she responded as though hungry for him there was nothing but the wind to stop them kissing for several minutes.

'Should I . . .?' Maserov asked. Jessica was hoping he was asking if he should come home with her but instead his next word was 'go'. She tried to hide her disappointment.

'Oh . . . I guess. It's late.'

'Yeah.'

They stood there in the street alternately looking at each other and away and then back again. She was wondering now why he hadn't continued kissing her, if he was going to start again and whether she had made a fool of herself by so obviously wanting him to once he had started. He was wondering if he had made a fool of himself, or worse, somehow taken the first albeit tiny step on the road towards behaving like Mike Mercer. He was thinking about the kiss, the first one he'd had in a long time. It was the first time he had kissed a woman who wasn't Eleanor since he had started dating Eleanor all those years ago. He was wondering if he had just been unfaithful to his wife and maybe even to his children. And he was wondering if they were going to kiss again before they got into their respective cars.

'So tomorrow you'll go to Malcolm Torrent to get the authority to offer,' she said, starting the whole thing all over again and returning to the assault as though it was all about that.

'Yeah, but first I have to go back to Freely Savage to satisfy HR's quota of fool's errands, wild-goose chases and the like.'

'Why do you still have to do this shit?'

'I figure it's easier to quickly do whatever bullshit they want me to do than to deal with the consequences of Hamilton finding out I'm not doing it.'

'So . . . I'll see you in the morning?' Jessica asked tentatively before adding, 'Or the afternoon, whenever. Let me know what Mr Torrent says.'

'Of course. You'll be the first person I tell.'

'Don't be nervous,' she said. 'Remember, he tends to listen to you and, frankly, you being the person on the other side is the best thing that's happened to Carla since the assault. So . . . I don't know if that came out right. You know what I mean.'

'You mean she's lucky there's such a lousy lawyer on the other side.'

'I mean she's lucky to find a man with so much integrity on the other side. Good luck.' With that she leaned in and gave him a peck on the cheek and, when she had returned to her pre-peck position, he pulled her back and began kissing her passionately just as he had a few minutes earlier. Jessica returned the fervour and neither was at all embarrassed, not in the street and not as they lay in their respective beds thinking of it all through the night.

V

Maserov was in his car driving into the CBD, where he would go, first, to Freely Savage in order to comply with the absurd demands of its HR department and thereby not re-enter Hamilton's consciousness any more than he had to ever since his meteoric rise to the status of target, and then on to Torrent Industries, where he would see Malcolm Torrent to try to get the authority to make the best offer to Carla and the other three plaintiffs that he could.

The traffic was barely crawling and sometimes not even that but it gave him time to survey his life and as long as his car didn't shudder more violently than usual between spasms of forward motion he didn't mind. Today was a new day. In this it was just like every other day. But this was the first day he had arisen, showered and put on a suit and tie knowing that a woman like Jessica Annand had wanted to kiss him passionately. In fact, it wasn't a woman *like* Jessica Annand, it was Jessica Annand. He hadn't been trying to charm or entice her. He didn't remember how to be flirtatious, couldn't recall when he had last been, if ever. No, Jessica had got to know him during a time where he had merely been himself, Stephen Maserov, a man in increasingly difficult circumstances, circumstances that he had never attempted to hide.

At risk of sleepily veering left into the lane meant for the airport, from which there would be no return other than by plane, Maserov tried to imagine how she saw him. He was a desperate man trying to save his job, his family and even his marriage while simultaneously attempting to negotiate a fair settlement for deserving victims of sexual assault for whom he felt sincere compassion. He had never tried to pretend to be any more than that. This was the man Jessica Annand wanted to hold and to kiss. And on a fading cracked leather seat that trembled under the burden of his car's twenty-seven years' service and its tortoise-like progress in the traffic on Kings Way, Maserov felt great. Then the lights changed.

Had he been unfaithful to his wife? The one thing he'd always had was his integrity. Was he on the slippery slope towards becoming Betga? But then, Eleanor had been unfaithful to him. Hadn't she? Probably, but he couldn't be sure. Anyway, all he had done was kiss Jessica, nothing more. But that was more than he knew for sure Eleanor had done with the drama teacher. Was it the drama teacher? Or was it the PE teacher? Was it a mitigating factor if he reasonably thought his wife had been unfaithful before he had kissed Jessica, unequivocally an act of infidelity but a trivial one, incredibly trivial? But perhaps it wasn't an act of infidelity at all. He was separated, after all. And the separation had been at Eleanor's instigation and against his will. If you kick your husband out of home what do you expect? What had Eleanor expected? They hadn't ever discussed it.

But the real guilt lay not so much in the act of kissing Jessica but in how much he had enjoyed it. He had replayed it in his mind over and over. But memories fray and need to be refreshed. He would have to do it again. But that's not a way to live, kissing someone repeatedly so as not to forget what it was like. Where was the future in this? Did Jessica envisage a future with this separated man with two children who would sooner or later probably be without a job? Did she want to be a mother? He already had two children. Would she want to be a stepmother and, if so, what kind of stepmother would she be? Perhaps she would agree to be a stepmother on the condition they have their own children together. Had he already left Eleanor in his mind? Wasn't it a bit early to be imagining a blended family with Jessica? He hadn't even reached Sturt Street.

The only things he knew for certain were that he didn't want to be without his children and that he wanted to kiss Jessica again, just once before he died. He was already living without his children, which felt like the beginning of a slow death. That had to change. Then the phone rang. It was Betga.

'She hasn't changed her mind?' Maserov asked before saying 'hello'.

'You don't say "good morning" or "hello" anymore?' came Betga's voice through speakerphone.

'Good morning, Betga. She hasn't changed her mind, has she?'

'No, not as of the time I left last night.' There was a pause. 'No, if you're wondering, she's still not letting me stay the night.'

'No, that wasn't where my mind was headed.'

'Where's your body headed, Torrent HQ?'

'It *will* be. First I have to appease the gods at Freely Savage by doing something inane for HR.'

'Is this Hamilton trying to fuck you up?'

'Yeah, I think so.'

'Listen, as long as you're going into Freely Savage, could you pop your head into Featherby's office?'

'What? No, why on earth should I do that?'

'Featherby keeps calling me. Says he's in a bad way and wants the support of the Freely Savage Survivors. He doesn't know it's me he's talking to. I keep telling him that he has to have left before he can join. But he calls 'cause he's convinced he's going to get canned. Says Hamilton's playing mind games with him.'

'Like what?'

'Oh, you know, walking down his department's corridor towards the end of the day, joking with the lawyers whose workstations sandwich Featherby's but never stopping to talk to Featherby. That sort of shit.'

'Is that all?'

'No, he says he gets told of departmental meetings after other people and then has to reschedule with clients. Then, when he comes late, Hamilton berates him for being late in front of everyone else at the meeting. Sometimes he comes into Hamilton's office to keep a scheduled appointment that Hamilton's secretary has called and Hamilton stays on the phone for up to an hour without acknowledging his presence in the room.'

'Betga, I would *kill* to be the victim of such benign mind games.'

'I don't know,' warned Betga. 'He certainly sounds freaked out.'

'Well, he might be but frankly if you guys, the FSS, aren't willing to help Featherby he sure as hell isn't my problem.'

'We're not willing to help him *yet*. Once he leaves he qualifies for our emergency assistance package.'

'Well, that distinction, important as it is for you, doesn't really change anything for me.'

'Okay, but if you see him while you're there —'

'Yeah, what? What should I do if I see him?'

'Observe and report back.'

'Will do, captain. Is there anything else I can help you with?'

'Actually, there is. It's in the nature of parenting advice. Do you mind?'

'No, not at all. Not that I'm holding myself out as any expert.'

'Okay, listen. You know I'm trying to improve my bond, my relationship with my daughter.'

'Marietta, yes.'

'Well, Carla is using me as a babysitter, which is fine, but it means I'm often alone with Marietta, I mean really alone, for long periods of time. And she's not yet two.'

'Where are you going with this?'

'Well, I don't know if I'm allowed to admit this,' said Betga tentatively over the phone, 'but . . . how do you deal with the boredom? I mean . . . I love her, I absolutely love her. But often, I mean not infrequently, it's like watching paint dry. She'll jump up and down, kind of sing, I suppose that's what she's doing. Roll around. She'll put two of her soft toys together in a kind of . . . I guess it's an embrace or maybe they're kissing. I'm supposed to be endlessly fascinated by all this. But I can't wait for her sleep time. Is there something wrong with me as a parent . . .?'

'No, there's nothing wrong with you.'

'Well, how do you deal with it?'

'So here's what you should do if you're getting bored. When you're certain you're completely alone and that no one but her can hear you, talk to her as you would to an adult. Have a conversation with her about how you feel about her, about Carla. Talk to her about your life, about your family, about the things you believe.'

'She's not yet two.'

'It's not for her in the first instance. But if it relieves the boredom then you'll be making it more pleasant for yourself and she'll benefit from that too. She'll feel it. Grab these moments with both hands before she grows up and you're an embarrassment to her.'

'Wow, that sounds like incredibly good advice.' Betga was impressed. 'Thanks, Maserov.'

'Glad to help. I'm at the car park now so I have to go. I'll call you when I've got the authority to make an offer but it may not be till late afternoon.'

'Okay,' said Betga. 'I've got a suggestion. If it's bad news, if you have any kind of problem, text me. Otherwise meet me at Carla's place and tell us the figure there. I'll have a bottle of something sparkling in the fridge and we can turn it into a celebration.'

'Are you sure?'

'Yeah, I think it will make her feel better about settling if we present it that way.'

'Okay, I gotta go now,' said Maserov. 'I'll text you if there's a problem. Otherwise, see you there.'

Maserov was reaching for his phone to end the call when he heard Betga say, 'You can bring your girlfriend.'

VI

Just walking through the street-level entry foyer, hearing the sound of his shoes on the marble floor as he made his way to the elevator, was enough to resurrect in his viscera the essential paradox of Maserov's professional life; he was absolutely terrified of losing a job he absolutely hated. When he reached his old floor he made straight for Emery in order to begin this morning's absurd task by visiting a friendly face. Seeing Maserov walking towards him, Emery stopped what he was doing and readied his body for a conversation with someone who would soon be kneeling beside him.

'They haven't fired you yet?'

'No,' Maserov answered in a low voice. 'I've been at Torrent Industries. I'm only back because HR have got me doing another stupid survey.'

'Is it good for you that you're the one chosen to conduct these surveys?'

'No, I don't think so. Not really. I think it's Hamilton trying to sabotage me, stop me from doing a good job at Torrent Industries.'

'Hamilton's trying to fuck you up?'

'Yes, I'm pretty sure that's what this is about.'

'I don't think he knows who I am,' said Emery.

'You're lucky.'

'Why don't I feel lucky?'

''Cause you're not really lucky. You're a white-collar wage slave and you're too smart to think you're lucky.'

'Yeah, I'm too smart to think I'm lucky,' said Emery, exhaling. 'Why don't I feel smart?'

''Cause you're a white-collar wage slave.'

'Yeah. Well, you know what my answer is.'

'Answer to what?'

'To your stupid survey.'

'You don't know the question yet.'

'No, but whatever the question is, make my answer the same as Fleur Werd-Gelding's answer. Are you asking Fleur Werd-Gelding?'

'Yes, of course I'm asking Fleur Werd-Gelding.'

'Then make my answer the same as hers. That's what I did last time and I'm still here.'

'Do you want to be here?'

'No, but I'm terrified of *not* being here, so make my answer the same as hers. Will you?'

'I promise I will.'

'Thanks Maserov. You're a good friend.'

It was only a few feet along the hall to Fleur Werd-Gelding's work-space but it somehow felt like a much better neighbourhood. Maserov wondered how she'd managed to do that.

'Fuck off, Maserov,' she said without looking up, affecting a manner consistent with being snowed under with work that was difficult, urgent and more important than other Second Years could ever understand, let alone assist with. But Maserov was a slightly different man following the events of the previous night and however transient the difference might prove to be, and however conflicted he might feel about those events, they formed a protective armour that Fleur Werd-Gelding wasn't able to pierce.

'But Fleur, you haven't heard the question yet.' She looked up at him and something made her abandon the perfect invective she seemed ready to unleash. Instead she paused as though registering some difference in him, a difference she wouldn't have been able to name but that generations of breeding had led her to notice, a kind of pre-rational recognition of someone else's self-confidence. Then she asked, 'Okay. What is it?'

'HR wants to know how you would feel if, at the end of each month, all employees, fee-earners *and* support staff, were required to anonymously write something positive about another staff member and place it in a jar. They'd call it an "Affirmation Jar" and the contents would be read out at random at a gathering of all members of the department during end-of-month drinks.'

Fleur Werd-Gelding considered whether it was worth her while to come back with something disparaging yet still clever but her heavy workload led her to fall back on, 'Fuck off, Maserov.'

'I thought you might say something like that but I just wanted to let you know that HR is monitoring your responses to these questions.'

'Yeah, I don't care.'

'No, but you might care that they've perfectly, I mean *exactly*, correlated all your responses with those of another fee-earner.'

'Yeah? I'm still not caring.'

'Fleur, as far as HR is concerned you're in a category with one other person.'

'Who?'

'Emery.'

'Who's Emery?'

'Emery! He's another Second Year.'

'I don't know who he is.'

'He's sitting about fifteen feet away from you on the same side of the building. If you walk that way you'll know immediately who he is. He's the man who won't want you to realise that he's looking at you as you pass by.'

'None of the men want me to realise that they're looking at me as I pass by.'

'He'll be the worst at hiding it.'

'And why do I care?'

'Because according to some metric HR has come up with, you and Emery think exactly the same way. Don't you think they'll have some say in who gets to go where, or even who gets to stay?'

'No, of course not. HR are the lickspittles of the partners.'

'Maybe. But when the partners are busy, which they always are, they delegate certain decisions.'

'Not *those* decisions. There'd be no point in . . . *doing* things for them. They know the power to make those kind of decisions brings them all sorts of . . . benefits. They wouldn't delegate that.'

'Can you *know* that? For each one? I mean, when they've *already* received the benefits? At precisely the time they're being asked to make a specific recommendation, can you be sure you can rely on them? Can you trust any particular one of them? After all, you can't sue them for breach of sycophancy.'

'What are you saying, Maserov?' She looked up at him.

'That you can't afford to alienate HR. Why do you think I'm doing *this*? Don't you think I know I'm going to be annoying the shit out of everyone I ask?'

Fleur Werd-Gelding now looked up at him in a way she never had before. Not only was there at least some superficial logic to what he was saying – he had to know his questions were indeed annoying the shit out of everyone he asked – but yet he seemed calmer, less afraid than other people and calmer than he himself had ever appeared before. Additionally, she'd heard some talk about his working inside Torrent Industries HQ. Unquestionably Maserov was different now. She couldn't ignore that. Perhaps it was *good* different. Was there any sense in befriending him? She could at the very least cease and desist talking down to him.

'So what exactly are you saying . . . about me and . . .? Emery, is it?'

'You should get to know Emery. Work with him. They think well of him and might ask him who he wants to take with him.'

'Take *with* him? Where?'

'They haven't told me that. Only *he* knows that.'

'When did they tell him?'

'Not long ago. Maybe as recently as this morning.'

'Do you think he'll choose me?'

'Hard to say. But you'd be wise to make sure of it.'

'Why are you telling me all this?' Maserov was saved from having to invent an answer to this by the ring of his mobile phone. He took it out of his pocket and held his hand up apologetically to Fleur Werd-Gelding and whispered, 'Got to go.'

It was Jessica calling him from Torrent Industries.

'Have you been to see Malcolm Torrent yet?'

'No, not yet. I'm still at Freely Savage,' he whispered into his phone. 'Is everything alright?'

'Don't see him till you've talked to me. Promise?'

'I promise?'

'As soon as you get back here, call me. Okay? I'll meet you in your office.'

'Is anything wrong?' he asked but Jessica had ended the call too early to answer.

Was that deliberate, he wondered in the elevator leaving the offices of Freely Savage. People with good news don't normally end their phone calls prematurely. Maybe it was the nature of her news, personal. But even if it was personal and bad, what could be so urgent? And if he was a good lawyer, shouldn't he be thinking first of his client's case and only then about his personal life? The two had become inextricably linked so perhaps he could be forgiven. But who was there to forgive him? Eleanor?

Maserov made his way from the east end of Collins Street to the west end via, first, a brisk walk down the hill to Swanston Street and then, as his anxiety rose and the gradient flattened, via an ungainly trot suggestive of an urgent need for knee surgery. But the aetiology of his ungainliness was not orthopaedic. It stemmed from the dissipation, like fog in the sun, of the protective armour of self-confidence from the previous night that Fleur Werd-Gelding at Freely Savage had been unable to pierce.

As he sweated with emphysematous exhaustion in a westerly direction towards the reclaimed Melbourne swamp that Uber drivers and the state government referred to as Docklands, he kept wondering why Jessica wanted him to speak to her *before* he spoke to Malcolm Torrent about settling the cases. Was it something about the sexual harassment claims or was it something personal between them? Which was better? Which was worse? He granted himself the luxury of not having to decide since Jessica was going to tell him whatever she had to say irrespective of his ranking of relative disasters.

He got to the Torrent Industries building and as he waited for the elevator he suddenly wondered if his kissing of Jessica the previous night had amounted to sexual harassment. Then he told himself that was ridiculous. She had initiated it. He was not her superior. Okay, at law their respective positions in an employment hierarchy was irrelevant. Even a subordinate could sexually harass you, although that hardly ever happened. But she had initiated their kissing, hadn't she? Was he on the slippery slope towards becoming Mike Mercer? He resolved to check the legislation.

'You look terrible!' Jessica said to him, waiting for him in his office.

'Of course I look terrible. I ran all the way here.'

'It's downhill.'

'Not after Swanston Street. Why do people forget that?'

'But it's flat till at least Elizabeth Street. How old are you again?'

'It wasn't just the running. I thought you were going to say . . . What *are* you going to say? Why did you want to meet me before I went in to see Torrent?'

'What did you think I was going to say?'

'I don't know. Is it . . . about last night?'

'Is *that* what you think?'

'No, of course not. Is it?'

'No,' Jessica smiled.

'Will you please tell me why I had to see you before I saw Malcolm Torrent?' he asked, trying to breathe normally again.

'Okay, relax. Remember Carla said that she reported the assault to HR? She said she wrote an account of it and gave it to the head of HR, my boss, Aileen van der Westhuizen.'

'Yeah? You said you'd never heard anything about it and I assumed Aileen van der Westhuizen would say that too.'

'*I'm* saying that because it's true, I *didn't* hear anything about it. But what if Aileen van der Westhuizen *did* hear about it? What if she did get Carla's written account but *said* she didn't?'

'Then it would be a matter of Carla's word against hers, just as in the larger matter, the events of that night, it would be a matter of Carla's word against Mike Mercer's. Mercer would claim it was consensual sex in the workplace, albeit embarrassing, but not criminal. Carla, of course, says it was sexual assault in the workplace.'

Jessica stood up and walked towards the window of Maserov's office. 'Has Torrent Industries denied not only that Mike Mercer sexually assaulted Carla but also that within a week of the night in question Carla had made the allegation in writing and given it to HR?'

'Yes, officially Torrent Industries denies not only the assault but that it received Carla's *report* of the assault. If we, that is, if Torrent Industries had Carla's report, we're meant to have noted this and given a copy of it to Betga via a process known as discovery.'

'And what if you didn't? I mean what if Torrent Industries hasn't?'

'Well, it definitely hasn't but Betga can't prove that Carla wrote the report and gave it to Torrent's HR department other than by calling Carla as a witness which he doesn't want to do to spare her having to give evidence of the whole thing in public. After which, of course, the lawyer for Torrent Industries, the one who'll come *after* me, will sanction the public humiliation of Carla in every conceivable way.'

'But if we could prove that Torrent Industries, through Aileen van der Westhuizen, *did* have Carla's report, how would that change things?' Jessica asked.

'Well, Torrent Industries, my client and your employer, would then be in breach of the rules of discovery and it would suggest a cover-up.'

'And would a cover-up be damaging to Torrent Industries' case?'

'Hugely damaging. Why?'

'Okay,' said Jessica, closing the door to Maserov's office and sitting down again. 'I had a casual conversation with Aileen van der Westhuizen this morning which I steered towards the whole Carla story. I told her I hadn't heard anything about it till the lawsuit and she said neither had she. I told her I'd heard that Carla's lawyer is saying that Carla submitted a report about the alleged assault to HR. I told her I'd never seen that report and she said she hadn't either.'

'So?'

'There was just something about the way she said it that made me suspect she was lying.'

'By the way, Jessica,' said Maserov, pondering, 'there's a whole group of in-house lawyers at Torrent Industries. Do you guys, I mean does anyone in HR, ever talk to them about these sorts of things, about any staff-related matters, personnel infractions, that kind of thing?'

'No, we don't bother them and they definitely try not to have anything to do with us.'

'Why not?'

'They say they're just completely flat out working on construction contracts, equipment acquisition and lease agreements and generally on matters they've assured us we wouldn't understand and, in turn, we do not take our problems to them.'

'So that's why Freely Savage was supposed to be handling the case. But there was no report from Carla on the file when I took it over from Featherby, the guy at Freely Savage who was running it before me,' Maserov observed.

'Well, anyway, I just *knew* Aileen van der Westhuizen was lying. She was incredibly uncomfortable and even got slightly aggressive in her tone with me.'

'What did she say?'

'It wasn't what she said. It was her demeanour.'

'Jessica, you might well be right but I don't know what I can do with this. I would need more evidence than your report of her demeanour during a discussion about it.'

'I knew you would.' Jessica smiled the way she must have when she had been a little girl and had arrived home to tell her parents she had come top of her class. 'There's a place on level three, in fact it takes up half the floor, where our HR department stores archived documents, not all documents, obviously, but some. Only people in HR have access to it and not even all HR staff, but I do and I went down there on a hunch. And I looked in the area where Aileen's file notes and notes of minutes are kept and searched around the week or two after the night in question. And I found this.'

Jessica handed Maserov four sheets of typed paper with Carla's signature and the date at the bottom of it. Maserov read it. This was Carla's report, stating in fairly graphic detail all that she alleged Mike Mercer had done to her.

'Oh my God!' Maserov said quietly under his breath.

'But it gets better,' Jessica said, handing over a piece of yellow post-it note paper that had almost lost its adhesiveness. 'This is Aileen's handwriting. It was stuck to the front page of Carla's report.'

Maserov read the handwriting on the post-it note. It read, 'Told Featherby of FS about Carla M typed complaint. F said hold on to it but keep it off the file.' The words 'keep it off the file' had been underlined.

'Carla reported it and Aileen van der Westhuizen buried it. It *is* a cover-up!' Jessica said in a triumph-coated whisper.

'Yeah,' Maserov agreed as he digested the implications. 'And Featherby told her to, or at least that's what she understood him to be saying.

Why would Featherby have told her to bury it, I wonder? That jeopardises *him*.'

'You can use this, right?'

'Well, I have to make it known that *I* now know that Aileen van der Westhuizen has Carla's report. It doesn't make Carla's report a true account of what happened but it certainly adds credibility to her account and the cover-up stinks to high heaven. A court would come down severely on Torrent Industries for this, I'd imagine, and the press would have a picnic with it. I think I'm obliged to tell Betga, obviously.'

'And he can use that against Mike Mercer, right?'

'Well, it won't affect Mike Mercer directly but it will affect Torrent Industries. Jessica, you know this is going to have implications for you. You've found a document that shows your boss to have lied, to have compromised her employer's case, and it could well cost her her job, maybe even her career. She'll fight this. She has to. And there's always a chance that she'll win or at least somehow try to take you down with her. Whistleblowers get hurt all the time, you know.'

'What about *you*?' Jessica countered. 'You're about to accuse another lawyer, a colleague, of burying evidence.'

'Yeah, but I think I have to. Ethically, I think I have no choice. I'm obliged to follow this through, to make it known. I'm an officer of the court. *You* don't have to, you're not professionally obliged.'

'Stephen, I want to do anything I can to help Carla and the others and to stamp this shit out.'

'Even at the cost of your job?'

'Absolutely.'

'Jessica, I could still use the document and the post-it note without implicating you directly. I could say that I asked you for access to the level-three archive, that you innocently let me in and that I ferreted around down there by myself and found this stuff.'

'But that wouldn't be true.'

VII

When Maserov called Betga he was looking after his daughter, Marietta, both to bond with her further and to assist Carla, who was temping across town that day for a greeting card and fine paper wholesaler in Thornbury. It was a brand new company whose advertisement – '*You* write it. *We* mail it. Beautiful greeting cards for all occasions.' – was trying to capture the market of creative, caring, expressive, self-indulgent and lazy people in the northern suburbs and it was giving Carla some extra work and a need for more childcare. Who better than Marietta's father? No one, other than Carla's mother and one of her sisters, was as motivated and as free.

'You are fucking kidding me!' Betga said over the phone when Maserov told him what Jessica had found. 'Oh shit! I shouldn't have sworn. I'm holding Marietta. Listen, is Jessica absolutely sure that this is in Aileen what's-her-name's handwriting?'

'Yes, she's sure,' came Maserov's voice over the phone.

'Fuck me!' said Betga, 'Oh! Sorry, sweetheart,' he said to his daughter as he bounced her on his knee. 'Daddy's just heard some very good news from Maserov, good news for Mummy and for you.'

'Obviously I'm going to tell all of this to Malcolm Torrent when I go to see him,' Maserov told him.

'Absolutely.'

'But first I want to hear what Featherby says about it. I want to show him her file note, the handwritten post-it note and see what he says.'

'Yeah but irrespective of what he says, you're going to tell Malcolm Torrent the whole story, aren't you?'

'Yeah, I am.'

'Good.'

'But I thought you might want to be somewhere close by. This is likely to finish Featherby's career at Freely Savage even if he's got some kind of explanation. Hamilton won't let him survive this. So, in your capacity as head of the Freely Savage Survivors, I thought you might want to be there to pick up the pieces.'

'I take your point but we don't usually come and scrape them off the pavement . . . so to speak. I mean they lose their jobs and *then,* only if they choose, they come to us for support, advice, counselling. But we're not ambulance chasers. And anyway, what do you mean by "some kind of explanation"? What possible explanation could he have?'

'Well, he could say that she's making it up, that he didn't say anything of the sort, maybe that he didn't even know about Carla's written account of the assault.'

'Why should Aileen van der Westhuizen verbal Featherby? What could she have against him?'

'She doesn't need to have anything against him per se. She might just be protecting her own arse.'

'But if he didn't tell her to bury the report, why would she?'

'No idea. But I thought I should ask him first before I go to Malcolm Torrent with this. He's more likely to tell us if you or someone from the Freely Savage Survivors is there, as though you're there in your capacity as his sponsor or counsellor or something. Isn't that how it works? And anyway, it seems the decent thing to do.'

'It *is* very decent. Uncle Stephen's a very decent man, little girl,' Betga said to his daughter. 'Gives lawyers a good name, if that's possible.'

'Problem is,' said Maserov, 'he's not in today. He's not at work. I checked with his secretary and she said he's at home, called in sick. So . . .'

'So you're thinking you're going to have to go to his house?'

'Yeah, and I was thinking you'd come with me.'

'Really?

'Not in your capacity as Carla's lawyer, in your Freely Savage Survivors capacity, given that he's going to be eligible to join any minute now. There's just one problem. No one at Freely Savage will give me his home address.'

'You're kidding?'

'No, apparently it's firm policy and, given that I'm an enemy of Hamilton's, no one is willing to cut me any slack. Jessica's working on it as we speak. She's trying to get it from Freely Savage HR in her capacity as a Torrent Industries HR executive, a professional courtesy between HR departments.'

'Yeah, well, even if she gets his home address, there's still one problem. I can't leave here. I'm meant to be looking after Marietta.'

'Oh no! Really? There's no one else you could leave her with?'

'No, believe me, I've been through this. And anyway, it would set me back weeks if not months with Carla if I dumped Marietta on to someone else when I've made such a big deal of wanting to help her and be back in their lives.'

'Hmm, then we *do* have a problem.'

'I could always bring her along.'

'What? To Featherby's house?'

'Why not?'

'When we tell him we've caught him withholding evidence?'

'Maserov, she's only two years old. There's plenty of time to teach her not to withhold evidence. But there's one other problem. I don't have a child seat installed in my car. *You've* got two kids. *You* must have one.'

'No, they're both in Eleanor's car.'

'Really, what kind of a father are you, not having a child seat in your car?' Betga asked him.

'I could say the same to you. You're the one trying to impress Carla with your devotion and fathering skills. You wouldn't even *be* a father if it wasn't for me. Why haven't *you* got a child seat?'

'I've bought one. It's just not installed.'

'Well, hurry up and install it.'

'I can't. I don't how to. Why don't *you* come over and do it? Then we can all go together.'

'What, you, me and Marietta . . . go uninvited . . . to Featherby's *house* . . . when he's unwell, and tell him we think we've caught him withholding evidence and knowingly permitting his client to swear a materially deficient affidavit of documents?'

'Yeah. What's wrong with that?'

'I'll tell you what's wrong with that, quite apart from it being highly unusual —'

'Yes, I'll grant you, it's highly unusual.'

'I don't know how to install a child's car seat either.'

'Didn't you install them in Eleanor's car?'

'No, my father did.'

'Where's your father now?'

'He's dead.'

'Well, at least he lived long enough to install the child car seats in your wife's car. What am *I* going to do? My father's dead too so I'm fucked. Oh sorry, sweetie, Daddy's trying to think outside the square and it's hard to do completely sober. How many lawyers does it take to install a child's car seat? That's not a joke. I really want to know how many we'd have to call before one us knows how to do it. Could Eleanor do it?'

'Yeah, probably, but that's not a good idea.'

'Maserov, this is an emergency.'

'Betga, this is my marriage. Besides, she's at work teaching sonnets to tomorrow's unemployed. Wait a second, Jessica's just texted me with Featherby's home address. He lives in Hawthorn.'

'Okay, let me think,' said Betga. 'You come over here and by the time you get here I'll have the car seat installed.'

'It's got to be safe. Are you sure you're going to be able to do it?'

'Not at all,' said Betga. 'But get here as fast as you can. I often do well under pressure.'

By the time Maserov arrived at Carla's house Betga had indeed solved the problem but not by himself. Teaching him how to shorten and lengthen the straps of his newly installed top-of-the-range child seat was Kasimir.

'Kasimir, you remember Mr Maserov?'

'Sure I do. How you going, Mr Maserov?' Kasimir nodded in place of shaking hands which he was unable to do because he was gently placing Marietta in Betga's car.

'I'm well, thanks, Kasimir.'

'Betga, she's such a pretty little thing,' said Kasimir with surprise. 'I didn't even know you had children.'

'I wasn't keeping it from you, Kasimir. I only recently found out myself.'

VIII

Featherby's heritage house was nestled among Hawthorn's tree-lined streets and manicured gardens only four miles east of the offices of Freely Savage. Betga, Maserov and little Marietta parked just outside the double garage that was once a stable.

'Wow!' said Betga, looking through the passenger window at Featherby's house as his car slowed to a stop.

'I've heard it said people in Hawthorn tend not to die because they're already in heaven,' Maserov commented, also looking at the house.

'Maybe,' Betga replied, scanning the street ninety degrees, 'but a lot of people round here do *look* dead. Actually, it's a look that stretches all the way to Canterbury.'

'They're not dead, just incredibly pale. It's not the same. I think I should go first and then text you if and when I need backup, or if *he* does. He's not going to appreciate my visit.'

'Not today,' said Betga in slightly sombre agreement.

Maserov opened the car door, sat there for a moment without moving, took a breath, exhaled, and then got out of the warm car. 'This isn't going to be easy. Wish me luck, Marietta,' he said and closed the door. He walked up the winding garden path flanked by trees, their leaves dappled in winter light and shimmering with traces of stubborn rain-drops, to Featherby's house. He stood at the front door in his winter coat, briefcase in one hand, containing photocopies of the incriminating documents Jessica had discovered, rang the doorbell and waited. What should he say as an opener? He watched his breath condensing a mere two leaves away from his face. There was no sound coming from the house. Perhaps Featherby was asleep in bed. He rang the doorbell again. Still no answer. Maserov was feeling worse with every second Featherby was making him wait.

'Come on Featherby, you bastard. I'm doing you a professional courtesy. Open the door so I can quickly get back to feeling better about myself,' he said under his breath. But still, nothing. Maserov walked back to the car, leaned down on the front passenger side and knocked on the window with two frozen fingers. Betga opened the car door.

'When is she going to call me "Daddy"? I mean, how long? She points at me and smiles.'

'Well, that's good,' said Maserov distractedly before looking behind him back up at the house.

'Yeah but then she says, "Betga!"'

'Listen,' said Maserov, changing the subject, 'he's not home. No one's home.'

'No? Maybe he's gone to get another job or he's fled to Argentina. Oh wait! You hear that?'

'No?'

'In the garage, there's a car starting up in the garage. Go and stand by the door. He must be on his way out somewhere. Go stand by the garage door and stop him. And don't let him run you over. But I'll be your witness if he does.'

Maserov, hearing the engine running in the garage, walked briskly to the garage door and knocked on it but there was no response. He figured that Featherby or whoever the driver was probably couldn't hear him so he waited at the door for it to open. He rehearsed his opening lines,

'Featherby, it's me, Stephen Maserov, from work. Sorry to bother you on your day off. Do you mind if we have a quick word? Well, yes, I'm afraid it *is* kind of urgent.' He thought it important that he stay diplomatic and polite as long as possible.

The car was still running but the garage door hadn't opened. Maserov tried knocking again but this still didn't achieve anything. Maybe he had gone back inside the house for something he'd forgotten, Maserov mused. But, if anything, the engine seemed to be revving up. Maybe whoever was in there was having car trouble. Maserov tried to peek in through a tiny gap between the garage door and the wall. He wasn't sure if he was actually seeing what he thought he was seeing.

From the car, Betga looked over in the direction of the garage and was shocked to see Maserov banging wildly on the door like someone having some kind of violent psychotic episode. He got out of the car, locked it leaving Marietta alone inside, and ran towards the garage, shouting at Maserov.

'Maserov, what the hell are you doing? You'll break the door down.'

When he reached the garage door Maserov was panting. 'Look through there.' Betga went to look through the now enlarged gap between the door and the wall and his response confirmed Maserov's assessment of the situation. There was a hose leading from the car's exhaust pipe into the interior of the car through the driver's window. It appeared the car's vents had been sealed.

'Fuck, he's trying to kill himself!'

'Have you got a jack in the car?'

Betga ran to his car, opened the boot and brought back a jack and, between the two of them, Betga with the jack and Maserov with his hands, they were able to get into the garage where the driver of a black Range Rover SUV was trying to asphyxiate himself. It was Featherby. At the steering wheel, still in his pyjamas, he had left the doors unlocked and they were able to drag him out of the car through the gap they had made in the garage door and onto the moist grassy verge between the garage and Featherby's house. The three of them coughing, Marietta looking on through the window of Betga's locked car, Featherby looked up at the two men who, in turn, looked at each other.

Within a couple of minutes they had him inside his house. There was no one else home. Maserov stayed with Featherby while Betga went out to the street to bring in Marietta. Featherby didn't pretend that they had come upon him doing anything other than what it looked like he was doing. The lawyer, lying on his back, face up towards the ceiling, had his head in Maserov's lap. He was wheezing but finally no longer coughing when Betga returned with Marietta in his arms. He looked up at Maserov with bloodshot eyes, perplexed, breathless, and asked him if he was dead.

'No, you're in Hawthorn,' said Betga.

'Who are *you*?'

'I'm Betga, A.A. Betga. This is my daughter, Marietta.'

'What are you doing here? I know that name. Do I know you?'

'You've been calling me practically every day. I'm here from the Freely Savage Survivors, although if your colleague here, Maserov, hadn't been determined to talk to you ASAP, you wouldn't have survived long enough to join.'

'I don't get it,' said Featherby, bewildered, now looking up at Maserov. 'Why are *you* here?'

'Well, I came here to talk to you about work, about a file. They told me, at work, they told me you were home, sick, so . . .'

'So you came here to . . . my *house*?'

'Yeah,' said Betga, 'And lucky he did.'

'And you?' he asked Betga.

'I was —'

'He was in the neighbourhood. I told him I was coming to see you, he knows me, and he was in the neighbourhood too, so he said he'd join me.'

'But you said you only see people who've *left* Freely Savage?' Featherby queried Betga.

'Well, talking to some of the other FSS board members, we thought we might make an exception for you.'

'Get him a glass of water,' Maserov suggested.

Maserov propped Featherby up in a chair in the Featherby family kitchen while Betga, with Marietta under one arm, went to look for a glass.

'Featherby, you need help, I mean *professional* help. What on earth were you thinking?'

'Not *those* glasses!' said Featherby. 'That's a Waterford Baccarat, my wife will kill me.'

'Well, where are the everyday glasses?' Betga called from the other end of the kitchen.

'In the cupboard above the kettle.'

'These ones?'

'Yeah.'

'Ooh, they're very nice too,' said Betga, holding one up to the light.

'Thank you.'

'Obviously more of an *everyday* glass though, isn't it?' said Betga, examining the glass more closely.

'Featherby, what were you thinking? How could you even contemplate something like this?'

'Maserov, I'm . . . I'm a mess. I'm not myself anymore.'

'Since when?'

'It's work, it's . . . Hamilton . . . I don't know. He's playing mind games with me and I don't even know what I did wrong. I've given everything to that place. Years! So many hours, weekends, but . . . I've lost . . . He's got me doubting everything I do. I'm constantly second-guessing myself. I hate going in there. I know they're going to get rid of me. *He's* going to get rid of me.'

'Featherby, is *that* all it is, just Hamilton?' Maserov asked.

'What do you mean, "Is that all?" It's my job.'

'You can't let Hamilton bully you into killing yourself.'

'Featherby,' Betga said, 'one in every hundred people is a psychopath. It's *that* common. But they're not all mass murderers. A lot of them end up in boardrooms and in large commercial law firms. They're what are known as *corporate* psychopaths. If you kill yourself, they win. You can't let them win. Your job is to survive them, get beyond them. And then to screw them if you possibly can. You've got to outlast them. If you let them push you into suicide you're letting everybody down.'

'What do you mean, who am I letting down?'

'The other ninety-nine. *We* win if we recognise who they are and tell as many people as possible, tell them the emperor isn't wearing any clothes. And that he's a cunt,' said Betga.

'No, I know him. He's a genius, an evil genius,' said Featherby, granting his tormentor an almost religious reverence.

'He's not a genius,' said Betga calmly. 'He was born with somewhat above average intelligence but no higher than you or Maserov.'

'What about you?' Featherby asked Betga.

'Oh, he's nowhere near *me*. He has certain attributes that have eased his way, I'll grant you, the biggest being that he was born with zero capacity for empathy or shame. This coupled with a restlessness, an impulsivity, a fondness for dishonesty and an enjoyment of others' distress, which of course all met with the good timing that only a true bastard can have.'

'Good timing? What do you mean?'

'Well, even for a corporate psychopath he rose to partnership early, quickly, but this was just because he happened to be in the right place at the right time. He was at just the right age to benefit from deregulation and the rash of amalgamations and acquisitions that followed the rise of Reagan's and Thatcher's free-market economics throughout the developed world. Trust me, he's no genius. And you can't kill yourself on account of him.'

'Featherby, think what you'd be doing to your family, your children,' said Maserov.

'What will I be doing to them if I lose my job?'

'They won't care about that.'

'My wife will, her parents will. *My* parents will. Our friends will.'

'So what if you lose your job! There are plenty of jobs out there,' offered Maserov.

'No there aren't,' said Featherby. 'Are you crazy? That's just the sort of shit they say to people to stop them from killing themselves.'

'Yeah, he's right, that's true,' said Betga. 'And they say it to people before elections too. But your job isn't *you*. You're more than that.'

'No . . . I'm not,' said Featherby, staring blankly at the space in front of him, a space that was empty all the way until the pristine white kitchen wall met the downlight-lit bench where the gleaming Faema e61 Legend coffee maker sat boldly, spread out triumphantly, braggadocio-ready with a head full of steam, colonising the countertop like it was Abyssinia, just waiting to spring into action the moment Featherby made some friends.

'Ah, now we're actually making progress!' said Betga. 'There's your problem. You *can't* let your job be you.'

'Featherby, do you have anyone professionally trained you can talk to, like a psychiatrist?' Maserov asked in a quiet voice.

'No.'

'Do you want me to call your wife?'

'Fuck no! What made you come here? What file? Was it the Torrent Industries sexual harassment files?'

'It doesn't matter,' Maserov tried to assure him. 'We can talk about work some other time.'

'It *was*, wasn't it?'

'Betga, you didn't get him a glass of water!'

'Oh shit, sorry! I got distracted by the Waterford. *Baccarat*, did you say?'

Betga got up and poured a glass of water for Featherby and asked, as though just remembering, 'Hey, Featherby, did you tell the head of HR at Torrent Industries to bury an account of the assault that was typed by one of the plaintiffs herself? The plaintiff's name is Carla Monterosso.'

'Betga! We don't have to talk about that now!' snapped Maserov.

'No, of course not,' shot back Featherby. 'Why would you say that?'

''Cause she's saying you did.'

'Betga, shut the fuck up!'

'The man deserves a chance to answer,' Betga argued in self-defence.

'Who's she saying this to?' Featherby asked, alarmed.

'No one yet but sooner or later it's going to be you or her.'

'Betga, for fuck's sake!' said Maserov.

'Look, we almost didn't have the chance to ask him.'

'I'm going to lose my job for this!' Featherby realised.

'Featherby, you said you didn't *do* it,' Betga said. 'Do you mind if I put her down on the floor? She's not housebroken yet but my arm's starting to spasm.'

'It doesn't matter if I did or not, Hamilton's going to have me killed for simply letting Malcolm Torrent even consider fleetingly that it's true. I mean, just to show Torrent he trusts Torrent people over his own. It's not going to matter at all if it's true.'

'No, it *will* matter if it's true. Maybe not to Hamilton but it will matter to the Supreme Court and to the Law Institute,' said Betga.

'Have you come over here to tell me you're going to report me to the Law Institute?'

'Will you drink your water and relax?' said Betga. 'I came over here to help you. I don't really remember why Maserov's here. But I should think you'd be glad he came exactly when he did.'

'Not if I'm going to lose my job,' said Featherby.

'Featherby, did you just hear what you just said? You'd rather I got here too late to save you, if living means losing your job,' Maserov told him, after which Featherby whispered something neither Maserov nor Betga could hear.

'What did you say?' Maserov asked.

Marietta was on the floor. 'Look, she's holding your leg,' Betga said. 'She *likes* you! It's okay, she doesn't bite.'

'He told me to,' Featherby whispered.

'What? Who told you to? Told you to what?' Maserov asked.

'Hamilton, he told me to bury it, told me to tell *her* to bury it.'

They heard the sound of a car pulling up outside the street.

'Fuck, that's my wife!'

'Why did he tell you to bury it?'

'Do you think I asked him? Don't say anything about this to my wife.'

'About Hamilton telling you to bury evidence or about the car and the hose?' Betga asked.

'About anything!' Featherby whispered in panic. 'Don't tell her anything about any of this!'

The car outside had its door slammed and someone was walking towards the front door. Maserov sat with Featherby in his pyjamas at the kitchen table while Marietta played under the table at Featherby's feet. They heard the front door open and Featherby's wife walked into the kitchen in her tennis dress, shouting, 'What the hell happened to the garage? You're home sick *one* day!' At which point Betga stood up and met her halfway between the kitchen entrance and the kitchen table.

'You must be Mrs Featherby?' he said, shaking her hand.

'Who are you?' asked the angry, sporty, flexible Mrs Featherby.

'Betga, A.A. Betga. Your husband called us about the insurance. You would have seen somebody's damaged your garage.'

'There's a little girl under the table!'

'Yes, that's my daughter. We were just testing her new car seat when I got your husband's call. We came immediately. It seems somebody tried to break in.'

'Through the garage door?'

'Yes. We've had a spate of reports of gangs targeting the area. They seem to be choosing houses with luxury homewares, Waterford crystal, Whitehill silver cutlery and suchlike. Do you have any Waterford crystal?'

'Yes, actually, we do. But how would they know?'

'Receipts, computer networks, online hacking, international crime syndicates. It's very complicated, a really sophisticated operation right up until they get to the houses with the Waterford products. *Then* the pattern seems to be for them to smash their way in via the garage, which is not very sophisticated. Fortunately for you, your husband fought them off with some kind of hose, which I'm afraid we'll need for our report, won't we, Mr Maserov?'

'Are they . . . ethnic, the gangs?' Mrs Featherby asked.

'Well, we're not really meant to say but . . .' Then Betga leaned in towards her as if to share a confidence. 'You've no doubt heard that most crime is economic?'

'Um, yes, I think I've heard that . . .'

'Okay, you didn't hear this from me but . . . they're economists.'

'What?'

'They're economists.'

'Economists?'

'Yes. They work in packs. Go unnoticed by most of the community. Wreak havoc on people everywhere. Today, sadly, it was you.'

'Economists . . . I'd never have guessed that.'

'No, they get away with murder. Now, if Mr Maserov can mind my daughter, I'd like to take you out to the garage, to the scene of the crime, if I may, to ask you a few questions.'

'Yes, of course.'

Betga led Featherby's wife to her garage and when she had left the kitchen, Maserov, whose gaze had fallen for a moment on photos of Featherby's children stuck to the door of the refrigerator, spoke to Featherby in a low voice to ensure his wife wouldn't hear.

'I'm going to get you the number of someone to call, a psychiatrist or a psychologist. If you call that person today and make an appointment to see them I won't tell your wife about any of this. But if you don't call the number I'm going to give you today, and I'm going to check, I will have to tell her what you tried to do. Understand?'

'Yes.'

'Do we have a deal?'

Featherby bent down and lifted Marietta to his knee and, looking at the little girl's face, his eyes began to well up.

'Deal,' he said, wiping his face with the back of his hand. The two men shook hands, Maserov receiving a not insubstantial fraction of Featherby's tear on the thin skin on the top of his hand. He pulled out his phone but stopped just before pressing his intended number and looked hard into Featherby's still moist eyes and asked Featherby, 'Are you a religious man?'

'No, we're Anglican.'

'Well,' continued Maserov carefully, 'none of us really know that much about death and even less about dying.'

'Are you Anglican too?'

'No, I meant none of us *humans*. How do you know you're not destined after death to keep re-living, re-experiencing, the agonisingly painful, frightening moment of your asphyxiation over and over again into eternity, broken only by scenes of your wife and your children learning of your death anew, over and over again?'

'You think?' asked Featherby quietly.

'Why risk it?' Maserov asked rhetorically. 'Listen to me, Featherby, you can't ever kill yourself. With all our scientific and technological advances, the entire human species can't even accurately predict the weather tomorrow. So how can any solitary person with a fear-clouded mind, seasoned with panic, stained by sadness, and burdened by the weight of their own history, how can one lone person know the spin of even one of our tomorrows? Things can change in a heartbeat, my friend. Your only *real* job is to nurture the heartbeat. It's a job for life.'

Marietta leaned in and touched Featherby's face with her finger.

'After all,' said Maserov, 'one never knows, maybe the horse will talk.'

'What?'

Maserov didn't answer but looked down at his phone just long enough to trigger the now frequently dialled chosen number. He spoke quietly to the recipient of his phone call.

'Jess, hi, it's me.' It was the first time he'd abbreviated her name. She noticed, he didn't. 'Don't ask me to explain anything now but do you have the number of a psychiatrist or a psychologist that someone could see without much delay?' There was a pause. 'What do I mean, "not much delay"? I mean . . .' Maserov looked at Featherby sitting helplessly in his stripy flannel pyjamas with Betga's daughter on his knee. 'I mean sometime . . . today.'

part seven

I

'Marietta, this is no way to live, pining for a policeman. Let me remind you, he's not Dada, *I* am. Perhaps later, when you're older, say sixteen, you can call me *Betga* in a kind of ironic or postmodern way, if they're still doing postmodernism then, if it's still a *thing* then or indeed if anything is a *thing* then, if they still have *things*. But for now, *I* am Dada, loving, highly entertaining *Dada*. And I'm not talking about the early twentieth-century European avant-garde art movement, either. I'm using it in the sense of a diminutive for *pater*. I probably should've chosen my words more carefully since, I'll grant you, there *is* some connection between postmodernism and Dadaism, but none at all between them and me, *your* dad.'

Betga was lying on the floor with two-year-old Marietta at Carla's house talking to her and simultaneously making a soft, white, fluffy, now broken, wind-up rabbit dance around her in jerks that could best be described as spasmodic. No music had ever been composed that would accommodate movements like these.

There was no one else in the house. They were waiting for Carla to come home from her temping gig across town in Flemington working for a week-old start-up that made plastic wishbones for people so starved of the opportunity to otherwise divine their own destinies that they were willing to pay three dollars per wishbone. When Carla realised what the company's core business was, she had managed to keep smiling but asked to be paid in cash. It was while earning this cash that her daughter's free childcare came courtesy of her father, A.A. Betga, who, after a full day with his daughter, found himself bored out of his mind.

The plan had been for Betga to take care of Marietta until Carla came home and then they would wait together for Maserov to come over with the paperwork necessary to formalise the settlement with Torrent Industries. Carla had softened her attitude to Jessica after she had learned from Betga all that Jessica had done to help her and that Jessica was even willing to jeopardise her job. She felt that now it was she who owed Jessica an apology. So Jessica had been invited to toast the settlement as well. It was only later during the day that Carla wondered if, in extending an invitation to Jessica, she hadn't unwittingly been disloyal to her new friend Eleanor Maserov but by then it was too late to revoke the invitation and, anyway, Carla was unsure of the precise nature of Jessica's relationship with Maserov, as indeed were Jessica and Maserov.

In the meantime, Betga had played every game he could think of with Marietta, told her every fairy tale he could recall from his own fractured childhood but then had suddenly remembered Maserov's advice to him when defending against an onslaught of boredom. He was to have a conversation with her as though she were an adult.

'You have to know, darling Marietta, that it was always my intention to be in your life, right from the time you were born. It was Mummy who insisted the three of us *not* be together although I don't want you to be cross with Mummy. We have to try to understand her. She was angry with Daddy for a moment of infidelity with a legal recruiter in a very tight job market. Already, I'm sure you can see both sides of this. Sometimes a man needs to be alone with a legal recruiter in order to do what he needs to do to safeguard the interests of his family. Additionally, and I say this in mitigation and because you might as well learn this now, when some socially under-evolved men see an attractive woman, certain regions of their brains light up in functional Magnetic Resonance Imaging. Researchers have found that when these regions of the brain are particularly active, these men's capacity to make moral judgments diminishes to an alarming degree astonishingly quickly. Believe me, I've seen it happen. It's a psychopathy that has been the cause of much suffering but it is treatable with cognitive behaviour therapy and education. Its precise neurobiology is something you might not learn till graduate school but you'll learn it experientially before high school.

'Then there was that study, I think it was in *Nature*, a study of the the nematode worm, which found that a neuron exists in its brain that allows it to memorise previous sexual encounters so strongly that they will override a conditioned salt aversion when they can't get sex without salt. I've no doubt one would find similar results with other condiments. So, while a lot of men are unscrupulous, immoral shits extremely often and should never be left alone without their gonads clearly observable on a live CCTV feed, sometimes, at least when it's your father, you have to cut him some slack.

'If you do this, if you do forgive me for the intimacy incident with the legal recruiter, I promise not to let you or your mother down again. You will never need to be ashamed of me, at least not till high school, when you're biologically programmed to be embarrassed and ashamed of both your parents. But you can always be proud to be a Betga. Betgas have fled Hitler *and* Stalin. Betgas have fought or agitated against Franco, General Jaruzelski, Erich Honecker and Jeff Kennett. We may not often have a lot of money but you can count on us to have all the right enemies.

'So I guess what I'm saying, my darling little girl, is that I love you with all my heart. I've loved you from the moment you were born and I will love you beyond my last breath. I also love your mummy with all my heart and am determined to prove it to her, no matter how long she treats me like a miscreant cocker spaniel. I guess, to some degree,

I deserve it but if you repeat that I'll deny it and never let you have your teeth straightened no matter in how many different directions they point. You and your mummy are the best things in my life and I want to live with both of you in a situation that, to the very best of my ability, approximates a conventional bourgeois family. I can't promise to be conventional but by the power vested in me to sign passport applications, I will do my damnedest to be bourgeois.'

Betga heard footsteps in the hallway closer than they ought to have been. His heart rate quickened slightly as he wondered how much of his monologue Carla would have heard. He looked at Carla's face in an attempt to discern where in his monologue her hearing had cut in.

'I was just talking to Marietta,' he said slightly nervously.

'I heard.'

'Really? What did you hear?'

'What did you say?'

'Nothing other than what you heard.'

'Then you know what I heard.'

'But not how much. What did you hear?'

'When I came in you had just described yourself as a cocker spaniel.'

'Oh,' said Betga, unable to hide his relief.

'Don't flatter yourself. You should be so lucky to be a cocker spaniel. They're famously loyal. You're infamously disloyal.'

But her tone was softer than it had been in a long while and she came over to him and kissed him. Betga tried as best he could to recall in sequence what he had just said to Marietta. If Carla really had heard what he'd said only from 'cocker spaniel' then she'd heard that he loved her, that she and Marietta were the best things in his life and that he wanted to live with them both as a family and she wouldn't have heard anything about a moment of infidelity with a legal recruiter in a very tight job market or about the male nematode worm. Certainly, the kiss was consistent with this. He breathed a little more easily now.

There was a knock at the door. They looked at each other and both wondered whether it was Maserov.

'Don't be disappointed,' Betga suddenly found himself saying.

'Why, do you *know* something?'

'No, but there's no guarantee Malcolm Torrent will behave rationally. He *should* but . . . you know . . . just in case. Don't be disappointed. We've got our family. That's more important than money.'

Suddenly two thoughts with opposing effects on her emotions competed for primacy in her consciousness; the possibility that not only would Mike Mercer escape punishment but that she might not even receive a remotely fair monetary compensation *and* the possibility that Betga could, after all, provide a ballast to her and Marietta's lives. And when she opened the door all possibilities remained alive. It wasn't Maserov.

'Hi,' said Jessica, handing Carla a chilled magnum of champagne. 'I hope you don't consider it bad luck for me to bring this before we know what Stephen is going to come back with. I nearly didn't bring it but then I thought, "What the hell? Why not be optimistic!"'

'Come in, come in,' said Carla, kissing Jessica on the cheek and taking the champagne towards the fridge. 'This is very kind of you. No, I'm not superstitious.'

'Yes she is,' called Betga. 'My God, she is. She goes to church although she's not otherwise religious.'

Carla turned around. 'That's not superstition, that's being rational. I'm hedging my bets.'

'So let's open the champagne then,' entreated Betga.

'Not till we hear what Stephen has to say. Being rational leaves no room for optimism.' Carla put the champagne in the fridge and then returned to Jessica. 'I want to thank you. It sounds like you really stuck your neck out for me.'

'To be honest, I'm not yet sure *what* it's done for me but there was no way I could find your account of the assault addressed to Aileen van der Westhuizen *and* her post-it note with the lawyer's advice to bury it, and then do nothing with it. I had no choice. I wouldn't have been able to live with myself.'

'No, but you *did* have a choice. You went looking for it in the first place, didn't you?'

'Yes.'

'You had a hunch they'd covered it up and then went looking for the evidence to prove it, even if it meant exposing yourself to some kind of payback from your boss. Your job is to sweep this sort of thing under the carpet and instead you dug it up.'

'Yes, I suppose so.'

'Then no matter what Stephen comes back with, I'll forever be grateful to you. I owe you an apology for the way I've spoken to you. I'll never be able to repay you, Jessica.'

'You don't need to repay me. Listen, unless we stick together we don't have a hope of changing things. And they've *got* to change. What kind of society is it where half the population feels vulnerable and then, if and when they report an incident, are likely to be silenced or disbelieved? The victim's very reporting of it gets more scrutiny than the assault itself. Decent men don't do this kind of shit. And when you find a decent one you've got to grab him with both —'

As if on cue, there was a knock on the door, an interruption that stopped her mid-sentence.

'Well, unless someone ordered pizza, that'll be Mascrov,' said Betga calmly, trying to mask a certain cocktail of impatience and anxiety. He too had a lot riding on the news Maserov had waiting on the other side of the door.

'Betga, can you let him in?' Carla asked. 'I won't be able to stop myself trying to read his face in the doorway.'

'Just leave the hall light off.'

'*I'll* get it,' Jessica volunteered.

Betga and Carla listened to Jessica open the front door and quietly greet Maserov and then ask him how it went. They didn't hear his answer because he didn't reply before the two of them were back in Carla's living room. Both Betga and Carla stood up and looked expectantly at Maserov who seemed to be searching for the right words with which to begin.

'Well, you saw him, right?' Betga asked.

'Yeah, finally.'

'And? You told him what Jessica found?' Maserov's face wasn't giving much away, if anything he looked a little shell-shocked, maybe almost sombre.

'I didn't just *tell* him what she found, I *showed* him.'

'Well, what was his reaction, what did he say?'

'He was pretty upset, to put it mildly.'

'Stephen, is it bad?' Carla asked. 'You guys said you thought I could get five or six hundred thousand. Is it a lot less? Is he going to make me go to court and testify in public?'

'Stephen, what happened?' Jessica asked.

'Okay, well, I'm not here with the offer we discussed.'

'Oh fuck!' said Betga under his breath.

'But,' Maserov continued, 'if you'll sign the offer I *did* bring with me, in full and final settlement of this matter, replete with a confidentiality clause, and with each side agreeing to bear its own costs, Torrent Industries will pay you . . . 2.6 million dollars.'

'You got him to offer me 2.6 million dollars?'

'Yep, that's right.'

'Oh fuck!' said Betga, no longer under his breath, before embracing Carla more strongly than he ever had before. When he released her she saw that Maserov and Jessica were also just coming out of their own embrace. Then Carla went over to Maserov to hug him.

'Stephen, I'm stunned! I can't believe you did this. I can't thank you enough.'

'Don't thank *me*. It's Jessica. I think I could have got you five or six hundred thousand, like I'd said. It was Jessica who added two million to this.'

'Jessica!' said Carla, now hugging her.

'*Now* we can open the champagne,' said Jessica, and the two of them went over to the fridge. 'Where are the glasses?'

'You get offers for Pauline, Lilly, and Monika?' Betga asked Maserov quietly.

'Yep,' said Maserov, handing him a slip of paper with figures corresponding to offers for the other three plaintiffs, all of them significantly higher than they would have been had Jessica not done her detective work. Betga smiled.

'Ooh! Good man! We can certainly live with *those* figures.'

'Again, it was Jessica's good work,' said Maserov, who put out his hand to shake Betga's hand. But Betga wasn't having any of it. He had Maserov in a hug too tight for Maserov to speak and only released him when he saw Jessica and Carla returning with the glasses of champagne.

'What did he say when you showed him Carla's report and the post-it note in Aileen's handwriting?' Jessica asked.

'He was furious. I think at that moment he wanted to fire every second person in the company's internal phone directory. I was even worried he might want to shoot the messenger. I still am.'

'What did you say?'

'I told him that, in my opinion, the immediate interests of the company were best served guaranteeing that these claims went away as soon as humanly possible.'

'And what did he say?'

'He saw the sense in this.'

'What's he going to do about Aileen van der Westhuizen?' Jessica asked.

'What's he going to do about Featherby?' Betga asked.

'I don't know. He said I've given him a lot to think about. As you can imagine, he wasn't happy. He asked me what I thought were the lowest figures that would make these cases go away in the next twenty-four hours.'

'He really put you on the spot.'

'Yeah, he often does.'

'But he always listens to you,' said Jessica. 'He always takes Stephen's advice,' she explained to the others with a small glint of pride.

'Well, he wants to see me in his office tomorrow morning at eleven. I guess he wants to talk through the ramifications of all of this.'

'Well, I'm pretty happy!' said Carla. 'To Stephen and Jessica.' And she and Betga drank to their guests.

'To Jessica and Stephen!' Betga added. 'And to your lawyer, too, who made everything but the original assault possible! Come on you guys, let's party like it's Y2K and we've just been engaged to perform a "due diligence" for Lehman Brothers!'

'Yes, let's party,' said Carla. 'Although we might well need to get more champagne. It's on me! I'm happy to spend at least as much as Mike Mercer would spend on his Indian *and* Iraqi marketing campaigns.'

'Marketing? He's not in marketing,' questioned Betga.

'No, I know, but every time he would go out for one of his boozy lunches with Frank Cardigan he'd tell me to get the marketing company to reimburse him.'

'Who was he marketing to?' Maserov asked.

'I don't know exactly but he'd tell me he was pitching to the Indian or the Iraqi government, part of one of the tender campaigns. He'd get me to invoice some marketing company and then send it through to Frank Cardigan. I always thought it was bogus but they always seemed to pay up so maybe it *was* legit. They even bought him a car.'

'What? The Torrent Industries marketing department bought him a car?' Maserov asked incredulously.

'No, it wasn't Torrent's marketing department, some other third-party marketing company. Can't remember the name. I don't know how he did it but Frank Cardigan always made sure Mercer got paid. I know because he used to make me do his banking, some of it anyway. I also had to get his dry-cleaning. Unbelievable perks that bastard got. Anyway, to hell with them both. I don't want to think about him.

Not even in therapy. We're going to need more champagne. But first I have to put this little one to bed,' she said, picking up her daughter off the floor. 'Give Uncle Stephen and Aunty Jessica a kiss goodnight.'

Carla brought Marietta over to Jessica, who kissed the little girl on the top of her head.

'Carla, she's such a beautiful little girl.'

'Thank you.'

'Well, she did very well in the genetic lottery,' Betga announced over his champagne.

'It's only a lottery for *you*,' said Carla. 'Everybody else has children intentionally, by design.'

'*You* didn't,' Betga shot back.

'Shut up, Betga. It's not too late for a paternity test,' Carla added.

'What if *I* go out to buy more champagne?' Betga volunteered. 'That's got to count for something.'

'Would it be alright if I came with you while you put Marietta to bed?' Jessica asked Carla.

'Of course,' said Carla. 'Let's see if she'll let you put her in her cot.'

Maserov watched as Carla gently gave Marietta to Jessica, who held the tired little girl carefully against her chest as they walked towards Marietta's bedroom. He couldn't help but smile to see the cautious way she held her. Then he thought of his own children and the smile vanished. They were eating their dinner in his house with his wife without him. He was back in the real world.

II

It was almost eleven o'clock and Maserov was due to be ushered into Malcolm Torrent's office by his inscrutable, elegantly dressed private secretary, Joan Henshaw, a woman who had been with the company so long that not only did she know where the company had buried its bodies but it was she who had signed for the acquisition of the shovels. Maserov wondered if she knew anything about the allegation he had brought to her boss concerning Aileen van der Westhuizen or about the advice the HR head had claimed to have received from Freely Savage's Featherby. He searched her face but found nothing there but a light-weight foundation, a dab of cream blush, a schmear of concealer and a fair quantity of concealment.

Despite the fact that Torrent was still on a phone call, she led Maserov into his office. Malcolm Torrent showed no sign of interest in his arrival other than to wave him into a chair opposite him. Maserov sat in the chair and waited for the call to end. The longer he waited the more he felt as he had when waiting for Hamilton. He tried to listen to the call to discern whether it had anything to do with any of the previous day's events but it was impossible to know what was being discussed because Malcolm Torrent was listening while the person on the other end did most of the talking. Then, after what seemed like a unit of time that had only a beginning, Malcolm Torrent uttered a sound that was part grunt, part snort and part affirmation in a language other than English before unceremoniously placing the receiver back in the cradle of his landline. Then he looked up at the separated father of two, the second-year Freely Savage lawyer who had gambled his way uncharacteristically out of the frying pan and into an office at Torrent Industry headquarters.

'Well Maserov, I have to commend you. I took a chance on you and it's certainly paid off.'

'Thank you, Mr Torrent.'

'You said you would make those sexual harassment suits disappear and you have.'

'Yes, sir. Thank you.'

'You're a bright young man who could be going places.'

'Thank you. *Where* . . . do you think?'

'But do you see how your success was inimical to your needs?'

'How?'

'When did we first meet, mid-April?'

'Yes.'

'Well, it's now only early July. You made the spate of sexual harassment claims go away before your twelve months were up.'

'So?' Maserov asked.

'You've thrust yourself back to a position of weakness.'

'That's my default position. I'm comfortable there.'

'You mean it's a tactic?'

'More a chronic condition.'

'Don't you see, Maserov, now that you've solved my problem so quickly, how are you going to ensure that you get what you wanted to get?'

'Mr Torrent . . . we had an agreement.'

'Which you would agree was unenforceable. You're the lawyer here.'

'But I did exactly what you wanted only faster than promised.'

'Exactly, there's your mistake right there.'

'So I'm going to be punished for —'

'No, no, the market doesn't *punish*. That assumes moral intention. Does water punish people who bought land at the bottom of a hill?'

'Are you the water or the hill in this?'

'I'm the market.'

'*You're* the market?'

'That's right.'

'*All* of it?'

'Usually. Look closely at our current situation; you've taken away my incentive.'

'To honour our agreement?'

'Maserov, you're hanging on to history. Look at the market *now*.'

'Look at you . . . now?'

'Yes.'

Maserov looked at Malcolm Torrent, who was smiling at him as though his apparent betrayal was a shining gift bestowed on a much-loved pupil.

'Trust me, you'll be better for this. You know what you have to do.'

'Yes. I have to . . . What do I have to do?'

'You need to look at the market as you find it *now* and ask yourself what you can do *now*.'

'To be desirable to the market?'

'Yes.'

'Which is you?'

'Might be a helpful way to think of it.'

'I have to make myself indispensable to you *again*?'

'I like your thinking,' Malcolm Torrent said, smiling.

'Or you'll shop me to Hamilton.'

'Maybe not.'

'How would I know?'

'Exactly! Don't take chances if you can help it.'

'Didn't you make your money taking chances?'

'Yep, worked for *me*. Although I inherited money so . . . All risk is relative. You know, I don't normally tutor people but I like . . . Oh, will you look at that!' Malcolm Torrent trailed off distractedly and started reading a newly arrived email.

'Me?' Maserov offered.

'What?' Malcolm Torrent asked absently.

'You like . . . *me*?'

'More than Hamilton', Malcolm Torrent said, still distracted by the just-arrived message.

'You like me more than you like Hamilton or you like me more than Hamilton likes me?'

Malcolm Torrent continued reading the email. 'Friendship's nice but like taxation it can distort the economy. Watch out for friendship,' Torrent volunteered. 'And don't trust in anything you can't trade. Okay, lesson over for today. I've got work to do. I think you have too.'

There had been no talk of Aileen van der Westhuizen or of Featherby, the compromised minion of Hamilton who, at least for a moment, hated and feared his boss more than he loved his children. Now Maserov was standing outside Torrent's office with one hand in a pocket, pretending to be fossicking for something while he tried to work out what had just happened. He'd done everything Malcolm Torrent could have wanted but too quickly.

III

'Betga was right, I should have been paying more attention to what was going to happen to me after the plaintiffs settled.'

'You're much too hard on yourself,' Jessica told him. 'You initiated countless delicate negotiations, many at personal peril, which at every turn looked like they were about to fall over and you arrived at an incredibly fair outcome for four women that even managed to be good for your client. I know, I was there too. And all while missing your children and virtually living out of a suitcase.'

It was the night after Maserov's meeting with Malcolm Torrent and they were back in the library section of Jessica's local cocktail bar, the Ghost of Alfred Felton, with the famously egoless bartenders. But there was one bartender who, having nurtured an ever-blossoming affection for Jessica, could not help but wonder if his ego had restrained his id for too long. To hell with the bartending job and its requirement that he not laud his skills with muddlers, tongs, shakers and shot glasses over any man who dared come within an arm's reach of this woman. He could shake crushed ice like the very best percussionist in the Banda de Ipanema during the Rio Mardi Gras. He could quip like the best late-night television sidekick and his innate understanding of people told him when to ask whether someone meant to order a traditional Negroni, a Negroni Bianco or a Negroni Sbagliato, and when to make the decision himself. But he now regarded himself as a fool for hiding his own feelings under the counter of an establishment in which he had no shares and where he was contractually forbidden from screaming when Jessica Annand looked with such unequivocal, heartbreaking warmth into Stephen Maserov's eyes.

'Personal peril . . . I know, I was there too,' Maserov repeated what she'd said and smiled. Jessica smiled in return and placed one of her hands on his forearm. The gesture was too much for the bartender. He knew that Jessica was going to find a reason, albeit thinly disguised, to take Maserov home for the first time. He knew it before Maserov did. He'd seen this kind of thing before. In fact he saw it several times every night. He was in its line of fire every working night and ought to have been paid danger money for it. Maserov hadn't seen this kind of thing for so long that he almost missed it. Almost.

Her flimsy excuse was that she wanted to show Maserov a draft of her policy recommendations to Torrent Industries to try to eradicate sexual harassment in the workplace. Of course, they both knew that she could have emailed them to him or, if she did want to discuss them with him in person, they could do that in one of their offices. But Maserov's description of his uncertainty as to the strength and now the terms of his deal with Malcolm Torrent had spurred her on. What if he suddenly stopped being available for her to see every day whenever she wanted? It made her feel like a lover in a time of war when what passes for the niceties of a peacetime society may well turn out be the passport to eternal regret. So they found themselves drinking more upstairs in her St Kilda apartment with their shoes off, pretending to be focusing intensely on the statutory definition of sexual harassment in the workplace.

At that point their shared look into the face of the other blocked out all thoughts of anything else. The sweetness of the shared smile triggered the memory of one thing only, the hunger of their kissing that first night, its ferocity. To be that close again and not in the street but alone on Jessica's couch, to be in private, to already know that neither of them needed to be embarrassed, at least not to kiss, because they were two people who enjoyed kissing each other. This had been established and this emboldened them. He undid the buttons of her blouse with one hand and then felt the contours of her breast with the palm of the other hand. Was she going to pull away? Was she going to ask him to stop, even politely, with gentle esteem-saving regret? Why should she? No, not only was she not going to stop him, she kissed him even more frantically, greedily. He returned her kiss with equal vigour. But in contrast, his cautious exploration of her breasts through her bra was like that of young man unsure of whether the very next step would be a misstep, a retrograde step that could lead to a reconsideration of what they were now, unequivocally, doing. Wanting to encourage him, wanting the fury of their kissing to be matched wherever they touched, she unhooked her bra and slid one strap off her shoulder. Then he slid the strap off her other shoulder.

She was now naked to the waist. He stopped kissing her for a moment and leaned back to take in the sight of her breasts, something he had so often fought not to think about, not to look at, not to imagine. She smiled. Her nipples were hard. She was not afraid at all and she put one hand to the crease of his suit pants and followed it all the way to the crotch where it was warm, hard. Then she stood up, took him to her bedroom, unzipped her skirt and proceeded to undress him.

She peeled the cover off her bed slowly and guided him down. This was her bedroom. These were her sheets. This was the smell of her and soon, at least for some unspecified time, of him, of his skin wrapped in her sheets. He wrapped himself around her, pressed against her tightly and then, slowly, entered her. He felt a radiant joy he hadn't felt since his early twenties.

For Jessica, here at last was the real thing. She hadn't had to preen or pretend to be someone she, herself, didn't much like. She had taken a chance on being herself to a man who was in many senses an old-fashioned gentleman, not in the sense of being a man of property or of a distinguished lineage, but in the sense of being a gentle man of integrity who possessed a strength he himself didn't know he had, an intelligent man, a compassionate man, who was honest to a fault, his own faults to start with. He was handsome in a way that, like his other qualities, didn't shout or draw attention to itself. But once glimpsed it was undeniable.

From the time Jessica discovered that men were attracted to her, which slightly preceded the time she first realised *she* was attracted to men, she had always sought the company and attention of men whose belief in their own worth, whose so often misplaced, unshakeable self-confidence had seemed intoxicatingly worthy of her own abasement. These men were the prizes, the ones you went after for the proof of your own prettiness and desirability despite your differences, even if you had to squint sometimes to avoid a clear-eyed recognition of their fetishisation of you and of your background and their sooner-or-later drunken mockery of the customs and accents of your family.

But Jessica had grown up. Here was the proof of that beside her. Stephen Maserov, the antithesis of those men, he was the real prize, and as she lay beside him there she celebrated finding him. And it wasn't just good fortune. He was devouring her again. It wasn't the act that animated him. Undeniably it was her.

And as finally somnolence overtook him, Maserov recognised what a miracle it was to have met someone like Jessica in, of all places, his place of work, the sort of place where so often the only thing people really had in common was the compulsion to contort the essence of themselves into a facsimile of someone else.

At one stage Maserov woke while it was still dark, thinking about his children. Whatever was going to happen, he couldn't live without them. He wanted the feeling he got from Jessica *and* he wanted to live with his children, children he would never try to separate from Eleanor. He even wanted Eleanor, but the way she used to be. And he wanted Jessica, breathing Jessica, urgently. Uncharacteristically, because logical inconsistency was an anathema to him, he was able to convince himself that all of this was possible and he fell back to sleep.

He was suddenly in some kind of pit, about to be executed by firing squad, when the light reflected from the bay across the St Kilda Esplanade woke him from a nightmare. His brow was moist with his own sweat. And he was alone. Jessica was not there.

Before he had a chance to imagine where she had gone, she came into the bedroom, showered, dressed for work and more beautiful than ever with a glass of freshly squeezed orange juice.

'I squeezed this for you,' she said, kissing his forehead as she gave it to him. 'You're wet! Are you unwell?'

'No, I think . . . I just had a nightmare.'

'What about?'

'I was going to be executed by firing squad.'

'Oh my God!' She sat down on the bed. 'You're worried about your job.'

'I guess so.'

She took his hand. 'You know, that might be premature, and even if it's not, you'll find something else. And maybe the first thing you find isn't ideal but it doesn't have to be the last thing, the thing you ultimately settle for.'

'I don't have any savings, not to speak of.'

'No one does. And just so you know . . .'

'What?'

'I don't care whether you have any money. I don't care whether you have a job. Those things come and go, faster than ever these days. I've seen who you really are. The qualities that make you the person I've come to know, they don't change.'

Now he took her hand. 'You're dressed for work, already?'

'It's already past *already*,' she said.

Maserov looked at his watch. 'Oh shit!'

'I've got a meeting,' Jessica continued calmly. 'You stay here as long as you like. There's a towel for you. Have a shower. Enjoy the view of the bay and call me when you get to work.'

She kissed him on the lips, turned, and he listened to the sounds of her leaving.

IV

There were brown thornbills and red wattlebirds in the trees and pink robins on the sagging overhead powerlines, all of them cheeping that morning when, coming back home after taking Marietta to the park, Carla found Betga waiting at the front door. She had been without work following the unsurprising collapse of the wishbone company. Betga kissed her cheek and lifted his daughter into his arms before kissing her too.

'Is something wrong?' Carla asked, as though his appearance in the morning without warning or invitation could be explained only by the need to break bad news in person.

'Nothing we can't fix.'

'What is it?' she asked anxiously.

'Well, it appears the council garbage truck has already visited the street. It collected everybody's garbage but inadvertently missed ours, I mean, "yours".'

'Oh shit! I forgot to put it out last night,' Carla remembered.

'That's okay, *I* put it out last night.'

'*You* did? When?'

'While you were on the phone to your mother.'

'Betga, that's so thoughtful. You're really trying to domesticate yourself.'

'Yes, I really am, but the council, or the people to whom they've outsourced Black Death prevention, are thwarting me at every turn. Or really just at one turn, the one into this street. But don't worry. I'll call them.'

She kissed him again and unlocked the front door and the three of them went inside. Betga wasn't very far into the house when he felt and heard his phone ring and he saw that it was Maserov.

'Top of the morning to you, Maserov.'

'Right back at you, Betga,' said Maserov glumly. 'Listen, I've got problems.'

'Do they impact *me*?'

'You know, I haven't actually turned my mind to that yet.'

'Do you want to call me back when you have? Oh never mind, I could use an excuse to delay my next call. I have to lecture a representative of the City of Port Phillip about the devastation of medieval Europe wrought by the bacterium *Yersinia pestis*. Again! Last time I tried, they thought I was making disparaging remarks about a young Greek woman.'

'Betga, what the hell are you talking about?'

'Carla's rubbish wasn't collected this morning. What's up, Maserov?'

'Well, I'm not sure about this but I think it's possible I might have lost my protection from Malcolm Torrent. I'm not sure he'd back me now if Hamilton tries to get rid of me.'

'You're kidding? What did you do?'

'What did I do? I found out exactly what was bothering him and I fixed it . . . much too quickly. I made what he saw as the spate of sexual harassment claims filed against Torrent Industries disappear well within the year in which I had to do it. Now he doesn't need me anymore. So he *might* get rid of me.'

'He *might* or he *will*?'

'That's the thing, Betga, it was hard to be sure. I didn't entirely understand what he was saying. He was kind of cryptic, enigmatic.'

'Maserov, he's an extremely powerful man. He has no choice but to be either cryptic or hostile. This is what power does to a man, pushes him into that corner. You need him to need you again.'

'You know, that's what *he* said . . . I *think*.'

'I'm at Carla's. Why don't you come over? Are you at Torrent headquarters?'

'No.'

'Are you at home?'

'No.'

'Where are you?'

'I'm in St Kilda.'

'You're in St Kilda?'

'Yes.'

'Could you be *less* specific?'

'Given time, yes. I could be there in five minutes. Are you sure it's alright with Carla if I come around now?'

'Maserov, you're her hero. When she hears you might be in trouble, especially on her account, she'll do anything for you. She'll knit you a chicken.'

'I don't know what that means.'

'Just get here. Oh wait! One more question.'

'Yes?'

'Does Jessica live in St Kilda?'

There was silence on the other end of the phone. 'How do you knit a chicken?' Maserov asked eventually.

'No further questions.'

Betga had explained Maserov's predicament to Carla, which accounted for the strength and duration of the hug she gave Maserov when she opened her front door and let him in. When they were all in Carla's living room she offered to make coffee and Betga accepted for both of them. Marietta was on the floor, playing with her cuddle friends, a menagerie of bears, bunnies and an echidna.

'I had a dream last night, woke up short of breath, in a panic,' said Maserov. 'I was taken to a quarry of sorts, an open-air salt mine, where I was to be shot on the orders of Stalin. In fact, Stalin was there, in attendance. He was right on top of the ravine giving the orders to a group of goons, soldiers or perhaps they were KGB men.'

'No, wouldn't have been KGB,' said Betga. 'In Stalin's time they were called variously the CHEKA, then the OGPU and then the NKVD.

And someone like you wouldn't have been shot in a salt mine. More likely in a courtyard or a cell in Lubyanka prison in Moscow, I'd say, but *do* go on.'

'Sorry Betga, I apologise for the historical inaccuracies of my unconscious.'

'Not at all. Please continue.'

'Well, there I was at this open-air salt mine type place, standing in a pit with my back to the firing squad, and they've lined me up next to Malenkov, Beria, Molotov, Khrushchev and some others I couldn't quite make out.'

'Wow, that's exalted company. And historically possible, but go on. Stalin's there. Is he in the pit with you?'

'No, like I said, he's above us on the ridge of the pit or the ravine or whatever it was. Talking down to us.'

'You realise,' Betga interrupted, 'Stalin is Hamilton. I mean, in your unconscious, that's who he represents.'

'You think?'

'Gotta be.'

'So I'm in the pit and I turn around and I call out. I tell Stalin I have a sleep mask, you know, one of those face masks you wear in bed to shut out the light and help you sleep? I tell him I have one in my pocket and I ask him if I may be permitted to wear it when they shoot me.'

'Even though they're going to shoot you in the back?'

'Yep.'

'What did Stalin say?'

'He told me to take it out slowly and to hold it up away from my body, which I did. And then he praised me for being prepared, praised me to everyone.'

'Wow! Hamilton would *never* have done that.'

'No, I know. For a moment I was feeling pretty good about things.'

'Sure, you got praise from Stalin. What happened then?'

'Well, it went quiet for a second and then there was a burst of machine-gun fire. The firing squad shot holes in my sleep mask. The sun burst through the bullet holes and I woke up with the sun in my eyes.'

'You know,' said Betga, thinking out loud, 'on second thought, Stalin *isn't* Hamilton, he's Malcolm Torrent. But the salt mine is Freely Savage.'

'Yeah, *I* could see that.'

'Did you notice the characteristics of any of your fellow lawyers in Malenkov, Beria, Molotov or Khrushchev?'

'No, not really. Oh wait, yes! Beria had a certain scent I recognised, incredibly alluring and yet terrifying.'

'Beria, chief of the secret police, smelled alluring to you?'

'Yes, I remember now. He smelled exactly like Fleur Werd-Gelding. She's another Second Year, known for her beauty and her cruelty. She smells great.'

'I see,' said Betga. 'Maserov, this has got you spooked. You need to get a grip, get back on the horse and go back fighting.'

'Back where?'

'Into Malcolm Torrent's office. You need to remind him that you're indispensable to him.'

'But maybe I no longer *am* indispensable to him.'

'We will make him see you as indispensable.'

'No one sees me that way, not even my wife. So how can I make this amoral, capricious construction tycoon see me that way?'

'Play to his fears and his dislike of Hamilton. You've done it once before but by chance. You learned what he was afraid of. Now milk that cow!'

'He was afraid of bad publicity from a spate of sexual harassment suits that would drive down the price of his company's shares and generally give it a taint. But I've settled, *we've* settled all the claims.'

'You want more? I could give you more. How many do you want?'

'Real or fabricated?'

'Real take longer but you know they're out there. Give me a week, I'll give you three more. That place is a white-collar cesspool.'

'No, he thinks I've solved his problem. If more sexual harassment claims start surfacing, what good am I? And anyway, he'll get suspicious if there's suddenly a flurry of them. Or he'll think that settling the first four has just opened the floodgates and that I've only made his problems worse.'

'You realise what you're saying?' said Betga. 'If you've *solved* his problems your situation's precarious and if you *haven't* solved his problems your situation's precarious.'

'Yes, I think that's what I'm saying.'

'Maserov, you need to identify problems he doesn't yet realise he might have and then show him that you have the capacity to solve them.'

'Have you got any ideas as to how to do that?'

'Sure. Of course I do. You should none-too-subtly warn him that someone could tell the Law Institute or even the court or, worse still, the media, what Hamilton by proxy ordered a Torrent Industries officer to do with Carla's report. After all, it might be possible to portray Mike Mercer as a lone sexual offender in a suit but the cover-up is institutional. The company could always try to hang him out to dry but there's no carpet they can sweep *this* under.'

'Well, the Law Institute and even the court won't care. The cases are settled and I cleaned it up for Featherby just by filing an amended affidavit of documents that included Carla's statement and then giving it to you.'

'Yeah, but only a lawyer would know that. Malcolm Torrent won't know that.'

'So you want me to mislead him?'

'Not in so many words.'

'You want me to mislead him through a series of hand gestures?'

'No, Maserov, you say it but you don't say it. You imply that the story of the buried incriminating document *could* get out. It might, one never knows. You're envisaging, foreseeing problems and helping him to avoid them.'

'What's my advice? What advice do I give him to help him avoid them?'

'You tell him what's likely to go down.'

'Which is?'

'Aileen van Beethoven is going to put the blame entirely on Featherby and he's going to shaft Hamilton because he doesn't want to wear this for the rest of his career and he's dead anyway, as far as Hamilton is concerned. I mean, why wouldn't he tell the truth and put it all on Hamilton if he's dead already, right? Hamilton would kill him for much less than this. So, to prevent Featherby going public, Malcolm Torrent needs to buy his silence.'

'You're suggesting that my salvation lies in advising Malcolm Torrent to bribe Featherby?'

'Not in so many words.'

'Betga, how many words . . . can I use . . . to suggest to Malcolm Torrent that he bribe Featherby?'

'Maserov, will you relax? Your tone of voice suggests tremendous agitation.'

'Betga, I'm in a salt mine getting shot by Stalin and his KGB henchmen!'

'Yes, and as I explained that's ahistorical and even *there* he's praising your foresight for having the face mask *and* you're standing beside the sweet-smelling Beria. It's not all bad. Look, Maserov, we're not talking brown paper bags or Swiss bank accounts in Mrs Featherby's name.'

'What do you want me to suggest to Malcolm Torrent to neutralise the threat of Featherby going public with this when Hamilton comes after him?'

'You should suggest to Malcolm Torrent that, when Featherby returns from General Anxiety Disorder leave, he be given a job in Torrent Industries' in-house legal department with the other survivors.'

'Betga, you're brilliant! A safe haven for Featherby, a soft landing on the condition that he never mentions Hamilton's instruction to bury Carla's report.'

'Yes, its brilliance resides in its simplicity and simultaneous comprehensiveness. In one blow it achieves many things; you've yet again demonstrated how much Malcolm Torrent needs you, you've found a problem for him before *he* did *and* found a painless solution for him. You even saved Featherby, which on behalf of the FSS, we thank you for.'

'What about Aileen van der Westhuizen, what's he meant to do with her?'

'Hmmm,' thought Betga. 'Keep her on but reprimand her, tell her she's being watched and had better tread carefully.'

'What exactly does that mean?'

'It means anything anybody needs it to mean. It will scare her. She's not likely to go to the media with her own dishonesty, especially not when her job depends on it. Maserov, all you've got to do is sell all of this to him. That's all. Oh, and one more thing, but this might well be the hardest part of all.'

'What's that?'

'You've got to tell him that as far as you can see, taking care of Featherby and Aileen von Ribbentrop is very *likely* to staunch the flow of negative information but there will still always be a tiny but everpresent danger of it getting out from that small group of unidentified people, that cohort of persons who both know what happened and who hate Hamilton.'

'A lot of people hate Hamilton,' said Maserov.

'Yeah, but how many of them know about the attempt to bury Carla's report?'

'You and . . . me.'

'Exactly,' said Betga. 'Malcolm Torrent's not stupid. He'll know what you're saying.'

'What will I be saying?'

'You'll be saying that you hate Hamilton *and* you know what he did. You'll be saying that Malcolm Torrent wouldn't want you to be unhappy or the story could get out.'

'You want me to blackmail Malcolm Torrent?'

'No. Not blackmail, certainly not, not in so many words. Do it right, you won't even need words. You're not blackmailing him.'

'No, I'd merely be *threatening* to blackmail him.'

'No, you'd be allowing him to consider that this is a theoretical possibility.'

'That I could blackmail him?'

'Yes, but not in so many words. Maserov, you'd be derelict in your duty not to point out all the potential dangers of which you have become aware.'

Carla returned with two coffee cups. 'How do you take your coffee, Stephen?'

'He needs it in something he can drink in the car.'

'Are you leaving already?'

'Yes,' answered Betga on his behalf. 'Maserov needs to talk to Malcolm Torrent again as soon as he can.'

'Do you mind if I just drink my coffee first?' Maserov asked.

'Of course not. But if you'll excuse me, I have to get the City of Port Phillip to see the error of its contractor's ways and come back for Carla's and especially Marietta's waste before the Black Death visits St Kilda.'

Betga picked up the phone and put it on speaker so that Maserov and Carla could hear the whole exchange. He was put on hold and eventually they all heard, 'City of Port Phillip, Yolanda speaking. How may we assist you today?'

Betga spoke slowly and extremely clearly into the phone but nonetheless his words were not immediately understood by the City of Port Phillip's Yolanda. He sounded a lot like a recorded message.

'Yolanda, thank you for taking the call of a resident of the City of Port Phillip. Your call is important to us. Please be aware that this call could be recorded for coaching and training purposes or for pillorying on social media. Should you wish to read *our* privacy policy please see the underside of the garbage bin designated for this house. This may prove hard to achieve since the bin is currently full despite it being collection day.'

V

Maserov agreed that he needed to put something along the lines of Betga's suggestion to Malcolm Torrent but he wanted a little more ammunition in the battle to present himself as indispensable. Without making an appointment Maserov went to the offices of Freely Savage and knocked on the door of the senior partner in Emerging Markets, Mr Radhakrishnan, a man Maserov thought had smiled at him in the hallway on more than one occasion. Mr Radhakrishnan's office had a window facing out into the heavens but somehow it was nowhere near as intimidating to Maserov as Hamilton's office. For a start it was nowhere near as big as Hamilton's office and, crucially, it didn't have Hamilton in it. It was widely known that the correlation between the square meterage of real estate and power was precise to a degree that could only be explained by quantum mechanics. It was not an insignificant office. No partner's office could be.

Maserov wondered what extraordinary abilities, faculties, insights, experience, connections or some combination of all of these had enabled this man, who was born in India, who spoke with an accent, who had not gone to school with any of the other partners, to reach the rank of partner, the only person with brown skin above the level of First Year and those in the mail room or IT section. He had a Masters from Oxford but was not a member of any club that would not have someone like him as a member, except one. He was a partner in the Melbourne office of Freely Savage Carter Blanche.

Maserov knocked on his door. 'Excuse me, Mr Radhakrishnan. I wondered if you had a few minutes.'

Mr Radhakrishnan looked up from the document he had been reading on his desk with surprise and, before he had a chance to say anything, Maserov felt the need to add, 'Sir, you probably don't know who I am but —'

'No, I do know who you are. I'm pretty sure I do.' There was that slight smile again.

'You do?' asked Maserov, who was now taking *his* turn to be surprised.

'You are Stephen Maserov, the Second Year who has fled temporarily to Torrent Industries HQ, having fuelled a vexation in Mr Hamilton the like of which no Second Year in the history of this firm has ever done.' The smile broadened to the point where even an uninterested observer would have concluded that Hamilton's vexation was at the very least entertaining to Radhakrishnan. 'Please come in,' the older man said, before adding, 'And close the door.'

Maserov was delighted to be asked to close the door although, since he had no expectation of his position at Freely Savage surviving any transient protection offered by Malcolm Torrent, it was arguable that whether or not the door was closed would affect his life far less than would the flapping of a butterfly's wings in Japan.

'Sir, I won't take up too much of your time. I have, as you said, been working at Torrent Industries and I wanted to ask you some questions that I thought might come under the heading of emerging markets.'

'Go ahead.'

'Well . . . when a company, say a construction company, an *unnamed* construction company, does business in, say, Iraq, after the invasion, after the toppling of Saddam Hussein, does it need to specifically *market* itself, its service to the new government?'

'To *market* itself? No, there's no need for marketing as such. If the new government needs a highway or a new bridge, for example, it might call for tenders and then select from the best of the tenders. That's generally how it's done, how it *should* be done.'

'So,' continued Maserov, 'there shouldn't be any need for a marketing spend, a marketing budget from within, say, the urban infrastructure department of said *unnamed* construction company?'

Mr Radhakrishnan smiled. 'Has a young lawyer, in the vicinity of, say, a Second Year, found evidence of an allocation of resources described as a *marketing* budget?'

'Young lawyers age rapidly these days so they're not so young anymore but other than that, the assumption in your question, sir, might be correct.'

'I see.' Mr Radhakrishnan smiled again.

'Another question occurs to me, Mr Radhakrishnan, a completely unrelated one.'

'Yes?'

'Is it illegal for a company, say a construction company, to bribe officials, bureaucrats or even members of a foreign government in order to win a contract?'

'Oh yes, most certainly. It is in *this* country.'

'That's what I thought. Thank you, Mr Radhakrishnan. I don't want to take up any more of your time.'

And with that Maserov got up and began to walk towards the closed door of Radhakrishnan's office.

'Just a moment, Stephen. I have a question for you. Is it really true that you made an offer to Malcolm Torrent to clean up his sexual harassment problems?'

'Yes, sir.'

'And it's this that has you working out of Torrent Industries HQ?'

'Yes, that's right.'

'And how are you getting along with that?'

'I'd think Mr Torrent would be pleased with my progress on that front.'

The older man smiled in appreciation of Maserov's audacity and gently nodded his head as if he'd just tasted the perfect example of his favourite dish, indicating unequivocally that he was no supporter of Hamilton's. Yet he hadn't said a word to that effect.

Maserov went back to his office at Torrent Industries headquarters and called Betga to tell him what he'd learned and what he suspected, namely that Mike Mercer was in some way involved in bribery in order to guarantee the Torrent Industries tender for various construction projects was successful and that this was illegal.

'*I* knew it was illegal,' said Betga. 'You didn't need a partner to tell you that. Bribery is illegal.'

'I wanted to hear it from a partner, okay! So sue me! Additionally, I wanted a partner to hear it from *me*,' Maserov said in his own defence.

'If that's supposed to mean what I think it's supposed to mean —'

'What do you think it's supposed to mean?' Maserov interrupted Betga.

'You mean that somehow by having one of the partners know that you suspect that someone at Torrent Industries has engaged in the bribery of a foreign government that your position at Freely Savage is somehow safer.'

'Yeah, when you put it that way, I guess it sounds kind of hopeless.'

'Hopeless? It's utterly stupid to the point of stretching the meaning of stupid towards "sad", after which it shatters into tiny pieces detectable only with a microscope. It's so sad it's not even wrong. Forget trying to find protection from any of the partners at Freely Savage. Wipe that possibility out of your mind. They're as scared of Hamilton as you are. And no one on their letterhead is going to stick their neck out to save your sorry arse. What you need to do is go to Malcolm Torrent with all this. Go and see him and tell him everything we discussed and now this too, about the bribery.'

'But I don't actually have any evidence of the bribery. I merely suspect it because Carla said that Mike Mercer and Frank Cardigan had a marketing budget. That's not enough to go to Malcolm Torrent with.'

'No, it *is* enough. Just ask him a few questions that suggest you're suspicious. That will buy you time.'

'I'm *always* trying to buy time. But I'm never safe.'

'Safety is relative, Maserov. It's a construct. It's no longer anyone's lived reality.'

'Hamilton's safe. Malcolm Torrent's safe.'

'Two people are not statistically significant, Maserov, not even those two. You should know that. Anyway, Tsar Nicholas II once thought *he* was safe.'

'Once he *was* safe.'

'Yes, that's true. Then a moment later he was overthrown and, before you could say "Felix Dzerzhinsky", he was shot and thrown down a mineshaft. Look, you're safer than Featherby. Go and see Malcolm Torrent. Bring him all that you know *and* all your unfounded suspicions. It will buy you time. Buying time is the new *safe*.'

Maserov did immediately try to get an appointment with Malcolm Torrent to do all that Betga advised but the tsar of Torrent Industries had gone to Lizard Island, off the coast of Far North Queensland, to repose, strategise, and look at fish the size of Mike Tyson, which, if no one was watching, he would kill, and he wouldn't be back for another two days. As things transpired this helped Maserov enormously because of a discovery he and Betga made in the interim. Carla, after the attack but before she left the company, had surreptitiously downloaded a trove of documents, including private emails from Mike Mercer's desktop computer.

'Why didn't you tell me you'd done this?' Betga implored her.

'I did it in anger, on the sly, but then I worried I could get in trouble for doing it. I didn't really know what use it would be or even why I'd done it. It was like stealing something of his, a kind of revenge, not very well thought out, a spur of the moment type thing. Look, I thought I could get into trouble.'

'Not from me and I'm your lawyer,' Betga replied.

'I didn't think to tell you because what relevance can documents have in a sexual assault case? *I'm* the evidence, my testimony, right? If people don't believe *me*, how can some document help? And anyway, he wasn't likely to have made a diary entry, "Attempted rape on Carla Monterosso last night. Try again Wednesday. Remember to buy wife flowers in re anniversary. Likes saffron crocus. Have rape victim place order."'

'Carla, I can't believe you did this. It's absolutely brilliant!'

'You sound surprised, like I wasn't capable of something so brilliant. Is that it?'

'Not at all! Although that's an entirely permissible inference to make and no one, least of all me, could fairly blame you for making it. But still, I can't believe you didn't tell me.'

'It *is* illegal, isn't it?'

'Absolutely! Especially given what *we* want to use it for. How did you do it?'

'It's not that hard. He always left his computer on so I just went into his office while he was at lunch. Remember, I used to do his banking sometimes. I knew he pretty much always used one of three passwords; MercyMike, MercyMike1 or MercyMikeMike1. I got lucky on the second try and then, as though it were a dagger, stuck a 128-gig USB stick into his computer, right clicked on Documents, clicked Copy and then pasted them to the USB. Did a similar thing again with his email and contacts via Microsoft Outlook. As far as I know, I got everything he had on his computer at the time I did it, which was within an hour of me leaving.'

There were so many documents to go through that, even working late into the night over two nights, the combined efforts of Maserov and Betga were insufficient to make anything but a dent in the quantity of documents to be read before Maserov's appointment with Malcolm Torrent. They hadn't been able to find Mike Mercer's banking records even though Carla assured them that she got everything from Mercer's computer.

'Now I know how the FBI felt with the clock ticking down in the days before Brett Kavanaugh was confirmed to the US Supreme Court,' commented Maserov, late into the second night at Carla's place.

'Yeah, but they had it much easier than us,' said Betga. 'They knew exactly what they were looking for and were expressly forbidden to speak to anyone who could help them find it.'

Maserov was shown into Malcolm Torrent's office without the smoking gun he wanted. In the previous hour he had rehearsed his strategy, which was to present himself as Malcolm Torrent's protector, an ever-vigilant professional who was looking out for the man, his company, its reputation and its value as perceived by the stock market, a sort of new-generation consigliere.

He opened with, 'In my capacity as your lawyer,' which was in itself audacious since Maserov was only a Second Year clinging precariously to his employment by a thread no stronger than that which secures a child's first baby tooth to its gum in the menacing presence of an arrogant, coked-up tooth fairy, whereas Torrent Industries had a division of in-house lawyers and an entire army of out-house lawyers at Freely Savage, led by the omnipotent Hamilton who, more than any other individual, was the one most aptly described as Malcolm Torrent's lawyer.

But when Maserov saw that Malcolm Torrent had neither flinched nor sought to correct his description of their relationship, he felt emboldened enough to convey to him that he perceived a danger to the company if word got out to the media that anyone at Torrent Industries had tried to bury an employee's written account of her sexual assault at the hands of a co-worker, a superior, a male, and notwithstanding the confidentiality clause that was part of the settlement agreement with the plaintiff Carla Monterosso, he, Maserov, would advise keeping others with knowledge of the 'burying' inside the tent, specifically Aileen van der Westhuizen and the Freely Savage lawyer, Featherby.

'If they did the wrong thing,' Malcolm Torrent asked with concern, 'why should I keep them "inside the tent", as you say?'

'Because if you don't, here's how it's going to go down,' Maserov began, surprising himself with his sudden unpremeditated immersion into a character more usually identified with Humphrey Bogart. But here he was, a latter-day Paul Muni look-alike, adopting the role with the same almost reckless gusto that had got him into Malcolm Torrent's consciousness in the first place.

'Your Aileen van der Westhuizen is going to say Featherby told her to do it. Featherby's either going to deny it or place the blame on Hamilton. Hamilton's going to deny it and then you've got an aggrieved Featherby, out of work, and thirsty for revenge.'

'Revenge? Revenge on who?'

'On Hamilton. So then he's a chance to go rogue, to go public with the allegation that Hamilton ordered him to bury evidence unfavourable to Torrent Industries. It might all be on Freely Savage, on Hamilton in particular, or those in the know, but it's going to stain Torrent Industries. Already Featherby's gone to ground.'

'Where is he?'

'Officially he's on stress leave for a mental health issue. Clearly he's dodging Hamilton but Betga says he can find him.'

'Find him!' said Malcolm Torrent sternly.

'Betga's on it right now. But when we do find him, we need to be able to tell him that he's got a nice soft landing as an in-house lawyer at Torrent Industries but only if he remembers who his friends are, only if he plays nice. Mr Torrent, we don't know *how* many people inside Torrent Industries *or* Freely Savage know about this. We need, as soon as possible, to get those two indebted to the good graces of the company and find out how many people know and who those people are because those people are a danger to your share price. In fact,' continued Maserov, now about to take a step that was potentially too far, a Betga kind of step, 'anyone,' he said with slow emphasis, 'anyone who knows about this and has a grievance against Hamilton should be looked after.'

He let his words hang in the air to see if he'd actually said them. He'd come this far in the service of a job to pay the mortgage to save his house to resurrect his marriage and be with his children. Maybe he'd just blown everything he'd been working for. So he decided to say more.

'Sir, you probably need to know why Mr Hamilton told Featherby to tell your Aileen to bury the document.'

'You're believing Featherby over Hamilton, are you?'

'Are *you*, Mr Torrent?'

'Let me ask the questions, Maserov. Do *you* believe that Hamilton ordered Featherby to hide the secretary's report?'

'Sir, no one at Freely Savage willingly, knowingly, does anything that goes against the orders, instructions or even the assumed predilections of Mike Hamilton.'

'*You* did.'

'Yes sir, I did.'

'Okay, so let's assume Hamilton ordered Featherby to bury the document. What's really so wrong with that, at least as far as I'm concerned? I didn't know anything about it and had the document stayed buried we would have been able to settle with the young lady at a much lower price. So he was trying to help me.'

'Yes, he was trying to help you, like he was trying to help you with all the sexual harassment cases. Your best-case scenario in terms of your bottom line would have been that no one in your employ rapes or sexually assaults anyone else. That's the gold standard. That's what we're aiming for. Next best case, if there is an attack and the victim reports it, the company employs an accredited outside arms-length body to investigate the matter. If the evidence is there, the company offers counselling to the victim, offers compensation from the company's insurance, sanctions the culprit and considers supporting the victim to take it to the police. Then you're morally, legally and financially covered.

'If you bury the report, however, you find yourself paying a premium to keep it out of court, out of the media and out of the consideration of investors. The premium isn't just the extra offered in settlement to the victim. It's also the cost of, say, buying the co-operation of Freely Savage's Featherby who's gone into hiding from Hamilton and even Betga's fee for finding him.

'Clearly Mr Hamilton's strategy was seriously flawed and is costing you, if indeed it was his idea to bury Carla Monterosso's report.'

There was silence and Maserov waited to see the older man's response but he didn't have to wait long. Malcolm Torrent was smiling. 'You have been doing your work, haven't you, Maserov?' he asked rhetorically.

'Thank you, Mr Torrent. Can I ask you a question on a separate but related topic?'

'Yes.'

'The firm obviously has a marketing department which would have a marketing budget, right?'

'Yes.'

'Does the urban infrastructure department have access to the marketing department's budget?'

'No.'

'So if someone from the urban infrastructure department was spending big on marketing, say, marketing to officials of a foreign government, that would surprise you?'

'What are you getting at, Maserov?' Torrent's brow was furrowed now and Maserov thought he should have quit while he was ahead.

'Is there a reason why . . .?' Maserov stopped. He had one foot over a ledge and was about to jump. A voice in his head was telling him to stop talking.

'What country are you referring to?'

Maserov almost whispered the answer and with the upward inflection often associated with a question. 'Iraq.'

Malcolm Torrent got up from his seat behind his desk and walked over towards the Second Year. Maserov thought he was going to be hit. Well, how much could it hurt? But then, sun-tanned and full of vigour, perhaps the old man could indeed pack a wallop. He didn't though but kept walking towards the door, leaving Maserov to wonder if he was simply going to walk out of the room. Should he say something? Should he apologise perhaps? But the old man didn't leave the room. He simply closed the door to his office and walked calmly back to his side of the desk and sat down again.

'As you might imagine, Maserov, this is a huge, sprawling company. I can't stay on top of everything, as much as I'd like to. I have to give my people a certain amount of autonomy otherwise nothing would ever get done. Now the boys in Urban Infrastructure, leaving aside this sexual assault business, they do a tremendous job. They don't market. They have to prepare tenders to the new government of Iraq. They're very good at it. They win the contracts. And I let them do whatever they need to do to get the job done. But I don't trouble myself with the nuts and bolts, the mechanics of how they go about things. One hears, from time to time, stories about the requirements of these governments, apparently they do try some outrageous stunts. But I'm sure they're often just cloak-and-dagger type stories to keep the chaps amused, war stories perhaps. Are you with me, Maserov? Just stories for the troops, I suppose. But I don't actually know anything about it, myself. You're certainly a hard worker, Maserov. I like that about you but don't work yourself too hard. You'll exhaust yourself and your judgment might suffer. You could see problems that aren't there. And neither of us would want that.'

VI

'They're bribing the Iraqis and Malcolm Torrent knows all about it,' Maserov told Betga when he returned to Carla's house.

'Shit! He told you that?'

'He did, not in so many words but there was no ambiguity in what he was and was not saying.'

'Well, if he knows all about it then we can't use this information to keep you safe but it sounds like you're already —'

'I thought nobody's safe anymore?' Maserov interrupted.

'Well, it sounds like certain members of the Iraqi government are safe, which is, you know, kind of ironic in its way, don't you think?'

'If buying time is the new safe,' continued Maserov unperturbed, 'I probably *am* a bit safer than I was before the meeting but when will that bought time run out? What's it really worth?'

'It would have helped if we could have found some irregularity in Mike Mercer's banking records,' Betga mused.

'Yes, but that would have required us finding his banking records, which don't appear to be in our possession.'

'Of course they are,' said Carla. 'I told you, I got everything.'

'Well, *show* me a file labelled "banking",' Betga implored her.

'He didn't have a file labelled "banking". He labelled his banking file something else.'

'What?' shouted Betga and Maserov in unison.

'Do you know what he labelled it?' Betga asked.

'Yes, I think so. I'd recognise it. I used to do his banking sometimes.'

'Why didn't you tell us?' Betga asked.

'I didn't know you were looking for his banking details. You didn't tell me that nor did you ask for my help in finding it.'

'We thought he'd file his banking file under "banking".'

'Yeah, when we couldn't find it we just assumed you hadn't got it.'

'No, I'm pretty sure I got it. I do remember he had some really annoying, masturbatory, juvenile, self-referential name for his banking file. Most self-respecting people would have been ashamed to let another person know the name but . . . Let me have a look.' Carla came over to Betga's laptop and started scrolling through the names of Mike Mercer's files, files she had copied before she left the employ of Torrent Industries. 'Yeah, there it is, "MercyMikeMike's swag". Such an arsehole!'

Betga took Carla's cheeks in his hands, kissed her, and began combing through the folder labelled 'MercyMikeMike's swag' to see Mike Mercer's banking history.

'You're right! This is the bastard's banking file, seems to be all his statements, everything.' He went all the way to the beginning and began reading just as Maserov called for his and Carla's attention.

'Hey, listen to this. There's a chain of emails between Mike Mercer and Frank Cardigan that sounds suspicious as all hell.'

Maserov read the email chain aloud. 'This is Cardigan: "You're right, $500 million worth of steel doesn't just disappear. It becomes worth a little bit more so it's not $500 mill of steel anymore." Then he's got a smiley face. Then Mike Mercer writes, "Where is it?" Cardigan replies, "It's been sold." Mercer asks, "For how much? To whom?" Cardigan writes, "Nothing outrageous. To the Iraqis. Don't worry. It's not missing, it's sold. You'll get your taste." Mercer replies, "Well don't fuck with me. I want the same percentage I get from your TOI deals."'

'What's TOI?' Betga asked.

'That's probably Torrent Offshore Industries,' said Carla.

'What's Torrent Offshore Industries?' Betga asked again.

'Don't know yet but I'll keep looking,' said Maserov, continuing to read.

'Torrent Offshore Industries,' said Carla, matter-of-factly, 'is a marketing company. It's the company Mercer and Cardigan use to market to places like Iraq.'

'But neither of those guys are either authorised *or* required to do any marketing,' Betga quizzed her.

'No,' said Maserov slowly, slower than any penny could ever drop. 'But they might well be authorised to engage in *bribery*!'

'This, I think,' said Betga, 'is a eureka moment. You really think Torrent Offshore Industries might be the vehicle they used to bribe the Iraqis? That's very clever, Maserov . . . if you're right.'

'Why are we even doing this?' Maserov asked in exhaustion. 'If Malcolm Torrent knows and even authorised and *funded* the bribery to win the tender, what do we gain by showing him that I know they've been bribing people? On the contrary, he seems to pay people for *not* telling him things. He's willing to pay top dollar for plausible deniability.'

'Maserov, you're tired and overwrought. We're looking for information that Malcolm Torrent *would* want to know. Find this and you buy yourself even more time. Do it long enough and it's called a career. You need to go and see him again and give him some information that he *didn't* have but *wants* to have. Be brave. And yea, though you walk through the valley of the shadows of Collins Street, you'll fear no evil.'

'Why not?'

'Because I'll be right with you, perhaps a little behind.'

'He'll be right there on your coat-tails, Stephen,' Carla explained.

'Hang on a second,' said Maserov, ignoring Betga. 'Carla, isn't Frank Cardigan *senior* to Mike Mercer?'

'Yes, Frank Cardigan is his boss, his manager, at least technically,' said Carla. 'Why do you ask?'

'Because Mercer is pretty casual, almost rude to Cardigan. Even in totally banal emails he's pretty dismissive of him, the tone leaps out at you off the emails.'

'Yeah, that would be right. He thinks Cardigan's an idiot.'

'Yes, maybe but . . .' said Betga, thinking. 'This is hardly uncommon. Most people think their manager is an idiot. The contempt in which you hold them is what allows you to continue working for them day after day. Do it long enough and you might just get to be someone else's manager and have *them* bottle up *their* contempt for *you*. It's all part of the life cycle of an employee. But most people don't make their contempt as obvious as Mercer does. You're right, Maserov, it does drip off his emails.'

'What can I say?' said Carla. 'His arrogance knows no bounds. It's like a wave that washes over all he sees, including Frank Cardigan.'

'Yet they seem to do an awful lot of work together,' said Maserov, thinking aloud.

'Well, you know what they say,' said Betga. '"Proximity to your manager breeds contempt." You heard that? It doesn't have the same fluency as, say, "absence makes the heart grow fonder" but it's actually more statistically reliable. Kasimir says a lot of his associates report that absence is directly responsible for the *end* of romance, even when it's an absence enforced by the state and so beyond the control of the absent loved one.'

Maserov looked up at his fellow lawyer with bewilderment. 'This is futile,' he lamented.

'No, well, possibly, but it's much too early for you to know that with confidence. I've had a thought, a new one, one that you haven't yet had. We're not getting the full story. We need to go back to his bank statements.'

VII

Within half an hour Betga had been proved right. An interesting pattern had emerged as far as Maserov could see. 'Mike Mercer seems to email Frank Cardigan whenever he feels he's owed money by Torrent Offshore Industries for "marketing services". It's not even a proper invoice. But it seems to work. Within twenty-four hours of asking Frank Cardigan for money allegedly owed by Torrent Offshore Industries for unspecified, un-itemised "marketing services", the money comes without fail and to the dollar. They're often substantial amounts, too. But they always come directly from Frank Cardigan's personal account.'

'Why,' Maserov asked, both out loud to Betga and rhetorically of himself, 'is Mike Mercer using Frank Cardigan as his personal banker —'

'Not his banker, his personal ATM,' Betga corrected.

'Okay, why is Mike Mercer using Frank Cardigan as his personal ATM, ostensibly for a "marketing service" he's performed for Torrent Offshore Industries, and expecting to be paid at the drop of a hat —'

'And getting paid in full by Frank Cardigan before the hat has dropped?' Betga interjected. 'He doesn't hide his contempt for Cardigan yet Cardigan always pays promptly.'

'Maybe they're the only two who know about the bribery, other than Malcolm Torrent himself?'

'Maybe they're skimming some of that bribery money off the top?' Betga suggested.

'Really? Do you really think they'd try something like that?' Carla asked, flabbergasted.

'He tried to rape you. This is a smaller leap of the imagination.'

'Yeah, I guess so,' she agreed.

'No, no, no!' said Maserov excitedly. 'Try this on for size. Frank Cardigan was skimming money off the top. His lieutenant, Mike Mercer, found this out and is blackmailing him. The size of the payments, the speed of the payments, the lack of proper accounting procedures, proper invoices and the undisguised contempt for his superior; there's your evidence. Malcolm Torrent knows and tacitly approves of the bribing of Iraqi government officials but he doesn't know that Cardigan has been stealing from TOI, the company set up to administer the bribes. Mercer found that out and is blackmailing him. Remember the theft of the steel by Cardigan? Mercer found out and was paid to keep quiet.'

Betga got up off the couch and kissed Maserov's forehead. 'Maserov,' he said, 'you're like a baby caterpillar that has burst through his cocoon to become an incredibly beautiful, translucent-winged commercial lawyer. The only thing that would make your theory better is me having thought of it.'

'How do we prove it?' Carla asked.

'Yes, how do we prove it? You know,' speculated Betga, 'there are often email conversations between Mike Mercer and Frank Cardigan that are incomplete for some reason. We'd know more if we also had all of Frank Cardigan's documents.'

'Well, we don't. We're lucky Carla was able to get *these*. We should just keep looking but maybe not tonight.'

'Yes, we should just keep looking but . . . What if we also got hold of all Frank Cardigan's documents? Do you think Jessica would be willing and able to download them?'

'You have got to be kidding?'

Maserov protested to protect Jessica from even the possibility of getting caught downloading Frank Cardigan's documents but Betga said he was merely planning to ask her. She should and would, he assured Maserov, feel perfectly comfortable saying 'no'. They all agreed to call it a night. Maserov left before he'd had a chance to see whether Carla was inviting Betga to stay the night but not before Carla had noticed Maserov's instinct to protect Jessica.

The next day Jessica told Betga that she did feel comfortable saying 'no' but that she wanted instead to say 'yes'. Maserov tried to talk her out of it on the grounds that it was dangerous, illegal and speculative. But she said it was so easily achieved that it was worth an attempt. She knew when Cardigan left his office for lunch and when he left to go home at the end of the day, because it was when she had suggested he go home. He left at four o'clock each day in order to test his idiosyncrasy credit. She had often been seen in his office working with him or dropping off her draft of the newsletter column he put his name to so, unless anyone actively saw her at his computer with a USB, she had an alibi for loitering and nobody would give it a second thought.

When she went to his office at lunchtime the next day most of his colleagues were out. His computer was on and she simply visited Dropbox. He always stored his passwords in Google Chrome so she breezed through the login then sat down at his desk and began to try to download everything he had onto the USB she'd brought along for the purpose. But he had so much data to download, Jessica began to worry that she wasn't going to have enough memory on her USB, so she started to curate what she was downloading, nothing with graphics or video. 'Oh well, there goes his collection of digitally remastered seventies porn,' she said to herself, sitting at his desk, and just as she said it her mobile phone rang in her jacket pocket. She took out the phone and saw that it was him, Frank Cardigan, calling her.

'Frank!' she said, trying to hide her nerves. 'Where *are* you?'

'I'm at work. Why?'

'Where exactly? You haven't left for the day yet, have you?'

'No, don't worry Jessie, I'm keeping it scientific, not leaving till four, just like you said. I've just stepped out to lunch. But that's what I wanted to talk to you about.'

'What, lunch?' she said, trying to hide her terror.

'No, but . . . Hey, do you *want* to have lunch?'

'I can't, sorry. Didn't mean to steer the conversation away from . . .' Jessica looked at the computer. There was still quite a bit left to download. 'Sorry Frank, didn't mean to steal the . . . steer the conversation away from . . .'

Now the rate of download seemed to have slowed. For the first time ever she began to contemplate what it would mean if she got caught. She'd have absolutely no defence, not one that was coming to her as she sat in Frank Cardigan's chair. Was this a criminal offence? It was feeling like one.

'Sorry Frank, what were you calling for?'

'Well, it's this "leaving" thing, you know, leaving early, the idiosyncrasy credit test?'

'Yes? What about it?'

'Well, people in the department have, I think, been leaving earlier since I started doing it, don't you think?'

'Yes, that's been my observation too. That's a good sign. It suggests they think of you as a leader.'

'Hmmm, see, that's what I was wanting to talk to you about. There seems to have been a marked drop-off in productivity in the department since I started doing it.'

'Frank, it's funny you called. You'll never guess where I am.'

'Where are you?'

'I'm in your department. I came in connection with the idiosyncrasy credit test, to see how many of the guys were already *not here*. A lot of them aren't here at exactly the same time as you're not here. This looks good for you.'

'Well, yeah, but it *is* lunchtime.'

'Frank, don't be so modest . . . Frank, I'm having trouble hearing you. Email me. Hanging up, hang-ing . . . up . . . *now*.' And with that she used her index finger to end the call. By then she had downloaded all she had come for and she withdrew the USB stick and put it in her jacket pocket beside her phone.

Maserov was amazed but Betga said, 'None of these guys in construction take IT security seriously. This is a salient lesson for them. Or it would be if they knew about it.'

'It's stunning,' said Maserov, 'that they could be so stupid, not about their plan per se, but stupid enough to leave a virtual paper trail, an email trail that could convict them both in about thirty minutes.'

Jessica and Betga nodded. Carla was the only one who didn't find this hard to understand. 'No, it's not really so amazing. Not really. Look, I don't know Frank Cardigan very well but, unfortunately, I do know Mike Mercer. He's an *entitled* piece of shit and the most arrogant man I've ever met. Went to all the right schools, joined all the right clubs and just takes anything he wants, always has.'

'Well,' said Jessica, 'Frank's thick as a concrete slab in a new Iraqi bridge and presents with a Jekyll and Hyde belief in himself as a leader of men who also fights not to see himself as the dumb unpopular rich kid everyone makes fun of.'

'See,' said Carla, 'if you give power to two men like that, give them access to huge sums of money so they can bribe people, at their discretion, and if they keep winning plaudits from their boss, who is the boss of everything, suddenly their brazen stupidity in terms of emails and IT security doesn't look so unlikely. It's almost predictable, don't you think?'

Both Maserov and Betga had been right. Maserov was right to speculate that Frank Cardigan was almost certainly the one, or one of very few people, responsible for bribing foreign governments and companies to ensure Torrent Industries' tender bids were successful. More importantly, as far as buying time from Malcolm Torrent was concerned, Cardigan was stealing from the funds allocated for doing this. Betga, in turn, was right that Frank Cardigan's files and Mike Mercer's files, especially when read together, pretty much proved it. Best of all, it appeared almost certain that Mike Mercer had twigged some time ago that Frank Cardigan was creaming a sizeable dairy-farm's worth off the top and was using the information to blackmail Cardigan. It was a good old-fashioned shakedown, classically elegant in its simplicity. Mike Mercer was extorting Frank Cardigan, knowing that Cardigan couldn't stop him without the risk of revealing his own crime.

'You've done it again! Brilliant!' said Carla to Jessica, who was now having trouble hiding her feeling of triumph.

'I can get some champagne if you think it's called for,' Jessica volunteered.

'When is it not called for?' asked Carla. 'This is going to stitch up Mike Mercer like I never dreamed of.' This was met with silence. 'Isn't it?'

'Well, maybe. Let's not get ahead of ourselves,' warned Betga.

'How could this possibly *not* fuck Mercer right up?' Carla asked.

'No, I think Betga's actually right to be cautious,' Maserov confirmed, 'Yes, Torrent will likely want both of them killed for what they've done but he's got a problem. If he, or anyone else, goes to the Feds with this it's going to be obvious very quickly that Torrent Industries has been bribing people left, right and centre. That's illegal. Even if he's able to plausibly claim he didn't know anything about the bribery, which, frankly, seems kind of doubtful, the share price will take a beating while Mercer and Cardigan are prosecuted and perhaps even longer while the company cleans house. It won't be able to do this overnight. Torrent Industries would be mud for quite a while no matter how well its core business had been doing. The board would almost certainly be thrown out. It will be a nightmare for him, a lot worse than having these bastards steal from him.'

'Are you saying he'd just let them get away with it?' Jessica asked.

'No, I can't possibly imagine that he'd let them get away with it. But he needs to find a way of punishing them that doesn't hurt him,' said Maserov.

'And that's where *we* come in!' said A.A. Betga, standing tall and clapping his hands in triumph just once before realising that this could wake his daughter.

part eight

I

Stephen Maserov knew there were certain things he wouldn't do that A.A. Betga would. But he didn't know what those things were. Time and Betga were about to tell. The first thing Betga did after that evening was ask Jessica if she could get Mike Mercer's home address, which she did within twenty-four hours, but only once he had assured her that he would not approach him or do anything remotely violent.

Although Carla was still not allowing Betga to come back to live with her and Marietta, she was now letting him stay overnight to sleep, and only to sleep, beside her. She welcomed the warmth and strength of his arms when he hugged her after her sleep had been broken by the violence of the nightmares that came in horrific variations of the same form several times a week.

And so she trusted him implicitly one morning as they drove out to a quiet street in the leafy suburb of Mont Albert where another woman, not known to either of them, had woken with a presentiment of foreboding. In the house beneath the red oak everyone admired for its robust health and spreading canopy, the attractive woman, in her early forties, whose husband had already left for work, awoke to read emails on her phone telling her variously that no matter how high their premiums, their private health insurer wasn't going to cover their daughter's speech pathology, that her new Cayenne E-Hybrid still hadn't arrived, that her son's anti-social behaviour had again attracted the attention of the vice-principal, and that a woman who had comprehensively out-campaigned her in the race for school council president was inviting her to join 'a few of the other mums' for a celebratory drink in South Yarra. Her husband had pushed her to nominate. He was always pushing her; pushing her to do better, dress better, lose a little around the hips and sometimes he pushed her up against the wall or down onto the floor.

So on this particular already dark morning for her the only saving grace to date had been the realisation that her husband had earlier left for work which was why she was alone when the doorbell rang and a man with a file filled with court documents inside an envelope asked if this was the home of Mr Mercer, Mr Michael Mercer. The envelope filled with documents was slightly torn so it was possible to see the first or uppermost document, which was Carla's report of her sexual harassment by the woman's husband.

'Nothing to worry about, ma'am. The case has settled. Just returning the documents to your husband.'

'What case?' Mike Mercer's wife asked Betga.

'Oh, I, um . . . I'm sorry. This is a private matter . . . these are . . . for your husband.'

From the car Carla saw Mike Mercer's wife begin to read her report to Torrent's HR department. She could see that the woman was learning about it for the first time and that Mrs Mercer, having long ago made her pact with the Torrent Industries executive, would believe every word Carla had written. The confidentiality clause in the settlement agreement did not contain anything to prohibit the return of the documents outlining the case against the alleged perpetrator to the man himself. So while it was unnecessary, it wasn't prohibited.

Betga closed the car door from the driver's seat without saying a word. They looked through the window at Mike Mercer's house one more time before Betga pulled the car away from the kerb, gently, without hurry or panic, and then without much conversation they headed south-west at a leisurely speed and managed to have Carla arrive five minutes early. Her psychiatrist wasn't even there yet.

Jessica was pivotal to what happened next. She arranged to meet Frank Cardigan in his office late one morning. He thought it was to discuss the idiosyncrasy credit test; his misgivings and her findings. But she was there to set the stage for what Betga described in a pep talk of sorts to both her and to Maserov as perhaps the greatest thing they would ever do in their professional lives.

'So how do you think I'm doing with this, the idiosyncrasy credit test?' Frank Cardigan asked her from the very same office chair she had sat in when she downloaded most of his files onto a USB.

'How do *you* think you're doing?' Jessica asked him back.

'Well, a lot of the guys *are* leaving early, aren't they? I mean, I know this because you've told me and you're watching them *and* because I can see it reflected in their work. Their productivity is down, in some cases way down.'

'Great sign, Frank.'

'Well, maybe, but I need them to be working. So it's kind of plus-minus.'

'I'm hearing you, Frank. Maybe it's time to end the experiment. We've already learned a lot from it.'

'Have we?'

'Oh, yes. It's staring at me like the nose on your face. We've proved beyond any doubt that you have leadership qualities. These men are following you.'

'Oh, that's great! Because I was worried, you know, that the department was simply experiencing a downturn in productivity for no good reason.'

'No, the reason is you're leading them. You're a leader by temperament, as we suspected. You've been leading them. They haven't even known it. You've been doing it without even being here. It's some of the most impressive leading I've seen since I left graduate school. I know it's not possible under the circumstances but if the experts could see the way you lead them —'

'To leave work early?'

'Yes. My God, you're the man, Frank. Now you know *they* know it. They're on what is known in the literature as the continuum, the hero-worship continuum.'

'The hero-worship continuum?'

'Sshhh! You can't let them know that *you* know or you'll embarrass, even humiliate them. A good leader allows his subordinates the space and creates the ambience around him to be comfortably hero worshipped.'

'Shit, I suspected they were just lazy pricks. And there they were adoring me.'

'That's the reading *I'm* getting. But I agree with you about the need to keep everyone working. So how about you discontinue leaving at 4 pm each day? Would you be comfortable with that?'

'Well, yes, but is there more we can do . . . to manifest my leadership and test *them*, the guys?'

'Frank, I'm so glad you asked me that, as a true leader would, because there's a lot more we can do, a lot.'

'Oh, that's good.'

'Frank, the leadership literature is a huge and growing body of scholarship, not all of it of equal merit or value. But some of the scholars in the area whom I most admire have come up with categories of leadership and that's important. We need to identify your natural leadership instincts and place them into one of the categories before we go further.'

'What are the categories?'

'There are six. They're fairly self-explanatory. They are: leaders as saints, leaders as gardeners, leaders as buddies, leaders as commanders, leaders as cyborgs and leaders as bullies.'

'That's a lot to choose from.'

'Well, Alvesson and Spicer, the scholars who've identified the categories, they weren't suggesting that you *choose* one but rather that you will naturally fall into one or other category.'

'Yeah, but couldn't a real leader choose which one he wanted to be?'

'No, that's not what they mean.'

'But if I'm a leader, couldn't I just choose the category myself and not have anyone impose it on me. As a leader, I sometimes see myself . . . you know, as kind of a *maverick*.'

'Which would you choose, Frank?'

'Okay,' Frank Cardigan said, looking down at the piece of paper on which she'd written the categories. 'I'm certainly not a saint. I don't have the temperament and, anyway, I'm not a Catholic. Do you guys have saints?'

'*Us* guys?'

'*You* know . . . Indians. I mean, the indigenous . . . the . . . Indians, native . . . Is that . . .? Shit, Jessie, you *know* I don't want to get it wrong. What are you called these days?'

'Jessica. I'm called Jessica.' She couldn't control the vigour of her exhalation, equal parts carbon dioxide and contempt. 'Okay Frank, so you're not a saint. I won't argue with that.'

'I'm not a cyborg either. I don't even really know what that is. I'm probably not a gardener. We *have* a gardener and he's certainly no leader. Barely speaks English. Barely *speaks*.'

'You know what, Frank? There are ways, tests, that will allow us to determine your natural leadership category *and*, at the same time, allow us to learn more as to where on the hero-worship continuum the other guys in the department see you. This is exciting and it's what I've been waiting to talk to you about for quite some time. I've taken the liberty of developing a protocol for the test in line with the incredibly stringent requirements of the National Association of Psychologists, South-East Region. But you might not be willing to conduct this test.'

'Why not?'

'Well, it takes a lot of daring. It's pretty out there, not for everybody.'

'Well, not everybody's a leader.'

'That's true. But even so, you'd really *need* to be the kind of maverick you sometimes suspect you are. There'd be no fudging this.'

'Do *you* suspect that . . . that I'm a maverick? Jessie?'

'Frankly, Frank, it would be good to test it, if you're up to it.'

'I'm up to it. You know I am. What have I got to do? Is it . . . does it involve boxing?'

'No, no boxing. It requires even greater daring than boxing. You would have to be willing to have your men think you're going over the wall, going rogue to help them, that in order to make things better for them you're willing to do something the federal police and the judiciary might even consider illegal. But this kind of leader doesn't care what a bunch of old lawyers think. Then the guys who go with you on this will thank you for helping them out, for looking out for their interests above and beyond the call of duty, and perhaps beyond the law, and we'll know then exactly which of them would follow you into battle and how far advanced each one of them is down the hero-worship continuum.'

'I'm willing to do that.'

'Frank, you don't know what it is yet.'

'You tell me and I bet I'll be willing to do it.'

'Okay, let's see. Obviously, I've given this some thought and have been waiting for you to show your readiness by calling off the four o'clock study. You've told me in the past that the company's been working on a plan for some kind of contract extension for . . . What was it? Was it for the southern oilfields project in Iraq?'

'Yeah, that's right.'

'Well, here's what you should do. You ask each of the guys out for a drink.'

'What, the whole department?'

'Yes, but one at a time. On different days, if necessary. Here's what you need to do. You take them, one at a time, to a cocktail bar or coffee lounge, and you put the following proposition to them. This is the test.

You tell them, "In a couple of weeks the company's going to announce a major contract extension re the southern oilfields project in Iraq. When that happens, obviously, our stock price will shoot up. None of us can be seen to benefit from this information, obviously, 'cause that's what they call insider trading. But with just a bit of care, we probably *can* still have a little taste. After all, we're the guys who did the work that got the contract extension, right?"'

'Jesus, Jessie! This is brilliant. It's actually how some of us talk in real life, you know, not just as part of a scientifically valid experiment. Psychology! Christ, who knew? Science has come such a long way, hasn't it?'

'Wait Frank, I'm not finished. You tell them, "I'm in touch with a party in the UAE who will buy and sell the shares for us when we tell them to, no questions asked, for a small cut. But they're big players and they only work with trades where the sum is big enough." So, you tell them, "I need to know right *now* whether you want a piece of this and, if so, for how much?" You'll be getting them to show their true colours right there and we'll be recording it, seeing what they answer *and* how fast they answer.'

'Jessie, that's breathtaking!' Frank Cardigan said, reaching for her hand but too slowly. 'I didn't know you had it . . . in you.'

'Frank, you do realise I'm only proposing that you say this in the interests of science and to help you make the department in your own image. This is, of course, illegal. I'm not encouraging you to do it. You do get that, right?'

'Yes, of course. But look where your mind went. I have to admit, I find that kind of —'

'Frank, eyes on the prize! Right? You want to actualise your leadership potential. You have to think to yourself, "I really want it, I don't just want to *talk* about it."'

'Who will I start with?'

'Well, I guess you'd start with the most senior member of your staff and work your way down.'

'That would be Mike Mercer.'

'Okay, start with him. The place I've got in mind is perfectly set up for this experiment. It's a chic bar called Romeo Lane. Do you know it? It's in Crossley Street, off Bourke Street.'

'Yeah, I've heard of it.'

'That's a great start. So, listen very carefully; you walk from Crossley Street into a passageway and turn left into the bar. Turn left again and sit at the second of two tables that abut the wall, the one closest to the window and to the right of the big circular mirror above the two tables. Are you getting this, Frank?'

'Yes. And . . . I find myself excited.'

'Don't breathe too hard, Frank. I'll have a microphone hidden in the overhanging downlight. I'll need you both as close to it as possible.'

'You'll be recording us?'

'That's the plan. Then I'll send you an email containing each recorded conversation and we'll make a time to analyse them, looking for people with the special qualities of a true follower.'

'Analyse them together?'

'Yes, together.'

II

The following evening Mike Mercer found a nervous Frank Cardigan waiting for him with two craft beers in an alcove at Romeo Lane in Crossley Street.

A tracking device, which days earlier Kasimir had placed on Mercer's car in the underground carpark of Torrent Industries HQ, alerted Kasimir that Mercer had arrived at the bar and allowed him to remotely switch on the recording device in the alcove.

'Frank, you look like shit. Did you mix your hayfever medication with alcohol? Did you do that again?'

'Always sticking it to me, aren't you, Mike? Listen, there's something I'd like to put to you on a confidential basis.'

'No, I'm not kidding, you really look like shit. What is it?'

'Oh, I just haven't been sleeping.'

'No, what is it you want to put to me on a confidential basis?'

Around the corner from the Romeo Lane cocktail bar, Betga and Acting Sergeant Ron Quinn, still in uniform, were at just that time having a coffee together at Pellegrini's. Betga, in his capacity as his life coach, had invited him there as part of a getting-to-know-you session.

'So, Ron, in order to do my best as your life coach, I need to know a bit more about you, what makes you tick, how you like to spend your free time. Do you go out much?'

'No, not really.'

'Not, say, to the movies?'

'Sometimes.'

'What about the football?'

'Not regularly.'

'Do you have any hobbies?'

'I'm a bit of a collector, I suppose.'

'What do you collect?'

'I collect single malt Scotch whisky. I like to think of myself as a bit of a connoisseur.'

'Ron, will you excuse me for a minute?' Betga had received a signal from Kasimir through the window that looked out onto the corner of Bourke and Crossley Streets. It meant that they now had a recording of Mike Mercer in conversation with Frank Cardigan conspiring to buy shares in Torrent Industries ahead of a public announcement that would increase the company's share price and then to sell the shares *after* the announcement to their mutual profit. It was a conspiracy to engage in insider trading, which was illegal and carried a maximum sentence of ten years' imprisonment and a fine of up to three times the value of the benefit attributable to the crime. The charge had a conviction rate of over

85 per cent. It was, therefore, statistically a lot more dangerous for the perpetrator than rape. It was almost thirty times more dangerous.

Jessica would send an email containing the recording to Frank Cardigan from a phony email address that had been created days earlier in an internet cafe. The address was TOI-MikeMike, a combination of the initials Torrent Offshore Industries, the entity Frank Cardigan used to bribe the Iraqis, and of Mike Mercer's secret name for his banking file.

On receipt of Kasimir's signal, Betga suggested that Acting Sergeant Ron Quinn and he go for a walk. It was, he explained, sometimes easier to talk while walking.

Betga suggested what might be missing in the acting sergeant. 'Look at that moon, Ron, almost full.'

'Yes, it's beautiful.'

'Beautiful, yet not quite full, *almost* . . . but not quite. A part of it is missing. It has no control over itself so we can't offer it any advice. But *you*, my friend, are a man, a man with agency, able to appreciate the finer and more subtle beauty of single malt whisky. And yet . . .'

'And yet?' asked Acting Sergeant Ron Quinn as they walked together at a pace slower than necessary for comfort.

'And yet, if you'll forgive me, you've failed to take advantage of your agency.'

'What do you mean?'

'To put it bluntly, Ron, I don't think you've lived up to your potential. I don't think you've seized the day.'

'Well, depends what day you mean. People outside the force under-estimate the need to stay on top of the paperwork. There's a spill-over effect, unintended consequences that nobody ever sees till it's too late.'

'Ron, don't feel the need to defend yourself here. Go with me on this. Take it as the compliment it is.'

'How is it a compliment?'

'A man of your calibre, a man with all your gifts, should have reached a higher rank. And I think it's because something has held you back.

Now, whatever that is we can examine over time but how about each day you set yourself the task of showing us, me and you, a certain drive? Set yourself the exercise each day of finding an opportunity to unequivocally show initiative.'

'What do you mean? What am I meant to do?'

'You're a cop. Solve crimes, catch people committing illegal acts. Show them that you can do it!'

'Show who?'

'The people above you, below you and the crime-committing public of this great state. You're not just fighting the war against paperwork, you're fighting crime, finding it wherever it's committed and fighting it. Do you know how many things are illegal in this state?'

'No, not the actual number.'

'A lot, Ron. *A lot* of things are illegal in this state. Yet people think they can get away with doing them. There are crimes waiting for you to find, everywhere you look. Here, look, even here! Look inside that car, for example,' said Betga, stopping now at Mike Mercer's Porsche. 'I can see what look like deal bags, probably heroin, just peeking out from under that document on the passenger seat. It's a prohibited substance. What are you going to do about it?'

'What *can* I do about it?'

'Impound this prick's car, Ron. You're the law! The public is counting on you not to let this guy thumb his nose at them . . . and at you.'

'Betga, I can't impound his car on suspicion.'

'Ron, you only need *reasonable cause* to suspect a crime in order to break into a car and seize stuff. That's *all* the law requires for a police officer. And there might be a laptop in there too with evidence that he's a dealer, a major player.'

'I can't see any laptop. There's nothing to suggest that he's a dealer, Betga.'

'No Ron, look carefully. I think there's a laptop lying on the floor.'

'Okay, so he doesn't value it. He's just rich.'

'Ron, look at today's economy. Who's really doing well out there? Only Rupert Murdoch, Jeff Bezos, Apple and drug dealers. Now, it's not Murdoch's or Bezos' car. You would have heard that Steve Jobs died. That just leaves drug dealers. Surely that's *reasonable cause* right there.'

There was indeed a laptop in Mercer's car, Frank Cardigan's laptop. Jessica had taken it from Cardigan's office and given it to Betga, who had made it available to Kasimir. Kasimir had put it in Mike Mercer's car together with the just visible deal bags of heroin. Mercer would think Frank Cardigan had planted the drugs there and Cardigan would think Mercer had stolen his laptop. Now they were guaranteed to be at each other's throats.

'No, I don't think that would be right,' said Acting Sergeant Ron Quinn. 'The public would consider it an infringement of their civil liberties.'

'Civil liberties? What kind of policeman are *you*?'

'Ron, the expensive foreign sports car, the laptop computer and what look like deal bags of heroin; *this* is the universe delivering you *reasonable cause* on a plate. You're allowed to make a mistake, Ron. People do it all the time, sometimes even the police. But you're also allowed to show some initiative. You can walk past this car because you're, of course, not sure what's going on in the life of the driver. Or you can take a deep breath, Ron, and you can investigate on behalf of the people of this great state. Will *you* be the one? What would your superiors say? Will the records, will the newspapers, will the television news show that Acting Sergeant Ron Quinn was the one who broke this case wide open? Who was it that found the dealer everyone had wanted caught for years? Was it Acting Sergeant Ron Quinn? Yes, turns out it *was* Acting Sergeant Ron Quinn. *He* did it.'

The ageing policeman's eyes had grown moist under the nearly full moon. Betga could almost see in the man an ingress of thoughts pertaining to possibilities long suppressed, so long in fact that they seemed to belong only to other people; people who had not been bullied by their colleagues, who had never been mocked or laughed at, whose opinions were valued, who were not always the last to learn about changes that affected everybody, people who had not spent decades gathering the detritus of their lives to build a wall to shelter them from the painful realisation of social and economic relativities, a sad cocoon in which a lonely man could feel safe. And there in St Andrews Place, a stone's throw from Parliament House, Acting Sergeant Ron Quinn took the first of several deep breaths that were the beginning of a chain of events that would ultimately see Mike Mercer and Frank Cardigan charged by the federal police with insider trading and Mercer with possession of heroin.

III

Maserov had arranged a meeting with Malcolm Torrent before the charges were laid. This meeting though was unlike any other he had ever had with the construction mogul. At Maserov's request, this one took place in the middle of Flagstaff Gardens where no one could record the conversation, the attendees, or even that there had been a conversation. The wind was blowing Malcolm Torrent's wispy hair awry when Maserov's phone vibrated. It was Eleanor. He couldn't take any calls now. If it was important enough she'd have to leave a message on his voicemail. This was an exceptionally bad time to call.

'This had better be good, Maserov. I'm not used to acting out scenes from *Gorky Park* in the course of my usual business day.'

'This won't take long, but nor will it be a usual day for you. We have just a couple of discrete topics to discuss. I suggested we meet here for your sake.'

'What's the first topic?'

'Michael Crispin "Crispy" Hamilton.'

'What about him?'

'I know you've trusted him for years. But *we* met because he was frustrating you by failing to take seriously your concerns about a spate of sexual harassment cases against executives at Torrent Industries. You didn't know why. I do now. Hamilton was sitting on his hands to protect his own interests.'

'What does that mean?'

'It means, sir,' said Maserov, 'that the senior partner at the law firm that you pay handsomely to advance and protect the interests of the company your grandfather started took risks that someone who had solely the company's welfare at heart would not have taken.'

'You can bring him out now,' Maserov said into his phone and Jessica and Betga came walking out towards them from behind the lowest part of the canopy of a Moreton Bay fig tree. She was holding the arm of a man who appeared to need her assistance to stand. He was the only one of them to be dressed casually, in loose-fitting beige chinos and a sports jacket that looked several sizes too big for him.

'Good morning, Mr Torrent,' said Betga. 'I found him for you.'

'Mr Torrent, I'm sure you remember Jessica Annand from your HR department?' Maserov said by way of confirmation of Jessica's identity.

'Hello Jessica,' he said as they shook hands.

'Hello Mr Torrent. This is Bruce Featherby.' Malcolm Torrent shook Featherby's hand. 'Mr Featherby was the Freely Savage lawyer acting for the company defending your interests against the sexual harassment allegations. He was directly answerable to Mr Hamilton. He's on leave at the moment but is of the opinion that when he returns he will be fired by Mr Hamilton.'

'Why, what have you done?' Malcolm Torrent asked.

'I . . . I followed his instructions . . . to the letter. But he will deny this. He'll blame me for . . . He told me to bury the report written by the plaintiff, Carla Monterosso. He told me to tell your HR department to bury it. And I did.'

'We've told Mr Featherby about a vacancy for an experienced lawyer in Torrent's in-house legal department but he seems to need to hear it from you,' Betga explained.

'Well, that depends on what you've got to say, Mr Featherby.'

Featherby swallowed cold air into his dry mouth and began. 'Hamilton told me to go slow on the negotiations with the sexual harassment cases, to test the resolve and the pockets of the plaintiffs.'

'Well, it might or might not be sage advice but it's hardly treason, is it? Did you ask him his reasoning?' Malcolm Torrent questioned.

'With respect, sir, nobody asks him that. I've never seen it, not in all the years I've been at the firm. But I suspected. He once said something. We'd been talking about the case and as I was walking out he said something to the effect of, "This ought to shut her up." I didn't know who the "she" was but I suspected it was his wife.'

'On the basis of Mr Featherby telling us this,' continued Jessica, 'I checked the HR file of Mike Mercer and, going all the way back, there's a personal letter of recommendation from Mr Hamilton. Then, on the basis of this, we did some further checking.'

'Where's this going?' Malcolm Torrent asked.

'Mike Mercer is the son of Mr Hamilton's wife's sister. He's Hamilton's nephew by marriage. Hamilton was protecting him at your expense,' Betga explained.

'Because of the family relationship,' Maserov explained, 'Mercer has acted for years as though he has immunity from any real-world consequences, that is, until these cases. And even then Hamilton put appeasing his wife ahead of the interests of Torrent Industries.' Malcolm Torrent was silent, taking it all in, but it was clear to all of them that he was furious.

'Sir,' began Maserov after a minute or two during which Malcolm Torrent silently roared his disgust at Hamilton, 'I will soon have nothing to do with Mr Hamilton when he ends my employment at Freely Savage but you will continue to. But, at least for now, it's currently still my duty to look out for your interests and I'm telling you this without fear or favour. He's a liability to you and to the company.'

'I see,' said Malcolm Torrent gravely. They were now all standing under the Moreton Bay fig tree that had earlier housed Jessica, Betga and Featherby. Malcolm Torrent looked at Featherby and nodded at the clearly broken man.

'When you've finished your . . . leave, you call Jessica here in HR. She'll set you up in our legal department.'

'Thank you, sir.'

'Is there anything else?' the construction tycoon asked.

'I'm afraid there is,' Maserov said. 'Ms Annand and Mr Featherby, you might want to get a coffee at the Radisson across the street?'

'Sure,' said Jessica, about to lead Featherby away.

'Just a moment,' said Malcolm Torrent, addressing Jessica. 'Are you working on recommendations, some kind of protocol to lessen the chances that we have to deal with any more of this . . . sexual harassment stuff?'

'Yes, sir, I'm working on that now as a matter of priority. It will be a detailed, nuanced paper for you.'

'Give me the gist of it now, one major recommendation, right here, right now.'

'Well, there'll be more than this but if you want a headline recommendation right now it's this. There need to be more women employed in the company generally and more women in positions of power. Each department needs a woman as either its head, but of course only if a woman is the best candidate, or as its deputy head.'

'Why? That's a pretty dramatic change. There'll be pushback. Could you tell me in one sentence, one sentence, why we should make that change?'

'Put simply, sir, people don't grope the boss.'

Malcolm Torrent thought for a moment and then nodded. 'That makes a lot of sense, Jessica.'

'Thank you.'

'It does sound a bit like affirmative action though. Need to think about that. Not sure how I feel about affirmative action.'

'No, Mr Torrent, with respect, it's not affirmative action. It's an end to affirmative action.'

'I don't follow you.'

'The firm's *current* policy is one of affirmative action where 50 per cent of the population is massively favoured in terms of hiring, promotion and pay. This would end that. Additionally, it would double the size of the talent pool for the company to recruit from, unleashing untold potential.'

'I see,' said Malcolm Torrent, smiling in what appeared to be agreement or at least understanding.

'Sir, my educational background and professional experience is in psychology and human resources and your primary concern is, understandably, the construction business. But where my background and your focus are increasingly meeting is in what finance people call risk-adjusted net present value.'

'Go on,' said Malcolm Torrent, intrigued.

'The share market is interested in what your company is going to be worth in the future, right?'

'Right,' said Malcolm Torrent.

'So,' Jessica continued, now emboldened and with Maserov and Betga watching her in awe, 'the share market projects your annual cash flow and has traditionally used things like interest rates and inflation rates to get the discount rate of your net present value. The higher a company's discount rate, the lower will be the present value of its future earnings and so the lower will be the company's share price.'

'Yes, I'm with you.'

'Well, this is where people like me come in and help you increase your company's share price, people who, previously, you tolerated but might have secretly thought were collateral to your main business activity.'

'I might've thought something like that at times,' said Malcolm Torrent, clearly warming to both Jessica and her line of argument.

'Increasingly, corporate behaviour is being factored into the discount rate of a company's present net value. So a history and culture of accepting sexual harassment or racism or bullying of any kind, in fact *anything* that opens up the company up to litigation, to payouts, to counselling and unnecessary costs across the board that are extraneous to its core business; these things will increase the company's discount rate and so lower its share price. Stamp out those things, set the gold standard for stamping out all of those things, and you'll see it reflected in your share price this financial year.'

'Will all of this be in your report?'

'Yes, I can put it in my report.'

'Please do. I'll want to hear more. Well, I'm impressed, Jessica, keep up the good work. I like where you're going with all of this and I look forward to reading the report. And I'm inclined to agree with you. This stuff just seems to be everywhere now. Just last night I saw on the TV that young actress, Helena Bagshaw. Said *she* had a dose of it. I like her. Did you see that . . . on the television?'

'I read about it.'

'We don't want any more of this.'

'Couldn't agree more, Mr Torrent.'

'Alright, Jessica, thank you.'

Malcolm Torrent, Maserov and Betga watched as Jessica led Featherby by the arm slowly but steadily towards William Street to get a coffee, stopping only when a homeless man approached Featherby and stood in the line of his trajectory, not far from the corner of William and La Trobe streets. Featherby wondered in horror why this ragged man had chosen *his* red-streaked eyes to look into, the eyes of someone who clearly did not want to be mistaken for being at one with him.

'Excuse me, sir. Don't be afraid. My name's Nick. I just wondered if you might have any spare change that I could use for food.'

When Maserov and Betga were alone they continued walking with Malcolm Torrent. 'Sir, I'm able to offer you the protection of legal professional privilege because I'm your lawyer so, obviously, I'm prohibited from repeating anything you tell me in confidence, even to a court. Mr Betga is, as you'll recall, also a qualified lawyer but since you've retained him only as a private investigator and not as a lawyer he's not currently able to offer that protection no matter how much he wants to tell you what he knows.' Torrent reached into his coat pocket, pulled a hundred-dollar note out of his wallet and handed it to Betga.

'Now you're my lawyer too.'

'Thank you, Mr Torrent. One of your employees has been bribing officials in the Iraqi government in order to win tenders for the company. You're not obliged to say anything to us about that. But we thought you'd want to know that he's been overstating the money required to do this and pocketing the difference. The employee is well known to you. It's Frank Cardigan.'

'Jesus Christ! The little shit!'

'Well before *we* found this out, someone else did, a man in the same department but subordinate to him. When this man found out he began blackmailing Frank Cardigan and quite successfully too. That man is also known to you, at least he is *now*. It's Mike Mercer.'

'Oh no! For fuck's sake! How much and for how long?'

'We don't yet know. The difficulty for you, sir, is that any press, police investigation or inquiry by the regulatory authority into this is going to raise questions about something you, of course, know nothing about and don't wish people to be asking about.'

'Bribing the Iraqis for tenders?'

'Yes, sir.'

'So you're saying I have to let them get away with this? I can't touch them?'

'No, you can but you won't have to. Sometime soon they're both going to be charged with insider trading.'

'You're kidding! On what basis?'

'On the basis of this recording.' Maserov handed the older man a USB containing a recording of the Frank Cardigan–Mike Mercer conspiracy to engage in insider trading recorded live in Romeo Lane, off Bourke Street.

'How on earth do you know all this?' Malcolm Torrent asked them.

'It's in your interests not to know,' Betga quietly explained.

They continued walking along the path among the Moreton Bay fig and elm trees in silence before Malcolm Torrent spoke. 'Gentlemen, you've done outstanding work.'

The meeting was over. As Malcolm Torrent walked back to his driver and Betga left to meet Jessica and Featherby in William Street, Maserov stayed back in the gardens for a moment, having remembered Eleanor's earlier call. For no reason other than a reflexive paternal anxiety now amplified by the separation, he suddenly imagined that it would be a report of some accident that had befallen one of his children. Yes, that would be it. Some disaster had befallen one or both of them and he'd ignored the call. With guilt and apprehension he played the message Eleanor had left for him.

'Hi Stephen . . . It's me.' There was a long pause on the line during which he thought he could hear her breathing although, with the wind unsettling the trees in Flagstaff Gardens, it was hard to be sure. 'Stephen . . . Um . . . Can we make a time to talk . . . sometime? It's nothing for you to . . . It's not the kids . . . directly but . . . Give me a call when you can. Please.' Then she hung up. What did she mean by 'please'?

Maserov looked at his phone as though reading Eleanor's name, the time of the call and its duration, might enlighten him in some way. It didn't.

IV

Maserov wondered who Malcolm Torrent had been talking to because, after their clandestine meeting in Flagstaff Gardens, another quite unexpected meeting was called but not with or by Malcolm Torrent. It was almost 10 pm and Maserov was with Jessica in a supermarket in St Kilda stocking up on milk, cereal, three-minute noodles and, at her insistence, sawtooth coriander, when a number he didn't recognise startled his phone. It was Mr Radhakrishnan, the partner in Emerging Markets at Freely Savage, apologising for calling Maserov at so late an hour and asking if he might have a conversation with him on the basis of the strictest confidence.

Maserov, stunned, agreed to meeting at 10.30 am the following day, at Degraves Espresso Bar, off Flinders Lane. Jessica speculated that Radhakrishnan would have chosen that place because it was midway between the Freely Savage offices and Torrent Industry headquarters. Also, consistent with his apparent desire for secrecy, it was unlikely anyone from either office would be there since the espresso bar's usual clientele would have long since left. And of those still there, none would have ever even aspired to, let alone undertaken, white-collar employment in the corporate sector. Additionally, Jessica could vouch for the coffee and the panini. But as to what Radhakrishnan wanted to discuss with Maserov, they were both completely unable to speculate. They had only one night to wait, during which time they managed to distract each other's attention from the following morning's meeting quite satisfactorily. Several times.

Radhakrishnan shook Maserov's hand and, contrary to Maserov's expectation, did not look at all discomfited by the location of the meeting or its apparent secrecy. He ordered a triple espresso and a mineral water and Maserov instinctively copied the order with one word, 'double', and a two-finger gesture that was almost a salute. He wasn't sure why he'd done that but nobody in Degraves commented. Then Radhakrishnan got straight down to business. It was very nice to see Stephen again. This meeting never happened. Did Maserov understand this? Maserov said he did.

'I've been asked to approach you on behalf of a cohort of partners at Freely Savage —'

'Really, who?'

'— who wish to remain nameless, at least for the time being.'

'Certainly, no names,' Maserov assured him.

'Do you know how the partnership works?' he asked Maserov.

'Not precisely but it's sort of like this, isn't it? If you're a partner you earn profits from the labour of all the people below you, you have an expense account, you can, it seems, humiliate people with impunity and you are virtually immune to any sanction for your behaviour.'

Radhakrishnan chuckled. 'Oh Stephen, that's *very* cynical and a little simplistic. That's true only for equity partners. Salaried partners can only dream of this. Would you like to be a partner? Of course I mean an equity partner. Is this or has this become your ultimate objective?'

'I hope you don't think me rude, if I ask why you ask.'

'Well, let's just say that your work with Malcolm Torrent has earned you some admirers among the partnership.'

'How does anyone even know about my work with Mr Torrent?'

'You'll forgive me, Stephen, I'm not at liberty to discuss that.'

'I'm intrigued but okay. But far from me becoming a partner, Hamilton is going to fire me as soon as the year is up.'

'Well,' Radhakrishnan began to explain, 'as I've indicated, a number of the partners have heard what you've been doing at Torrent and there is, at least among this cohort of partners —'

'The ones who should remain nameless for the time being?'

'Yes, among those same partners, there is an understanding that you've become something of a golden boy, Malcolm Torrent's golden boy.'

'Well, that's very flattering, Mr Radhakrishnan.'

'Allow me to explain a little further how the partnership works,' the more senior man continued. 'All partners, both equity and salaried, get voting rights, which are directly tied to the billings from all the files for which they are the responsible partner. Of course, equity partners also get additional voting rights which are tied to the equity they hold in the firm. Mr Hamilton, as you well know, is the partner directly responsible for all the Torrent Industries files. Torrent Industries is by far the firm's biggest client in terms of billings. Frankly, this is how Mr Hamilton comes to tyrannise the other partners and, indirectly but unambiguously, the rest of the firm.'

Radhakrishnan went on to explain that if Maserov could get Malcolm Torrent to agree to make him, Maserov, the lawyer responsible for all Torrent Industries matters, then Radhakrishnan and the other members of the secretly conspiring cohort of partners would propose Maserov for partnership. Once Maserov was a partner, with his voting rights from control of the Torrent Industries files, Maserov, Radhakrishnan and the cohort of other partners would together hold a majority of the partnership vote.

'Then Mr Hamilton's reign of terror will be over and you will be a partner.' He smiled and sipped on his mineral water.

'What happens if something goes wrong?' Maserov asked, still not believing what he was hearing.

'Well, there are a limited number of things that can go wrong as I see it. But you said yourself that Mr Hamilton will sooner or later get rid of you so, by your own reckoning, you probably have nothing to lose. This cohort of partners that I speak of has, of course, everything to lose. This is why our meeting now has never happened and why, in the event that something does go wrong, you will be, I believe the expression is "hung out to dry". But Stephen,' Radhakrishnan said in a voice Maserov wanted to sink into, 'your history suggests that you do extremely well when you have nothing to lose.'

Maserov thought for a moment and looked around the cafe to see if there was anything or anyone to suggest this was some kind of set-up. Then he asked, 'So someone will go to Mr Torrent and propose that I become the lawyer responsible for all the Torrent Industries work?'

'Yes. You will.'

'Me?'

'Yes, this way there'll be no record of any of this should it not go our way.'

'"*Our* way," Mr Radhakrishnan?'

'Yes, Stephen, *our* way. Call me on this number as and when the need arises.' And with that, Radhakrishnan stood up and smiled, with a barely perceptible nod, leaving a fifty dollar note on the table and a business card on the saucer of Maserov's triple espresso. The business card had Radhakrishnan's landline and a mobile phone number that had been crossed out but on the other side there was a handwritten mobile number that differed from the printed one. There would be no record of any calls between the two ever having been made as far as anyone at the firm could tell. But by the time Maserov had realised this, Radhakrishnan could be seen turning left, out the door into Degraves Street, where he began the walk back to the hilly part of Collins Street where the specialist chocolate stores were nestled and the dentists liked to graze.

V

'You are fucking kidding me?' was Betga's response to the news over the phone of Maserov's Radhakrishnan meeting. He was delighted for his friend and colleague and also saw the likely benefits for himself. Perhaps best of all, it represented a kind of David slaying of Goliath wherein Hamilton was the Philistine unexpectedly brought down.

'Maserov, this is unbelievable! This is the stuff of legend, it's a once-in-a-generation event. You'll be telling your grandchildren about this.'

'I think my grandchildren would rather know why I did nothing to ameliorate climate change.'

'Forget climate change, Maserov, we're talking about making partner in a depressed economy. And as a Second Year . . . one with a target on his head. I'm honoured to know you and to have been a not insignificant part of this. I've got to hand it to you, Maserov. This hurts Hamilton more than anything I ever *dreamed* of doing to him.'

'Listen Betga, you've never actually told me what Hamilton did to you. What did he do?'

Betga exhaled. 'Okay, so first of all, I was a victim of all of the shit that you and everyone else has to put up with from him; the mind games, impossible deadlines, late nights, humiliation in meetings, you name it. But then there was something, something way out of left field. You know he always calls his secretary "Joy"?'

'Yeah.'

'Well, she . . . Oh shit! Hang on, Maserov. Wait. Marietta's crying. She's just woken up and she's crying . . . probably hungry or . . . maybe . . . I need to change her. Listen, Maserov, I'm going to have to call you back.'

'This is wonderful, Stephen! I can't believe it!' exclaimed Jessica when he later told her of the proposal Radhakrishnan had put to him. 'But is this what you want? I'm not saying it shouldn't be. You'd be cementing yourself into Freely Savage. Don't get me wrong, this is amazing news. But is it what you really want?' she asked hesitantly.

'What are you going to do?' Eleanor said when he told her.

'I don't know,' Maserov told his wife.

'You're their sacrificial lamb. These "heroic" partners who choose to hide behind you finally get a chance to de-fang Hamilton at no cost to them. If it doesn't work or if word gets out, *you'll* suffer the consequences and they'll be back in business as usual.'

'Yeah, it's pretty clever on their part, isn't it?'

'It manages to be ruthless and yet cowardly. If it works, these will be the distinguishing characteristics of your partners.'

'Not all of them, just the best of them.'

'Aren't you worried that they're just using you?'

'Everyone there is just using everyone else there.'

'Stephen, I worry about you.'

'Do you?'

'Of course, don't you know that?'

In a quiet voice, without anger or recrimination he asked Eleanor, 'How should I know that? Really, I mean that. How *should* I know?'

It was a voice she found irresistible and she began to cry. 'Stephen, I think we should try to be together again, to live together.'

'How long have you thought this?'

'I don't know. It's been a gradual dawning, I suppose.'

'A dawning of what?'

'A realisation that I don't want the kids to be without their father.'

'That's funny because for quite a few months now you were fine with it.'

'And I . . . don't really want to live without you either.'

'So what should I do?'

'I think you should move back in.'

'But what if you change your mind again?'

'I won't.'

'Should I just come and go from my own house and my own children depending on how you're feeling about things? Should I keep a suitcase packed?'

'I've earned that. I mean, I deserve that you should say that. I was going to work and doing all the work at home and with the kids. It felt like I was doing everything. I hated it. You didn't seem to get it. You didn't seem to hear me.'

'You've never apologised, Eleanor, never even admitted you'd done anything wrong. You know, I *still* couldn't explain to someone what exactly you claim I did that was so wrong that I deserved to be kicked out of my own house.'

'Who do you want to explain it to?' Maserov turned away but it hurt him to do this. His wife was in tears.

'I was talking to Carla. She told me about the amazing result you got for her. I was proud of you. She said that even though you were meant to be opposed to Betga, you actually kind of worked *with* him.'

'Yeah, I suppose I did.'

'And she said you worked with someone else too.'

'Yeah, there have been three of us working on all this.'

'Is that . . . who you want to explain what I did to?'

'Eleanor, for an English teacher, that's a terrible sentence.' Maserov wasn't ready to talk about Jessica to Eleanor. He didn't know what role he wanted Jessica to take in his life and he wasn't sure Jessica knew what she wanted either. His mouth was dry and his head was spinning with exhaustion and the nervous excitement of possibilities he'd never imagined and so had never hoped for. 'You mean to say, "Is that to whom you want to explain what I did?" Sorry to correct you but the children might be listening and we don't want them to hear their mother setting fire to the rules of grammar.'

'Am I too late, Stephen?'

'No, I think they're asleep.'

'Stephen, I'm sorry.' Eleanor ignored his use of humour to delay discussing anything that mattered. 'I do owe you an apology. As time's gone on *I* have trouble explaining it too. I was angry. I was lashing out. I asked you to leave because you never seemed to hear me.'

'I did hear you. I couldn't do anything about it without quitting my job. And we needed my salary or we'd lose the house. Still do.'

'Can you forgive me? Will you come back? The children would be in heaven.'

'They never wanted me to live somewhere else.'

'Of course they never wanted you to live somewhere else. I've hurt them too.' Maserov went over to the kitchen counter and poured himself a Scotch, one Acting Sergeant Ron Quinn would have approved of.

'Stephen?'

He took a sip from the glass.

'Stephen, what are you going to do?'

He looked at her and he didn't know.

'Am I too late?' she asked. 'Isn't this what you've been wanting?'

'Eleanor . . . It's lucky you're not a musician 'cause your timing is awful. Do you have any idea what's going on for me right now . . . at work?'

'Well, I'm kind of concerned . . . that I sort of . . . do. Am I too late? Is that what you're saying?'

'No.'

'I'm *not* too late?'

'No, that's not what I'm saying.'

'What are you saying?'

'I'm saying that we need to talk but that I just have to . . . I am *so* tired. Right now I just need to sleep. Then tomorrow morning I'm going to see if I can get an appointment to see Malcolm Torrent, see if I can get him to agree to make me, a lowly Second Year, the lawyer responsible for all Torrent Industries matters at Freely Savage. *Then* we should talk.' Maserov finished his drink.

VI

The argument was simple. 'I know that I'm a very junior lawyer but you've seen what I can do. You've seen what I've done for you and for the company in a very short space of time. You wanted me to demonstrate that you need me around. Well, sir, I think I have.'

'It is quite stunning what you've done for me, Maserov. There's no doubt about that. But what you're asking, it's very —'

'When I met you, even apart from the sexual harassment problems, you had a meta-problem. You didn't much like Hamilton, in fact, between us, I think you loathed him even then, but you didn't want to go to the trouble and the expense of taking all your work away from Freely Savage to another law firm, pouring all that historical and institutional knowledge down the drain with the move and waiting for the new firm to get up to speed. Now you don't have to make that choice. You can keep all your work in the same place.'

'But I *do* have to make a choice, don't I?'

'Yes, sir, you do. It's Hamilton or me.'

'You're smart, honest, hard-working and you've got balls no one would ever suspect you had.'

'Thank you. Yes, it's true, few people have ever speculated much at all about my testicles.'

'But you're a Second Year, for Christ's sake.'

'Yes, I'm a Second Year, a mature-age one. And Hamilton's a narcissistic, sociopathic bastard. And you know it.'

Malcolm Torrent got up from his desk and walked over to his window and, with his back to Maserov, looked out high above the world that almost everybody else lived in. He stood there for some time. Then he turned around.

'You draft the document, I'll sign it.' He smiled and the two men shook hands. Then Malcolm Torrent leaned into his desk, pressed a button to ask his private secretary, Joan Henshaw, to come in and 'show Maserov to the door before I gift him one of the grandchildren'.

Maserov could hardly believe what had happened. Nothing like it, nothing of this magnitude ever happened to normal mortals and as Malcolm Torrent's inscrutable Joan Henshaw rode down in the elevator with him, he wanted to scream, not make small talk. Fortunately for him she, quite uncharacteristically, began to chat.

'Are you a coffee drinker, Mr Maserov?'

'Coffee? Yes, I love a good coffee. How about you?'

'Yes,' she said, before adding pointedly, 'Whenever I can manage it, I like to get to Degraves Espresso Bar.'

'Degraves? I was just . . .'

She looked briefly at her shoes and then, as she looked up again, she betrayed the smallest smile he had ever seen.

'How's your Mr Radhakrishnan?' she asked suddenly. 'Now *he's* a gentleman.'

VII

Maserov called the handwritten number on Radhakrishnan's business card and told him the good news, Malcolm Torrent was prepared to make Maserov the lawyer responsible for all Torrent Industries files.

'Mr Torrent is prepared to sign a document to this effect,' Maserov explained as calmly as he could, hardly believing the words he was saying. Radhakrishnan showed little emotion during the call as there were still several stages to be satisfied in order for what was in effect a silent coup to be accomplished. He calmly explained that in order to validly effect the change there was a specific form that needed to be filled in and then signed by Malcolm Torrent himself. He cautioned against leaving this form unsigned anywhere.

'You should not take the form to his office until you have a face-to-face appointment with him that would permit you to bring the form into his office unsigned and take it out again with you once he's signed it. It's better to wait with the unsigned form in your safekeeping for however long is necessary than to rush over to his office without an appointment and leave it somewhere, insecure. The importance of this, coupled with its secrecy, warrants patience. That said, Stephen, the sooner you're able to get the document signed the better. Do you understand?'

'Yes sir, I do.'

'For your own sake, I strongly advise you to follow these instructions to the letter. Should something go wrong, no one in the partnership will confirm having entered into any prior arrangements or agreements with you and you will be seen to have acted on your own initiative with all the negative consequences that such a course of action would entail.'

'I understand.'

'Now the form itself,' Radhakrishnan continued, 'is not one of those available as a standard precedent for all fee-earners to access. Only partners have access to these forms because of their value. Rather than trouble you with the mechanics of this, my secretary will print two copies for you, one as a spare in case something happens to the first one. She will place both copies inside a plain white envelope, which she will, in turn, secrete inside a copy of a magazine, say, the *Law Institute Journal*. Then she will put the *Law Institute Journal* inside a larger white envelope, which will have your name typed on it.'

'Got it! Where will she leave the envelope? She could leave it for me at reception?'

'No, I don't think so,' said Radhakrishnan. 'Is there anyone in the firm you could trust with your mail on a no-questions-asked basis?'

'Hmm,' Maserov was thinking. 'Yes, a Second Year named Emery, he's currently in the litigation department. I can ask *him* to hold it for me.'

'Can you trust him to keep the envelope safe for you without opening it and without your needing to tell him *not* to open it, which could arouse his suspicion?'

'I trust him. And if I tell him it's my copy of the *Law Institute Journal* he definitely won't open it.'

'Do the Second Years not enjoy the *Law Institute Journal*?'

'There is the view that they are not its target market. They like getting it but they don't read it.'

'If they don't read it why do they like getting it?'

'Several reasons. It's frequently used as professionally sanctioned camouflage to cover whatever the given Second Year is *really* reading. Additionally, it can be brought out when waiting for someone in a bar or cafe to signal to everyone else there that the person occupying the table or seated at the bar is a lawyer. And, finally, the Second Years do like getting mail personally addressed to them. It's an uncommon happening in the work setting. They show it to their parents.'

'I see. And you're absolutely sure you can trust this *Emery*?'

'More than I can trust anyone else in the firm, other than you, sir, of course.'

'No, for this you would need to trust him *more* than you can trust me.'

'Certainly, if you advise it.'

Maserov was to give Radhakrishnan an hour to do all he had described with the required form and its insertion in an envelope containing the *Law Institute Journal*. In the meantime Betga had called and convinced Maserov to leave the spare copy with him for safety's sake. Then Maserov called Emery, casually, to see if he would be around if Maserov had to drop into the office in the next hour or so.

'Well,' said Emery, 'I was thinking that if I got enough done in the next hour I would duck out to the Rainbow Mountains of China, which are said to be spectacular. But otherwise, yes, I'll be at my workstation.'

'Listen, Emery, if I get my copy of the *Law Institute Journal* delivered to you, can you hold it for me?'

'You read it too?' he asked Maserov with surprise.

'Do *you* read it?' Maserov asked with equal surprise.

'I check the obituaries to see if anyone in the firm that I haven't seen for a while has died and they're not telling us. Listen, there's something I need to talk to you about but I can't do it right now.'

'Okay, I'll see you in about an hour.'

Maserov's heart went out to Emery when he approached his work-station from the elevator but before he could get there he was set upon by Fleur Werd-Gelding.

'Maserov!' she whispered. 'Thank God! He won't look at me. Emery won't look at me.'

'Have you approached him?'

'I've tried but he won't look at me. He turns away. There's no way he's going to tell HR to take me with him if he won't even look at me. Am I too late?'

'Relax, Fleur, you're probably not too late.'

'"Probably" means *possibly* I am. Am I or not? I'd rather know.'

'Fleur, other than Bradley Messenger in HR, only Emery would know that.'

'But he won't even look at me.'

'Okay, look Fleur, I can't stay long. Let me try to talk to him on your behalf. If I give you a nod, you need to be brave and do two things. First, approach Emery and, whether he looks at you or not, you need to ask him out for a drink. You know what to do.'

'What's the second thing?' she whispered.

'Once you've got Emery in your corner, you need to go to HR and tell them you want to share the role of Second Year rep with me. Oh hell, you can volunteer to take the whole thing from me. I don't care. They'll never entrust it *all* to you, anyway. Unless . . .'

'Unless what?'

'Unless Emery tells them to.'

'You think he would?'

'Well, that's kind of up to you, Fleur.'

'And you'd let HR make me the sole Second Year rep?'

'Yeah, HR already knows I'm completely loyal. I'm in their pocket. You need to get there too. Let me go to Emery now. Remember, if I nod, it's all go.'

'And if you don't?'

'Well, Fleur, obviously it's your call, but you may want to look at another firm before the end of the financial year. Discuss it with your agent.'

'My agent? I don't have an agent!' she whispered in panic.

With this, Maserov walked over to Emery's workstation. When he saw the envelope with his name on it on Emery's desk all he wanted was to get away as fast as he could without arousing anyone's suspicion, not even Emery's.

'Maserov,' Emery whispered, 'Fleur Werd-Gelding keeps looking at me. It's unnerving.' Emery looked around and saw Fleur Werd-Gelding looking at him. 'She's doing it now! Is she going to fire me?'

'Emery, she can't fire you. She's a Second Year just like you. In fact, if I give her a nod right now, she's going to ask you out for a drink.'

'She would never do that.'

'She would. All I need to do is nod.'

'Why?'

'Because she thinks you know things about the running of the firm that she doesn't and that you have sway with HR.'

'Why would she think that?'

'She's confused. I think I confused her.'

'How?'

'I told her you know things about the running of the firm that she doesn't and that you have sway with HR. Let me nod to her then I'll go. Thanks for looking after my *Law Institute Journal*.'

'Wait!' said Emery in panic, holding on to Maserov's sleeve. 'What will I do if she takes me out for a drink and finds out I *don't* know things about the running of the firm that she doesn't and that I *don't* have sway with HR?'

'Your mission, Emery, should you choose to accept it, is to take this whole thing as far as you can and report back to me.' Maserov turned towards the eagle-eye of Fleur Werd-Gelding and gave her an unambiguous nod. Then he stood up with the envelope that had been addressed to him, gave Emery a tiny pat on the back and headed back towards the elevator. When he was safely out of the building and blocks away from the Freely Savage offices, Maserov called Malcolm Torrent's secretary and got the first available appointment with him, which was the following afternoon.

On returning to Torrent Industries, Maserov called Jessica to his office.

'Where did you get all that finance talk about "risk-adjusted net present value" or whatever it's called? You blew me away with all that. And Malcolm Torrent too, I think,' he asked her.

'You know the bartender at the Ghost of Alfred Felton?'

'The tender bartender, the one who idolises you and can't take his eyes off you?'

'Yes, *that* one. Well, he used to work in finance before he was laid off and decided to make his living watching me drink. I got talking to him about what we're doing at work and he started explaining this stuff, put it on a cocktail napkin too, along with his phone number if I needed to discuss it further.'

'Have you been going there . . . without me, to the Ghost of Alfred Felton?'

'Well, I always used to. I meet friends there . . . sometimes. I mean . . . I don't see you every night.'

Jessica immediately regretted reminding him that she didn't spend every night with him. She hadn't wanted to sound needy or vulnerable and, in any event, while her feelings had developed to the point that on any given night she did want to spend her time with Maserov more than she wanted to be with anyone else, she knew that to do that, to be with him every night, would inevitably unleash a cascade of consequences for a lot of people, including children. Even to say it out loud was dangerous. It could lead her to stumble into a future she was unsure of.

Maserov, for his part, was about to ask her if *she* wanted to see *him* every night. But he caught himself just in time. He knew not to drive the conversation when he didn't know where he wanted it to go, not when he wasn't going to be able to erase the words and feelings that had fuelled the journey. They both felt that whatever was going to happen between them, they each wanted to be the one that made it happen. They didn't want to be rejected, however honourable the reason. Equally, neither of them knew how far they wanted things to go notwithstanding that they both shared an unspoken horror of them ending. So, simultaneously, and with all the absurd illogic and contradiction inherent in the business of being human, they also longed to have the decision made for them by the other. And as this amorphous clutch of incompatible wants became ever clearer via the space framed by the words they did *not* say, Jessica went back to her office.

VIII

That evening Eleanor had parent–teacher night and had to go back to school and be a teacher well into the night. It was a private school so the children were her customers and their parents doubled as the customers' financiers and the school's shareholders. This was like an AGM and Eleanor and her colleagues had for weeks been preparing a reconciliation between the educational fantasies of the stakeholders and the truth. Ultimately, their jobs depended on it. She had asked and Maserov had agreed to stay with Jacob and Beanie after the nightly routine of bath, bed and storytelling. He had, however, forgotten to tell Jessica this when they had met at work during the day.

He was on his way there when his phone rang. He thought it might be Jessica. He was going to have to tell her that he wouldn't be able to see her that night due to family obligations. The call wasn't from Jessica but from Betga.

'Have you heard the news? We've got a few problems but I want you to stay calm.'

'What news? I haven't heard any news. What are you talking about?'

'Malcolm Torrent's in hospital. He's had a stroke.'

'A stroke!'

'Don't worry, we're not finished yet.'

'How bad is it?'

'I don't how bad it is. I'll know more soon. I'm on my way down there. Don't worry. We're not finished yet.'

'What? What are you talking about?'

'Don't get upset, Maserov. It's not going to help anything.'

'You're on your way where?'

'To the hospital. He's in the ICU. I spoke to his private secretary. She told me which hospital. Don't worry.'

'Why are you going to visit him in hospital? They won't let you into his room.'

'Don't worry, I'll get in.'

'Why do you want to get into his hospital room?'

'You've got to get his signature, don't you? I'm taking the spare form you left with me for safekeeping.'

'Betga, you're crazy. Don't do this!'

'Do *what*? I'm visiting a sick old man. There's nothing wrong with that. In fact, it's admirable.'

'Betga, it's fraud, it's obtaining financial advantage by deception, it's forgery, falsification of documents, it's —'

'Maserov, you need to relax. First, it's not obtaining financial advantage by deception because there's no deception, ditto re fraud. *You* know this because you know what his intentions were before his stroke and what they will be again, if and when he recovers. It was his intention to make you the lawyer at Freely Savage responsible for all Torrent Industries files. Anything that furthers that intention is hardly deceptive or fraudulent. It's giving effect to his wishes; it's the opposite of deceptive.'

'Betga, the Supreme Court wouldn't like this.'

'No, they'll love it. They love cases like this. Trust me. And second, it's not forgery if it's in his own hand.'

'You're going to put a pen in his hand?'

'It's too early for me to know the extent of the assistance he requires, but yes, of course I'm going to help him effect his wishes to the best of my powers as his legally retained personal lawyer, and, of course, as someone who cares. Remember the hundred bucks he gave me. I won't forget that in a hurry. I, for one, will not desert him.'

'Betga, you're going to put a pen in the hand of a stroke victim!'

'I'm going to try, yes.'

'I don't want any part of this.'

'Maserov, you've done all you need to do, my friend. I've got the form to be signed, I've got the pen and I've got the resealable ziploc bag. I've even brought him his favourite bible. It's a Gutenberg special, autographed. You relax with your family . . . or your lover, whomever . . . Know that I won't judge you.'

'A resealable ziploc bag?'

'Yeah, it's for the pen . . . after he signs it.' There was silence at the other end of the phone. 'Preserves his DNA on the pen. Everyone loves DNA evidence. It's so reassuring. Listen, Maserov, I've got to find somewhere to park the car. I'll call you when I've been in to see him. I'll give him your love.'

IX

When Betga arrived at the hospital and found a sizeable contingent waiting to check on the welfare of Malcolm Torrent, he went back to his car and took himself out for an Italian dinner in North Melbourne that lasted until it was much too late for people who respected convention to still be in a hospital waiting room. At around 10 pm he returned to the ICU nurses station, introduced himself, flashed his driver's licence faster than a speeding bullet, and enquired gravely in an almost whispered tone, 'Okay, you can level with me, what's the prognosis? How bad is this?'

'Are you family, sir?' the nurse asked Betga without looking up. 'Or do you work with Mr Torrent?'

'Actually, I'm both. We tend not to talk much about the family connection because, frankly, there are people in the firm who are jealous enough of our closeness as it is and it really can get in the way. And I have to remind myself that most people will have trouble understanding a relationship like ours; in and out of each other's offices, private jokes, knowing what the other's thinking without the use of words. We have been blessed. Until now. Where *are* we? And don't sugar coat it because of our relationship.'

'Mr Torrent presented unconscious with the typical features of a stroke. He's in the process of being investigated and managed appropriately.'

'What does that mean re his prognosis?'

'I'm afraid it's too early to speculate on the timing and extent of any recovery or even if there will be a favourable one.'

'Oh my God! Can I see him?'

'I'm afraid not. Visiting hours are over and he needs to rest.'

'Are you sure I can't just . . . for a moment?'

'Yes, I'm sorry, sir. I know this must be a terrible time for you.'

'It is, it is, Nurse . . .' Betga peered at the nurse's name tag, 'Nurse Penberthy. I've had a hell of a day, as you probably have every day. It's kind of hard to imagine how we'll proceed without him, if we have to, which I hope we won't for a very long time. Would you mind if I just sat here for a moment?'

'No, not at all.'

'It's just been such a shock. I still can't quite . . .'

'Of course,' Nurse Penberthy said, allowing him to trail off while she looked at a computer screen in front of her. She was somewhere between forty and forty-five and her experience and clinical education as an intensive-care nurse suggested to Betga that this was not going to be as easy as it might have been. He was going to have to wait.

X

Eleanor had headed off into the night, back to the school where she taught English and history. Maserov was in the house they had bought together all those years earlier. He looked at the furniture, no longer new and never so alluring once it had left the catalogue. But it was theirs, held their history, absorbed it, soaked it up, a history only they knew or cared about; the artefacts of a shared life. Or was it just a chapter within a life? And was this distinction a choice, his choice?

Why did she want him back now, suddenly? Was it really simply because of the children? Why just now? And was getting back together again solely because of the children a good enough reason? Maserov dismissed the possibility that she was influenced by the prospect that he might be made a partner. This wasn't the Eleanor he knew. He'd been an underpaid teacher when she'd agreed to marry him and a lawyer when she'd asked him to leave. Maybe she had found the drama teacher wanting. Or was it that Carla had hinted that the possibility of reconciling, a choice that had been Eleanor's ever since she'd kicked him out, might be taken away from her? After all, Eleanor now knew at least of the existence of this mysterious female work colleague, someone Carla herself thought well of. It was likely more than one thing, he reasoned. If they got back together he'd have the chance to find out. If not, perhaps it wouldn't matter. Until perhaps one day it would. And then it would be too late.

With the children asleep, at least for now, his mind was free to wander and he wasn't sure it should. Rightly or wrongly, he thought of taming it with an update from Betga, who was apparently camped out in the reception anteroom of the Intensive Care Unit housing Malcolm Torrent.

'Hey Betga, any news?'

'Not yet,' said Betga quietly. 'I'm earning my bona fides with the nurse in charge. It takes time. She's on a call now anyway. What are you up to?'

'Eleanor's had to go to parent–teacher night and I'm at our house minding our sleeping kids, wondering what's going to happen to Mr Torrent, to my job, to my life. Eleanor's said she wants me back. I'm looking at our furniture, remembering when we bought it, missing Jessica, missing Eleanor, the one I married, wondering if I move back in will she be the Eleanor who used to greet me with a kiss and an almighty hug or will it be the one who prefers to watch *The Bachelor*. And I'm missing Jessica. Did I mention that? Betga I'm tearing my hair out. I don't know what to do.'

'About what?'

'About Jessica and Eleanor. Have you been listening?'

'Yes, I have. Here's my advice: enjoy the moment. Do nothing!'

'Do nothing?'

'Look, Maserov, whichever option you choose, there will be times in your life, and knowing you, *many*, when you will regret the choice and feel guilty you made it. Yes, of course you will. We're all of us only human, especially you. You're nothing but human.'

'What a talent you have for making an innocuous comment with the remote possibility of a slightly positive interpretation sound unbelievably negative and belittling.'

'Yes, I really should be in management. Do nothing for as long as you can. Enjoy the sweet nectar of possibility before you make a choice and fuck everything up.'

'That's really your advice?'

'Yes, why does that surprise you? It's because you keep looking for safety, by whatever name, in every corner of your brief and compromised existence. How many times do I have to remind you, dear Maserov, the very best you can do these days is to try to buy a little time before your worst fear becomes your neighbour, after which it becomes your overcoat, then your shirt, then your skin. If you *really* want to buy some time, learn how to write the algorithms that are taking every other bastard's livelihood. But even that will be short-lived. There will eventually be an algorithm to write the algorithms sure as bribery follows day. You can occupy yourself, distract yourself trying to wake people up, prodding them into recognition of their own learned helplessness. But there's no money in this and a person like you will be crushed to see just how fast your audience swipes left.'

'Thanks, Betga. I feel much of my anxiety transforming into a kind of numb resignation with still just enough in reserve to resemble a living creature, albeit an immunosuppressed one, an ideal host for a homeless virus or two, a renovator's dream for a couple of nucleic acid molecules in protein coats hoping to settle down and start a family.'

'Will you stop worrying? At least you're not bored. Look, whatever you do, you'll always have me.'

'Betga, you never told me what Hamilton did to you.' There was an uncharacteristic silence.

'Well, that's another story . . . which I'm happy to tell you . . . Oh, got to go now! She's off the phone. Wish me luck. I'm going to buy us all a big chunk of time. This could be the start of a brand new chapter in your life . . . and mine. Got to go.'

'Betga? Betga?'

Betga had returned the phone to his pocket but whether deliberately or not, he hadn't ended the call. So Maserov did.

He went for a walk around his old house. It was quiet. When he reached the kitchen he decided to pour himself a drink, Scotch on ice. Did he want to be a partner at Freely Savage? He was a guy who tried to hang on. Partnership wasn't compatible with his self-image. Could he change his self-image? He tried calling Jessica to tell her what had happened to Malcolm Torrent. Or was it more important to tell her where he was? The call went through to voicemail, which was perhaps just as well since he couldn't talk loudly for fear of waking the children. What did Eleanor drink now? Was there still the Scotch he liked or had she given it to the drama teacher? No, there was some. But it was a brand new, unopened bottle. Was that an enticement to come home or just a reflection of guilt? He was getting himself some ice when he was startled by his elder son.

'Beanie! What are you doing in the kitchen?'

'What are *you* doing in the kitchen?' his son asked. His father hadn't lived there in a while. It was a legitimate question for a five-year-old.

XI

Betga had been in the Intensive Care Unit anteroom for almost an hour, alternately pacing and drinking cups of water from the water cooler adjacent to the hand sanitiser. And when he wasn't doing this he was reading the bible. There was a large, mute television suspended from the ceiling, showing what was either a news magazine show devoted to the entertainment industry or else the network's late news program. Betga couldn't tell and hadn't really paid the television much attention. Instead, he'd been hoping to impress the nurse with his apparent religiosity, studying the bible he'd brought along. But this was hard given she had barely looked at him for the previous forty-six minutes.

'Are you a religious person?' Betga suddenly asked Nurse Penberthy outside Malcolm Torrent's room. She looked up as though startled anyone was there.

'What?'

'Are you a religious person?'

'No, used to be . . . when I first started, but it's not really possible to remain religious after you've worked here for years.'

'Is it confronting mortality day after day, does it test your faith to breaking point?'

'Sure, it's that and all the rest of it.'

'"All the rest of it"? The physical toll of the work?'

'Yes, the daily reminder of suffering and mortality, the physical toll, the fact that you can come into this career so full of enthusiasm, so well educated and trained and be so poorly treated as a matter of course.'

'By management?'

'By management, they who periodically line us up against the wall for rounds of jobs cuts, wave after wave of job cuts, then make those who survive do the work of all the people they've just fired. Then there's being treated like dirt by the doctors and by the family and friends of the patients who don't make it and allow their grief to morph into anger. There's not a nurse here who hasn't been abused in some way, verbally and physically assaulted, some of them even sexually.'

'Jesus! I'm so sorry to hear that,' said Betga. 'I really . . . am.' He glanced up at the television screen, momentarily distracted.

'Oh, look, it's that actress, Helena Bagshaw,' said Nurse Penberthy, 'the one who was sexually assaulted. She's got herself lawyered up. Good for you, honey!' On the screen, standing beside the mute young actress, was her new lawyer, taking questions from the press, Mike Hamilton of Freely Savage Carter Blanche.

'You know,' began Betga, looking away from the screen, 'all the nurses I've met tell me they love what they do. They speak of the tremendous job satisfaction they get from nursing. I can't help but admire them. And,' he added cheekily, 'I've met a lot of nurses in my time.'

'Why, are you chronically ill?'

The woman was not easily charmed. She was too exhausted, not just by the day, but by the sum of all the suffering it had been her task to try to mitigate and by the inappreciation with which that endeavour had so often been met.

'No, I was just trying to be funny.'

'Yeah, you're funny, mister,' she said, unimpressed.

'Betga, A.A. Betga.'

'Look, Mr Betga, I can't let you in to see your friend till tomorrow, no matter how much you sympathise with the plight of working nurses.'

'I empathise, it's better than sympathy,' said Betga.

'And I'm not giving you my phone number so you can put your bible away.'

'Nurse, that was the furthest thing from my mind.'

'Mister, I'm too busy and too tired for your bullshit. You want to know how things *really* are for people around here? This will probably sound crazy to you but . . . more than half the nurses here, pretty much everyone employed in the hospital, certainly everyone below doctor, most of them are absolutely terrified of losing a job they absolutely hate. Does that sound crazy to you?'

'No, that doesn't sound crazy to me at all.' He looked up at the television screen. Hamilton was still there, talking.

'If I might speak frankly, with your experience and your post-graduate training as an ICU nurse, you could really earn a packet working directly, I mean privately, for the patient, one patient, a grateful patient, say, a high net worth patient. I'm talking really high net worth, high enough to build his own hospital. You could recruit colleagues to share the shifts, take a cut as a finder's fee and, well, you could have a much improved life, should the circumstances arise. You just need to be on the lookout for the right opportunity. Granted, the kind of opportunity I'm talking about doesn't come every day, but if ever one does come, you wouldn't want to miss it, Nurse Penberthy. Would you?'

She looked at him and, for the first time, paused to consider what he'd said. Then, abruptly, she turned her attention back to what she was doing. 'I need to check on my patient,' she told him.

Betga wondered if he'd just played his last card. He'd gone all-in and was looking to fold.

It was late and he was tired. It was not a good time to be tired.

Just then Nurse Penberthy came out of Malcolm Torrent's room newly animated. She closed the sliding door and started walking away from both the room and Betga at speed.

'What's wrong?' Betga called to her.

'You can't go in. I need to get the ICU registrar.'

'Why?'

'He's woken up.'

XII

Eleanor still hadn't returned home. Beanie couldn't sleep and negotiations had led him back to bed in return for some patting and a 'pretend' story, by which Beanie meant an impromptu story created live by the storyteller as opposed to one read from a book. It could be told in total darkness which promoted sleep but it also required greater effort than mere narration from his father. That was the deal. Beanie was lying on his side in the dark while his father patted him through his blanket.

'What about the story?'

'Okay, once there was a little boy who had a bear and —'

'No, not that one, the one about the jester, the king's court jester.'

Maserov's phone lit up. It was a text from Jessica that read, 'That's awful about Mr Torrent! Can you talk now?'

'Not really,' Maserov texted back. He didn't want his son to see the text but he wasn't quite sure why.

'I don't know one about a king and a jester.'

'Yes, you do. The king was going to get rid of the jester but the jester said if he was given a year he would be able to make the king's horse talk. Remember?'

'Able to make the king's horse talk?'

'Yeah.'

'Talk later?' came another text from Jessica.

'Yes. Will talk later,' Maserov texted back as fast as he could. He tried to imagine how she would feel on reading his reply and winced at the apparent lack of priority he was according her but he really wasn't sure he was going to be able to call her later. Nothing at all was within his control as far as he could see. He couldn't remember the last time anything was. He wasn't sure where he would be sleeping that night. He wasn't sure where he wanted to be sleeping that night.

'Oh yeah, *that* one. Once upon a time,' Maserov began in a quiet soothing voice, 'in the thirteenth century in a far-off land now called

Turkey there lived a jester whose job it was to entertain the king. He'd gone to court jester school years earlier to learn how to be the best court jester he could be. He never wanted to be a partner and certainly not the partner responsible for all the Torrent Industries files. All he ever wanted was to be safe, a safe jester.'

Beanie was breathing heavily now in a rhythmic pattern that suggested he was close to sleep. He crept out of his son's room as quietly as he could. Soon Eleanor would be home. Soon he would have to call Jessica or be ready to explain why he hadn't. Which was it going to be? He didn't know. Was that Eleanor's car?

Now Maserov's phone was ringing. It was Betga. But when Maserov answered there was no reply, as though Betga couldn't hear him or simply wasn't listening, and Maserov quickly surmised that Betga must have called him by mistake, a pocket-dial, the world's fastest growing form of interpersonal non-communication. Maserov was about to hang up when he realised he could hear Betga talking to what must have been Malcolm Torrent's nurse.

'Can I tempt you, perhaps . . .?'

'What do you have in mind?' she asked. Maserov heard a loud but muffled whooshing sound as though rapid excited movement was taking place through material of some kind.

'Oh, Jila mints! Thank you!' came the woman's voice, genuinely delighted.

It sounded as though Betga had poured at least two mints into the palm of the woman's hand. Then nothing but breathing, Betga's breathing, footsteps on a linoleum floor and the sound of a door squeaking, just slightly. The breathing got louder. Then Maserov heard Betga's voice, a muffled whisper, but the words were clear and unambiguous.

'Maserov? We're going in!'

acknowledgements

For their help in various ways (sometimes unknown to them) during the gestation of this book the author wishes to express his gratitude to: Simone Abel, Jin Auh, Jane Banting, Peter Bartholomew, Tracy Bohan, Sarah Chalfant, Nikki Christer, Françoise Delivet, Danny Dexter, Maggie Doyle, Tamara Eichel, Emma Felman, Rick Goldberg, Liv Perlman Handfield, Toby Handfield, Johannes Jakob, Dorothy Kovacs, Bob Lamb, Sharon Lewin, Evi Meisa, Danny Mahendra, Niki Maartens, Brendan Miller, Robert Milstein, Gil Orski, Dan Pearce, Donna Pelka, Alexander Perlman, Janine Perlman, Nicholas Perlman, Rodrigo Pintos-Lopez, Adam Pozniak, Gabriel Pozniak, Gideon Pozniak, Micah Pozniak, Samara Prosser, Anne Sarzin, Lisa Sarzin, Zara Sarzin, Alan Schauder, Rachael Schauder, Suzie Sharp, Gabrielle Williams and Andrew Wylie.

Harry Perlman deserves to be singled out for the critical attention he lavished on the many incarnations of this book over the many years of its creation. For not the first time, his close reading and thoughtful advice proved invaluable and cannot be repaid in words alone.

Praise for Elliot Perlman

THE STREET SWEEPER

'Excellent . . . harrowing, humane and brilliant.'

The Times

'A wonderfully rich, engaging and multilayered story . . . [from] an author of rare erudition and compassion.'

Washington Post

'This epic about racial persecution employs similar techniques [to *Seven Types of Ambiguity*] but scales up the ambition . . . The interleaved sequences set in Nazi Germany and Fifties America are so searingly potent . . . As he depicts both the kindnesses and the unspeakable cruelties of the concentration camps, Perlman fleshes out his research with a moral and imaginative force that feels revelatory . . . It demonstrates how history and fiction can converge to tell stories that cry out to be remembered.'

The Telegraph

'An expertly told novel of life in immigrant America – and of the terrible events left behind in the old country . . . Perlman's long tale, spanning decades, is suspenseful and perfectly told in many voices, without a false note. It deals with big issues of memory, race, human fallibilities and the will to survive against the odds.'

Kirkus Reviews (starred review)

'Perlman deftly navigates . . . complicated waters, moving back and forth in time . . . In so doing, he brilliantly makes personal both the Holocaust and the civil rights movement, and crafts a moving and literate page-turner.'

Publishers Weekly (starred review)

'*The Street Sweeper*, Elliot Perlman's monumental and, at times, mesmerizing novel, is a meditation of memory – and its relationship to history . . . Perlman burnishes his reputation as a masterful storyteller who captures the cadences of consciousness and conversation and the varieties and vagaries of cruelty, courage and compassion . . . You will, in all likelihood, find it unforgettable.'

Jerusalem Post

'A big, bold international work with a piercing moral sense . . . striking and enlightening . . . The novel illuminates the small acts of individual kindness, memory and compassion which must stand against the human capacity for cruelty and inhumanity.'

Prospect

'Acclaimed Australian writer Perlman is a master at meshing characters' streams of consciousness with social tsunamis of hate and violence. In his intensely detailed world-within-worlds third novel, this discerning and unflinching investigator of moral dilemmas great and small takes on the monstrous horrors of racism in America and the Holocaust . . . Perlman's compulsively readable wrestle-with-evil saga is intimate and monumental, wrenching and cathartic.'

Booklist

'In the best kind of books, there is always that moment when the words on the page swallow the world outside – subway stations fly by, errands go un-run, rational bedtimes are abandoned – and the only goal is to gobble up the next paragraph, and the next, and the next . . . [*The Street Sweeper* is] a towering achievement: a strikingly modern literary novel that brings the ugliest moments of 20th-century history to life, and finds real beauty there.'

Entertainment Weekly

'On the one hand the focus is intimate, concerned with the surprisingly inter-connected lives of a small number of characters in New York some years past. On the other it encompasses and – in a series of vivid primal scenes, exposes – some of the worst horrors of the 20th century . . . Some will recall . . . *Les Miserables*. Perlman certainly has, in this novel that shares Victor Hugo's unrepentant digressiveness and compassionate span.'

The Age

'This is a big fat novel filled with empathy and indignation. Every page of it dramatizes American race relations, 20th-century Jewish persecution, or class conflict – or all three . . . Perlman's preeminent skill as a novelist seems to be for stitching together scenes and histories, in gradually interlacing the disparate strands.'

Boston Globe

'*The Street Sweeper* is an epic tale that spans decades and bridges generations while chronicling the predominant chapters of racial persecution perpetrated in the darkest hours of the 20th century . . . [Perlman] shines a fresh light on the struggle of the American civil rights movement . . . The narrative pull is breathtaking [as he] pulls off the supreme feat of articulating the unspeakable . . . This stunning novel works and matters, because of the expert way Perlman has recorded both the agonized howl of the past and the plaintive echoes of the present.'

San Francisco Chronicle

'The power of memory sits at the centre of Australian writer Elliot Perlman's *The Street Sweeper*, a superb multistrand epic that stretches across continents and over a century of history as it depicts racial prejudice and its consequences . . . If it's not enough to focus on two events that could intimidate many writers – the Holocaust and the African-American civil-rights struggle – Perlman intertwines them in a way that brings out their similarities and renders them intensely personal . . . He stays in full control of his material, creating a sprawling yet tightly woven book that aims high and succeeds . . . The novel zips along and proves impossible to set aside . . . There are moments of unremitting despair, but also of strength, unsung bravery and hope that arrives when all seems lost . . . An extraordinary tale powerfully told, *The Street Sweeper* reveals how individual people matter in history, how unexpected connections can change lives, and how the stories we hear affect how we see the world. It's a tremendously moving work that deserves to be read and remembered.'

The Globe and Mail

SEVEN TYPES OF AMBIGUITY

'Compulsively readable.'

New Yorker

'Bustling, kaleidoscopic . . . There are traces of Dickens's range in Perlman and of George Eliot's generous humanist spirit . . . This is an exciting gamble of a novel, one willing to lose its shirt in its bid to hold you . . . Stay with it for the long haul. It's worth it.'

New York Times Book Review
(Editors' Choice and Notable Book of the Year)

'This is a love story in the 19th century tradition, the kind that makes the real world seem a bit dim . . . George Eliot down under.'

Kirkus Reviews (starred review)

'Nuanced, dynamic storytelling, layered with essential digressions on everything from psychiatry to the stockmarket.'

Washington Post

'Dazzling . . . a page turner, a psychological thriller that is, in short, dangerous, beguiling fun.'

Newsweek

'Elliot Perlman's *Seven Types of Ambiguity* is an exemplary novel in the tradition of Thomas Hardy and the earlier D.H. Lawrence. Perlman's power is in conveying the strife between personality and character in each of his protagonists. His prose, like his story itself, is vivid, humane, and finally optimistic in a manner that strengthens the reader's perceptiveness.'

Harold Bloom

'Motives are tangled, perceptions unreliable, and outcomes unexpected . . . [Perlman] has created a novel with just the right amount of meaning, intelligence, and beauty.'

Boston Globe

'Perlman writes with such convincing simplicity – his sentences read like whiskey-fueled confessions . . . We can't trust ourselves because Perlman makes us care too much.'

Esquire

'[A] sophisticated psychodrama.'

Wall Street Journal

'The scope of [Perlman's] ambition and the strength of his achievement in portraying the psychological state of [the developed world] is unrivalled . . . We feel ourselves spiralling closer to a truth that we could not have reached through other means . . . [from] a voice in the wilderness burdened with seeing the truth.'

Times Literary Supplement

'A colossal achievement, a complicated, driven marathon of a book . . . The opening section is a tour de force . . . At the end, in a comprehensive, an almost Shakespearian way, Perlman picks up every loose thread and knots it.'

The Observer

'One of the best novels of recent years, a complete success.'

Le Monde

'Has the virtues of the great modern European novel.'

Süddeutsche Zeitung

'Where, critics have asked, is Australia's equivalent of Jonathan Franzen's *The Corrections*, or Philip Roth's *American Pastoral*? Now, with Perlman's achingly humane, richly layered and seamlessly constructed masterpiece, it seems that we have it.'

Canberra Times

'My novel of the year . . . Captures the Zeitgeist of contemporary Australia every bit as powerfully as *The Corrections* anatomised that of America.'

Sunday Telegraph (UK)

'[A] wise and generous book, a kind of less showy and more deeply humane version of Jonathan Franzen's *The Corrections*.'

The Guardian (UK)

'One of those rare works of art that makes you realise the world is both a simpler and a more complex place.'

Evening Standard (A Book of the Year)

'This book's true size is in its scope, its ambition, its emotional richness . . . Certainly, no novel has made this reviewer feel quite so sane in a long time.'

Glasgow Herald

'Remarkable . . . Perlman builds up an unsettling, often sympathetic but always memorable picture of [his characters'] emotional lives, and of the coldly mercenary world they inhabit.'

Sunday Times

'[A] complex and perfectly nuanced study of idealised love turned sour.'

Daily Mail

'Remarkably well-written . . . funny, moving, and constantly surprising . . . It is impossible not to care what happens to Eddie, Tanya his wife, and Abby, their adorable daughter . . . Perlman is echoing Auden's cry, "We must love one another or die."'

Time Out (UK)

'Constructed like a catchy pop song . . . a quirky cautionary tale that feels like a wake-up call.'

New York Times Book Review

'Perlman moves deftly from the personal to the political, from intellectual debate to near farce to edgy tenderness. His novel gradually builds into a study of a whole generation, a sad, angry, disconcertingly funny reflection of the way we live now.'

Times Literary Supplement

'Funny and dramatic, literary yet accessible . . . what a find this is!'

Marie Claire (Australia)

'[The novel's] blend of self-deprecating wit, caustic social comment, spirited sensitivity and big heart carries the narrative in beautifully controlled passages that brim with insight, humor and feeling . . . Rich with the pleasures and pains of love, family, friendship and marriage . . . Perlman's sheer storytelling virtuosity gives this essentially domestic tale the narrative drive of a thriller and the unforgettable radiance of a novel that accurately reflects essential human values.'

Publishers Weekly (starred review)

'Perlman is a marvellous storyteller.'

The Observer

'Few novels ever dare to fuse emotional and economic life with the passionate intelligence of this one.'

The Independent

'Elliot Perlman's new novel is priceless . . . With admirable subtlety, Perlman satirizes a world in which suburban paradise and homelessness are just a single missed payment apart.'

Christian Science Monitor

'It's such an enormous relief to discover Elliot Perlman's *Three Dollars*, a novel that is unequivocally about our times.'

The Age (Book of the Year)

THE REASONS I WON'T BE COMING

'Stunning . . . by turns hilarious and heartbreaking.'

Baltimore Sun

'Invigorating stories . . . enlivened by Perlman's intelligence, verbal energy, and mischievous wit.'

Entertainment Weekly

'Unashamedly various without being feeble, a series of exercises in voice, perspective and style, it deals in violence, exile and much else besides . . . Deftly switching perspectives is his most impressive technique . . . yet Perlman's work isn't all juggling tricks: at times, he manages to pack whole lives into a few paragraphs . . . Perlman's plots seem effortless, which makes his surprises all the more affecting.'

New York Times Book Review (Editors' Choice)

'Perlman writes fiction with muscle . . . It's provocative stuff.'

People (Critic's Choice)

'All of Perlman's stories remain undeniably assured and carefully devised, and hold out nine complete and whole worlds for us to discover and contemplate.'

San Francisco Chronicle

'The nine tales here don't just suggest an emerging voice, they show it well developed, stretching and flexing . . . marvelously realized, evocative and utterly original . . . Perlman continues to amaze and move.'

New York Post

'The details are perfect throughout . . . Perlman excels at creating tension . . . These stories are like walking down the hallway of an old hotel and eavesdropping on sad confessions. It's hard not to be moved . . . These stories are love letters, really, and their protagonist, we come to learn, is none other than the human heart.'

The Washington Post

'Perlman's voices draw you in and hold you . . . The order of the stories makes *Reasons* a sort of literary sample tray, a gradual introduction to the full breadth of Perlman's talents. "A Tale in Two Cities" [the final story in the collection] is almost worth the price of the book by itself.'

Boston Globe

'Hopelessly conscious of embarrassing personal truths – the sort we realize, then yearn to forget – Perlman's characters are erudite specialists of anomie. Hyperliterate and brutally funny, alternatively self-assured and self-loathing, they are mostly noble and deserving of our sympathy, even if we're implicated in our schadenfreude. The effect might be depressing if Perlman didn't show such care in imbuing his characters with devious charm . . . Scant evidence exists to suggest that casual flirtation with Perlman's fiction will not end in total obsession.'

The Believer

'Fans of Perlman's grapplings with both the minutiae and the sweeping "big questions" of modern life won't be disappointed . . . As a writer, Perlman's obsession is with epic yet individual moments of truth when everything – from marriage to career to a person's innate sense of right and wrong – seems up for grabs . . . compulsively readable.'

Elle (US)

'Perlman mines pure narrative gold . . . insistently readable . . . provocative and powerful fiction from one of the best new writers on the international scene.'

Kirkus (starred review)

'Coldly luminous . . . dead-on . . . Perlman in full: mystery, tight dialogue, layers of irony.'

Publishers Weekly

'The nine stories serve as a varied introduction to an accomplished stylist and storyteller.'

Seattle Times

'Impressive . . . Evident in all of these stories are the writer's talent and ambition . . . Perlman shows he has the skills to fully manifest the ambitions, ideas, perspectives and plots for the stories he wants to tell . . . Perlman [is] a restless, thoughtful, and interesting writer.'

The Miami Herald

'Perlman has a winner with this collection of nine eloquent short stories that examine the various natures of the human condition via a cast of remarkable characters.'

Sacramento Bee

'Readers . . . will be delighted with nine stories whose characters range from lawyers to immigrants . . . This story collection showcases the talent of . . . Australian-born Perlman . . . expansively written with admirable control and generous detail, this is an excellent collection and is highly recommended for fiction collections.'

Library Journal